To my editor, Leis Pederson, who bought
the book I really wanted to write.

To Megan. If I knew you were coming, I'd have baked a cake.

As always, to Mark, who is living proof that
love at first sight is real, and lasts.

Finally, to my mother, the original Ann. Your love remains a
steady source of inspiration and comfort. Thanks, Mom.

continued . . .

"Scintillating sexual chemistry, wonderfully drawn characters—a total winner."   —Lauren Dane, *New York Times* bestselling author

"Beautifully written and emotionally charged, Anne Calhoun's romances define the erotic."   —Alison Kent, author of *Unforgettable*

PRAISE FOR THE NOVELS OF ANNE CALHOUN

"Anne Calhoun is one of the best writers of contemporary erotic fiction."   —*Kirkus Reviews* blog

"One of the best erotic romances I've read in a long time . . . An emotional read with two characters that I can fall in love with."
                                                              —*Dear Author*

"Absolutely fabulous."   —*The Romance Readers Connection*

"A must-read."   —*Smexy Books*

"Fresh and imaginative."   —*The Romance Studio*

– THE –

ANNE CALHOUN

HEAT | NEW YORK

THE BERKLEY PUBLISHING GROUP
Published by the Penguin Group
Penguin Group (USA) LLC
375 Hudson Street, New York, New York 10014

USA • Canada • UK • Ireland • Australia • New Zealand • India • South Africa • China

penguin.com

A Penguin Random House Company

This book is an original publication of The Berkley Publishing Group.

Copyright © 2015 by Anne Calhoun.

HEAT and the HEAT design are trademarks of Penguin Group (USA) LLC

Library of Congress Cataloging-in-Publication Data
Calhoun, Anne.
The list / Anne Calhoun.—Heat trade paperback edition.
p. cm.—(An irresistible novel ; 3)
ISBN 978-0-425-27689-1)
1. Mate selection—Fiction. 2. Man-woman relationships—Fiction. I. Title.
PS3603.A43867L57 2015
813'.6—dc23
2014035518

PUBLISHING HISTORY
Heat trade paperback edition / March 2015

PRINTED IN THE UNITED STATES OF AMERICA

10 9 8 7 6 5 4 3 2 1

Cover photograph: "Woman with feather" © Nilufer Barin / Trevillion Images.
Cover design by Diana Kolsky.
Text design by Kelly Lipovich.

ACKNOWLEDGMENTS

This book took shape during a months-long rambling conversation with Megan Mulry; settings and characters were kick-started by a Perry Street stay in the West Village with Megan and Miranda Neville. Once again, Robin Rotham read the rough draft, and this time talked me back up on a ledge. With friends like this, a writer can go anywhere.

Attention is the most basic form of love.
Through it we bless and are blessed.

—John Tarrant

– ONE –

The window air-conditioning unit clicked twice, then whirred to life. Cold air drifted through the swath of sunshine that faded the ancient Oriental rug's reds to a brick shade. Special Agent Daniel Logan took up position at the left end of the love seat and braced his elbow on the arm as he noted the way light fell on the monument in Washington Square Park. Back in his NYPD days, before he left for the FBI, he'd trained himself to note not just date and time but the weather, moon, and astronomical events in his reports to anchor things in his memory. It was useful when he testified in court.

At this very moment the sun was at its highest point in the sky, and the summer would only get hotter.

Today he noted the solstice not because he'd be called to testify, but because he'd met Tilda the preceding summer solstice. One year had passed, the year of Tilda. They'd met, started dating or whatever Tilda called it, gotten married, and were now sitting in front of a marriage counselor, because Tilda thought they needed to divorce.

She folded herself into the opposite end of the love seat, as pale and textured as fine paper, wearing a sleeveless black sheath, her bare legs crossed. No wedding ring. No birthday bracelet. The therapist, a tall, thin man with dark brown eyes and a turban covering his hair, shook both their hands as he introduced himself as Dr. Bhowmick, then settled himself across from them.

"Daniel," he said in a lightly accented voice. "Do you prefer Daniel or Dan?"

"Daniel."

"The interpreter of dreams," Dr. Bhowmick said. "Word origins are a hobby of mine. What do you do?"

"I'm with the FBI." It wasn't all that different from interpreting dreams. As an agent assigned to investigate white-collar crime, he reconstructed people's dreams after they'd been stolen.

Dr. Bhowmick transferred his gaze to Tilda. "And Tilda. An unusual name."

"It's short for Matilda," she said, but she lacked her usual smile.

"Ah," the therapist said genially. "Do you know the origin of your name?"

"I do," she said. "It's German and a combination of two words meaning strength and battle."

Her face wore her most pleasant expression, as if she batted away idle observations and trivial facts all day, deflecting the conversation down shallow gullies until everything they had left dissipated into the air.

"What brings you here today?"

"I think we need to divorce," Tilda said.

"I think we don't," Daniel replied.

She smiled at Dr. Bhowmick. "And there you have it." Crisp, clean, precise, the upper-class British accent the same temperature as the room. She must be freezing, in her sleeveless sheath. Daniel was comfortable in his suit, and he ran much hotter than Tilda, who lived like she could spontaneously combust at any moment but was always cold.

Dr. Bhowmick turned to a clean page in his legal pad, and wrote something at the top. Daniel's gaze flicked to the words. He could read most handwriting from all angles, but Dr. Bhowmick appeared to be taking notes in some form of shorthand. Tilda was also studying the pen and paper, but Daniel doubted she was trying to read the handwriting. *Cheap legal pad, a ballpoint pen that came in packs of ten at the Duane Reade* is what Tilda, who owned an upscale stationery store, would see.

"How long have you been married?"

This information was on the intake assessment Daniel filled out before the appointment. He'd do the same thing to a suspect or witness, take information, ask again from a slightly different angle, then ask again from another. It's how he pieced together the stories that solved crimes. Simple or complex, financial or physical, a crime was always about a story. People had goals, motivations, conflicts that escalated into theft and violence. Stories and numbers were his specialty. "Six months," he said.

Dr. Bhowmick halted midscrawl. "You've been married six months? How long have you known each other?"

"A year."

"Eleven months," Tilda clarified.

Daniel slid her a look. "It's the solstice. We met a year ago today," he said, standing on the only solid ground in his earthquake-rattled world. That day was written on his bones, as real and solid as the love seat under him, the light on his skin, Tilda's even breathing beside him.

"So you've been together for almost a year, and married for most of that time. Why don't you want to be married to Daniel any longer?"

She looked away, out the large rectangular window in the living room. NYU students were crossing the square, pausing by the chess games going on at the south end of the park. Daniel remembered his student days, the freedom to explore everything body and mind had to offer. Tilda, four years younger, hadn't crossed his path.

"Tilda," Dr. Bhowmick prompted gently.

"I'm not comfortable opening our marriage to a stranger."

"Neither am I," Daniel pointed out.

The look she shot him was swift and fierce, like a silver blade. When she returned her gaze to Dr. Bhowmick, he straightened almost imperceptibly. "We married in haste. It was an impulsive decision that, in hindsight, was the wrong one. It would be foolish to repent at leisure, when both of us could be free."

Words mattered to Tilda; she chose them carefully. She didn't say to meet other people. She didn't say she didn't love him. She didn't say it was a mistake. She didn't even say she wanted a divorce. *We need to divorce.*

"Daniel?"

"I love her. I want to be married to her for the rest of my life."

Tilda's unreadable gray gaze never left the window. Her slender, pale fingers, bare of any rings at all, sat unmoving in her lap while the rest of the session passed in silence. Daniel was comfortable with silence, knew how to use it during an interrogation, so he sat and watched the sun shift on the rug as the seconds crawled by. When their time was up, Tilda collected her purse as she stood.

"I have an appointment. Thank you, Dr. Bhowmick," she said, and walked out the door.

"Tilda," Dr. Bhowmick mused. Reflecting on her name, Daniel thought, not pining for her. He said it that way often enough. "These things take time, Agent Logan. Would you like to schedule a recurring session?"

"I need to talk to Tilda first. She travels for work."

When he reached the street, Tilda was standing by the curb, her tote slung over her shoulder, one slender arm outstretched to hail a cab. Without looking at him, she asked, "Do you want to share a taxi to Midtown?"

Startled, he laughed. None of this was like Tilda, except it was. She was perfectly capable of walking right up to a ledge, a cliff, and peering over the edge to assess the landing. He loved surprises, loved pitting himself against the unexpected, loved even more his unpredictable wife. To get a better angle on oncoming traffic, she stepped off the curb between two parked cars. He took a moment, just a moment, to admire the taut swell of her calf in four-inch heels, the way her dress hugged her hips, the play of her shoulder blades, the seemingly vulnerable nape of her neck, exposed by the riotous tumble of chin-length black curls.

"I assume you're still having lunch with the runners club?" she said over her shoulder. "I'm meeting Colin at Barneys before we leave for London. Do you want to share a cab?"

A cab slowed for her, the availability light flicking off as it braked. Her words were a challenge, a dare, a gauntlet thrown down onto the steaming city pavement. She was exactly the same as the day he'd met her, except she thought they needed to divorce. "Yeah," he said, and slid into the backseat next to her.

"Sixtieth and Madison," she said, then sat back and tucked her purse in her lap.

The cab crawled through midday traffic. Daniel stared out the window and thought. Tilda didn't talk about emotions with him, much less strangers, some vestigial remnant of her English upbringing. In an era of constant oversharing on social media, it took months for Tilda to give him even the thinnest slivers of her story. When she did tell him something, she was ruthlessly honest.

"An impulsive decision to marry isn't a solid foundation for a marriage," she said, as if she could read his mind. Maybe she could. "We never really meshed as a couple. Your work and family. The deal is about to close, the situation with Sheba snowballed out of control, and I'm worried about Nan."

Her grandmother lived in a fishing village in Cornwall, England, where Tilda had lived as a child. Two weeks earlier Nan had stumbled off the ramp leading to the henhouse and broken her ankle. If Tilda hadn't been in the middle of a business opportunity that could make or break her, she would have been in Cornwall already.

The cab pulled to a stop on the east side of the street. She handed a twenty through the sliding window, while Daniel, seated on the sidewalk side, got out of the cab so she wouldn't exit into the traffic rushing up Madison. Without thinking about it, he held out his hand; he suspected her taking it was equally a matter of habit. He stayed where he was, trapping her between his body and the cab door, and let her forward momentum bring her right up against his body.

It was far too blatant and possessive for an on-duty FBI agent wearing his gun and his badge and standing on one of the busiest street corners in Midtown Manhattan. He was working the case of the decade; even a verbal reprimand could get him yanked back to investigative support. But this was Tilda, his wife, who said there was nothing between them worth building a marriage on.

Then he kissed her.

His mouth landed a little off center, her lips parting in surprise and then softening, heating under his. Her fingers spasmed as if she would pull away. He neither tightened nor relaxed his grip on her hand, but rather slipped his tongue between her lips to touch hers. Then it happened, a hint of flint and tinder, sparks flaring, the hitch in her breathing as she tilted her head just enough to align their mouths.

With one quick jerk she freed her hand and stepped back, her eyes dark with an anguish that triggered a sense of déjà vu. "Don't, Daniel. If you really knew me, if you really *knew me*, the last thing you would have done is schedule an appointment with a *therapist*."

She pushed past him onto the sidewalk, and disappeared around the corner. Daniel closed the cab's door and tapped the roof twice with his fist. As the cab pulled out into traffic, Daniel withdrew his notebook and pen, and took refuge in habit. He made a list.

Risks Tilda Takes

1. *Sitting on ledges*
2. *Sliding over cliffs*
3. *Going after the deal that will make her a global brand*
4. *Asking for a divorce*

He walked the few blocks to meet the ultramarathon runners for lunch, his mind only half on the discussion about training schedules, nutrition, hydration, and war stories. Instead he thought about the divorce rate for law enforcement officers, which was well above the national average. Just about every cop or agent he knew well enough to swap stories with fell somewhere on the spectrum from marriage counseling, separate rooms, separations, filing for divorce, to actually divorcing. Then, just out of curiosity, he walked back to Barneys, got an iced coffee from the coffee shop across the street, and stood in the shade under the awning of the coffee shop next to Judith Ripka, just in time to watch his wife get into another man's car.

Colin Wilkinson, Quality Group's director of North American acquisitions, had spent the last nine months negotiating Tilda to partner with them. The deal agreement sat next to the divorce agreement on their dining room table. Colin aimed the clicker at a Mercedes that cost more than Daniel made in a year. Tilda called him posh. Daniel would have called him slick except for the fact that Colin had the cheerful optimism and manners of a well-trained, well-bred Labrador. Tilda stood on the sidewalk, her hair curling in the humidity, accentuating her cheekbones and her lush mouth. She reached for the door handle of the rear passenger door; when it didn't open, she shot Colin a glance across the roof of the car. Colin said something Daniel didn't catch, but Tilda's smile didn't light up her eyes.

The lights on the Mercedes flashed, then flashed twice, then the alarm went off. This time Daniel caught Colin's *buggering fuck* even over the traffic between them. Daniel took another sip of coffee. Tilda switched her clutch from her left hand to her right. More impatient thumbing at the key fob, the Mercedes's lights blinked like it was taking fifty thousand volts from a Taser, and finally Colin silenced the alarm and got the doors unlocked. Tilda folded herself into the passenger seat. For a split second, Daniel let himself drink in the pleasure of watching Tilda get into the car, all clean lines and sharp angles. She could stop him dead in his tracks, the bolt of lust paralyzing him as swiftly and effectively as it had the first time he saw her.

Impossibly, unapologetically, effortlessly stylish, his wife. At West Village Stationery she sold exclusive, handmade paper, couture stationery, invitations embossed or engraved. By twenty-eight she had established herself as the trend-setting expert for millennials fascinated by the art of pen and ink. The shopping trip with Colin, scoping out the luxury goods trade, potentially looked incriminating, but there was no sex involved. Daniel knew this for two reasons: Tilda's cheeks, throat, and collarbone turned a very specific shade of dark pink when she had sex, and her personal code of ethics had no room for anything as cheap as infidelity.

Was that the only thing he knew about her?

Colin managed to start the car and turned on his blinker to merge into traffic, only to have a fast-moving cab slam on its brakes, then begin the requisite honk-showdown. The blinding sunlight slid off the windshield, and for a split second Tilda's face was visible. She wore an expression of such naked anguish, her enormous gray eyes dark with despair, that Daniel's thigh muscle clenched to take a step forward and intervene. A jolt of primitive awareness shot up his spine, straightening his vertebrae as he remembered exactly where he'd last seen that look on Tilda's face.

The taxi swerved around Colin's Mercedes, freeing room for Colin to merge into traffic. Sunlight flashed off the windshield like a blade, blinding Daniel for a moment. When his pupils relaxed, they were gone. His heart started slowing back into a normal resting rate, and he forced himself to relax, lean back against the building.

The last time he saw that look on Tilda's face, they were at the Waldorf, the night of her birthday, after he'd given her his gift. It should have been a lovely night, and it was, except for one moment when he'd thought it was a trick of the lighting, the dim pool of soft white light casting shadows across her face, the downturned corners of her wide eyes, the desolate set of her mouth just after he gave her his gift, a Cartier LOVE bracelet, purchased in a rare fit of romantic possessiveness.

Hey. You okay?

I'm fine. It's lovely, Daniel.
You sure? We can exchange it if you'd rather have the cuff.
No. No, I like it very much.

He'd let it go. Taken her answer on faith. Chalked it up to lighting and the desire on a slow simmer since they sat down, her ankle pressed against his calf during dinner, her gaze heated with promise. He knew how desire could tendril through the pit of your stomach, heating the marrow from your bones. It was who she was, and he loved her that way.

He automatically walked with the lights, avoiding the heavy foot traffic on Fifth Avenue for the quieter stretch of Madison. Anguished look. The divorce papers were sitting on their dining room table, anchored in place by an expensive paperweight that was a wedding present, and a framed screen of two eighteenth-century silk-embroidered robins. The skin at the nape of his neck hummed with awareness, a sensation he'd long ago learned to respect. He didn't believe in coincidence, or in rescuing damsels in distress. Tilda didn't need rescuing. She needed someone to stand next to her, toes over the abyss, while she took a good, long look.

He had two problems. The first was obvious. Making an appointment with a marriage counselor was a knee-jerk impulse that proved to be the wrong thing to do. The second was that Tilda thought they were wrong for each other, that six months of marriage proved not lifetime compatibility but fundamental, irreconcilable differences. Which meant he'd misunderstood something.

He hated not understanding something.

The direct hit to his ego landed in his gut. He'd built his reputation as a cop, FBI agent, and a man on taking puzzles apart, piece by piece, datum by datum, and reassembling them so they made sense. But when it came to his marriage, he'd missed something big, something bone-deep, something life changing about Tilda Davies.

That was on him. The end of the marriage wouldn't be. He needed to think. He pulled out his phone and sent a text to their mutual friend Louise, who came from old New York money, and was the most down-to-earth person he'd ever met.

Can I borrow your terrace tonight?

The reply came almost immediately.

I'd suspect you're going to propose to Tilda except you
two lovebirds already got married. I haven't forgiven you
for eloping, but of course you can borrow the terrace. Will
leave key with doorman. Come over anytime. xx L

He needed time, and space, a literal and metaphorical distance from his current life so he could think things through. In order to get answers, he would have to go back to where it all began.

― TWO ―

June, 1 year earlier

"Lady Matilda?"

Oh my, that was a lovely voice, licking at her skin like a cat's tongue and sending a shiver down her spine. She forced herself not to turn and look for the man who owned that voice. "It's Tilda," she said, and tipped back her bottle of beer. Early in her days in the city some wit in awe of her British accent christened her Lady Matilda; she used the nickname in one specific area of her life. But people who really knew her called her Tilda, and while she wasn't getting her hopes up, a man with a voice like that might be someone she wanted to know.

"Okay. Tilda. How about you come back off the ledge?"

Dull. "I'm fine where I am, thanks." She looked out over the city. A stiff breeze sent clouds scudding across the full moon, mirroring the unsettled, restless longing inside her and flinging her curls against her cheeks. She needed something new, something exciting, something big.

She *needed*, and the air was so tempting.

"It is a little loud inside, Tilda."

The repetition of her name in that slow, rich baritone made her pause. She turned to look at the man balanced on the balls of his feet, within arms reach but not so close he'd startle her off-balance. He wore slim jeans, a blue-and-white checked Oxford, and a dark blue velvet blazer that looked as scrumptious as his voice. The Chinese lanterns strung from Louise's lattice arbor didn't quite give away the color of his eyes. His blond hair was cropped close, except for a slightly longer section at the front that was styled back off his forehead.

"I'm not going to jump."

"I didn't think you were," he said. He had a long face with strong bones—cheekbones, forehead, jaw—and a full-lipped mouth that looked like it rarely smiled. She found herself wondering how his smile transformed his face, if it made it foolish, or charming.

"Yes, you did. You're using my name like I'm holding someone hostage, which, if I'm suicidal, I am. I'm holding myself hostage and am therefore a threat to myself. Using names establishes a bond. I'm smoking, and I'm sitting on a ledge two hundred feet over Park Avenue South, which means I've a death wish. I'm drinking, which makes it more likely I'll go through with it because my inhibitions are lowered. You're not too close to crowd me but you could reach me if I shifted my weight forward."

She didn't pretend to do that. He'd grab her and pull her to safety, and she really wanted to keep sitting on the ledge. Her heart rate was up, and delicious little shocks gathered between her thighs. This was the most arousing thing she'd done in months, and she wasn't ready to let it go just yet.

"Or if you lost your balance. Which is more likely than you jumping. More people die of stupidity than suicide in this city."

"I'm not stupid, or suicidal."

"Prove it," he said. Despite the smile in his voice, he was deadly serious. She wondered how much further she could push him before he ordered her off the ledge.

"I'm also not very susceptible to childhood taunts turned into tactics to get me off this ledge."

"I'm out of tactics."

He sounded amused, not on edge, and his smile rendered his face into something that was charming, but more than that. He was laughing at himself, at her, at the whole situation, very much a point in his favor. She rubbed her chin on her bare shoulder, not bothering to disguise the slow up-and-down look she gave him. He stood under it, let her gaze travel the length of his legs in jeans. Strength harnessed for the purpose of endurance. A distance runner, she'd wager.

She shot him a smile. "If you can't beat them, join them."

He sat on the ledge, swung those long, long legs over as he swiveled, then sat up straight. "Je-sus."

The hair had lifted on his forearms. She took the last drag from her cigarette, then leaned back to stub it out in the ashtray behind her.

"Thanks."

"For what?"

"Not littering."

"You're a police officer?"

"In a manner of speaking."

"The blazer and jeans are an effective disguise. You look like a college professor. Or a poet," she added, smoothing her palm over the velvet at his shoulder. Strength carefully hidden. She liked that.

"Now that you know my official capacity, will you get off the ledge?"

"You're out here with me, so . . . no."

"Are you trying to provoke me?"

"I'm not seventeen, nor do I have problems with authority figures."

"You're not getting off the ledge."

"Exactly."

He thought about this for a minute, watching a television set flicker in an apartment across the street. Two floors up from the television set, a man swept up a small child bouncing on a bed and blew a raspberry into the boy's tummy. Everyone lived a public life in Manhattan. "So you're not suicidal, seventeen, rebellious, stupid, or Lady Matilda."

"Correct." She offered him the bottle of beer.

He tipped it up and swallowed, then gave it back. "Then what are you?"

The wind caught her sleeveless top, pressing it to her breasts and belly. Her nipples stood out hard against the silk, and his gaze flicked down, then back up again. "Adventurous," he said, answering his own question.

"Among other things. An observant man like you can do better than that."

"Aroused."

"Very."

"Is it the danger? The risk?"

She closed her eyes and inhaled slowly, taking in the smells of the city, exhaust and hot brick and dreams. He smelled like sandalwood and clean male sweat. "How do you know Louise?" she asked, curious to know whether he'd keep the conversation focused on her desire.

He let her divert him. "We went to college together. Her brother is a friend." He looked into the distance, his eyes flickering from lit window to lit window, letting the words linger in the air. She was so distracted by his resonant voice that it took a moment for the penny to drop. When it did, the emotion that drifted through her was so unfamiliar it took a moment to identify it as disappointment. He'd not come out to get to know her, but rather to get on Lady Matilda's list.

She provided a quiet, discreet function for people she knew, friends of friends: an introductions service. Despite the presence of a global communications infrastructure in every cell phone, people still longed for and yet were increasingly unprepared for face-to-face connections. The human brain still responded to things like eye contact, a smile, a stance, a laugh. If you wanted to meet a specific kind of person, one with similar tastes and interests, she would help connect you. Sometimes people wanted to meet someone to discuss the classics, in Latin. Sometimes the desires were more elaborate, more secretive, more sexual. She didn't filter, didn't judge, and more important, she didn't advertise. The service was for friends, and friends of friends, intimate, discreet, exclusive, and effective. Couture stationery was her labor of love, but connecting people with unusual desires was her passion, her specialty. Given enough time, she managed to match most people who ended up on her list.

Finding a place on her list wasn't without work, however. You must own what you wanted and lacked, write it down in your own hand, on paper, and put it in the mail. There was no immediate gratification of email, or worse, a text; no Dutch courage, only clear-eyed desire faced willingly. She set aside her disappointment and considered him. He certainly didn't lack courage, and his eyes were confident, unclouded.

Whatever he wanted, whatever he'd ask for, she had no doubt she had a name on her list for him. "There's a process—" She cocked her head. "I don't know your name."

"Daniel."

"Daniel, there's a process. I give you a card with a post-office box address on it. When you're ready, you mail me a handwritten letter explaining what you want. I do my best to match you with an individual with like needs. Sometimes a need cannot be met. Sometimes writing out what you long for is enough to satisfy the longing. The process can take hours, or months, but I will succeed. Would you like my card?"

"Yes," he said. No hesitation, no doubt. "Now can we get off this ledge?"

The thrill she'd felt only minutes before was gone, or perhaps had changed, gotten wrapped up in Daniel's voice, the heat steaming from his body to hers. "Yes," she said, and ruthlessly stamped down the lingering edge of disappointment. The people on her list belonged to each other. She didn't poach from them.

In seconds his feet were back on the terra firma of the rooftop garden. Then he extended his hand to her. She pulled her feet under her hips and stood, leaning back to counterbalance over the very precipice.

His grip around her waist was like iron, like he'd hooked her out of the sky, and for a long moment the length of her body pressed against his. The velvet lapels under her hands felt as delicious as she'd anticipated. His fingers flexed against her waist, and he exhaled slowly, releasing the tension only when she was safe. She walked over to her purse, resting on Louise's cafe table, pulled a card from the pocket, and offered it to him. He took it, skimmed the words, turned it over, and then slid it into his back pocket.

"Thanks."

"Don't thank me yet. I haven't done anything for you." But she would. She was good at it, a small victory won each time two like-minded people found a soul mate in the electronic chaos of the twenty-first century.

He tipped his head toward the ledge. "I was thanking you for the most exciting thing I've done in weeks."

"I find that hard to believe. You're a police officer."

"Believe it," he said, and flashed her a smile. "I work white-collar crime with the FBI."

Somehow knowing that made it easier to ignore the disappointment. Her name wasn't on her list. Daniel was a friend of Louise's, and she would do her best to match him up with someone who was right for him. "I'll be in touch. Excuse me, please," she said, and went back to the party.

Later in the week a handwritten note appeared in her mail. The return address was Brooklyn, and the handwriting the square, blocky print of a man who fills out reports comprised of little boxes for name, address, offense, summons to appear in court. In front of her rested two brown leather card files, one for requests received, the other for matches made. She slit the end of the envelope and tugged out the folded note card, preparing to read Daniel's request and file it until she could match him.

Dear Tilda,

I'd like to take you to dinner.

Best,
Daniel Logan

His phone number was printed neatly beneath his name. She picked up her phone from her desk and thumbed in the digits.

"Logan."

Men the world over answered the phone with their last names, something that struck her as quintessentially British, until she moved to New York. "It's Tilda."

The sound of voices diminished, then a door closed.

"I thought Louise sent you to me because you needed a connection."

"No. I saw you sit on the ledge and thought I'd . . . get acquainted."

Or save her. A knight in a sumptuous blue velvet blazer. Charming, but the last thing she needed. "Why didn't you simply ask me out while we were on the roof?" she asked, puzzled.

"Because you started talking about *the process*, and I liked the idea of sending you a letter," he said. His voice was slightly amused. "Are you going to keep me hanging by writing me back, or will you give me an answer now?"

"Yes," she said.

"Yes, you'll keep me hanging?"

"No."

"Yes, you'll give me an answer now?"

"Yes."

"And your answer?"

She thought about his broad shoulders, his easy manner, his wide smile, the way heat flickered through her when his arm locked around her waist, all the ways she could ruin someone like him. She thought about that luscious voice, and mentally calculated the odds a nice, white-collar crime specialist like him would know how to use it during sex. "No. Thank you for the invitation," she said gently, and disconnected the call.

– THREE –

July

I want to go down on you.

The text banner glowed against Tilda's screen background. Without breaking stride in the conversation with a man purchasing a gift for a client, she pushed the power button to deactivate the screen and slid her phone onto the shelf under the counter.

"The paper is made from one hundred percent cotton, of course," she said, "and the recipient's name or initials can be added by engraving, thermography, or letterpress." She held out options for each so he could feel the difference. Quality died even more slowly than tradition, and in the high-end goods market shopped by both old blue bloods and new money, nothing was more traditional and elegant than paper. Calling cards. Business cards. Personalized notecards. Thank-you notes. Invitations to events ranging from a quiet dinner to a ball. In the last year a placement in *InStyle*'s accessories section led to an inclusion in O magazine's Favorite Things spread. For millennials with money, she'd become an arbiter of taste with a caliber of luxury normally reserved for royalty.

Her phone lit up again.

Correction: I want to tie you to the bed and go down on you until you can't talk.

This time Tilda took the split second necessary to find out who was sexting her.

Daniel Logan.

"What size do you recommend?" the customer asked, thankfully oblivious to the heat rising in Tilda's cheeks at the pornographic texts appearing on her screen.

"Cards are a traditional and very safe choice, but some men prefer what's called a social sheet," she said. "He'll have more room to write a note, and it's folded then inserted into the envelope. I suggest ordering a selection with his monogram or name, then extra plain sheets for longer notes."

Her phone vibrated again. Tilda ignored it, because there was clearly some mistake. Daniel Logan would no sooner sext her than voluntarily sit down on a ledge twenty-two stories over the city streets.

Except, he'd done exactly that. When the client made his selection, she compiled the order on her tablet, emailed him a receipt, and tidied the sample books. Her assistant, Penny, was engrossed with a bride across the store, but no one else needed her attention. She closed the door to her office and scrolled through what she'd missed on the phone.

> Or fuck you. You won't know which you want more, but
> you'll be begging.

Gobsmacked, she stared at the screen. Without her permission her brain thoughtfully provided images: Daniel's head, light glinting in his sun-streaked hair, his face buried between her thighs. Her hands, restrained by . . . velvet bands, she decided. Something elegant, silky, unbreakable.

She shifted in her seat.

Several weeks had passed since their phone conversation, so he must be texting his current lover. That was the only explanation. Also, they were completely unexpected, shockingly blatant foreplay, not meant for her. If it were, he would have prefaced the initial text with something apologetic. *I know I shouldn't do this, but . . . I can't stop thinking about you. . . . Don't be angry with me. . . .* Not the bare, explicit, *I want to go down on you.*

> I can't stop thinking about it. You'll be salty and damp and
> wound up after a long day. You'll taste like frustration and
> woman.

Clearly, she'd underestimated Daniel Logan. Who was he dating now? He'd not asked her for another connection, and she'd not given him any names.

> Touch yourself for me. Now.

Impossible. All of this was impossible. But she could clamp her thighs together more tightly, flex the muscles, feel the faint, resonant pulses of desire. She should stop this. He was texting the wrong woman, probably someone whose number was next to hers in his phone.

Are you touching yourself? I'm hard thinking about that.
Sitting at my desk, head down in paperwork, thinking
about you.

That was a compelling image in itself, Daniel pretending to work while thinking about sex. An FBI agent would wear a suit, not a uniform; factoring in his blue velvet blazer, she came up with a dark navy suit, a slim cut, with a formfitting Oxford underneath, a subtle tie.

But he wasn't thinking about sex with her. Couldn't be.

Is your clit hard? Slick? I can't wait to watch you come.

Disappointment deflated her lungs. Definitely someone else. He'd never seen her get herself off, something she'd done far too often lately. Heat flickered through her pussy. All work and no play was making Tilda edgy and restless. She'd turned him down because every instinct she had told her he'd want something she couldn't give him.

When we're alone, I'll do it nice and slow, until you're
moaning. But do it fast, now. Don't want you getting in
trouble at work.

She couldn't get in trouble at work. She was the boss, this was her shop, the door closed on the outside world. She could hike her skirt up, wriggle her panties down, and rub off to these texts. Knowing these texts were meant for someone else should have jolted her back to reality. Instead, the vaguely voyeuristic feel added another layer to the erotic tension crackling in the air. This was a peek into a completely different side of Daniel than the man who had asked her to dinner.

Don't come.

God, a firm command. Who exactly was this man?

Save that for me. When I spread your legs and lick you, I want to taste how desperate you are.

She began composing the text she'd known all along she'd have to send.

Daniel, you're texting Tilda Davies. I'll delete this—

Another bubble appeared.

I can't work like this. I'm going to take care of this.

Backspacebackspacebackspace. Face-to-face was the only way to do this, because she had to see his face when he realized what he'd done. She had to see his face and know if she'd made a mistake, refusing to go on a date with him. A trick of the moonlight made him look more innocent than he was.

She picked up her clutch and opened the door. Penny glanced over at her, rocking back on the four-inch-heeled ankle boots that lifted her to five feet two. In her four-inch heels Tilda stood five eleven, and felt like a Great Dane next to Penny's teacup Yorkie size. "Can I redo the front windows?" Penny asked.

"Absolutely," Tilda said. She did the business side and the product selection but had no flair for creative design, so she hired Penny, straight out of Parsons and a seemingly endless fount of creative window displays. "I'm going out for a coffee," she said. "Can I bring you back anything?"

"A latte," Penny said. "Extra shots."

She hailed a cab and directed the driver to Federal Plaza. "Everything okay, miss?" the cabbie asked.

"Fine," she said. Just the unexpected from a man she'd written off.

She took the stairs to the front doors, and asked the uniformed officer staffing the front desk for Agent Daniel Logan.

"He expecting you, ma'am?"

"No," she said, and left it at that.

The officer rang through, then said, "Tilda Davies is downstairs."

Daniel walked out of the elevator, into the lobby, finishing a conversation with two individuals in jackets and suits. He made eye contact with Tilda and beckoned her to come with him without halting the conversation. Intrigued by the difference in his demeanor, she waited quietly by his side while he finished issuing instructions. Then he put his hand under her elbow and guided her into the elevator, then through open desks to an office at the back of the room, where he closed the door. He braced his bum against the edge of his desk, crossed his legs at the ankle, folded his arms, and said, "What can I do for you, not–Lady Matilda?"

She'd been right about everything from the color of his suit to the subtlety of his tie, and now she could add a dark brown leather belt and matching brown wingtips to the ensemble. The wave in his hair was tamed to lie flat above his forehead, but held furrows, as if he'd been shoving his fingers through it. She held out her phone, the bubble announcing that he was going to take care of his arousal. "You've been texting the wrong woman."

He didn't even look at the screen, just kept his gaze focused on her. "No, I haven't," he said. "The old-fashioned method of asking you out didn't work. I took a different tack."

She stared at him. He looked different at work, in his suit and tie, less open, less likely to smile. Like he was the one sitting on a ledge, inviting her to join him.

"Did you come?" he asked, without a hint of modesty or embarrassment. As if it were perfectly reasonable for him to sext her in the middle of the day, for them to have this conversation in his office with other FBI agents working outside.

You told me not to hovered on the tip of her tongue, but what she said was, "I was in the middle of a consultation with a client."

"I'll take that as a no. Did it make you hot?"

She flicked him a glance. "What do you think?"

He bent forward and put his lips close to her ear. "I think it did. Even better, I think it made you curious."

A shiver coursed down her spine.

"Would you do it now?"

"Do what?"

"Get off while I watch."

She had been wrong, so very, very wrong. He knew exactly what to do with his voice. "We're in your office, which has rather large glass windows."

"And you were sitting on a ledge two hundred feet above the street. You were shaking so I thought you were cold, or afraid. Then I thought it was the adrenaline. I was wrong. It was desire," he said, looking away from her as he spoke. From the outside this looked like . . . well, maybe it looked like he was talking to her about a case. Maybe it looked like his girlfriend dropped by for a visit.

"Do you have a girlfriend?"

"If I did, I wouldn't have texted you. No," he added, cutting her off. "I don't have a girlfriend. The last woman I asked out turned me down flat. Can you do it?"

"Why would you think I can?"

He shot her a grin full of mischief and a rather dark amusement. "You like risk. Based on the way you're looking at me, you're no more satisfied than you were a couple of weeks ago. Come on," he said, lowering his voice, just enough to send goose bumps up her arms. "Show me what you can do."

She crossed her legs. "Talk to me," she said quietly, then activated the screen on her mobile. From the outside, she hoped it would look like she was scanning her phone while he talked. She closed her eyes.

"Why?"

"Because I like your voice."

He chuckled, low and deep. "Do you have any idea how hot you were on that ledge? I should have yanked you back onto the patio. I should have arrested you for public endangerment, made up some law. But you were glowing in the moonlight. I could see your nipples under your top, see the flush on your cheeks. The moon was as bright as a streetlight up there. You'd been biting your lips, too. I wanted to do that. I took one look at your mouth, and I got so hard."

She exhaled soft and slow, rhythmically clenching the muscles of her thighs. Her lace panties were caught up against her clit, and the pressure and shift of the lace provided a tantalizing rough edge to the flex and release. Oh, yes. "Oh, I do love being wrong," she said with a laughing gasp.

"Waiting made it worse," he said. "I made another mistake with the letter I sent you. I backed off, went with something too gentle, too traditional, *I want to take you to dinner.* Something any idiot would say."

"What did you start with?"

Her voice was low, not breathy, almost inaudible. The pressure coiled behind her clit, arousing the nerves in her sex, and she closed her eyes, the better to see what he described.

He hesitated, then said, "I want to get you in my bed, naked and defenseless, then take you apart. I want to find the rhythm that draws you under, the angle that layers pleasure until you can't breathe under the weight."

She could imagine it, white sheets, blank like paper, his body caging hers between arms and legs, shades drawn against the afternoon sunlight and the ever-present city noise, her body bared in his bed, tangled with his, the slick stretch as he slid inside. The nerves in her vagina ached in anticipation. She added a subtle swivel to her hips, the lace tugging at her clit until she was close, so close, so fucking, *fucking close.*

"Sounds like sex to me," she murmured.

He bent closer. She could smell him rather than see him, the scent of man and sweat and skin and the city. "It's not sex, Tilda. I want to white out your thoughts, turn your muscles to jelly and your bones to light. I want to taste your come, my come, our sweat. It's annihilation. That's what I want to do to you."

She came, silent, restraining her shudders to abbreviated jerks of shoulders and hips, her muscles clenching around nothing, nothing, the pleasure centers in her brain glowing white-hot. After a long moment, her muscles relaxed and she opened her eyes.

He was watching her, jaw taut, expression feral. "You look like you want to hoist me onto your desk and have your way with me."

"Fuck you," he said. "Hard and fast. Not enough time to annihilate you."

Her heart gradually slowed. She inhaled shakily, exhaled more smoothly, inhaled again. "What a shame," she said.

"You'd do it, wouldn't you?"

An aftershock tumbled through her. "You'd lose your job," she said. "I'd be arrested, which isn't the adrenaline rush I crave."

"A limit. I wasn't sure you had them."

She rose, steady on her heels. "I don't date," she explained. "That's my limit, and why I turned you down."

His brows drew together. "You don't date. Are *you* in a relationship?"

"No. I just don't like dating."

"You don't like dating."

"It's prelude to sex. I know whether or not I want to have sex with someone. Dinner and a conversation beforehand aren't necessary, and are frequently counterproductive."

This time his eyebrows shot up. "Okay. So you hook up."

"Is that what you'd call what we just did?"

He thought before he spoke, a point to his advantage. "No."

"What I do is what we just did."

"Take a risk. A dare. A challenge."

"Exactly," she said, and slid her phone into the pocket of her jacket.

"Hmm," he said, soft and considering.

"I have to get back to the shop. I told my assistant I'd bring her a latte"—she checked her watch—"thirty-five minutes ago. Not even Starbucks is that slow."

"I want to see you again."

She stopped with her hand on the doorknob, and considered him. He waited, silent, unmoving. Through all of that, he hadn't moved, his arms still folded across his chest, his legs still crossed at the ankles. If he was aroused by what they'd just done, he kept it contained. She remembered his first impulse, the one he revised. She was sure he'd started with something sexual, not a decorous dinner invitation. They'd had a couple of discarded drafts, but hit their stride with his texts.

She opened her clutch and withdrew a silver card case, then a business card. Her name was engraved on one side in Garamond. The other side was blank. On it she wrote her address, then held it out to him.

"I'm having drinks with a friend," she said as he took it, "so I won't be home until after nine."

He traced the edges of the card, then looked at her. "You're serious."

"About sex? Always." She opened the door to his office. "Have a pleasant day, Agent Logan."

— FOUR —

Did that just happen? Did that really just happen?

Turns out his second experience of Tilda Davies in the flesh was no less of a kick to the head than the first. Daniel was supposed to escort visitors back to the reception desk when they left. The brass frowned on unescorted civilians wandering through the office, but he couldn't move. His feet were nailed to the floor, his butt glued to his desk while his body battled a dozen conflicting urges. Getting off was priority number one. Not happening. Not with Tilda Davies walking down the rows of cubes like it was a runway. Her legs were steady, her shoulders straight, her neck exposed. She didn't look back, didn't throw him a teasing bone or a coy bone or a sultry come-over-and-fuck-me-soon bone. She swept through the door a dumbfounded agent held open for her, and disappeared.

If he didn't have her card in his hand, he wouldn't believe what just happened. Her card. Thick, made of stiff paper slightly rough to the touch, with just her name in bold, clear letters. No address, no phone number, no job title. Matilda Davies, with her address handwritten on the back. She'd pulled out a pricey pen to write it down. He automatically registered the cross streets. Perry Street between Bleecker and Hudson. West Village. Nice. What passed for quaint residential in Manhattan.

Who did that? Who still handed out cards like they were in *The Age of Innocence*? Everyone their age just pulled out a phone and entered a number into the contacts, then sent a text to establish the connection. Letters and personal cards, handwritten in ink, suggested Tilda wanted a more permanent connection than pixels on a screen forming a number. She had a cell phone, but she gave him a card. Not a business card for West Village Stationery. A Tilda card. He had her cell phone number, and now her address. It felt like a victory, and not a small one, either.

Outside the glass, a couple of agents clustered in a group around a desk turned to look at him, then mouthed, *Lunch in ten?* Daniel pulled himself together and picked up his phone. He had voice mail. He always had voice mail. New York City was the hub of the financial world, leaving more than enough crime for the FBI, the SEC, the DOJ, Treasury, and the NYPD to share among them.

Time seemed distorted, the leaves rustling in slow motion, twisting and dappling the sidewalk as they walked to the restaurant. He surfaced enough to order, but didn't remember eating his food, too busy imagining what it would be like to get Tilda Davies in bed. He talked, but what he said, or what anyone else said, didn't really register. He went back to work, made more phone calls, reviewed reports, got in a heated argument with his boss over a plea bargain for a repeat offender specializing in work-at-home scams. It wasn't the high-profile financial services fraud he wanted to work, but he'd left the NYPD to come to the FBI prepared to do his time before moving up the food chain.

The office emptied out as the light melted from day to the

burnished gold of evening. Daniel looked up at the clock again to find that six o'clock had come and gone. He hadn't felt this out of time and place since . . . ever. But, in his defense, he'd never met anyone like Tilda Davies before. In the privacy of his office, with his notebook before him and a pen in his hand, he noted the date, the time, the weather, and then started a list of pertinent details.

Black hair, curly, exposed nape.

Eyes that could only be described as gray, not blue, not green, certainly not anything in the range of brown. Thick black lashes.

Pale skin. He knew it had seen sunshine, because a faint smattering of freckles dotted her nose and her cheeks, but she looked like a woman who disdained the sun.

Thin, wide lips, the barest hint of color over the natural pale pink.

A slim, angular body, bordering on bony.

She'd come alive in the night, something he knew now that he'd seen her during the day. A nocturnal animal, he finally decided, out of step with the natural rhythm of day and night.

He left the precinct just before seven, not enough time to head back to Brooklyn before knocking on Tilda's door. Instead he walked over to the High Line and strolled the length of it, watching the shadows lengthen as the sun set over the Jersey shoreline. Sitting on one of the rolling benches, he wondered if Tilda liked this park, or if she liked green spaces at all. He wondered what he'd have to do to find out.

He knew this feeling, knew it well, recognized it from sense memories burned into his nerves. The swoop and tumble of his gut the first time he arrested someone, the first time an arrest went bad, the first time he put handcuffs on a murderer. He liked puzzles. Solving them was better than trying to get promoted or get laid or get rich. Tilda Davies was pure risk, and he was an addict.

Promptly at nine he rang the bell at Fifteen Perry Street. She appeared wavy and disjointed through the leaded glass windows until she opened one half of the double door, then leaned one shoulder against the opposite side and tilted her head. She was all angles and opposites, body moving one direction, head moving another, cheekbones and chin and collarbone visible in the dip of the same sheath dress she'd worn this morning.

"Hi," she said.

He'd expected something profound, something astonishing, so the mundane greeting made him huff. "Hi," he said.

"Something tells me this isn't your first time doing this."

"Showing up at a woman's house for sex? No. Sorry. Were you hoping for a virgin?"

"Quite the opposite," she said, the same little smile on her face.

He had a sudden urge to wipe it off her mouth with his. God, she was tough. "You going to let me in, or are we going to do this out here?"

Another pause. "The slate will be quite hard on your tailbone and my knees," she said, and stepped back to admit him.

The double door was only the width of a typical front door, so he had to angle himself through, into the foyer. The walnut flooring gleamed in the low light, drawing the eye to the back of the town house. The stairs and handrail were made of the same polished material, but the risers and rails were painted white. Black-and-white prints framed in black mirrored the handrail's progress to the second floor, but he couldn't see the images, just the contrast.

"Nice," he said.

"It's my mother's," she replied, and stepped out of her heels.

He bit back the automatic questions because she'd bent to pick up her heels and was climbing the stairs. He followed her, up to the second floor, around the bend, past two closed doors to another set of stairs. On the third floor, the doors were open. He saw a desk and a chaise through one door and a big bed through another. She walked into that room. He took five seconds to peer out of the floor-to-ceiling windows down at the tiny private garden below, added another quarter of a million to his estimate of the town house's value, then followed her into the bedroom.

"Does your mother live here, too?" he said to the empty room.

She emerged from the closet, still in the dress but without the shoes. "She lives in London," she replied, and walked around the bed to the nightstand. "Were you serious about the restraints?"

"Yes."

"I'd prefer not to use handcuffs. They'll scratch the wood."

"Fine," he said.

He caught a quick glimpse of the drawer's rather interesting contents before she withdrew two satin cords and tossed them on the mound of pillows at the top of the bed. She flung the white comforter to the foot of the bed, then reached behind her for the zipper.

"Stop."

She stopped, her head tipped forward, as if bending her head made it easier to reach the tab, then looked at him. There was another second of odd alignment, where he realized his brain was automatically filling in the movement of hair, to hide, to tease, the obvious mark of femininity. But Tilda was all cheekbones and spiky eyelashes, shoulders and elbows, the collar of her dress gaping forward to reveal her collarbones.

He walked around the foot of the bed. "Let me do that," he said quietly.

Her hands dropped to her sides. Permission granted. He pressed a thumb and index finger to the tab and drew the zipper down. The still air in the house seemed to absorb the noise. It was so silent here, Manhattan's energy dampened, no radio or iPod, just the tap and swish of the leaves against the windows at the other end of the hall, and Tilda's spine, revealed in the white light.

He slid his palms over her shoulder blades and eased the fabric forward, watching the bumps and fibers catch the light before dropping down her arms to the floor. She wore sheer white underwear but of a surprisingly modest cut, the cleft between her buttocks a shadowy secret, a hint of lace at her hipbones and between her breasts as he bent forward and set his mouth to her nape.

"I've wanted to do this since the moment I saw you."

Goose bumps shivered under his lips, down her arms, pebbling her nipples in the sheer white fabric. "Kiss my neck?"

"Yes," he murmured into her nape, then licked each bump on his way down to between her shoulder blades. She arched and flexed like a cat.

"Ticklish?"

"Sensitive."

"Good." He unfastened her bra and let it drop onto the dress. He set his fingertips on her hipbones, then drew them up her ribs, along the swell of her small breasts, then curving around over her shoulder blades to press both thumbs on either side of her spine. At the pressure her head tipped forward. He slid one hand around to lay his index finger and thumb on either side of her jaw and wrapped his other arm around her waist to hold her exactly where he wanted her. Her hands gripped his forearms as he explored the sensitive, vulnerable skin. This didn't work for everyone, but for some people the nape was wired directly to the sex drive in the brain. They got off on the submissiveness of this, a primitive response left over from the animals humans had once been, where baring the nape meant surrender, where biting it, as he just bit Tilda's, meant ownership.

All her angles melted into sinuous lines, and she undulated in his grip, seeking contact where she didn't have it. Her nipples were swollen, but he ignored them, instead sliding his hand under the elastic stretched across her abdomen and stroking the outer lips of her pussy. The curls there were damp enough to make him moan.

"Is this now, or from earlier?" he growled.

"Yes," she said, and spread her thighs.

He shook his head in disbelief, but didn't oblige her. Instead he cupped her breasts and squeezed, avoiding the nipples, which tightened at the touch, before letting go and stepping back.

"Lie down," he said.

She turned to face him, eased her bottom back on the bed, then swung her legs up. There was a natural grace to the way she moved, a completely unselfconscious way of getting from point A to point B. He toed out of his shoes, shucked his jacket, and rolled his sleeves to his elbows, then caught her smiling at him.

"What?"

"You look like a man getting down to work."

He knelt on the bed beside her and picked up the silk cords. "You're sure you're okay with this?"

In response she lay back and stretched her arms to the head-board. The movement was part surrender, part challenge, all paradox, and somehow entirely Tilda. He was thoroughly experienced, but he'd never seen anything like her before. Untouchable, and yet utterly available to him.

He looped the silk around her wrists and tied the cords in loose bows, then tapped the end against her palms. She watched him, eyes wide open, content in the silence. "One tug and you're loose," he said.

"Thank you," she said seriously.

"Anything I can't do?"

"You mean, do I have an odd quirk, like you can tie me to the bed and go down on me until I scream but you can't kiss me? I won't know until you do it," she said.

The calm response surprised him until he remembered the way she swung her legs in the air twenty-two stories over the street. "You'll let me know if I need to stop."

"That wasn't a question," she said, amused.

"No, it wasn't," he said, and straddled her hips.

The amusement disappeared. For a long moment he studied her, the slender length of her arms hollowing to the curve of her underarm, then swelling again at her breasts. Her nipples were small, pale pink, and distended, and her skin was pale cream but for a bit of color in her cheeks and her mouth. He palmed his jaw and rubbed, hearing a day's worth of growth scrape against his skin. The sound rasped into the room, and her mouth opened slightly.

He bent down, braced his forearms on either side of her head, and gently nuzzled her cheek, drawing rough skin down to her jaw, then turning his face to hers, chin to chin. Her lips parted in anticipation but he didn't close the gap, just drew his lips above hers in a parody of a kiss before stroking opposite cheek to opposite cheek. A short puff of air aimed at her earlobe earned him an answering exhale that drifted over the juncture of his neck and collarbone. He retraced his steps, this time using his parted lips on her chin, a dry, open kiss of sorts.

"You have very pale skin," he murmured into her ear. "I'm going to mark it."

"Yes, please," she whispered in return.

He chuckled, then pressed kisses into her eyelids, feeling her lashes snag in his five o'clock shadow as her lids fluttered. He continued down her cheek, over her jaw, to the pale skin of her neck. A very faint perfume tempted him to linger there before he slid one hand under her head and tightened his grip in her hair. One tug arched her neck. He set his lips to her pulse point just under her jaw, then moved back up over her chin to her mouth.

This time he let his lips graze hers, again and again, slowly deepening the pressure but without using tongue, detouring to her ear or the hinge of her jaw or her cheek, until her mouth was wide open. She shifted restlessly under him, her thighs pressing against his knees, her hips lifting into his, softening, opening, flooding with desire.

The rhythmic lifting movements stopped when he touched his tongue to hers. He gave her one slow lick and withdrew, and watched as she bit her lip, licked the spot, then whimpered. He bit the same spot, kissed his way down the tendon in her throat to the hollow between her collarbones, and worked his way back up again. He licked his way into her mouth, granted access to his, and felt her breasts lift as she inhaled deep need.

His hand left her hair, and he smoothed his palm along her jaw, fanned his fingers over her now-swollen lips, then flexed it against her throat. She arched into the touch, lifting her breasts toward his hand. He smiled, even though she couldn't see it, and trailed just the tips of his fingers over one mound, avoiding the nipple. She purred at the back of her throat, but the sound held an edge, not of desperation but of demand.

"Did you think I'd come over and service you?"

"The possibility—" She paused as he took her nipple between his thumb and forefinger, and lightly pinched. "Occurred to me," she finished when he released the pressure.

"Disappointed?"

Her eyes opened slightly. "Do you always ask questions to which you know the answers?"

He bent down and flicked lightly at the other nipple with his tongue. "Not always," he said. "But I am now, because I want to hear you say it."

She undulated under him, her legs closing, her hips writhing. "I'm not at all disappointed."

"Good," he said, and sat back, then shuffled down the bed, using his knees to spread her wide. Once he was sitting on his heels between her legs, he unbuttoned his shirt and tugged it off. She watched him, her pupils blown wide, her body moving unconsciously, hips lifting in demand, back arching in search of pressure on her nipples and breasts.

He gave her none of that, instead shifting down to scrape his face over her hipbones and belly and mound. The bristly hairs rasped against the sheer fabric of her panties. Here, the scent of her arousal was so strong, making his mouth water. He traced the elastic edge of her panties with his tongue, and watched her arch, then pressed his open mouth to the curve of her mound and exhaled. He left her panties on and lapped at her, pausing to lick the elastic at her inner thigh. He pushed his tongue against the soaked panel of her panties, and heard her moan.

"Take them off," she commanded.

"No," he said, and worked his arms under her hips. For a few more minutes he traced his fingers from hipbone to hipbone, absorbing the dip of flesh, the way the skin quivered under his fingertips. He hooked his index finger in the elastic and tugged it down, let it spring back while he worked his tongue against her clit, hidden in her folds. Her gasps went higher in pitch as he did, eased back into deep, slow exhales when he backed off to trace the leg edges with fingers and tongue.

"Daniel. Now."

He laughed, extracted himself from between her legs, and leaned up to kiss her. She moaned when he left, a sound he cut off with his mouth. This time he kissed her thoroughly, a physical promise of what lay ahead.

"You're demanding," he said.

"And you're a tease," she replied, chasing his mouth with her own.

He checked her over quickly, running his palms along her

triceps, sliding a finger under the silk cord to make sure the restraints weren't too tight. She'd released the dangling ends, refusing to set herself free and renegotiate the terms of this encounter.

"You think so?"

"I do."

"You want to argue with me? I don't multitask well. I can think about it," he said, then circled her nipple with his tongue. He rested his chin on the upper swell of her breast and looked up at her. "Or I can do that. Totally up to you."

"You're a right bastard," she moaned. "Get to it."

"Bossy," he said. "Now I have to work my way down there again."

She was hot to the touch now, the scent of her skin, the taste, the sight of red washes of color at her breasts and thighs creating a sensory overload. A primitive urge swamped him to pull off her panties, release his cock, bury himself so deep inside her she would feel it for days. He stopped, breathed through it, and gave himself the treat of hooking his fingers in her panties and working them down her thighs.

She planted both feet on the bed and lifted her hips. He resettled himself between her thighs and resumed teasing her, a progression of touches from gentle grazes of fingernails to inner thighs, then flat strokes with his fingers over her trimmed curls, kisses along her outer folds, before he put his open mouth to the top of her slit and darted his tongue out. The folds parted easily and he circled her clit once. Her hips bucked, catching him off guard, so he flattened his hands on her hipbones and held her down.

A few moments of exploration taught him what he needed to know. Then he backed off and settled into slow circles just outside the most sensitive tissue, closing in for a few moments, building the pleasure, then letting it ebb again, using the tension in her thighs, the quivering muscles under his fingers, the tenor of her moans as his guide. When they took on a helpless, pleading quality, he relented and gave her what she needed.

When she came, she went utterly silent, her body jerking in his arms.

She'd be sensitive, so he pulled back and rested his head on her thigh, stroking her belly with one hand and her inner thigh with the other. "Can you do that again?"

"Oh, yes," she breathed.

He chuckled. The scent of her, clean and tangy and primitive, clung to his lips and jaw, drifted from his nostrils straight to his back brain. When she'd shimmied on the bed, he traced the swollen folds with his index finger, then gently pushed inside. Her inner walls tightened around his finger, so he waited until she relaxed, then worked a second finger inside, doing nothing more than feeling the silky heat and strength.

When he added a third, she groaned. When he twisted his wrist up and curled his fingers gently, spreading them to stroke across the top wall of her sex, she let out a sobbing little laugh.

He coaxed her next orgasm out of her using just his fingers, blowing gently on her clit, watching the nub swell and redden again as he stroked and curled. His pinky finger pressed into her cleft so when she started to come the second time, he felt the contractions inside and out.

After the third orgasm, she cried out, "Stop. Oh, please, no more!"

He was lightheaded with need, blood pooling dangerously in his cock and balls. She filled his senses, taste and sound and smell and vision and touch, so much touch he thought she was seared into his skin. He couldn't remember anything but her, this room. He crawled up her body, clumsy with desire, fumbling with the cords until she had one hand loose. Then he collapsed beside her, half crazed, wanting her, refusing to take her.

She unfastened the second cord and rolled him to his back. "That was," she murmured against his mouth, "unbelievably hot."

He couldn't answer, because her tongue was lapping at his lips and jaw while her hand went to his belt buckle. His brain couldn't process multiple stimuli, so he forced himself to focus.

She was licking her juices from his face, chasing every smear of fluid down his jaw, across his throat, kissing it back into his mouth. He groaned, then heard a zipper, felt her hand shove at his trousers and underwear, trying to lower them down his hips. He used the hand not wrapped around her shoulder to help her, and groaned again when his cock sprang free.

She palmed the tip, spreading his precome to ease her way. He jerked and groaned into her mouth when she gripped him firmly and began to jerk him off, starting out loose and fast until he tightened her grip and slowed her movements.

She was a quick learner. "God," he groaned. "Like that."

It was over embarrassingly quickly, his shoulders lifting off the bed, his fist tight in her hair to hold her mouth to his as the contractions clenched muscle to bone. "Yes," she whispered. "Oh, yes."

He slumped back against the bed. "Sorry," he muttered, aware that he was gripping her shoulder hard enough to bruise and was holding her by the hair like a caveman.

She kissed him gently. "Stay where you are."

"Not a problem," he said, because only a citywide emergency involving helicopters and SWAT and maybe the National Guard could get him off this bed in the next few minutes.

She disappeared through a door he assumed led to a bathroom because he heard water running. When she returned she was wearing a gray silk robe and had a wet washcloth in her hand. He took it and cleaned himself up, then collapsed again. When he opened his eyes next, she was sitting cross-legged at the foot of the bed.

"Well," she said.

"Yeah." His hearing was almost back to normal. She didn't sound like she was at the far end of a tunnel, and he could hear car traffic on Perry Street. He breathed for a little longer, just to remind himself he still could, until he realized she wasn't lying down next to him. "You want me to go."

"Yes," she said. "I have a breakfast meeting."

He laughed at the outright dare in her words, and struggled into a sitting position, then assessed her. "Going to walk me out?" he asked, seeing her dare and raising her one of his own.

"If you insist on it," she said, and reached for his shirt. Her thigh muscles quivered tellingly when strained.

"Your legs not quite up to the stairs?" he asked as he shouldered into his shirt.

"A gentleman wouldn't point that out."

"Let me know when you find one and I'll ask for etiquette lessons."

He fastened everything that needed to be fastened to avoid sidelong stares on the subway, then hooked his jacket with one hand and his shoes with the other.

Using the bannister for support, she followed him down the stairs, and sat on the steps while he untied his shoelaces. A soft, satisfied smile curved her lips.

"You didn't try to have sex with me."

"I didn't," he agreed as he worked his foot into his shoe.

"I'm surprised," she said, watching him with all the self-consciousness of a cat.

He looked up from tightening his laces, and smiled, then leaned forward to graze a kiss along her cheek. "Good."

Her breath caught. He heard the snag, the soft, unconscious, longing noise she made with the air left in her lungs, and drew back just as she turned her mouth to his.

"Thank you for a very enjoyable evening, Tilda." The words

should have felt stilted or ridiculous, but he meant it. He should be sleepy and relaxed. Instead he was humming with adrenaline.

She leaned back on her elbows, the soft robe pooling at the tops of her thighs, her hair a tousled wreck, falling to her eyebrows, snarled at the back. Her eyes were lazily amused. "You're welcome," she said.

He almost asked if he could see her again, could see the way her eyebrows lifted, anticipating the question, but he didn't. There was absolutely no doubt in his mind that he would fall farther, faster, and harder than she would. She would have to make the next move. He didn't need much, a text, a call, a casual request for coffee, and he had no idea whether or not she would make that move. With this woman, darkness and danger walked hand in hand.

"Lock up after me," he said, and stepped out into the hot summer night.

— FIVE —

September, Autumnal Equinox

"Paper? You sell paper? Who uses paper anymore?"

Tilda tore her attention from the door and focused on the small group gathered back of the expansive, high-ceilinged SoHo loft. A man, tall, heavy, squinted at her in what she assumed was an effort to be charming, but came across as a leer. The man withdrew his cell phone from his pocket and waggled it at her. "I have everything I need here. Paper kills trees, and you have to store it and carry it around."

"Stationery, actually," she said, and wondered if she could sneak out to the balcony for a cigarette. "Good quality paper and your handwriting, in ink, on one hundred percent cotton paper, require discipline, self-control, clear thinking, and a fair bit of artistic interpretation. From fonts to apps, that," she said, nodding at his phone, "is someone else's artistic vision, even with your customized screen and cover."

"Handwriting isn't art," he objected.

"It's actually drawing," another woman said as she cut herself a wedge of Brie to go with the crackers on her plate. "Forgers see not letters and words but strokes in certain angles and widths, and replicate them as they'd replicate an artist's brushstroke technique. Your signature used to be seen as a measure of your education, your standing in society, your manner. An elegant hand was considered to be critical to a lady or gentleman's persona."

The man downed the last of his beer and sidled off. Tilda glanced at the door, then reminded herself she wasn't looking for someone in particular, and certainly not the very surprising Daniel Logan. No, she was here to meet people, make connections. Perhaps someone here was right for someone on her list.

"Are you an artist?" Tilda asked.

"I took some classes in college, about a hundred years ago," the woman said. "I was repeating what my drawing instructor said. Do you sell anything besides stationery?"

"Handmade couture paper, bespoke greeting cards, accessories, that sort of thing," Tilda replied.

"That's not exactly what I was thinking," the woman said, and licked a bit of Brie off her thumb. "I have a friend, an artist who lives in my building, who's been out of the scene for a while. She used to be famous, then interest moved on, that sort of thing. She never stopped creating, and she wants to know if there's a market for her current work."

Dollars to euros she'd end up sifting through the equivalent of dogs playing poker, but Tilda never turned down that kind of introduction. "I'd be happy to take a look," she said. "If they're not right for my shop, I might know someone who would be a more appropriate distributor."

"Great, but she's anti-gallery at the moment, so keep that in mind. Bathsheba Clark. Here's her number," she said, smiling as she used a pen from her purse to scrawl a phone number on a napkin. "Not quite art, but it gets the job done. I'll tell her you'll be calling."

"Ah, here she is." Her hostess, Dierdre, peered around the wall separating the SoHo loft living space from the kitchen, a suit-clad young man in tow. "Excuse us for a minute, Lisa. Tilda, let me introduce you to one of your fellow countrymen, Colin Wilkinson."

Standing beside Dierdre was the perfect example of a cheerful public schoolboy. He had tousled brown hair, a slender frame clad in a Bond Street suit, and despite the fact that they were probably the same age, projected an innocence she'd never had.

"Tilda sells gorgeous, unique stationery she finds all over the world," Dierdre said in her best hostess form. "Colin heads up North American acquisitions for Quality Group."

Tilda's smile never changed, even though her heart thunked hard against her breastbone. She'd been trying to get an introduction to someone at Quality for the better part of a year. The London-based arbiter of taste and style the world over tended to stick with known quantities like Smythson of Bond Street, Cartier, and Mrs. John L. Strong, but like any business serving the rapidly changing consumer market, they kept their finger on the pulse of the up-and-coming as well as catered to the traditional. Quality's distribution channels and connections in the high-end sales markets could take her business from a single shop in Manhattan to a global entity.

"Hello, Colin," she said, and held out her hand.

"A pleasure," Colin said.

Dierdre excused herself to greet a newcomer, leaving the two of them on the edge of the party. "It's nice to hear a familiar accent," Colin said.

"Have you been in the country long?"

"A few weeks. You?"

"I went to university here, and never left," she said. "How do you know Dierdre?"

"Trent plays racquetball at my fitness club. He mentioned the party at the juice bar. I'm not sure I was meant to be included in the invitation, but he was quite insistent I come."

"He meant it," Tilda said. "That's exactly the sort of thing he'd do. They host parties like this every few weeks. It's one of the few places you'll find where New York's social circles overlap."

"Dierdre says you're in stationery?" Colin asked.

She had her elevator pitch down pat. "Yes. I sell the standbys, Crane and Company, Dauphine Press, Smock, but I also search out companies with an artistic edge."

"Who are your latest finds?"

"A couple of really interesting, independent letterpress companies in Chicago and Brooklyn, a papermaker just outside Paris, and another in Istanbul," she said. This was not the time to go into specifics, but rather the time to radiate confidence and sophistication, not an easy task when the one thing she wanted more than anything else in the world stood in front of her in wingtips and a Bond Street tie.

He quirked an eyebrow at her. "Interesting."

"I'd be happy to show you my current stock," she said. From her silver Cartier card case she withdrew a business card for West Village Stationery and offered it to him. "Stop by anytime," she said, resisting the impulse to offer to put together a portfolio of samples eminently suitable for Quality's distribution channels.

With a smile he took the card. "I was there last week, actually. Your reputation precedes you. I've been here less than a month and heard 'you really should meet Tilda Davies' half a dozen times."

He'd taken the time to scope out the shop and determine if the introduction was worth pursuing. She respected the approach, as she would have done the same thing. "I'm sorry I missed you."

"Penny was very helpful. I'd like to talk to you further. May I call you?"

She reclaimed the card and added her mobile number to the back. "I'll look forward to hearing from you."

Colin tipped his head in an old-fashioned leave-taking and faded into the crowd. Tilda found Dierdre against the windows, pretending not to watch the conversation. "Thank you," she breathed.

"He asked to see *you*," Dierdre said. "I just plowed through the crowd in search of you. Good connection?"

"Maybe life changing," she said.

"We're even, then," Dierdre said with a nod at Trent. Tilda had introduced Dierdre to her adoring husband three years earlier, and toasted them at their wedding the previous summer. It wasn't a formal list connection, simply a matter of chemistry. She'd thought they would be good together, and they were. "Get yourself a glass of wine and celebrate."

She made her way back to the island bristling with wine bottles and glasses. As she poured herself a fresh glass she felt a tremor ripple along her nape moments before a male voice spoke.

"Hello, Tilda."

At the words her whole body went into a little humming alert, like a tuning fork gently tapped. She didn't need to turn around to know Daniel Logan stood behind her, but she did anyway, peering over her shoulder to offer him a little smile. "Hello, Daniel."

He leaned against the island that formed the boundary between the loft's kitchen and living space, a bottle of beer in one hand. Tonight he wore a lightweight linen blazer, Oxford, jeans so faded and washed they were white at all the interesting places, and a pair of running shoes. She'd not seen him, nor heard a word from him, since he left her town house. A dangerous spike of need shot through her at the sight of him. She wasn't often wrong about people, but she'd been very wrong about Daniel.

"I think there's a fire escape at the back of the building," he said. "If you're feeling the need to get your feet off the ground."

After that conversation she felt like her feet were twelve inches off the floor. That was an introduction that could change her life. "We're on the second floor," she replied. "That's hardly worth it."

"What is worth it?"

"Ten flights," she said, picking a number at random.

"You pulled that number out of thin air," he said. She could hear the smile in his voice.

"I did," she said archly. "Getting a rush is largely situational. The second floor might be enough, given the right circumstances."

"So these aren't the right circumstances. But the last time I saw you was," he said, not asked, the confident bastard, as if he were narrowing down the world into two categories: what got her off and what didn't. How had she mistaken him for a college professor?

Across the high-ceilinged room Dierdre directed two men carrying her rolled-up rug to the entryway while her husband pulled the iPod from the speaker dock, cutting off the background music mid-Adele. Trent scrolled through the menu, then set the iPod back in the speaker dock. Something heavily Latin pulsed into the air, and he swept his wife into his arms. Tilda felt an odd combination of emotions, satisfaction tinged with just a hint of envy. Normally she was satisfied to connect people who were meant to be together. Every time she sold someone the tools to memorialize everything from gratitude to love, every time she matched someone on her list, or simply introduced two people who might enjoy knowing each other, she'd proved that she understood that most basic of human needs, to see someone and be seen by them in turn. Tonight, however, she wanted the thing she'd resolved never to want: something for herself.

"I introduced them," Tilda said, apropos of nothing.

Daniel shifted his weight, drawing close enough for her to feel his body heat, smell soap and skin. No cologne or aftershave, just his unique scent. Tonight his towhead hair was standing up in a crest that on a lesser man would have looked ridiculous but on Daniel looked effortlessly stylish. "As Lady Matilda?"

"Yes."

"Stationery and introductions. I guess the two go together. Why do it?"

"Connect people?" She flicked another glance at him. "I have a knack for it. I can tell what will work for someone, and what won't."

"Yes, but why do it? Why do *you* do it?"

"You said it yourself. Stationery and introductions go together," she said, watching as loose groups of dancers formed among the couples.

"Dance with me," he said.

"I don't dance," she replied.

At that he came to stand in front of her, feet braced, arms folded, obviously amused. "You don't dance."

"I do not."

His smile widened. "Like Darcy."

"Perhaps," she said. She tried not to stare at his mouth, or let her face flush as she remembered exactly what that mouth had done to her. "A Jane Austen fan?"

"I wouldn't go as far as fan, but I've read her."

"Why?"

"I've got an English degree," he said.

"I wasn't far off with a college professor guess, then, was I?"

"I considered it, but academia wasn't really right for me."

"But police work was?"

"I want to understand why things happened, and do what I can to make them right."

And there was all the proof she needed that getting involved with him was a very bad idea. "Still, it's an odd choice for a police officer."

"Not really. You wouldn't believe how much writing goes into police work," he said, then reached past her to set his beer bottle in a cluster of other empties. Her nerves lit up again, sparks trickling from the point of near contact between his upper arm and her shoulder. "Shame you don't dance. I love it. Nice to see you again, not–Lady Matilda."

Then he walked away, his hair glinting in the lights as he said his good-byes to Dierdre, collected a sisterly kiss on the cheek, and walked out the door. Tilda told herself she knew exactly what she was doing, and why. She told herself she appreciated that he respected her wishes. She told herself that going home alone didn't bother her at all.

Except it did. Only meeting Colin Wilkinson salvaged the night. That was going to work. She just knew it, the way she knew when two people were meant for each other, as friends, as lovers, as life partners in all the beautiful, glorious iterations that phrase took on. She and Colin Wilkinson were going to get on extremely well, and that would make up for the hollowness left by Daniel Logan's abrupt departure.

She waited a few more minutes, then collected her purse and left the building. Outside the building she paused by the door and lit a cigarette.

"If the ledges don't get you, the cigarettes will."

Daniel was standing in a shadowy doorway. He stepped down to the sidewalk, into the harsh glare cast by the streetlight.

"That's an easy choice," she said mildly, and flicked the butt into the trash can on the corner. "Done."

"Giving up a vice is that easy for you?"

"Yes."

"It wasn't for me."

"You were a smoker?"

He ducked his head in a way that was almost shy, almost abashed, then nodded as he leaned against the lamppost. "Smoking was my lone act of rebellion in college. I gave it up when I started training for marathons," he said. "Some people can run and smoke, but I'm not one of them."

"That was your *lone act of rebellion*?"

"This surprises you?" he countered.

"You're proving rather surprising," she said.

He looked away, around the street, then up at the sky. The cloud cover parted to reveal a full moon, a couple of bright stars visible through the light pollution, as if he were committing the moment to memory. "It's like you make the weather."

She didn't know what to say to that. "Lost your way?"

"Definitely."

"Were you waiting for me?"

"Maybe."

"You don't seem happy about it."

He didn't say anything, just looked at the base of the streetlamp he was leaning against. He was like something out of an old movie, wearing a blazer even though it was still warm, hands shoved into his jeans pockets. She thought of all the things she didn't do, like dance, or date, or tell her secrets, then thought about who he was, what she would do to him. But there was no denying that her heart beat a little faster while she looked at him. There was also no denying that no matter how badly she wanted this to work, it wouldn't. Men like Daniel wanted things that were not in her power to give, much less feel. "I really am more trouble than I'm worth, Daniel," she said gently. "No hard feelings."

"I can handle a hell of a lot of trouble," he said. "Take me home with you."

"Why?"

"Because I've been thinking about what it will be like to be inside you since I left your house the last time."

Heat flared along her spine, curled around her ribs to drip and pool low in her belly.

"Because I can't stop thinking about it."

Exorcising demons she understood. She knew all about that, wanting and helpless to stop the wanting, until the only solution left was to take it in great greedy dripping handfuls until you were satiated, then pay for it afterward. "And you want to."

"Because I want *you*."

He said it like it meant something. Her face must have changed, because he turned north and held out his elbow. She slid her hand into the crook and set off beside him. They walked slowly up West Broadway, through Washington Square Park.

"I went to school here," he offered in the park.

"As did I."

"I had my ten-year reunion last year. You?"

"Six."

"You're making your mark on the world for six years out of college."

She shrugged. "One keeps busy," she said.

They stopped in the shadowy space between lights on the path. He slid his palms along her jaw, such an old-fashioned gesture, then bent his head and kissed her, almost tentatively at first until his lips urged hers to part and admit his tongue. Then heat flared between them. Tilda found herself gripping his belt, felt the shift of muscle and bone under her palm. There wasn't an ounce of fat on him.

"It's as bad as I remember," he breathed.

She drew in a shuddering breath, then captured his mouth for one last kiss. His arm slid around her shoulders as they set off again, turning west along Waverly Place to Perry Street. In the dark doorway to a thrift shop he backed her into the wall and ground against her, hiking her skirt up to get his hand to the curve of her bottom. His fingertips found lace and silk, then he pushed forward, hips tipping and sliding against hers in a delicious parody of sex. He broke off the kiss to bury his face in the curve of her neck and groan.

"I would take you right here," he said.

His old-fashioned language charmed her, and she doubted that swearing was a vice he often permitted himself. "I'd let you. I'd let you have me right here." It wouldn't be the first time she'd picked shards of brick from the skin of her back. Sometimes the pain made the pleasure that much more exquisite.

One arm braced beside her head, he drew back to look at her. "Is there anything you won't let me do?"

"Do I seem like I have boundaries?" she countered.

"Everyone has boundaries," he said. Her eyes were adjusting to the darkness in the doorway. She saw pale flashes of blue as he searched her face. She could have told him it was pointless, but she didn't. Instead she turned her wrist and slid her palm over his erection straining against his jeans.

His eyes closed as he ground against her palm. His teeth caught her lower lip. She delicately licked his upper lip, rubbing his balls with the tips of her fingers in time to the strokes. He groaned, the sound low, tight, helpless, and released her lip.

"This is going to be so good."

This time his hand rested on her waist as they crossed Bleecker and transitioned into the angled, tree-lined streets of the West Village. When they had to stop for a short line of traffic, he pulled her close and kissed her like no one was watching. One hand on her jaw, the other wrapped all the way around the small of her back while his tongue rubbed against hers. She hooked her elbow behind his neck and pressed in close, luxuriating in the heat coursing through her body, in the sheer abandon of kissing someone who loved to kiss.

He stood at her back, hot and breathing deeply while she fumbled with her keys, then dropped them entirely when he palmed the back of her head, tipped it forward, and set his teeth to her nape. "Let me . . . let me open the door," she half chided, half laughed.

He crouched, picked up her keys, unerringly jammed the right one in the lock, and opened one half of the narrow double door. She stepped inside, and he slammed her up against the wall.

"Third floor . . . two flights of stairs . . . that's a long way." His voice was like the purr of the big cat, coming from his chest as much as from his throat.

She shoved his jacket to the floor. "The wall?"

"No," he said, and dragged her halfway up the first flight of stairs. She stopped one step above him and threaded her hands through his cropped blond hair, holding him for her mouth. It was crazy, the way she wanted him. She was slick and hot, nerves tingling with anticipation.

"Here," she said, and sat down, hiking her skirt to the tops of her thighs.

"No," he said again, and hoisted her to her feet. "This happens in a bed."

On the landing she unbuttoned his shirt while he jerked open his cuffs. Desperate to get her hands on his cock, she opened his belt and jeans at the bottom of the next flight of stairs, tugging down boxers and jeans until she could grip it.

"*Stop,*" he said. "Do that and this will all be over."

Possessed by a demon, she turned her back to him. "Unzip me," she said.

He did. She shrugged. The dress dropped to her feet. Without turning around she proceeded up the stairs in nothing but four-inch heels and lace panties. "Coming?" she said.

"Just admiring the view," he said.

He caught up with her at the top of the stairs, taking them two at a time by the sound of his bare feet on the wood. Without breaking stride his hands slid over her ribs to cup her breasts, teasing her nipples as they walked. The sensations were so strong she had to brace herself on the doorframe. His hands skimmed down her torso to hook in her panties and urge them down her legs. She stepped out of the lace and her heels, then pulled the duvet to the end of the bed before sprawling back on her elbows.

He'd stripped off his jeans while she prepared the bed, and joined her on the bed, kneeing her thighs apart. While she watched him he rolled a condom down his shaft, then reached for her hands and pinned them to the bed next to her head as he nudged into place.

And waited.

"Daniel," she said.

"Shh," he said. His mouth hovered over hers, their lips barely brushing. Tilda felt her eyes close as her awareness shrank to the slight pressure of Daniel's cock against her slick folds. He was going slowly, so slowly, torturously slowly, and every time she lifted into the pressure he pulled back. With her hands pinned she had no leverage. Trying for some, for anything that would make this happen, she wrapped both legs around his hips and pulled, moving him not one whit.

"Easy," he said. "Shh. Wait. Feel this."

She groaned and went limp. When she stopped fighting for what she wanted, the sensation of him stretching her, easing into her half an inch at a time, filled her senses. His fingers, clasped with hers. His chest hair brushing her nipples; the increasing slickness of their skin; the rough but nearly invisible blond stubble on his jaw; the heated, damp caress of his breath against her lips, her cheekbones, her eyelids, her ears.

Then he was finally all the way inside, pelvis pressing against her, abdomen brushing hers with each rapid inhale. "Still with me?"

She opened her eyes. "Of course."

He shifted the minute distance necessary to rub his shaft against the bundle of nerves inside her. Every muscle in her body tightened, her eyes flew closed, and then he drew out and thrust in, smooth and deep and unhurried. The whole stroke slid over that ache inside, tip to base, and she moaned helplessly.

The pace he set wasn't hard and fast or slow and deep. No, nothing so contrived. It was simply relentless, and perfectly timed to keep her riding the tight curl of energy. Her face was hot and flushed, her pulse pounding in her throat and cheeks. Someone was whimpering and it couldn't be her, but it was too high pitched to be Daniel.

He was, she realized at the back of her mind, getting off not on the sex, not on having sex with *her*, but on how sex made her feel, making her lift, tighten, go molten. He wasn't taking something from her, using her to get off. No, he was exerting an astonishing willpower to own her. This wasn't as ordinary as *she comes, he comes, find your clothes, and leave.*

The friction was indescribable, adding some punch to the unrelenting strokes.

The air when she remembered to breathe smelled like sweat and sex.

The slick sounds of skin on skin punctuated her gasping little cries.

She gripped his hands and clung to his hips, lifting up, up, up, until the world whited out. He came almost immediately after, grinding into her.

"Oh my bloody God," she said.

He laughed, a response she felt in the bellows-like action of his ribs against hers and in the huff of air against her damp hair. The sound was almost tertiary to the experience of feeling Daniel Logan laugh while he was inside her.

He released her hands, then pulled out to sprawl beside her. "Exactly."

She made a little sound of agreement. He got up, went into the bathroom, then untangled his boxers from his jeans. She pushed herself up on her elbows.

"Worked me out of your system?"

"I figured I'd save you the trouble of kicking me to the curb again."

His voice was carefully emotionless, as if he didn't really care whether he stayed or left. In thinking over their time together his voice hadn't changed much at all, but she didn't make the mistake of thinking that a limited vocal range meant a limited emotional range. No, Daniel Logan was simply very, very careful about who he showed his emotions to.

"You can stay," she said, surprising herself.

Completely unselfconscious about his nudity, he paused with his underpants in one hand and his jeans in the other. A sex flush faded on his throat and chest. "I can."

She shrugged. She'd wanted like that before, knew it didn't last, but she'd learned to hold on to something until it got too hot to hold. Right now she had the tiger by the tail. Letting Daniel Logan spend the night held no threat at all.

His eyes narrowed ever so slightly as he studied her. "All right, but we go out for breakfast and have a conversation."

She blinked. "That sounds serious."

"Not that kind of conversation. A *get to know you* conversation."

"The kind we should have had before we started sleeping together."

He didn't move from his position by the door. She openly admired his runner's body, lean, muscled, the sparse hair on his chest tapering to a line that thickened again around his cock. She could see ribs, hipbones, the bulge of muscle by his knee. As she studied him his cock twitched and lifted.

"Ah," she said. It came out rougher and throatier than she expected.

"If we're going to do this again, we talk to each other first."

"The last time we did this I was fairly clear about what I do and do not do."

"You were," he agreed, his smile creasing his cheeks. "Now I'm being clear about what I do and don't do."

"I don't like ultimatums."

"Tilda," he said very seriously in that voice like dark, melted chocolate, "it's not a marriage proposal. It's not even dinner and a conversation beforehand. It's breakfast and a conversation after, and you don't have to tell me your whole life story over hash browns."

"Deal," she said, and scooted over to make room for him.

"Breakfast," he said.

"Sarabeth's."

He crawled onto the bed and sprawled on his stomach beside her. "Eggs Benedict."

"With salmon," she said, and heard him whisper *ornery* before she drifted off.

− SIX −

September

"I let myself in," Daniel said. He stopped in the doorway to her office and braced his shoulder against the white-painted frame. The room, like Tilda, was a hidden surprise, windows taking the entire back wall, then continuing halfway up the roof. When the trees were in bloom the effect was a bit like a greenhouse, sunlight dappling the room through the thick leaves of the oak tree. Her desk faced the wall, more conducive to work, she said, and the chaise lounge angled toward the windows, the better for sorting through the card file she kept of people who'd asked for Lady Matilda's help with a connection. He often found Tilda up here, curled on the chaise like a child hidden in a tree fort, rereading letters. Today the antique brown leather card files sat on the carpet by the chaise, as if she'd been reviewing paperwork, refreshing her memory, perhaps even celebrating successful matches. She wore jeans and a gray cashmere sweater, and her curls spilled away from her face against the throw pillow. Rain plunked steadily against the windows, the kind of steady drizzle that made the fallen orange and yellow leaves gleam on the Perry Street sidewalk.

"You've got to stop leaving the door unlocked. It's not safe," Daniel said.

She turned her head and smiled but said nothing, just went back to looking out the window. He stretched out beside her on the chaise, slotting himself between her body and the back then wrapping his arms around her to pull her close. Her exposed arms and bare feet were chilly against his skin. He sucked in air, then said, "You're cold."

"I thought it would be warmer," she said distantly.

"The cold front came through sooner than they said it would," he replied, and reached for the silver-gray throw behind him.

"What are you working on?"

"Just rereading the letters. These two," she said, tapping two folded note cards lying on the floor by the chaise, "have been on my list the longest."

"What do they want?" he asked. After she ascertained that he didn't want to be put on the list, they didn't discuss it, but Daniel could tell how much it meant to her. She took the list seriously, puzzled over the notes, in a way that told him that connecting people wasn't just a sideline. It was a compulsion.

"They want what everyone wants, deep down," she said. "A soul mate."

"That's a lot to ask of Lady Matilda. Of you," he said.

"Ask and ye shall receive," she said, but her tone lifted a little at the end, making the statement a question, or at least indicating a hint of doubt. "You have to ask. If you don't ask, you don't stand a chance of getting what you want."

"You don't believe in fate, or serendipity, do you?"

"Not really," she said.

"Do you ever review successful matches?" he asked, looking at the second card file, with its smaller assortment of cards.

"No," she said. She shifted restlessly. "I hate this weather."

He smiled and kissed the back of her head. He'd never heard her express that much emotion about anything. "Why?"

"This is England for about eight months of the year. Dreary, rainy, cold. One's feet are always wet unless one wears ridiculous ugly boots."

Daniel felt his smile broaden. She must be tired. She got a little more English when she was tired, as if she filtered herself to sound more American when she was awake and alert. "What have you been up to today, besides working on the list?"

"Thinking about a business proposal, and working on a letter to Nan. You?"

"I ran in the rain."

"Do you run in all weather?"

"Anything short of a blizzard or a thunderstorm," he said. "I've slipped a couple of times on the ice, but never broken anything. Marathon training won't happen if you don't run."

Her feet were still blocks of ice against his, the cold seeping through his socks to his skin. They'd been lovers for a couple of months now, the newness of it still shocking and visceral. He thought of himself as the man who kept her warm, who brought the blood to the surface of her skin, turning it pale pink, a darker red at her lips, cheeks, nipples, throat, sex. The image bloomed in his mind and sent blood pumping south, hardening his cock. He did nothing as gauche as grind it against her bottom, but it was impossible to miss. The corner of her mouth lifted in a smile, and she said, "I've a million things to do."

"A million," Daniel said, and cupped her throat with his hand, thumb by the bolt of her jaw, tips of his fingers brushing her ear on the other side of her head.

"Perhaps half a million."

"Slacker."

She smiled and made a soft sound, low and deep in her throat, somewhere between a purr and a laugh. He couldn't name it, but with his hand against her throat, he could feel it under his palm. A few months into their relationship, he was learning that the best way to explore her was through touch, as if he could draw the answers to who she was out through her skin. And it blew his mind that she'd let him palm her throat when the only difference between caressing her and choking her was pressure.

No self-protective instincts at all. "What's left on the list?"

She shifted a little, tucking her feet into the throw's lower edge. "Work. Call a few people. Make a connection. I may need to go to London in a few weeks."

"See your family?"

"Talk to people at Quality Group about a potential business deal. I'll take the train to Cornwall to see Nan while I'm there, yes."

He made his own soft noise, indicating he'd heard her. Family wasn't her favorite subject, and he wasn't clear on the details of her childhood, except that for a woman who collected friends and acquaintances and people to connect, she could count her living relatives on one hand and rarely brought up friends from home.

Or former lovers.

"You have any ex-boyfriends in the UK?"

"No," she said.

"No," he repeated, a little surprised. "How old were you when you left?"

"Eighteen. I skipped my gap year to start at NYU. You sound surprised."

"I am surprised."

"You asked about boyfriends. I had one lover before I came to America."

He mulled this over. In high school he'd had girlfriends, not lovers. It was an oddly mature word to use to describe what he thought of as a typical teenage experience.

"How many since?"

"Do you keep score, Daniel?"

"I've lost count," he admitted.

"As have I."

The colorful leaves of the oak tree dipped to the glass, smearing the water streaming off the glass ceiling before springing up. She wasn't relaxed in his arms, but she wasn't getting up, either. "Fine," he said. "Your first kiss."

"Rory Freeman, in his father's shed."

"How old were you?"

"Twelve. He lived on the next farm over from Nan's. I was with her on and off that summer, based on Mum's schedule. You?"

"Tiffany Lubbock, thirteen, both of us, on the way home from junior high school. I'd had a crush on her since the fourth grade. She had braces, and it was very awkward. Neither of us knew what we were doing."

She peered over her shoulder at him. "You're quite good at it now."

He kissed her. "Thanks. Lots of practice. How was it?"

"I also made up for inexperience with enthusiasm," she said. Her eyes went out of focus. "It was a toolshed. Rory and his dad fixed motorbikes for extra dosh, so it smelled of dirt and oil and petrol. His hands were rough. I remember that. He liked to hold my face while we kissed," she said.

He drew his finger along her jaw. Tilda's jaw was so strong, not square but distinct, with a stubborn chin, and somehow knowing a boy of twelve had been the first to feel the clean bones of her face under his hands sent a swift pang of jealousy through Daniel's gut. "He had calluses. The contrast of rough skin and soft lips fixated me. I wanted to learn everything he could teach me."

"At twelve he couldn't teach you much."

Her eyes remained unfocused. She was lost in memory, and somehow Daniel doubted he'd be thanking Rory for anything. To cover the flood of emotion inside him, he kept going. "When did you lose your virginity?"

"Virginity is a cultural construct," she pointed out. "Given the many, many ways two people can have sex, limiting the question to the penetration of penis into vagina is a rather narrow approach. Anyway, why is it a loss? I gained knowledge, experience."

The thought of wild, barely restrained Tilda growing in experience sent a bolt of desire tinged with a now gut-deep jealousy through him. "It's just a figure of speech," he said mildly.

"An interesting one. I didn't lose anything."

"Fine. When was the first time you had sex?"

"Proper sex? It was a step up from a toolshed. A very posh hotel room, actually. Smelled of expensive linen detergent and a stupidly big floral arrangement."

"Rory sprang for a hotel room?"

She turned her face away to stare out the window. The rain was too steady to be showers but too light to be a storm, and he once again pondered the possibility that Tilda made the weather. Today she was quiet, still, reflective, and it seemed perfectly reasonable that water would coalesce into clouds, then shed their excess weight to let the entire city know Tilda Davies's frame of mind. The curve of her jaw needed to be kissed, so he kissed it, then slid his hand to span the soft space between her hipbones. "Not Rory. Another student," she said lightly. "Very careful with me. He didn't rush, didn't push. I set the pace."

"Not a typical teenage boy," he said.

The corner of her mouth he could see lifted. "No," she said.

"Are you still in touch with him?"

"No. Are you still in touch with your first lover?"

That word again. Lover. Maybe everything was more sophisticated in Tilda's world, public schools and high-class stationery. Her eyes were the color of the sky beyond the trees, dark, cloudy, opaque.

"Most people as intently curious as you can't keep their mouths shut. But you never tell anyone's stories."

"I respect that people have desires, and that they want to keep some of them private."

"Which would you miss more? Making connections or collecting stories?"

"They're the same," she said. "Stop changing the subject. Are you still in touch with your first lover?"

"No. Mindy Carlyle," he said. "Prom night. I was a sophomore, she was a senior. She knew exactly how she wanted it to happen, so there was a mix CD for background music and a bottle of champagne I had to bribe my cousin to buy for me."

"And how was it for you?" she said, clearly amused.

He shrugged. "She knew what she wanted. I respect that."

"Sounds a bit artificial."

He stroked her hair back from her temple, watched the play of black silk stream through his fingers. "Self-conscious," he said. "Wasn't it for you?"

"I had my first orgasm when I was eight," she said. "Sex didn't seem mysterious to me."

He felt his eyebrows shoot up. "Eight?"

"Horseback riding," she said in explanation.

"You were eight."

She hummed, her gaze avid, bright, probing, testing. "When did you first experience orgasm?"

"I was probably ten or eleven when I had my first wet dream. A little older when I managed it myself."

"As was I. Are you judging me, Daniel?"

"Just surprised," he said. "I haven't had this conversation with a lot of women, but none of them were sexually aware that early."

"It's entirely possible they were lying to you," she said. "Americans are barely comfortable with a grown woman owning her sexuality, let alone the thought of her being aware of it as a child. First love. Mindy Carlyle?"

She was relentless. Suddenly shy, he ducked his head and kissed her shoulder. "No. Not Mindy."

"You knew you didn't love her then, or you know now that you didn't?"

"I knew then," he said.

"How?" she repeated.

"You just know," he said. "What about you? First love? Rory with the motorcycle? The guy with the dish for the hotel room?"

"Dosh," she corrected. "No. Neither."

"Someone else, then."

"I don't think I've ever been in love," she said, looking right at him. "Something to look forward to. God knows I don't have many firsts left."

His heart began to pound against his sternum. To hide his expression he nuzzled against her ear, breathing heat and humidity into the soft fall of hair. She made a soft sound, then turned her face away from the rain and kissed him, an openmouthed brush of lips interspersed with flicks of tongue. She turned onto her side on the narrow chaise, the cashmere throw crumpled between their bodies as she tucked her leg over his. He worked his lower arm under her shoulder and draped his upper arm over her hip and pulled her as close as he could get her. The throw tangled between their legs until Daniel impatiently tugged it from between their bodies.

Tilda gasped when he rolled her to her back, and he had to put out a hand to stop them from tumbling to the floor. Her hands fumbled with his belt and zipper. When he regained his balance he took off her sweater. Her hair sparked and crackled in the gray light, and stayed in an eerie halo around her head even as he tried to work her jeans lower on her hips.

"Not here," she said. "It's silk. I'll never get the stain out."

He slid to his knees on the floor in front of her, gripped her jeans, and pulled them off. "Fuck," he said. "My wallet's in my jacket pocket."

Naked except for her bra, she crawled to her desk and pulled open the top drawer, tore a packet off a strip, and handed it to him, then wrapped the throw around her shoulders as he sheathed himself. "Off," she demanded, pulling at his shirt hem.

Sweat made the cotton cling to his back as he yanked it off, but the moment he did Tilda straddled his thighs and gripped his cock. He steadied her with both hands on her hips, looking down between their bodies for that indescribable moment of lush, hot pressure, groaning as what he saw and felt blended in his mind.

She wrapped her arms around his neck, enfolding them both in the throw, and started to roll her hips into his. Even with miles of leg, she couldn't get her knees on the floor for the leverage she needed so she clamped them to his hips. He thought of horseback riding and orgasms and groaned again. She gave a little laugh, as if she knew what he was thinking, and he opened his eyes, because he had to kiss her and the last thing he wanted to do was head butt her while blindly trying to find her mouth.

But she wasn't looking at him. She was looking over his shoulder. He turned to see a pale reflection of them in the glass. His back, bared to his backside, the throw's fringe clinging to his skin, Tilda straddling him. She looked like a fierce anime character, big eyes, pointy chin, jagged edges of hair, a red mouth that pressed to his as he watched. She was staring at him, unblinking, unflinching, eyes as dark as they were that night on the ledge. His head dropped back and he groaned, felt the sound start between his hipbones and rumble through his chest, into the air. She laughed like a witch or a wild woman and kept up her pace. He had to be hurting her, as tightly as he gripped her, thrusting up into her body in short, sharp jerks, thinking of *nothing, nothing at all* in a desperate effort to stave off the inevitable, until her head dropped back and she cried out. The pulsing contractions around his cock set him off. He held her hard against him and ground up into her body, tremors ripping through him.

The aftershocks left him light-headed and curled around her. "You're going to kill me one of these days," he said.

Her smile curved against the spot where his neck and shoulder met. "I hope not," she said.

She didn't so much get up as tumble backward onto the Turkish rug. He got to his feet and hitched his jeans up enough to let him walk to the bathroom, where he flushed the condom. When he got back to her office, she was dressed and running her fingers through her hair in an attempt to tame the curls. He braced his shoulder against the doorframe and folded his arms. "I expected you to be back on the chaise."

"I thought we might see a film."

He cocked his head and looked at her. "Really," he said, and it wasn't a question. "I thought you didn't want to go out in the rain."

"I'm energized now," she said, focused on her phone. "The theater in Union Square is showing a Clint Eastwood retrospective. *Hereafter* starts in twenty minutes. If we dash we can get there in time."

She'd never suggested a date. She texted him to let him know she would welcome a late-night visitor, and he did the same, keeping things far more casual than he would prefer. "Sure," he said.

"Do you have plans?"

"No," he said.

"Let's go."

She darted into her bedroom to snatch a pair of Wellingtons from her closet, then hurried down the stairs. He followed, shrugging into his blazer while she stomped into the boots, belted her trench coat around her waist, and plucked an umbrella from the stand. He took her hand at the top of the stairs to the sidewalk and they jog-walked through the rain to the theater.

"Popcorn? Junior Mints?" he asked. She shook her head, and they walked into the nearly empty theater as the lights dimmed. She kept her jacket on, and hooked the umbrella over the seat in front of her, and watched the movie, a tale of the ultimate severed connection, with a near-feral intensity.

When it was over, he took a chance. "Dinner?"

"Sure," she said.

He took her to his favorite Ethiopian place, and since she was feeling chatty, probed a little while she studied the menu. "You have art on the walls, but no pictures. None of you, your friends, vacation snapshots, selfies in unusual places, your family, nothing," he said. Earlier in the afternoon he'd taken the time to look at the art on his way up the stairs. Normally he was too focused on getting Tilda naked and in bed to do anything as contemplative as look at pictures.

"They got lost in one of my moves," she said, flipping from the appetizers to the vegetarian dishes. "The originals are in Cornwall with my grandmother, and between school and work, I never got around to replacing them. Fancy a starter?"

"Depends on what a starter is."

"An appetizer."

"The sambossas are good here," he said.

"That and doro wat sounds delicious," she said, and closed the menu. The waiter took their orders and left a bottle of wine.

"You mentioned a business proposal," he said, his voice lifting just a little to indicate that it was a question.

"Yes, I met someone at the same party where I saw you for the second time. He's in charge of North American acquisitions for a luxury goods global conglomerate. I haven't called him yet, but if things go well, there's a good possibility that I would take West Village Stationery to the next level."

"I still don't fully understand why stationery," he said as he poured her a glass.

With one elbow resting on the table, she played with the stem of her wineglass and smiled rather wryly at him. "Two reasons, I suppose. Do you know how really good paper is made?"

"No," he said, and prepared to sit back and enjoy every second of learning.

"It's a rather vigorous process by which the fibers are separated from the junk, beaten into pulp—that's where the expression came from, by the way—screened through mesh to eliminate still more unwanted materials that affect the paper's quality, then pressed and dried. Making one sheet of paper requires three gallons of water, more as the quality increases. The finest paper in the world has been through a purifying crucible. I admire that, and respect the result."

He blinked. Her face, her tone, were far too intense to reflect casual interest, but then again, in his experience people with obsessions were intense about them. "And the second reason?"

This time the smile softened. A better memory. "It began in childhood, as these things so often do. I went to boarding school when I was eight, and was terribly homesick for the first year. The housemistress suggested I write a little bit of a letter each day, to

Nan, my grandmother. I did, and it helped. Eventually." She smiled at him. "Now it's a habit I can't break. Cheers," she said, and tapped her glass to his.

"You don't email her?"

"Nan never made the leap into the digital generation, and I like writing. It feels more real to me," she said, then glanced at him. Like she'd admitted something she shouldn't have. "I suppose that's why I make the connections. I know chemistry when I see it. Computers can match people based on interests or activities or hobbies, but I match people based on something far harder to quantify. It's the human elements, like stationery. You just can't replace the human touch."

"So if I want to make something real to you, I should write it down?"

"Not necessary. You feel very real to me."

There was a simmering silence that smelled of cumin and cayenne in doses intense enough to make his eyes water.

"As long as we're asking the why questions, why the FBI?"

"I started with the NYPD, but went over to the FBI. Better stories," he said.

"Hmm," she said. "Explain. You studied English at school."

She'd remembered. "I have a double major in English and accounting," he said. "My mother said reading books was great but almost no one got paid to do it, and I should be employable. The way I see it, numbers tell stories, too."

"The current story?" she asked, toying with the wineglass.

"The usual sordid attempts to circumvent laws and make more money than any one person or family needs."

Her smile broadened. "Insider trading?"

"It's always happening," he said equably. Tilda knew everyone. She probably sold stationery to the crooks they were trying to catch who partied like the one percent. "We're always two steps behind," he said. "Convincing legislatures to close loopholes takes years, and as fast as we get them closed, really smart guys with MBAs from Ivy League universities find another one to exploit. That doesn't mean we shouldn't catch them."

"So you like stories, and you like numbers."

"I like stories in any form. Numbers tell stories," he said.

Her smile widened.

"I get the feeling that, until now, you didn't think I was that interesting."

"Oh, I thought you were very interesting," she said. "You ask good questions. You listen. You're patient. Persistent. You spend months putting together cases against white-collar criminals, and you run marathons. How many?"

"Twelve," he said. "I'm stepping up to ultramarathons next year."

"Ultra?"

"Fifty miles or more. I'm starting with fifty. We'll see how that goes."

"You are a very interesting person, Daniel Logan."

Her attention felt like a searchlight sliding over his skin, and he understood why people went to Tilda Davies to ask for their most secret desires. She looked at you like you mattered, like she saw who you were and judged not at all. He wasn't about to deny that the attention was addictive. Every time he got a bit of her, he wanted more, more, more.

"Who connects you?" he asked. The question seemed like a non sequitur, but it wasn't. He'd been puzzling over this since the night he met Tilda Davies. In a city like New York, or London, people lived literally one on top of the other. A certain level of intimacy was unavoidable. He overheard conversations, watched dramatic breakups and reunions all take place on the subway in rush hour traffic, and yet despite all that intimacy, everyone was looking for that elusive thing: a meaningful connection.

Everyone except Tilda Davies.

"Sorry?"

"Louise says you're the woman to see if you want an introduction. For any reason. Who does that for you?"

She rested her chin on her fist and smiled at him. "I'm the woman who knows everyone. I don't need introductions. People come to me."

"Everyone needs something," he said.

"I have everything I want."

The thought saddened him a little. She was so young and so alone, and yet she thought she had everything she wanted. The statement also sent up a red flag, because people who had everything they wanted did not sit on ledges twenty-two stories above the street. But for tonight he simply smiled and topped off her glass of wine.

They walked home from the restaurant through a fine mist. Tilda kept her umbrella furled, and her curls coiled in the damp air. Standing on her front steps, he shoved his hands into his pockets to keep from touching her. "Good night, Tilda," he said.

"You don't want to come in for a nightcap?"

"I have to be on a train to Long Island early tomorrow for my niece's birthday party," he said, because there had to be a limit to how this happened. Suddenly dry-mouthed, he bent to kiss her cheek, his hands fisted in his pocket linings. "Go inside and lock up."

She opened the half door, then turned back to face him. "Thank you for a lovely day, Daniel," she said, and closed it behind her.

– SEVEN –

October

"**A**re you keeping your name?"

Tilda sat at the maple table in front of West Village Stationery's front window across from Marin Bryant, a professional dancer and one of her former introductions. She sifted through the personal notecard samples and withdrew one, nudging it forward for Marin to take a second look.

"Professionally," Marin said. She smiled a little, secret smile, and tucked her straight blond hair behind her ear as she considered the card, bronze and port ink on ecru two-ply cotton paper. "I'll still dance and choreograph as Marin Bryant, for as long as people want to see me on stage. Personally, I'll be Marin Bryant-Fleming."

Tilda offered another sample of card stock, this time from an up-and-coming designer out of Rouen. Marin and her husband, Cole, were one of her most successful connections. Marin, with her demanding, intense life as a dancer in service to art and beauty, needed a situation in which she was in complete control. Cole, the son of an old New York family and Marine turned trader, wanted the risk of the ultimate surrender. Both demanded absolute secrecy, and therefore arranged their encounters through Tilda, until the requests stopped abruptly the previous year. Tilda had noted their end without surprise, given the hothouse, intense nature of their relationship. In her experience things like that burned too brightly to last.

Marin appearing at her shop to order personalized stationery shocked her. She'd bowed to her mother-in-law's request to order the wedding invitations from Mrs. John L. Strong, a choice Tilda would never begrudge her. Tilda knew all about tradition, and expectations, but sincerely appreciated Marin buying her notecards from West Village Stationery. Marin represented her target market, the younger generation accustomed to texting and email, who wanted something less iconic and more personal.

"Those," Marin said decisively. "The pear logo. Is gold too pretentious? It feels pretentious, but—"

Tilda shook her head wordlessly, and smiled. She felt a deep connection with Marin, one based on growing up poor and suddenly finding oneself in a world where money was no object in the pursuit of luxury and quality. She was very good at recognizing the Imposter Syndrome in other people, because it was carved so deeply into her bones after years of attending boarding school with girls who went by their last names but in the outside world had titles in front of their proper names.

"No? Then gold. How many should I order?"

"One hundred cards with envelopes," Tilda said, and noted the order in her iPad. "That's one of her standard dies but each card is made by hand, so the order will take six weeks or so. You can order more via our website. Just sign in to your account and we'll take care of the rest."

Marin smiled at her. An absolutely stupendous diamond glittered on her ring finger, constantly slipping to one side or the other from the weight of the stone. Invited but unable to attend due to travel, Tilda had read about the wedding in the *New York Times* Weddings section's full-page description. That kind of fairy tale wasn't in her future, and she knew it, no matter how easy it was to lie with Daniel on the chaise lounge in her office and spin stories out of her past.

It was a mistake, relaxed, warm, watching rivulets of rain trickle down the greenhouse glass that comprised the back wall and ceiling of her home office. She'd let down her guard. Let him in, dangerously quickly, surrendering to impulses she'd learned the hard way were untrustworthy.

"Thank you," Marin said.

"It was my pleasure," Tilda replied automatically.

"I meant for introducing us," Marin said, her voice soft. "I had no idea he was out there. Without you, our paths never would have crossed."

"Oh, you might have met," Tilda said lightly. "He might have come to see you dance. You might have made an appearance at a fundraiser, and caught his eye. You were clearly meant to be."

"But we wouldn't have known what we know about each other," Marin said. "Meeting like we did, in the dark, in secret, let us be who we were. You made that possible."

"It was my pleasure," Tilda said again. "I'm very happy for you both. I'll call you when the order arrives and make arrangements to drop it off."

"That's not necessary. I now have people who pick things up for me. My dry cleaning, my groceries, anything I buy now appears in my drawers or closets like magic. The one percent lives in a completely different world. Rather like this one," she said, looking around the shop. "I guess it's my world, now. I'm a long way from sharing a sixth-floor walkup with three other dancers and an incontinent, eighteen-year-old cat whose hair fell out when it got stressed."

"Enjoy it," Tilda said gently as she followed Marin's gaze around the shop, the clean, shining maple floors, the white walls, the shelves spotlit by individual lights. Most card and stationery shops overflowed with merchandise, greeting cards, packaged thank-you or sympathy notes, journals, day planners, calendars, desk accessories. Tilda opted for a simple message: I sell only what's worth buying.

She was a long way from a three-room farmhouse in Cornwall. The trip had cost her dearly, and she intended to get her blood's worth of it, including the improbable, hard-to-define relationship with Daniel Logan. There would be no happy ending for them. Cole and Marin may have found a way to burn without consuming, but so far that particular skill had eluded Tilda.

She escorted Marin to the door, then walked over to Penny, standing behind the glass display case that served as a counter. "I'm going out for a bit," she said to Penny. "I've an appointment with an artist with the improbable name of Bathsheba Clark. Have you heard of her?"

Penny tucked her hair behind her ear and frowned. "From the seventies, maybe? I have a vague memory of a few pictures in a textbook in an art history class."

"Someone I met at a party said her work might be suitable for the shop."

"You're expanding into art?" Penny said, her eyes widening slightly.

"Perhaps," Tilda said. "When I spoke to Ms. Clark she said she was working on palimpsests."

"A manuscript that has been reused. A work in progress, repurposed," Penny intoned. "Graffiti and bumper stickers layered on street signs comprise a palimpsest. It's an interesting field at the moment, and wildly divergent from your current selection. I have some ideas, if you're interested in that market."

Tilda slid her bag to the crook of her elbow. "I'll let you know when I return."

Outside her front door was a gorgeous New York fall day. The air when she walked to work held just a bit of a chill, but the sun warmed it pleasantly. She made her way through the Village to the busier streets of SoHo, slowing her pace to cross the brick-paved streets. She'd been waiting out the sensible three to five days before contacting Colin when he called and took her out for burgers at the Broome Street Bar. After the requisite small talk covered the weather and traffic, he moved straight into the business portion of the lunch. It was a high step for a girl from Cornwall, but she'd spent her three days preparing a pitch that shot for the stars, settling for nothing less than retail space for West Village Stationery in upscale malls and airports around the world. She'd not planned to make the pitch at SoHo's famous dive bar, but she was a Davies. She made do with what she had, and kept her eyes on the prize.

A global brand by thirty. That's what she wanted, to be internationally renowned, not just memorable, but unforgettable. Quality would expect not just the unique but the truly sublime, *objets d'art*, and palimpsests were as good a place to start as any. She needed to position herself as exceptional in her current field, with an eye able to see the extraordinary in other disciplines. Colin took her proposal back to the management team, and promised to be in touch. When she'd described the meeting in her letter to Nan, she was so excited her handwriting lacked its usual swoops and curls. Nan would know exactly what this meant to her.

"Eighteen, sixteen, fourteen," she said to herself, then stopped and rang the buzzer for 5B.

She heard a click, but no welcome. "Hello?"

"Who is it?"

"It's Matilda Davies. We had an—"

The buzzer rang out, cutting her off. She pushed through the door into a foyer that hadn't been cleaned since the building went up, and began climbing stairs. Two doors faced the top of the fifth-floor landing. She knocked on the one that wasn't labeled *A*.

The door cracked open.

"Lady Matilda?" Her drawl was from the American South.

The woman standing in front of her was Tilda's height in her heels, which meant she had five inches on Tilda in flat feet. Her face was the color of good coffee, lined but in that ageless space between forty and seventy. Her hair was shorn to her scalp, leaving only a tight crop of iron gray. Her face was free of makeup, and she wore a man's Oxford shirt, loose pants, and Birkenstock sandals so old dirt molecules from Woodstock were likely embedded in the cork.

"It's just Tilda," she said.

The woman opened the door. Tilda walked into the kind of space most New Yorkers dreamed about. The flat occupied one-half of the fifth floor, and featured sparkling-clean floor-to-ceiling windows facing east, south, and west. The light was stupendous, sunshine pouring into the vast, cluttered atelier, the space so airy Tilda had the odd sensation of sitting on Louise's ledge again. She shook it off and looked around.

Paintings, framed and unframed, were stacked against the north wall. A table that had to be six feet by ten feet stood nearest the east windows, and on that table lay a number of implements and tools Tilda didn't recognize. But she recognized the ubiquitous artist's companion, the Moleskine sketchbook, stacked ten high and three deep in the middle of the table. Loose, large sheets of one hundred percent cotton drawing paper lay scattered on the table like a giant's game of Fifty-Two-Card Pickup.

Without conscious thought, Tilda drew closer to the enormous table, which held works in varying states of completion, some containing elements seemingly torn from the notebooks, layered watercolors or ink drawings, and handwritten notes. The mature trees of Central Park overlaid a series of poppies, another of the Brooklyn Bridge, yet another of bodegas along Broadway.

The process was completely foreign to Tilda, so she started with what she could sincerely compliment. "The light is amazing." Unless she was in her third-floor office, she didn't get this kind of light in her town house. "The whole space is brilliant."

"Rent control," Ms. Clark said with immense satisfaction. "They'll have to carry me out of this apartment in a body bag. Can I get you some tea?"

Indeed, this was not a situation where one got straight down to business. "I'd love some," she said.

She made the effort to look at the canvases on the easels around the large room, but by the time the tea had steeped and Ms. Clark poured two cups, Tilda was back at the table, all but clasping her hands to prevent herself from touching the pages.

"Thank you," she said and wrapped her hands around the cup, holding it carefully to avoid spilling tea on the . . . "Ms. Clark, what, exactly, are these?"

"Call me Sheba." Tilda felt like she'd been given an immense privilege. "I've got fifty-five years of journals, sketchbooks, finished canvases, unfinished canvases. Good old-fashioned experiments. It was time to start doing something with them. Look back at my history, see where I'd been, where I might be going with what's left of the time God's given me."

Tilda hadn't felt so off-balance in years, except, perhaps, with Daniel, who in one afternoon knew more about Tilda than any other single person alive except Nan. With a fine disregard for the materials on the table, Sheba set her mug down and pulled forward three pages bound. "Take a look. Stop worrying about the tea, child. If you spill it, the color would just become part of the page."

Tilda lifted one of the canvases. Sheba had scraped the painting of the Sheep Meadow in Central Park down to smears of paint on canvas, layered the text from what appeared to be a treatise on botany over it, then somehow erased the text to near invisibility and added several rough sketches and watercolors of the same spot to the canvas.

The palimpsests both intrigued and confused—or perhaps annoyed—her. Any attempt to make sense of the words and sketches was thwarted by the seemingly random placement, or the juxtaposition of colors, materials, and jumps through time. On the surface, it had no place whatsoever in West Village Stationery.

Tilda set it down. Picked up her mug of tea, now cool enough to drink. Sipped it. Waited in the silence and sunshine. Picked up a different page in progress, for the moment mostly sky and the Brooklyn Bridge. They made her uncomfortable, with their jumbled images, blended colors, not certain where to rest her eye.

She couldn't stop looking at them, and the paper. Thick, sturdy, textured, the edges torn to expose the fibers. She trailed her fingers along one edge, then couldn't stop touching them.

"I'm not sure these are right for my shop," she said finally.

"I understand," Sheba said.

"I'm not sure they're *wrong* for my shop," Tilda said.

"I understand," Sheba said again.

What she was sure of is that she had to have them. Couldn't place why, but the feeling was unmistakable, both discomfiting and commanding. Rather like Daniel, in fact. "Why not use a gallery to sell these? They'd certainly get a more discriminating buyer, have the connections."

"Galleries left me behind decades ago," Sheba said, but her voice wasn't angry, simply stating a fact. "I don't see any need to go crawling back to them now. And I like your shop."

"You've been to my shop?"

"Walked past," Sheba said. "The windows are works of art in themselves."

"Penny, my designer, does them." The current displays were

of hot air balloons created out of thin papier-mâché, spilling cards into the updrafts to soar with hawks and ravens and other birds of prey over a replica of the city. Penny had a gift Tilda admired but didn't hope to replicate.

"I gathered as much. You're also a work of art, child, but you didn't create those windows. You've got an eye, though, if you hired her."

"Thank you, I think," she said, amused, and sorted through the top layer of pages on the table. Sheba didn't try to sell her on the work, or dissuade Tilda. She simply waited while Tilda made up her mind. She decided what to offer based on two broad categories: things people expected in a couture stationery shop, and things they didn't expect but would want once they saw them. It was the second ability that caught Colin's eye. People would want these. Tilda might not understand them, but when she thought about someone else selling them, her stomach sank. "Let's give this a trial run. How many do you have ready to sell?"

In response Sheba walked over to a double door and swung it open. Inside were stacks and stacks of pages in a twisting spiral of edges and angles, all different sizes, all unmounted.

"Excellent," Tilda said. "In cases like this we would work on consignment. I supply the space and display the product; in return I take a percentage of the selling price."

"That's fine, child," Sheba said.

"They need to be mounted. A friend of mine runs a gallery in the West Village. I suggest she mount them. I'd also like to ask her opinion on pricing them, and possibly about having a show of the larger pieces. A two-pronged approach, double the exposure, that sort of thing."

"All right," she said. "We'll see how they do. Just put them out for sale and see what happens. I'm done with them."

With an eye toward the space on her walls, Tilda selected ten larger pieces and twenty smaller ones. Sheba wrapped them in tissue and slid them into a brown carrier bag. Back down the five flights of stairs, to the SoHo street that now felt crowded and far too noisy. She walked back to the shop, picking up a container of miso soup along the way.

"What did you get?" Penny asked, eyeing the bags. "Miso soup in that one."

Tilda set the soup on her desk and drew out the pieces she'd taken on consignment. "These. Tell me what you think. In this you have rather more experience than I."

The soup had cooled on the walk back. Tilda slid her thumb under the lid's lip until it came free, then dropped it in the trash. She drank her soup while Penny respectfully unwrapped pages.

"I did some research on Bathsheba Clark while you were gone. She was big in the late sixties and early seventies, then fell out of favor when the times changed and she didn't. And, I think she had a child out of wedlock, which was still rather sketchy in those days. Are these . . . ?" She looked at Tilda. "Are these sketches from Bathsheba Clark's *journals*?"

Tilda nodded.

"Oh my God. This sketch looks like her architectural phase from the early eighties. It looks like . . . is this an early draft of her cathedrals series?"

"Possibly," Tilda said. "She's curating her history, she said. Is this unusual?"

"Of course it's unusual! Her *journals*? Her history, the foundation of her *career* as an artist, the growth, the shifts, the transitions? Most people can't bear to do something like that, destroy the thing that charts their progression as an artist."

"Are these something we should have in the shop?"

"*Of course they're something we should have in the shop!*" Penny flipped to a second page, and stroked the tips of her fingers over the rough edges. "I'm holding Bathsheba Clark's thoughts in my hands. She made this, and I can touch it. How much? I want all of them. How much?"

That was exactly the visceral reaction Tilda hoped for in a customer, from viewing to wanting in under ten seconds. "I need to talk to Edith about pricing them."

"More than I can afford," Penny said. "A friend just casually mentioned her at a party, and you find these? You and your introductions."

"I didn't meet her before today. My friend just said I might be interested in her work. I don't understand them," she said, eyeing the palimpsests. "They're rough and uneven and somewhat bizarre."

Penny was staring at her, incredulous amusement in her eyes. "So why take them?"

"I hated the thought of anyone else selling them. It's a gut reaction I've learned to respect."

It was inexplicable, really, this mixture of possessiveness and wary vigilance, as if the works had some power she didn't recognize and she'd just let that into her shop. Her life. She felt the same way about Daniel Logan. She didn't understand him, with his logical, methodical approach to life as a series of puzzles to be solved. He used columns and rows and the law to make things plain, while she used paper and ink to hide what she didn't want anyone to see. But the thought of him with anyone else left her shaky, cold.

Tilda finished the soup and dropped the container in the trash. "Run them over to Edith to see about getting them mounted and framed. We'll take them in stages, hang them as she's got them ready," she said, then picked up the phone to call Edith.

– EIGHT –

Late November

Daniel pushed open the front door to Fifteen Perry Street, then locked it behind him before taking the stairs two at a time to the third floor, past the black-and-white pictures of the Eiffel Tower, the Brooklyn Bridge, the kind of art you could buy from any street vendor. Tilda had pictures of recognizable landmarks from all over the world—Oxford's dreaming spires, Tokyo's endless neon—but none of her family.

She'd texted him an hour ago: Meet me at Perry Street. He was used to her commands, but earlier in the week an average-looking guy in a bespoke suit had walked in off the street, and asked to talk to someone about an ongoing fraud. Daniel was the guy not on a call or in a meeting, so he sat across from an I-banker in a conference room who told him a story of greed, fraud, and deception that, if it panned out through to indictments, would make headlines around the world. A couple of days to check out his story, and Daniel went from routine duties to a career-making case. He hadn't talked to Tilda since he'd picked her up at the airport after a trip to London, and frankly, he could use a quickie over lunch. He was uncharacteristically jacked, his brain dumping adrenaline into his system every time he thought about what this could mean for investors, for the department, for his career.

"You've got to stop leaving the front door unlocked like that," he said as he swung into her office, expecting to find her at her desk. No Tilda. He walked into her bedroom, and found it empty as well. The bathroom door was closed.

"Tilda?" he said as he knocked.

Silence. He could hear her breathing behind the door. He squared up on the balls of his feet, put his hands on his hips, and stared at the locked door. Any number of possibilities had crossed his mind when he saw her text—Tilda in lingerie, Tilda naked, Tilda with lunch because he was hungry, too—but Tilda locked in the bathroom wasn't on the list.

"Are you trapped in there?" he asked, trying to figure out if he had to call the FDNY or if he could jimmy open the lock with a credit card or a screwdriver.

"No."

"So open the door."

No movement, just a shaky inhale.

"Tilda."

Silence.

His brain spun up an increasingly wild range of scenarios: being held hostage, a sudden psychotic break on her part, a sudden psychotic break on *his* part. He checked his phone. Yes, she'd texted him. He leaned against the doorframe, and tried to figure out where to start. "What's wrong?"

"I'm late."

"Well," he said with a laugh, "you're going to be even more late if you don't come out of the bathroom."

"Not that kind of late, Daniel."

His grin disappeared so fast his jaw muscles tensed in protest. Emotion careened through him, shock, with a primitive possessiveness hard on its heels when the image of Tilda, pregnant with his baby, bloomed in his brain. He cleared his throat. "How late?"

"I'm not sure. My cycle has been off lately, with the travel."

"How can you be sure you're late, then?"

"I am. I have other symptoms, too."

"Such as?"

The silence crackled with irritation. Tilda, She Who Sat On Ledges, didn't talk about personal things. Finally, "My breasts are tender, and I'm bloated."

"Those are PMS signs, too, right?"

"Yes. This is different. I feel sick."

"It's the adrenaline rush. Five days isn't that late," he tried.

"Five days is a generous estimate from the latest likely time for my period to start. If I'm counting precisely, I'm two weeks late."

Oh, fuck.

He leaned his head against the bathroom door. Now her voice was steady, as always, giving nothing away. He shrugged out of his jacket and loosened his tie as he automatically started a mental list, recording date, time, weather. *Twelve forty-seven, November twentieth, gray, cold, windy day.* Then he made a list of the range of emotions she'd ricocheted through since he knocked on the door. *Flat, irritated, precise.*

"Do you have a pregnancy test?

"Yes."

"Have you taken the pregnancy test?"

"No."

"Why not?"

"I'm afraid to." *Testy.* A hint of shaky nerves in her voice.

Involuntarily, he smiled. "Tilda, sweetheart, open the package and take the test. It's not going to change anything. It's just going to tell you what's already real."

He heard cardboard tearing, then the fan clicked on, obscuring any other sounds. He wasn't so stressed he couldn't find her reticence amusing. After everything they'd done together, she wouldn't let him hear her peeing. Water ran, the slick sound of soap lathering, rinsing, drying, all while he waited outside.

"Tilda. Let me in."

She unlocked the door. He saw the pregnancy test stick sitting on the counter. Tilda perched on the edge of the bathtub, legs crossed, arms folded protectively over her abdomen, the side of her ring finger in her mouth.

He'd never seen her bite her nails, much less her cuticles. "Hey," he said quietly. "It's okay."

She cut him a glance through her lashes. *Pissed off.* Tilda would not be patronized.

"A couple of minutes, right?"

"How do you know that? Don't touch it! It has to be level."

Hysterical. This was like watching a kaleidoscope made of razor blades spin. Trying to remember his suicidal jumper training, he eased to the floor with his back to the cabinet, avoiding the stick with its purple cap on the end. "Remember that conversation we had about first times? This isn't my first time sitting in a bathroom with a panicked woman, waiting to see if a line appears."

"It's my first time sitting in a bathroom, panicked, waiting to see if a line appears."

"You've never had a pregnancy scare?"

"The point of taking the pill and using condoms is to prevent pregnancy scares." *Pedantic.*

"Did you miss a day?"

"No."

"So, we're probably fine."

"You say we—"

"Because *we* are *we*. Especially in this."

She peeked at the stick. Let her breath out in a shudder and went back to biting her cuticle. Stopped. Smoothed her skirt down. *Nervous.* Nervous about being left alone, or nervous about being forever tied to a man because she accidentally got knocked up?

"I went to England two weeks ago. Perhaps jet lag threw off my cycle."

"We didn't have sex while you were in England," he pointed out.

"We did when I returned."

Against the door, if he remembered correctly. Her skirt at her hips, his trousers undone just enough to release his cock. She'd rubbed him to hardness on the way home from JFK. An hour on the LIE with Tilda's hand gripping his cock, blood thumping in his veins. She'd relayed details of her business meetings, a party attended by several well-known actors, which a friend of a friend invited her to that lasted until dawn, a contact she made with an investor who liked what he'd heard about West Village Stationery, reestablishing herself in a world she'd left behind a decade earlier, all the while subtly jacking him. He'd parked illegally, thrown his badge onto the dash, and all but dragged her into the house. It was their first time without a condom, and when he emerged to park the car like a law-abiding citizen of the city of New York, his entire nervous system was lit up like Times Square.

"We'll deal with it together," he said quietly. "We have options. It's not a terrible thing."

She said nothing. "The point of taking the pill is that it won't happen."

"Nothing's foolproof except abstinence."

He meant it as a joke. The look she slid him had an edge that cycled back through pissed off.

"Quality Group kicked my proposal up a level to talk about bringing me into their premier brands division, which means I'm going to spend the next six months flying all over the world. You work sixty hours a week on a good week. Morning sickness and nappies and nursing aren't in my business plan. Who else?"

Now wasn't the time to tell her he'd be lucky to work eighty hours a week for the foreseeable future. Wait, *jealousy*? "Lindy, my college girlfriend. A one-night stand texted a month later, but she got her period a couple of days after the first text."

"Texting does seem to mean trouble for you."

One corner of her mouth lifted as she spoke. A fragment of humor. He ran his hands over his scalp and blew out his breath. "Neither of those things were trouble. They just were. Life happens, Tilda. You don't know if it's a good thing or a bad thing until later."

"I'm not in the mood for a philosophical discussion, Daniel."

Her voice was strained. He took a chance and shifted up to sit on the edge of the tub with her. "Hey," he said. "Hey. It'll be fine. We've got this. We'll get married."

A silence he couldn't describe. Did he say what he thought he'd just said?

"We'll get married?" *Incredulous.*

"Uh," he said.

"Did you just ask me to marry you whilst sitting on the loo floor, waiting for a pregnancy test result?" *Really incredulous.* Was it that crazy?

"Well, technically, I didn't ask. I just presumed."

"Because it's the right thing to do? People don't get married because they turn up pregnant. This is not the seventeenth century, or even the nineteen seventies."

She was laughing, or maybe about to cry. It was hard to tell, because Tilda not quite in control of her emotions wasn't something he'd seen, ever. "Yeah, because it's the right thing to do, but because I want to marry you."

"You don't want to marry me." Point-blank *certain*.

"I do," he said, relieved to hear he sounded pretty certain himself. *Irresistible force, meet immovable object.*

She skimmed her hair back from her face. "You really don't. You really, really don't. You're saying this because you've got a savior complex and I might be in trouble."

"I've been through enough psychological testing to know I don't have a savior complex, I have obsessive tendencies. I'm saying this because I love you, and whether or not you're pregnant, I want to marry you."

"You love me."

"Yeah," he said, more defensively than he should. "I love you."

"Oh, Daniel," she murmured.

Remorse. Nothing else. He waited, as the seconds ticked by, waited for the test to hand them an answer about their future, waited for her to say something. Anything. Instead, she turned to him, fisted her hands in his shirt and leaned her head onto his shoulder. Resigned, he wrapped his arms around her narrow back, and felt her relax into him, bit by bit.

He checked his watch surreptitiously. Four minutes. More than enough time. He straightened his spine and reached for the stick.

"No line," he said.

"That's a line," she said, pointing at the stick.

"That's the control line to show the test is working. Did you read the directions?"

"No," she said. "No line?" *Relief.*

"No line," he repeated. "Chalk it up to a body clock out of whack from travel."

She took the stick from him, looked at it, looked at the instructions, then back at the stick. "What if it's not accurate?"

"If you're a week late, that's plenty of time for the test to come up positive."

"Daniel, really, your knowledge of pregnancy tests is rather—"
Manic relief.

"My sister Angie had trouble getting pregnant, so I know all about cervical fluid and luteal cycles and HCG, plus just about every man I know has gone through this at one time or another. It's not complicated. Five days to two weeks late and four minutes of waiting is plenty for a definitive answer." He got to his feet and held out his hand to help her up. "You're not pregnant."

She slid the stick back into the wrapper, dropped it in the trash can under the sink, then went up on her tiptoes and kissed him gently. "Thank you for coming over," she said quietly.

"You're welcome." He tried to keep from sounding *royally pissed off*, and failed.

"Do you have to go back to work right away, or can you stay for lunch?"

He looked at his watch, tried to figure out what he wanted to do. He'd just told her he loved her, and asked her to marry him, and gotten not a negative but no response, *no fucking response at all*, to either statement. His ego could use a break.

"Please," she said quietly. "Daniel. Please stay."

Apologetic, but not apologizing. Say hello to being in love with Tilda Davies. "Fine," he said.

She squeezed his hand, then turned and nuzzled into his palm, pressing a kiss there, then to his wrist, all the while watching him with her gray eyes. He'd come here intent on a noontime quickie, and the events of the last ten minutes hadn't changed that, just added layers of dangerous complexity to the near-constant heat simmering in his blood. Lust, love, and wounded masculine pride made for a potent aphrodisiac.

He stroked his fingertips along the fine skin covering her cheekbone. When he reached her hairline, he wound her curls around his fingers and held her for his mouth. Her lips parted under his almost immediately, and he could taste her emotions, relief and desire, as her tongue rubbed against his. He curled his fingers in the fabric of her skirt and drew it up as she backed him to the edge of the bed. When his knees hit the edge, he sat down hard. She went to work on his belt and zipper, freeing his cock through the opening in his boxers. He glanced at the drawer that held sex toys, lubricant, condoms, and a selection of books with cracked spines, Dorothy Sayers. Tilda read herself to sleep with *Gaudy Night*. She followed his gaze, then looked back at him, one black brow arched.

"Up to you," he said. He'd just asked her to marry him. He didn't give a damn about condoms.

Unsurprisingly, she tore a condom from the strip in her nightstand and rolled it down his shaft while he worked her panties down her thighs and off. With a knee on either side of his hips, she held her skirt at the tops of her thighs with one hand and braced herself on his shoulder with the other. He held his cock, and bit back a groan as she enveloped him in tight heat.

She wasn't very wet yet, so he waited while her body adjusted to his. She bent her head until their foreheads touched, her fingers gripping his nape through his collar, tie. "Daniel," she whispered.

He smoothed his hands up her hips, under her rucked-up skirt. "It's better without the condom," he said.

"I know," she said. "But this is good, right?"

Her curls tumbled in her eyes as she moved. Hell, yes, this was good. He leaned back on one hand and held his shirt and tie out of the way with the other so he could watch his cock disappear into her body with each slow stroke of her hips. She lifted her fingers to his mouth and watched him lick the tips, then circled them over her clit. Almost immediately the sex flush bloomed on her throat and cheeks. Black hair, gray eyes, pink cheeks, and her mouth swollen from kissing him. Each gliding stroke drew his orgasm up his shaft. He let her please them both, unabashedly focused on the way her fingers moved in slow, tight circles, and tried to be grateful for the deadening effect of the condom.

Her head dropped back. He leaned forward and closed his teeth on the tendon in her neck. She gasped, laughed, shuddered, and tipped her head down to kiss him. Her tongue in his mouth, her fingers brushing his abdomen, her sex slick and grasping around him, and a particular needy tone to her soft inhalations as her muscles tightened. He gripped her hip and thrust up into her, again, again, and then she unraveled, her lips soft and hot against his, her weight a sweet heat and pressure, just enough to send him over. He ground up into her as his release pulsed through him.

She kissed him, waiting out the aftershocks, then scooted off him and back into the bathroom. A quick cleanup, then she emerged. "I'll put together a quick lunch," she said, and went downstairs. He cleaned up, zipped up, and heard the fridge door opening and plates clattering against the granite countertops as he followed her. She'd brought out containers of hummus, cheese, crackers, sliced peppers, some deli meats, olives, and pita. He opened lids and found serving spoons and forks while she got them glasses of water. They sat at the counter and ate, watching the light dapple the trees in the back garden.

"Did you go into work today?" he asked finally.

"For a couple of hours. I was working on receipts from my trip, and between looking back at last month and counting days, realized I was late. I went to Duane Reade and bought the test, then came home. I'll go back after lunch. You?"

"The case of the decade walked in off the street a couple of days ago," he said. He didn't usually talk about work, much less make it sound like he was on rooftops, fists on hips and chest thrust out, saving the world, but he needed to salvage something out of this. And, if it panned out, it was huge.

Her eyes widened. "That's wonderful," she said. "What's it about?"

"Greed," he said shortly. "In my line of work it's always about greed. Sometimes the biggest problem people have is knowing when they have enough." His voice trailed off and he looked at her over the hummus. "Do you know anyone looking to moonlight as a whistleblower?"

"Not I, said the little red hen," Tilda said, her tone light. "I would have told you if someone had come to me asking to be connected with you and your professional capacity."

"Good."

"Your whistleblower is in good hands," she said quietly.

Daniel wished she'd give him the same trust. He shrugged, and finished his lunch. She escorted him to the front door, and waited until he was on the pavement. "Yes."

He turned back to face her. "Yes, what?"

"Yes, I'll marry you. If you still want to marry me, that is."

He couldn't read her now, which at least felt familiar. Tilda cycling through the emotional spectrum was beyond disconcerting, into unreal. "Of course I still want to marry you."

"Even though I'm not pregnant."

"Even though you're not pregnant."

"Even though I didn't say yes right away."

"Even though you didn't say yes right away."

"When?"

He looked at his watch, then at her. "What are you doing later today?"

She laughed.

"Don't laugh. I know judges," he said. "Do you want a big wedding?"

"I'd really prefer to elope," she said.

This didn't surprise him. "I'll text you."

It took him longer than he anticipated to get everything set up, but toward the end of the week he texted her.

Noon. Judge Power's chambers at courthouse.

To Do

1. ~~Get ring~~
2. ~~Get license~~
3. ~~Arrange judge~~
4. *Get married*

— NINE —

December, Winter Solstice

"You're going into the shop today?" Daniel asked without turning away from the armoire, where he was messing about in a shoebox he'd brought with him when he moved into the town house the previous weekend. Suspecting the shoebox held her wedding ring, she turned her back on him to give him privacy.

"I am," she said. She needed something to ground her. The days between Daniel proposing and their wedding day had passed in a blur not all that dissimilar from jet lag. She wasn't quite sure where she was, or who she was, and kept getting lost in the neighborhood she'd lived and worked in since graduating from college.

She tossed her phone on the bed, toweled her hair into a wild mess, then ran her fingers through it. "I have two morning appointments with brides, a shipment arriving from Paris, and I need to go over some things with Penny before taking the weekend off."

"Okay," he said, then shoved something into his pocket. Definitely the ring. "You're sure this is how you want to do this?"

She peered at him as she wriggled into her panties. "My mother is hardly going to drop everything and fly here for our wedding. Nan doesn't travel. Given my history of relationships, my friends expect me to elope. The more important question is whether you want to elope. Your family is only an hour away."

He closed the armoire door and buttoned his white shirt. He wore a gray suit with a deep red tie, a black belt, and wingtips. "After watching Angie get married, I have no interest in a big wedding."

"Neither do I," she said from the closet. She slid her arms into a long-sleeved wrap dress of garnet wool, tied the belt, then zipped up black leather boots. He snagged her on her way out the door to drop a kiss on her nape. The strength of his arm contrasted with the tender touch of his mouth sent a shiver down her spine.

"I'll meet you at the courthouse. You know where it is?"

"Yes," she said.

So she walked to the shop under a low, threatening gray sky, and worked. She helped customers, fielded email requests, sorted orders, talked to Edith about the upcoming show for Sheba. The day had an aura of unreality about it, humid air and a cold breeze that boded of a coming storm, mirroring the mix of secretive joy and utter terror inside her.

Married. The one thing she'd never thought she'd do. She didn't put her own desires on her list, much less think about a wedding day, or a lifelong commitment. No wonder the gathering darkness of the winter solstice made her feel like she'd slipped down the rabbit hole.

Daniel got to the courthouse before she did. He was waiting on the other side of the metal detectors, making idle conversation with the officers on duty while his gaze never left hers. Her stomach flip-flopped when she looked at him. Was this love? She didn't know, honestly wasn't sure what she felt, only that it was powerful, deep, dangerous, and reciprocated.

"Hi," he said, and gave her a quick kiss. "Judge Power's chambers are upstairs."

She held his hand on the way up the stairs, where Daniel walked into the secretary's office. "Daniel Logan and Tilda Davies to see the judge," he said.

Judge Power poked her head around the door. "Come in, Daniel," she said, then introduced herself to Tilda. "Congratulations to you both. Did you bring witnesses?"

"No," Daniel said, and withdrew what she assumed was the license from his jacket pocket.

"Mary, could we borrow you for a few minutes?" the judge asked.

The clerk appeared in the door with a takeout container of falafel in one hand and a fork in the other. There was some fussing over the license. Drawn to the thunderclouds, Tilda wandered over to the window and looked out at the sky.

"Hey," he said gently.

She turned to face him and buried her face in his chest, the scent of his clothes so familiar. She felt so tall next to him, but at moments like this, their size difference became clear.

"Are you sure?" She didn't look up at him, so he bent at the knees, clasped both her hands in his, and sought her eyes. "Tilda, are you sure? We don't have to do this."

She wasn't sure. She'd said yes because she wanted him with a desperation that was equally familiar and frightening. But the alternative, saying no and eventually losing him, was equally familiar and frightening. She'd denied herself for so long. Deep down, she knew how it would end, but couldn't refuse herself the here and now.

Her shoulders shuddered with her inhale, less so on the exhale. She turned their hands so his were palm up with hers palm down in his. Together they looked at her long, thin fingers, the nails trimmed and buffed to a high shine, bare of rings except for the gold band gleaming on her left thumb. The ring she'd chosen for him.

"Oh," he said, almost helplessly.

"Yes," she said. She looked up at him, and saw joy in his eyes. "I'm sure. Yes."

When they turned back to the room, the judge was turning off her computer, and the clerk was finishing her falafel. Daniel dropped both of Tilda's hands to guide her with a palm at the small of her back. They stood in front of the judge. Tilda held out a book with a white leather cover embossed with *Book of Common Prayer* in gold. "Use this, please," she said. "The wedding rite is marked."

Judge Power didn't blink an eye, turned to the pages marked by the ribbon. Tilda clasped Daniel's hands and faced him. When it came time to exchange rings, he pulled a pale blue box from his pocket, opened it, and pulled out a thin platinum band. No diamonds, no precious stones of any kind.

It was perfect. Exactly what she would have chosen for herself.

"Daniel, you have taken Matilda to be your wife. Do you promise to love her, comfort her, honor and keep her, in sickness and in health; and, forsaking all others, to be faithful to her as long as you both shall live?"

Without hesitation, he slid the band onto her left ring finger. "I do."

She did the same with his ring, transferring the simple band of gold from her thumb to his ring finger, and smiled when his thumb worried at it. Neither of them wore rings. Wedding bands would take some getting used to.

"You may kiss the bride," Judge Power said with a smile.

Daniel laid his fingers on Tilda's jaw and kissed her, soft and sweet. Her hand rose to clasp his wrist and hold him close.

"Congratulations," Mary said.

Handshakes all around, then Tilda picked up her bag and

withdrew neatly wrapped gifts for Judge Power and Mary, boxes of notecards stamped with gold bumblebees. Judge Power seemed genuinely touched.

"Tilda, you forgot to sign the license," Mary said. Without hesitation, Tilda uncapped her fountain pen and signed her name in a swirl of script. *Matilda Elizabeth Agnes Davies.*

"Your middle name is Agnes?" Daniel asked as they headed for the stairs to the main floor.

"One of my middle names is Agnes," she said as she pulled on her coat and buttoned it.

"You're one surprise after another."

"It's Nan's name. Agnes Elizabeth. Mum's name is Elizabeth Agnes Mary, for Nan and her sisters."

"Who picked Matilda?" Daniel asked as he claimed two overnight bags from the officer staffing the metal detectors. "It's quintessentially British, but now seems out of place given the family naming conventions."

"Apparently, my father did," she said. "Where are we going?"

"It's a surprise," he said, and surprised her then and there by kissing her in full view of everyone coming and going from the building.

They took a cab to LaGuardia and caught a flight to Charleston, South Carolina. On the plane she pulled her letter to Nan from her purse and added a few lines.

You're the first to know that Daniel and I are married. We eloped today, just a quick ceremony in a judge's chambers, and a short honeymoon. I'm still planning to come home after Christmas, and can't wait for you to meet him.

It felt strange to put it on paper, make it real. She'd married Daniel, and was going on her honeymoon. She looked out the window as they followed the Atlantic coast south, the greens and blues welcome after New York's autumn and the first gray sleet of winter. When they disembarked they picked up a rental car and drove into the heart of the old town. Tilda looked out the window with great interest as he parked in front of the John Rutledge House Inn as the sun was setting. A wide two-sided staircase led up to the main entryway of the three-story inn. Green-painted wrought iron scrollwork curved under her hand as they climbed the stairs, and framed the second-floor windows and balcony. "Oh, it's warm," she sighed.

"Not as warm as Miami or the Virgin Islands, but closer for a quick getaway," he said. "I thought you might like the history. I tried to book us into the Belmond but they were full."

"That's all right. I'd prefer a quaint bed-and-breakfast over a luxury hotel any day."

The host showed them to a tiny cottage tucked away at the back of the property. Enormous lilac bushes bracketed the path to the door. "You're our only carriage house guests," she said as she opened the drapes overlooking the patio, dotted with wrought iron tables and chairs next to palm trees and magnolia trees. "Perfect for honeymooners. We're expecting a storm tonight, but it should blow through by tomorrow morning. Let me know if you need anything, otherwise, we'll see you at breakfast."

After she left, Tilda walked right up to Daniel, who stood with his hands in his pockets in front of the marble fireplace. "It's beautiful."

"I'm glad you like it," he said. She peered up into his long face, saved from terminal gloominess by the intelligence and compassion that was as much a part of his bone structure as his cheekbones or jaw. The permanent furrow between his brows deepened a little as she looked up at him. "We have dinner reservations at seven, but I can cancel them if you want to stay in."

"No," she said, and surprised them both by kissing the slight dent in his chin. "I'll just freshen up."

She came out of the bathroom with her makeup touched up, a fresh coat of lipstick on her mouth, and pulled a cashmere wrap out of her overnight bag.

The restaurant was exquisite, and only half full in the off-season. Their table overlooked the water. Tilda wore her wrap to ward off the chill, and kept up a steady stream of quiet conversation about the food, the view, the area, the business. Daniel watched her, his long fingers toying with the stem of his wineglass, his face slipping into the expression that frightened her, tender, curious, relentless.

"Tilda," he said.

"Yes?"

"Are you *nervous?*"

Denial shaped her lips until he lifted one eyebrow. "Yes," she said.

"Why?"

"It's . . . we're different. Commitments change things."

He clearly tried to fight the smile, and lost. "They do," he said. "I don't know how to do this."

"I don't, either. We'll figure it out together."

She pulled her wrap more tightly around her shoulders, hunching in on herself against the fear bubbling inside her. *Let me have this,* she pleaded with herself. *Let me have this, have him.*

He reached across the table and covered her hand with his own. "We can get coffee to warm you up, or we can go back to the inn, go to bed, and warm you up that way."

"The inn," she said without hesitation. What would happen at the inn, on a wedding night, was very familiar territory.

He signaled for their server. "The check, please, and two slices of that chocolate cake to go. There's a coffeemaker in the room," he explained. "We'll have dessert afterward."

Rain and wind lashed at the car, the windshield wipers barely making headway against the driving rain. Daniel drove slowly, carefully, Tilda guiding him with the GPS and the landmarks.

"The storm's getting worse," she remarked.

An umbrella was useless in the wind. He parked at the back of the lot and together they dashed along the brick path to the cottage, then tumbled inside. She worked her fingers through her rain-spattered hair, slicked droplets down her arms, then flicked the damp from her fingertips. She stood for a moment, her eyes closed, letting the storm's energy surge at her skin.

Then Daniel backed her into the wall and kissed her, swallowing her delighted gasp. Her hands fisted in his suit jacket lapels, pulling him close only to shove him back and work the jacket off. He jerked off his tie while she unfastened his shirt buttons and tugged that material down, leaving him to wrestle with the cuffs while she yanked his undershirt free from his trousers and dropped to her knees.

"Tilda, yes," he muttered as she opened his belt and fly, and then he was in her mouth. He gave up on the cuffs and braced one forearm against the wall, needing the support with his suddenly weak knees. With his other hand he smoothed her tousled hair, then worked his fingers into the damp strands. She whimpered, maybe because he pulled, maybe because the air between them suddenly heated to the flash point. When she looked up, her lips stretched around his thick shaft, he was looking down. A low groan left his mouth, and a hint of salt seeped onto her tongue. She wrapped fingers and thumb around the base of his shaft and started to move her hand and mouth in unison.

He pulled out with a wet pop. "Come on," he said, and urged her to her feet. They stumbled to the bed. He finally managed to undo his cuffs on the way, and yanked loose the tie of her wrap dress.

"Yes," she gasped, twisting onto her back and scrambling for the center of the bed. She lifted her hips so he could pull down her panties, leaving her in her bra and nothing else. "Now, Daniel. Yes. Now." Speed was her friend, anything to stop her thinking about what they'd done, the commitment she'd made, the sheer drop of terror that line of thought inspired.

He nudged inside her, the slick stretch so erotic and carnal she squirmed under him until he pinned her with chest and hands. Her legs drew up with each thrust, her body tightening under his until her head arched back and her heels dug into the small of his back.

"Oh!" she cried, and arched off the bed, burying her face in his collarbone. He cupped the back of her head with his hand, holding her as close as he could, thrusting through the wrenching contractions of her orgasm.

Once, twice, again, and he came, eyes closing as he shoved that extra bit deeper inside her, burying himself to the hilt. It was better, more powerful, more erotic, to have him bare inside her, a risk she'd allowed with no other man, and suddenly craved with Daniel.

He bent his head so his forehead rested on hers. His muscles loosened and his breathing evened out. As if sex set things aright, she relaxed. This was no different than what they had before. This she understood. This she knew.

This she could do.

– TEN –

Christmas

The half-empty train slowed to a crawl as it closed in on Huntington Station. Beside him, Tilda capped her fountain pen and tucked her ongoing letter to Nan back in her bag. "What do you write to her?" Daniel asked as the train jerked to a stop at the station.

"Everything," she said. "I keep the letter with me and update it as I go about my day, especially when I'm seeing something new or interesting, something that takes my fancy. She's traveled so little, you see."

"That's nice," he said. Thoughtful, caring, kind, a little like the mental list Tilda kept of people who needed someone special in their lives. Sunlight reflected off mounded snow, giving the platform and parking lot a pristine, festive air. Tilda pulled on her gloves. Out of the corner of his eye Daniel watched as the thin platinum band disappeared into black leather lined with cashmere. "You haven't told your family?" she asked.

"No," Daniel said. He stood in the aisle and reached up to grab their bags from the overhead rack. "I wanted to tell them in person. With you."

Because everything was different. He wanted to tell his parents he'd eloped four days earlier, on the winter solstice, with the woman they'd never met by his side.

"Who's picking us up?" she asked. Serene. Unruffled. Maybe years of boarding school taught her how to handle anything, including holidays with people she'd never met.

"Angie. Come on," he said, and held out his hand.

Tilda tightened her scarf around her neck then took Daniel's outstretched hand. She wore slacks, boots, and a slim-fitting green wool turtleneck with a thick collar; with her dark hair, pale skin, and gray eyes, the whole combination reminded him of an evergreen tree. He wore jeans, a gray V-neck over an Oxford, and a blazer, and for a moment he had the unreal sense of being in a commercial, the man bringing home his elegant new bride to spend the holidays with his family. He carried the canvas bag he'd owned since college, while Tilda's change of clothes, toiletries, and laptop were in a battered Louis Vuitton weekend bag. A third bag held presents for the family.

They cleared the turnstiles, pushed through the doors to the kiss-and-ride circle, and crossed the parking lot to a monster SUV. Angie was waiting beside it, the engine running. Her blond hair was pulled back in a sleek ponytail, and her jeans, red cable-knit sweater, and flats matched Tilda's sense of clean style, which cheered Daniel for some inexplicable reason, as if a similar sense in fashion would bond them like sisters. Through the tinted glass of the third row of seats, Daniel's niece and nephew waved frantically; the only thing keeping them in the car was having to work their way out of the Tahoe's way back. Angie's husband Jason gave Daniel a wry salute. Daniel doubted he could hear a thing over the high-pitched childrens' voices in the car.

"We're on our way, Mom. Yes, I've got the pies. Yes . . . yes, Mom. He's here. Yes, she's with him. I have to go." She reached out to Daniel with the arm holding the phone and hugged him tightly. "Merry Christmas! Hi!" she said.

Daniel hugged her, then stepped a little to the side and put his arm around Tilda's shoulders to draw her forward. "Angie, this is Tilda Davies."

"So nice to meet you," Angie said with a smile. "Are you a hugger? I'm a hugger. Don't mind the imps. They've been up since five, and they're high on candy from their stockings. It's one day a year, I mean, I normally wouldn't let them eat chocolate at seven in the morning, but they said they were trying to keep Max, he's our goldendoodle, from eating it, and it's Christmas, you know?"

Tilda leaned in for a swift hug. "Hello. Happy Christmas," she said.

Jason picked up their bags and tossed them in the back of the Tahoe. "Be careful of the pies!" Angie called.

"The pies are fine," Jason said. "Let's go, before your mother calls the police."

She scanned their bags as she clicked open the locks on the SUV. "You're staying the night?" she asked. "That should be fine. Mom was going to keep the kids, but she can throw sleeping bags on the floor in the basement. She'll be thrilled. She wishes Daniel got a job with a local police department."

This last remark was aimed at Tilda, who smiled.

"How about we get in the car now," Jason said.

"If Mom had her way, neither of us would have moved out,"

Daniel said as he opened the door for Tilda. "They'd just keep adding on to the house until it looked like something out of a fairy tale, and she could see her grandkids every single day."

"She sees them almost every day of the week as it is," Angie said as she swung up into the passenger's seat.

"Merry Christmas, Jessie, Kiernan," he said, using Little K's full name for Tilda's benefit.

"Who's that?"

"This is your uncle Daniel's friend," Angie said from the front seat.

Tilda shot Daniel an amused look, but wisely didn't try to interrupt the chatter from the backseat.

"Uncle Daniel! Uncle Daniel! I got a Thomas play set." Little K held up a zipped clear plastic tote containing towers, tracks, and an orange plastic turret. Two train cars he could identify as Thomas and Percy.

"Looks pretty cool, Little K," Daniel said. His eardrums were vibrating already. It was a wonder Jason wasn't stone deaf. "What did you get, Jessie?"

"New soccer cleats," Jessie said, then stuck her sucker back in her mouth. At nine, Jessie was acting fourteen, maybe older. "And a regulation goal so I can practice in the back yard." Back went the sucker.

"Did Santa bring you anything, Uncle Daniel?" Little K asked.

"No, kiddo," Daniel said. "Santa doesn't bring presents to grown-ups. Only good kids."

"Were you bad?"

Tilda stifled a smile. "No," he said. "I'm just grown up."

"Oh."

The train station gave way to a four-lane road lined with big-box stores and the occasional strip mall. The fresh snow left streets and yards and bushes carpeted in white but wasn't enough to snarl holiday travel. Daniel had worked enough winter storms and holidays to give thanks for seniority and a desk job.

Tilda looked around with interest as they wound their way into his parents' neighborhood. Halfway down the street they pulled into the driveway of a white two-story house with black shutters on a street lined with mature trees. His father had the driveway shoveled, but with the cars parked two deep, they had to park on the street. Daniel climbed out, helped Tilda out, then stood back so the kids could explode out of the Tahoe and up the sidewalk to his mother.

The front door stood open, showing a staircase and a quick flash of dining room as his mother gathered the kids into a big hug. "Go on inside," she said. "Santa left you a couple of presents on the fireplace. Leave everything else for after dinner!" she called.

Jason handed Daniel their bags and a fourth shopping bag stacked with presents. Angie collected the pies and yet another bag stacked with plastic containers. "Fruit salad, green bean casserole, and rolls," she said over her shoulder to Tilda as they made their way up the sidewalk. "Mom says she wants to do all the cooking, but she really shouldn't. Daniel ordered the floral arrangements for the table and they're gorgeous, holly and evergreen . . ."

"Come inside, come inside," his mother fussed. There was a big moment of confusion in the too-small foyer while his mother and aunt and a couple of cousins took bags and dispersed them. All the while Daniel tried to keep Tilda close by. His heart was pounding in his chest, and he couldn't get a word in edgewise with his mother chattering away at Angie about food and dinner plans. She came over, arms extended, and Daniel dutifully lowered his head for a cheek-smacking kiss. His father held out his hand and Daniel shook it. They both turned to Tilda.

"I'm Judy," she said. "Daniel's mother."

"I'm Tilda." She took off her glove and shook his mother's hand.

"My wife," Daniel added.

All movement in the foyer stopped. The abrupt silence spread along the hallway lined with forty years of family pictures into the living room, where the rest of his extended family was gathered, eggnog and hot chocolate in hand. Behind him, Jason turned a laugh into a throat-clearing cough.

"What?" Angie said. Her eyes flicked down to Tilda's left hand, then to Daniel's. "You're *married*?"

Her shocked tone carried into the kitchen at the back of the house. Heads peered around the doorway. "What's going on?"

"Daniel's *married*," Angie said in a tone of utter disbelief.

"*Married*? To who? To her?"

"My goodness, I don't know what to say," his mother said. "What . . . ? When . . . ? I mean, congratulations, and welcome, Tilda. Welcome to our family. Let's get you introduced to . . . everyone."

"Thank you," Tilda said, and let herself be drawn down the hallway, toward the kitchen.

Jason clapped a hand on Daniel's shoulder. "Congratulations. Want some eggnog?"

"Skip the eggnog," Daniel said over his shoulder.

"Whiskey it is," Jason said.

Angie cornered him in the kitchen. "You got married and you didn't tell anyone? Did Todd know? Or Dusty? Dad?"

Todd and Dusty were his two best friends from college. "No one knew."

"You *eloped*? Did you go to Vegas or something?"

Daniel watched Tilda chat with his aunt in the living room that ran the length of the back of the house, into a sunny porch furnished with overstuffed chairs. Wooden toys suitable for small children were strewn under the tree and on the hearth; the older cousins were making an attempt to keep shredded wrapping paper from taking over the floor. His mother's ancient Persian cat had retreated to the top of the entertainment center and hissed at anyone who stood too close. The room overlooked an enormous lot rolling back to a tree line. A second set of sliding glass doors opened to a multilevel deck that ended in pavers leading to a sand box and swing set currently frosted with snow. The noise level had passed full volume, and was rapidly approaching rafter rattling. He wondered how Tilda was holding up.

"We got married last week by a district court judge in Manhattan." Solstice to solstice, one half of a complete cycle of the earth around the sun. He liked the symmetry.

"Why?"

"Because that's what we wanted to do," Daniel said.

"You'll have another reception later in the spring," his mother said.

Something tapped his shoulder. He turned to see Jason holding out a tumbler half full of whiskey. "Probably not, Mom," he said. "Tilda's in the middle of a really big deal and I'm doing something I can't talk about but involves seventy-hour work weeks."

His mother pulled the meat thermometer out of the turkey, set it down on the stove, and pulled off her oven mitts. "Angie, come help me downstairs," she said as she opened the door to the basement, then started down the stairs.

"Daniel, you *idiot*," she hissed, then smacked him. "Mom's going to be upset because she won't have anything to give Tilda for Christmas. Or as wedding presents. None of us do."

"We don't want presents," Daniel said. "We don't need anything."

"It's what people do, Danny. It's a big deal to us. You know this," she said, staring at him. "You bring presents, celebrate. It's what you do."

He shifted his weight, and sipped the whiskey. Angie had no difficulty holding his feet to the fire, and this was very much out of character for the way they did things in his family. But this was what Tilda wanted. He tried not to think about how he'd been eager to elope because he was afraid that she would change her mind. But while it was perfectly in character for Tilda to elope, it was very out of character for him. He came from a loving, close-knit family, one that helped each other through the difficult times as steadfastly as they celebrated joys and successes. Eloping may have been a misstep on his part, because it would be easy for his family to interpret that as Tilda taking him away from them, when that wasn't the case at all. It was sheer, primitive possessiveness on his part. She said yes, and he wasn't about to let her get away. "It's done, Angie. We wanted it this way."

"You did or she did?"

"We did." Emphatic. No room for discussion.

"Okay, okay," Angie said. "We'll get to know her, and I'm sure we'll love her as much as you do."

"Angie!" his mother called from the basement.

"Coming, Mom." Angie gave him a little shove. "Go make sure your *wife* isn't pinned in the corner with Uncle Kiernan. He's lost his hearing aids again."

He tracked Tilda down in the study not with Uncle K but with his cousin Marie, who held a family reunion photograph in which the various family branches wore color-coordinated T-shirts. There were so many Logans, Murphys, and O'Hanrahans the photographer needed a cherry picker to get everyone in the shot.

Tilda was nodding and smiling. "Let me borrow her for a moment," he said to Marie.

He offered her a coffee with Baileys in it. "Holding up okay?"

"I'm fine," she said. She sipped the coffee, gave him an appreciative smile over the rim of the cup, and sipped again. "Your wife?"

To his surprise, he colored a little. It was possessive, a statement of ownership, tightening the connection begun months earlier in Louise's rooftop garden. His wife. Daniel Logan's wife. He'd introduced her in the simplest possible fashion, conveying everything about who they were in two single-syllable words. But she was looking at him like she'd never thought of it that way before.

"You are my wife," he said.

"Are you sure it was best to hit them with it like that?" she asked quietly.

"Better than sitting around with rings on, wondering when they were going to notice," Daniel replied.

"I didn't think there would be this many people," Tilda said. "You said a family Christmas."

"This is a family Christmas," he said. "What's Christmas like in your family?"

"Smaller than this," she said. "Quieter."

"We're killing two birds with one stone. Everyone we'd invite to a reception is here, so Mom won't fuss about throwing another party, and the kids are wired up for gifts, so we fade into the background."

Marie approached them, one of the albums open. "I found one," she said. "That's Daniel just after college," she said, pointing at a picture of Daniel, shirtless, before he'd cut his hair for the academy.

"You look so young," she said quietly, then looked at him, as if trying to find that boy in his face. "So innocent."

He leaned over to murmur in her ear. "I wasn't."

She laughed.

"Time to open gifts," he said.

They left the seats of honor for the kids and the kids' parents. Tilda volunteered to track who gave what to whom, earning a grateful smile from Angie. Several hastily wrapped things came to them, a candle, an elaborate wrought iron tree with picture frames dangling from the branches. The twin hung on the wall, obscured by the Christmas tree, and held wedding pictures from Daniel's parents, grandparents, and great-grandparents. A second one hung in Angie's house, with her wedding picture and a rotation of shots of Jessie's and Little K's school pictures in the frames. Inspired by the lack of pictures in her town house, he gave Tilda a framed picture of herself and her grandmother, one he'd hastily written to Nan to obtain. She went silent when she opened it. "You didn't have any pictures up," he said. "You said they got lost in a move and you hadn't gotten around to replacing them. It's a good start."

She touched Nan's face carefully, as if afraid to smear the glass. "When did you do this?"

"At the last possible minute. That's why I had to run out last night."

"Can I see?" Angie asked, her hand out.

"That's my Nan," Tilda said. "My grandmother. She lives in Cornwall, England."

"I'll get you copies of our side," his mother said.

"It's lovely," Tilda said quietly. "Thank you."

"I didn't know you had one for me," Daniel said with a nod at the photo family tree Tilda had opened a few minutes earlier.

"Of course I did," his mother said. "I wasn't giving up hope."

– ELEVEN –

Tilda found it interesting that she wasn't the center of attention. Yes, her impromptu, unexpected marriage came up frequently, but as Daniel explained, people hadn't seen each other in a while and everyone was focused on the kids, so she found herself able to drift from group to group without garnering much attention. When she did touch down with a group, people asked the same questions.

What do you do?
Where are you from?
How long have you lived in the US?
How long have you known Daniel?
How did you meet?
Will your family be upset about the elopement?

Everyone was too polite or yet too sober to phrase the question so bluntly, but that was the unspoken subtext. Wouldn't her family want a wedding of any size, a chance to celebrate this transition in her life? She explained how her mother was teaching, her grandmother too frail to travel, and that no, not all weddings in England were as elaborate as Will and Kate's. Alone for a second, she thought about Daniel's gift. Nan had sent two pictures, one of her and Tilda when Tilda was seventeen, another when Tilda was about eight. A wild mop of curls and big eyes, elbows and knees, just her and Nan. Thank God for a chaotic family Christmas. No one asked too many questions.

She looked past the enormous Christmas tree and saw Jessie and Kiernan kicking a new soccer ball around in the driveway.

"Just need some fresh air," she said to a group gathered around the fireplace. Impulsively, she opened the door and made her way down the steps. She wasn't running. Or escaping. Just getting some air. Air was in short supply in that house right now.

"Hello," she said to Jessie and Kiernan.

"You sound funny."

"Shut up, Little K," Jessie hissed.

"I likely do sound funny to you," Tilda agreed.

Kiernan looked at her. "Do I sound funny to you?"

Only because he was missing his two front teeth, but Tilda didn't say that. "Not really. I've lived here for quite some time, so I'm used to your accent. How long have you played soccer?" she asked Jessie, purposefully choosing to call it by its American name.

"Since I was three," the girl said proudly. She kicked the ball up and began a quite accomplished game of keepy-uppy, managing nearly thirty seconds before she lost control of the ball.

"Well done," Tilda said with a smile. "Can I have a go?"

"You play soccer?"

"Not for ages, but I did when I was in school."

"My age?"

"Older than you. Your equivalent of high school."

"Sure," the girl said.

The girl flipped the ball into the air and Tilda tapped it up with her knee. She managed slightly less time than Jessie, not bad for ten years without touching a ball, and the rhythmic pace of her breathing calmed her.

"Nice," Jessie said magnanimously. In an automatic move Tilda recognized from her own player days, Jessie twitched her ponytail free of her shirt, dropped the ball, and kicked it toward Tilda. Tilda dribbled it toward the makeshift goal and let Jessie steal it just before she reached it.

"Don't let me take it," Jessie said, mightily offended.

Tilda promptly stole it back. Taking advantage of Tilda's boots, Jessie fought for the ball, then took off with it, heading for the opposite goal.

"Why did you marry Uncle Daniel?"

Focused on the ball, Tilda danced around Jessie, and the question. "Why do you think I did?"

"My mom says maybe you're knocked up."

To keep from laughing, Tilda concentrated on blocking Jessie's progress. "I am not knocked up."

"What's knocked up?"

"Ask your mother."

"I wasn't supposed to hear her say that."

"Best not to eavesdrop," Tilda said.

"What's eavesdrop?"

"Listening to conversations you shouldn't."

"In all the movies the prince comes and saves the princess and they get married and she wears a big white dress and then it's over. Mom says her wedding was the best day of her life. I don't want my life to be over. Did you wear a white dress?"

"No," Tilda said.

"I don't want a big dress and a party. Boys smell, and I play soccer better than most of them. They don't listen to the coach, and they're all focused on scoring, not teamwork."

"Bad news, Jessie," Tilda said. "They still smell when they get older. But they will get better at soccer."

Jessie shrugged. "I'll be the best, though."

"An excellent goal."

Jessie beamed. "Will you come see me play in the spring? I'm in the elite league."

She wasn't going to make promises she might not be able to keep to this sprite of a girl who reminded her of herself. "I'm going to be traveling a lot in the spring, but I'll try," Tilda said.

Daniel stood with his parents, Angie, Uncle Ralph, and Marie at the front windows overlooking the driveway. Jessie and Tilda had wrestled the net from the back of the Tahoe, and were using the open garage as one goal and the net at the end of the driveway as the other.

"You didn't know she played soccer," Angie said without looking at him.

His sister could read minds. "I did not," Daniel said.

Silence. Angie finally said what he knew everyone was thinking. "Is she pregnant?"

"No."

"She's a beautiful girl," his mother said. "What does she do?"

"She owns West Village Stationery, but she's in talks with a British company about a global deal."

"So she's a successful businesswoman. She's smart, and look how good she is with Jessie."

The outlier in a family of girly girls. Daniel wasn't sure whom she was trying to convince, herself, or everyone else. "I love her," he said to no one in particular, and to everyone in general. "I love her, and I married her."

"And that's all he has to say about that," Angie said in a sing-song voice.

Daniel snorted.

Tilda's skin seemed to vibrate as they climbed the stairs to the second floor. Daniel flipped on lights in various bedrooms. "Angie's room. It used to be mine until I got caught climbing out the window," he said, nodding at the branches of the big maple tapping at the glass. "Now it's the girls' sleepover room." He walked down the hall and flipped on another light. "The boys' sleepover room."

Tilda peeked her head inside. Two single beds made up with cartoon character sheets were pushed against opposite walls and covered in dark blue comforters. The bookshelves were old but carefully painted and held worn books ranging from the Hardy Boys to Harry Potter. Tilda walked inside and looked at the trophies and medals.

"Is this the room you were moved to?"

He shook his head. "I got moved to the back of the house, where there's a two-story drop to the patio. It's the guest room now, quieter for people who are staying a few days. But that's my furniture from childhood, and some of my awards."

"You were on the track team?"

"Cross-country, too. I wasn't much for team sports, but I liked to run."

She continued through the ribbons, medals, and trophies hanging from decorative bulletin boards, then looked around the room again. Likely it wasn't all that different from when Daniel was a boy, simple, comfortable components of childhood. Character sheets. Books designed to appeal to boys, games in case books were boring. A poster of a baseball player shared wall space with a poster of the solar system, and another one of the Milky Way with a yellow arrow labeled *You Are Here* pointing to an indeterminate star at one of the ends of the spiral. Daniel belonged here, in this room, in this house, in this suburb, in this family, and while most people were too polite to say it out loud, the subtext running under the entire day was that Tilda wasn't what anyone expected Daniel to bring home as his bride.

She'd visited enough friends' homes to know that Daniel's room held fairly typical trappings of a middle-class suburban upbringing, but her friends weren't her husband. Her friends never came to Cornwall with her, as Daniel would in a couple of days.

The odd sense of unreality, similar to jet lag, made her sway on her feet.

"Are you tired?"

"A little," she said.

"Long day. Lots of people to meet."

"Everyone was very nice."

"You'll get to know them," he said.

The idea seemed incomprehensible, but it was late, very late. After the noise of the train, then a house overflowing with people, the late-night silence vibrated against her eardrums. "Well," she said brightly. "Do you want SpongeBob sheets or Star Wars sheets?"

One corner of his mouth lifted. "We're in the guest room."

The room was furnished in sage and a pale yellow, very comfortable, very soothing, and overlooked the back yard. Daniel switched on the lamp on the nightstand and lowered the blinds. Someone had brought their overnight bags up and left them on an old mariner's trunk. Above the trunk hung a wooden placard with the phrase *Home is where your story begins* painted in quaint letters over a drooping tree and a New England–style house fronting a split-rail fence. The sign made Tilda smile when she recognized the foundation of such a key component of Daniel's character. Daniel was all about stories, the stories money told, the stories people told. Real-life stories were complicated, full of twists and turns, sleight-of-hand, red herrings. He loved nothing more than slowly, carefully teasing apart the separate strands until he understood the whole story.

"Bathroom's through there," he said, tipping his head toward a door she'd mistaken for a closet.

Hurriedly she pulled her nightgown and toiletries case from her bag and ducked into the bathroom. She washed her face, brushed her teeth, and emerged to find Daniel in bed, reading, one hand tucked behind his head and the covers at his waist. He glanced up at her, then back at his book, then did a very gratifying double take.

"Happy Christmas," she said in a low voice.

"Uh," he said.

She smiled at his inarticulate response, then turned in a slow circle. Rather than her usual functional satin set she wore a camisole made of sheer gold lace and matching cheeky panties. "I found these at a gorgeous shop in the Fashion District called Irresistible. We should go back together sometime. The dressing rooms are enormous, with mirrors *everywhere*, and the owner seems to mind not at all. She's French. Very Continental."

Daniel seemed not to hear her, adding credence to the argument that men's focus narrowed when presented with a pretty, nearly naked woman. "That's for me?"

"They're for us," she said, and knelt on the bed. The box spring squawked under her weight. "Rather selfish of me, perhaps."

"Not at all," he said, and reached for her hand to draw her close. His thumb found her wedding ring, still unfamiliar on her finger. "It's a little loose," he commented.

"It's fine," she said. "It won't slip over my knuckle."

He gave her a little smile, then lifted her fingers to his lips. The gesture never failed to surprise her, so old-fashioned and courtly and completely Daniel. "Warm," he said, but blew on her fingertips anyway.

His tongue traced the sensitive edges of her fingers, licked each of the tips. He let her press gently against his lower lip, feeling the give that would disappear as they fucked, as friction and pressure swelled his lips with blood, all the while holding her gaze. The heat simmering in his eyes covered a complex tapestry of emotion. Some she could identify, laughter, the sheer pleasure of a day with family. Others were unfamiliar, harder to discern.

Slow steps made their way up the stairs and down the hall. Tilda tried to tug her hand free from Daniel's grip, but he tightened his fingers. "They won't come in," he said in a low voice.

The hall light flicked off, then the door to the master suite closed. The silence felt all encompassing as Tilda leaned forward to kiss Daniel. "We shouldn't," she whispered.

She felt his smile form under her mouth. "You just have to be quiet."

He used his body to tip her onto her back and tuck her under him, a move her animal brain responded to from deep inside, that of the powerful male covering the smaller female. The box spring squeaked again as they shifted into the middle of the bed. "We can't," she said even as she arched her hips against his erection.

"Shh," he said, and kissed her.

The wind picked up, scraping the bare branches against the window. Cocooned in the sheets and blankets, she held Daniel's shoulders while he kissed her, slow and deep, as noiselessly as possible, a rub of lips, tongue sliding against hers before he licked and nipped his way along her jaw to her ear. She wasn't used to being quiet, expected it to be a turn-off, but found instead that restricting herself from moving, from moaning, heightened her sense of touch and taste and smell. The scent of sweat bloomed between them, dissipating in the cool room. He took her earlobe between his teeth and bit down slowly, increasing the touch until it became pressure, then a sweet, hot pain that rolled along her nerves to her nipples and clit. She whimpered, turned her head to the side. He relented, kissed the hollow under her jaw, then her neck, palming her forehead and tipping her head back to expose her whole throat to his mouth. She ground her head against the pillow until he fisted his hand in her hair and held her still. Demanding heat pooled between her thighs.

Without releasing her hair, moving at a snail's pace, he shifted down, licking at her nipple through the delicate lace. She reached down to pull it up but the mattress creaked and he wouldn't lift, keeping the fabric trapped between their stomachs. "Stay still," he murmured.

His voice hung in the air. Her nipples were tender and achingly sensitive by the time he lifted his head. They tightened harder in the cooling air. She wanted to pinch them herself but the creaky bed kept her immobilized, Daniel a heavy presence between her thighs. Even lifting to press her mound into his body set off another jarring set of noises.

"This is not amusing," she hissed in a stage whisper.

"No," he replied. Keeping his weight braced on one arm he trailed his fingers along her hip and began to edge up the camisole. "It's hot." He made a *tut-tut-tut* noise. "You're wearing panties."

It took some doing to get his hand positioned, long moments during which she shamelessly spread her legs and sucked in her stomach, the better to stretch the elastic between her hipbones and give him room to maneuver. He chuckled, and if movement were possible she would have smacked him for that masculine laugh. As it was, the raspy sound combined with his fingertips moving lightly over her mound tightened every pleasure center in her body—nipples, clit; the empty, needy walls of her sex.

He parted her folds and circled her clit. When she moaned, he bent and covered her mouth with his, not hard, just lightly enough to remind her that she needed to be quiet. His movements were torturously slow, around and around, calculated to tease and provoke without much promise of release. His tongue traced the edges of her teeth, dipped inside to rub against hers, then withdrew again.

When his fingers slid lower, inside, she gasped, a sound he almost managed to stifle.

"Shh," he said, then stroked her G-spot and pulled out.

"Don't be a tease," she said, a threat in the words.

"Don't be so loud," he replied, and resumed his lazy circles.

He brought her to the edge of orgasm twice, each time stopping to glide inside her and feel the ebbing flutters while she cursed him. By the third time she'd lost her words but for *please* and *no*, which she sobbed breathlessly into his mouth when he once again left her hanging on the edge of the abyss. He reached between them and gripped himself, nudging aside the panel of her panties to expose her cleft, then covered her mouth with his hand. The scent of her own arousal made her mouth water. The first touch of his cock to her tingling opening made her tense up. The first sliding stroke, gliding over nerve endings teased into hyperawareness, seated him fully inside her, made her arch her back and cry out against his palm clamped tightly over her mouth.

He stopped, embedded deep inside her, and once again let the tension ebb from her muscles. She undulated under him, set off a quacking in the box spring, and sobbed. Endlessly patient, he waited until she subsided.

"I'll make you come, but we have to be very, very quiet," he murmured in her ear.

It was a steady, relentless, prolonged movement, all in his hips, heightening her senses. She could feel the slow drag of the flared head of his cock as he pulled out, the slightly increased pressure on her G-spot each time he slid back inside. A single touch of his finger to her clit and she'd come, something she could have done herself if she'd had the presence of mind to think of it. Instead she focused on the way her damp camisole rasped against her nipples, the growing stretch of her inner thighs as she held herself open for him, desperate, taking only what he gave her, unable to reach for more without alerting everyone on that floor to exactly what they were doing.

Her legs drew up by his hips, her heels dug into his buttocks. Blood pounded in her cheeks, her throat, and her muscles trembled from being flexed for so long. When she tipped over the edge into release, each contraction jerked her rigid, her sobs once again caught in his mouth. She had a vague sense of him burying himself deep inside her and grinding his hips until he came without a sound.

All her muscles trembled as he breathed deeply above her. Then he pulled out. "That's going to leave a mess," she mumbled.

"I'll put the sheets in the wash before we leave," he said.

This she understood, the heat, the desire, the way her body recognized him as a risk every time they had sex. The room settled into a familiar spot in her mind, the purposefully charming atmosphere of a bed-and-breakfast. The rest of the day seemed like a dream.

"Have you brought anyone else home?"

He slid a glance at her, amusement tugging at the corners of his lips and eyes. "Why? Jealous?"

Yes. It was an unfamiliar emotion, and not one she was willing to admit to. "No. Just curious."

"Yeah," he said. "Lindy. Allyson, the woman I dated for a

couple of years while I was on patrol in the Bronx. We run together two or three times a month. Sandy, who came after Allyson. She moved to Detroit with her new boyfriend, so I don't see her at all."

"That's a relief," she said, and hitched the covers more securely under her arm.

His golden brows drew down. "Why is it a relief?"

"I'm not special. Remarkable," she amended. "You've done this before. Brought home a somewhat surprising individual."

He tucked his train ticket into the book and closed it. "Yeah, I've brought home a tattooed Goth drummer and a vegan sous chef," he said. He slid down under the covers and arranged himself to mirror her, on his side, head braced on his hand. He reached out with his right hand and picked up her left, tipping her wedding band back and forth with his thumb. "But I've never brought home a wife."

That word again, that odd, unfamiliar word. The reverberating silence was back, Daniel's even breathing echoing in her head.

The next part wouldn't be so easy. She was taking him home, to England, for New Year's.

— TWELVE —

Late December

"Right, then, who shall I list as the primary driver?" Daniel rubbed his eyes with the thumb and forefinger of his left hand and fumbled for his wallet with his right. An hour of sleep on the flight from New York to London left him with the discomfiting brain slosh that characterized near-complete exhaustion. "Me," he said.

"I'll drive," Tilda said.

They stood at the rental car counter at the airport, their bags clustered around their feet. Winter sunlight filtered through the windows, washing everything out. The airport bustled along, travelers coming home from Christmas or leaving to ring in the New Year somewhere warm or exotic. The holiday decorations felt out of place given the unseasonably warm temperatures that had settled over the UK the week before. Based on the weather forecast, he'd brought a jacket with a zip-out lining. The jet lag, the warm weather, and the holiday decorations added up to his perception of being out of time, out of place.

He looked at Tilda as he added yet another item to the list of things he was learning about her. "You drive?"

"Of course I drive," she said. Perhaps the jet lag was affecting her differently. After two flights to London in the last month followed by late-night phone calls all over the world, her body clock had to be completely jacked.

"I just didn't know you did." He'd seen her on the subway, in taxis, on the train to Long Island, but never behind the wheel.

"I don't drive in New York, but who does? It's the whole point of the city, not needing a car."

"I drive," Daniel said firmly, attempting to regain control of the situation. "I am a licensed driver, a sworn officer of the law, and scored first in my class on the training course."

"Yes, but you're jet-lagged whereas I'm accustomed to travel, and you've never driven in the UK, while I have."

"I assume you rent to first-time American drivers all the time," Daniel said.

"We do, sir," said the unflappable clerk behind the counter. "As long as they present a valid driver's license, proof of insurance, and a valid bank card, we rent to anyone. Even Americans."

He turned to Tilda. "Do *you* have a valid driver's license?"

Tilda pursed her lips. "I did."

Daniel narrowed his eyes at her. She smiled back, firing on all twelve cylinders. Maybe she was just running on adrenaline. She looked a little wild around the eyes. "I'm driving," he said to the clerk, and slid his driver's license out of the clear slot in his wallet.

"Of course, sir."

The clerk typed information into his computer. "It's a rental car counter," Daniel said. People could talk all they wanted about globalization, but this was definitely England. "LaGuardia has one, Kennedy has one, and they all feel pretty much the same. But this one feels different. It's definitely not home."

She looked around, as if seeing the place for the first time when she'd been in and out of Heathrow ten times in the last six months. "It's the teeth," she said.

He laughed. "Teeth."

"Americans are obsessed with perfect teeth."

"We are?"

"Braces, whitening, crowns and caps. You can tell an American by the smile."

He looked at her slightly crooked lower teeth, the hint of a gap between her incisor and her front teeth. "So this feels like home to you?"

She looked around. "Airports certainly do," she said.

Twenty-five minutes later they stood behind a car not much bigger than his mother's bread box. "You might have to ride on the roof," he said.

"You should let me drive," she said, watching him attempt to cram their suitcases into the trunk.

"Number one, you don't have a license that's valid in either the US or the UK. Number two, and perhaps more important, the thought of you, who happily sits on ledges two hundred feet above the street, behind the wheel of anything more powerful than a golf cart makes me break out in a cold sweat."

She laughed delightedly, as if it were the highest compliment he could pay her, a frisson of terror skittering over his nerves, and opened the driver's side door. The passenger side door, actually. This was going to take some getting used to.

"You think this has more power than a golf cart?"

"I think you might have to get out and push," he said. "Buckle up. How are you with maps?"

"I am brilliant with maps," she said.

His brain preoccupied with shifting with his left hand and steering with his right, he paid little attention to anything other than traffic signals and other cars on the road until they cleared the heaviest of the London suburbs. They stopped to get coffee, then got back in the car. "Did you drive yourself back and forth from London?"

"I took the train, then a bus," she said, then gestured to the left. "The motorway entrance is just there."

He turned on his blinker, pulled past a line of waiting cars, and merged into traffic. Tilda dissolved into laughter, sliding down in her seat and holding her stomach.

"What?" he demanded. "What's so funny? What did I do?"

"You just bypassed an entire line of cars waiting to make that left-hand turn. You were in the oncoming traffic lane!"

"Jesus Christ." That explained the shocked looks from the drivers, who were actually passengers.

Giggles shuddered through her shoulders, and she clapped her hand over her mouth.

"Stop it. I need to focus."

That set her off worse. He gritted his teeth, kept the car at precisely the speed limit, and waited for her to laugh herself out. "I can't wait to see how you handle roundabouts."

"I can handle a roundabout," he said grumpily.

"I have complete confidence in your driving ability, Daniel," she said. She smiled and turned her attention to the scenery.

"Excited to see Nan again?"

"Very."

The road followed twists and curves through rolling fields. Occasionally he could see the sea, glinting through a valley in the distance, the grassy land dropping sharply away to rocky coves and cliffs. They drove past seaside hotels and luxurious estates, and through villages, where they stopped for a picnic basket from

Darts Farm, the contents of which cost more than an expensive dinner for two in the city. Either city.

Her energy changed as the sun rose in the sky, like she was drawing strength from the land and sea. Her knee bounced until she flattened her palm on it, forcing it to stillness.

"How much longer?"

"Not long. A few minutes," she said, as much to herself as to him. "It's the most beautiful place on earth," she added, without a hint of irony. "I've traveled all over the world. But there is nowhere, *nowhere*, as beautiful as Cornwall."

"It's pretty spectacular," he agreed.

"Turn here," she said.

They exited the main road to a narrower, more winding road that wound through a cluster of well-kept shops and freshly painted municipal buildings. Daniel carefully navigated the car down the single-lane road. The harbor, not much bigger than a cove, peeked through the roofs and white-painted houses. Stretched to the end of the chains, boats rested on the rocky bottom while the sea lapped at the breakwaters constructed a dozen yards farther out. "That's some tide," Daniel said.

"The breakwaters were constructed during Henry VIII's reign," Tilda said absently.

"They're older than the United States," Daniel mused.

"Most of England is older than America. That's our inn," Tilda said, pointing at a charming stone house perched behind a stone wall protecting the village from the sea. The water was placid, pale green shading to deeper colors as it stretched to the horizon, but he had no doubt a winter storm would hurl the ocean at the inn's windows. "No, don't pull in. Nan's expecting us. Up the side of the harbor, along there. I just wanted to show you the town before we go on to Nan's."

Above the village she directed him along a hedged lane to a

dirt path leading to a tumbledown little cottage. The house had the barely claimed look of a place losing the battle with nature. Tall grasses waved in the yard not fenced off into a small, dormant garden layered with manure. Chickens clucked and squawked in an enclosure, and a few sheep dotted the hillside that swept down to the ocean. He'd imagined Tilda growing up in a London town house, or in a Harry Potter version of suburbia. Now that he'd seen Davies Farm, he couldn't imagine her anywhere else.

Tilda stumbled out of the car with uncharacteristic clumsiness and closed the door. "Nan?" she called.

"Round back," came a strong voice.

Tilda hurried up the front path, which was flat stones set right into the sod, and followed a branching path around the house to the back yard. Daniel followed more slowly, stretching his back and legs, giving Tilda a moment with her grandmother. He heard a cry of unadulterated joy, and smiled as he strolled around the house. The back yard, or garden, as Tilda would call it, sloped gently to an orchard of twisted fruit trees and a tangled bramble of bushes. His imagination supplied the scent of fruit. An uneven stone patio held a weather-beaten wooden kitchen table painted a bright pink, and mismatched chairs. A stone wall extended from the house before tumbling into the ground. Climbing roses grew everywhere.

He found Tilda hugging her grandmother, eyes squeezed shut. The older woman had Tilda's height, or did before age hunched her back. What little of her hair he could see under an enormous straw hat was white, not gray. Lines bracketed the soft skin around her mouth and eyes the same color as Tilda's. Sturdy pants, a pilled, shapeless cardigan in a faded red, and a barn jacket hung on her nearly skeletal frame. A pair of Wellingtons that looked old enough to have been worn by the duke himself, slapped against her calves.

"Daniel, this is my Nan. Nan, this is Daniel."

"A pleasure to meet you, ma'am," he said.

She studied him for a moment. He stood quietly under her gaze, hands in his pockets, and let her draw her conclusions.

"He's a handsome one," she commented without looking at Tilda.

"Don't spoil him, Nan. It'll go to his head."

He smiled at them both, content to let them tease him.

"You both must be starved. I'll make tea," she said, and drew the dirt-smeared gloves from her hands.

"Nan, we've been sitting since we left America, and we brought a picnic basket. Shall we eat outside? The weather's gorgeous."

It wasn't that warm, but after a night in a plane, Daniel understood the desire to be outside, in sunshine and a sea breeze. "I'll help," Daniel said.

"No," she said. "I'll do it."

He dropped the keys into her outstretched hand. She trotted back along the flagstone path to the car, and returned with the picnic basket, then slipped through the back door, into the tiny house. "Would you like a tour of the farm?" Nan asked.

"I'd love one," he said.

They walked down the slope, into the trees. The air was crisp, sharp, scented of both land and sea, a scent that reminded him of Tilda. It rose from her skin, he realized, like her bones were made of the same wood as the trees, like the blood in her veins was the ocean. Nan named the varieties of fruit, patting the trunks like old friends.

"Do you make jam from them?"

"Oh, yes. It keeps me busy, and out of doors. Raspberry, Cornish gilliflowers, and black currants. Some strawberries, but they don't often do well. The climate's stressful for the plants, so we don't get much fruit but what we do get has great flavor. How was your flight?"

"Fine," he said.

"And when do you leave for London?"

"A couple of days. Tilda wants to look over some locations for the expansion. Her mother is hosting a dinner party for us."

"I'm sure it will be lovely." Nan stroked her hand along the branch until it reached the tip. "Elizabeth missed so much of Tilda's childhood. She was such a dear little thing. Big eyes, black hair, like a sprite in the forest. She was constantly dirty. Did she tell you that?"

"No," he said, trying and failing to imagine cat-clean Tilda smudged with dirt.

"Wild as a mink that girl was."

"That I can imagine," he said with a smile. "Have you lived here long?"

"In the village or in this house? The village, all my life. The house, since I married, although it's a good deal older than that."

"And your husband?" he asked as they strolled back up the hill to the house. He kept a sharp eye on her, worried about the uneven terrain and her loose boots, but she walked slowly, her gaze on the ground.

"Long dead. Tilda never knew him. He was also a good man. She has cousins in the village, but they're not close."

They reached the transition where scrubby grass became tended garden. The table was covered with a linen cloth frayed at the edges and faintly stained. Bone china cups, saucers, and plates were neatly set, the butter dish matching the pattern, but wisteria, not lilies, ringed the creamer and sugar bowl. He held a wooden chair for Nan, waiting until she found an even spot on the stones, then sat down next to her.

Tilda came out with plates balanced on her inner arms and carried in her hands. Daniel lifted one eyebrow. "I waited tables in college," she said in explanation.

"We're still getting to know each other," he said to Nan.

"A lifetime job with her," Nan replied.

After a prolonged look at the murky depths hidden by Tilda's bright-burning surface, he was beginning to agree. Unmistakable differences characterized this casual tea in the late-afternoon gloaming and the polished perfection of New York's cocktail parties and dinners.

Tilda set a sturdy teapot in the center of the table. "There," she said, satisfied, and sat down.

"My dear, this is lovely. What do we have?"

"Well," Tilda said. "We've got cheddar made near Exeter that seems to have won some sort of award, olives, freshly baked bread, two quiches, yogurt, scones, crackers and chutney, charcuterie from a local farm, and dessert."

They ate while the sun traced a slow arc in the sky. Nan didn't ask the questions about how they met. In fact, she seemed to know all about Daniel, his job, his family, his history with Tilda, which surprised Daniel in his jet-lagged state, until he remembered the letters, crossing the Atlantic once or twice a week for over a decade. He felt a little like one of those letters, flattened, colorless, only thinly connected to New York now that he was in Cornwall. Nan brought Tilda up-to-date on the latest news from this tiny, unknown, almost forgotten part of the world, a running conversation about people and places. Daniel watched, and listened.

And learned. Because this was a completely different side of his wife. She was so gentle with Nan, matching her bite for bite, cajoling her into another slice of sweet bread, or a sliver of the spiced peach tart, spreading the crackers with some of the chutney, making a second pot of tea. Most of it was the same, the wild restlessness alive in Tilda seemingly from birth. There were stories about wrists sprained falling out of trees, knees skinned tumbling down rocks near the sea. Tilda belonged in this old house, full of sunshine and sea air. She belonged here in a way that was deeper and more powerful than the way she made New York her own. Suddenly her life in New York seemed like a profound dislocation.

"How old were you?"

"Oh, six, I think," she said.

"Five," Nan corrected. "Five, and nowhere to be found from sunup to sundown."

"It was summer," Tilda objected.

"And what about the times the head teacher called, 'Matilda's not here yet, Mrs. Davies, have you any idea where that child's got to this time?'"

Tilda laughed. "I always turned up."

"Down some path to the sea, or under a bush. You'd turn up dirty and late, brazen as you please."

"But I did turn up."

"Near feral, your grade-one teacher said. Unruly, undisciplined, unable to sit still two seconds together, and brilliant. You were bored, you didn't like it, and you didn't care who knew it."

"I still don't."

"You solved the problem with dirt and fresh air, and running. She never walked anywhere," Nan confided to Daniel. "A little whirlwind. Ran with the boys from an early age. She had them wrapped around her little finger. They couldn't sort her out, you see."

"She hasn't changed much. I'd love to see more of the pictures like the one you sent me before Christmas," Daniel said.

Nan's face brightened, but Tilda went blank, like a fire brutally quenched, before laughter trilled from her throat. "Oh, Nan doesn't keep anything like that. Besides, all this," she said with a sweeping gesture that took in sea and sky, "and you want to look at old snaps of me?" she said.

"Where are you staying?"

"At Cliff House, where you'll be having supper with us. I want to have a look at your bank statements while I'm here," Tilda said.

Nan put her hands on the table to rise. "I've got this," Daniel said when Tilda started to gather the dishes.

The interior of the house was as small as the outside hinted, a single story with very low ceilings. The kitchen ran along the front wall, a couch and table the length of the house and a small table in between, a bathroom, a cupboard, and a single bedroom off the main living area. The room seemed locked in time. The taps were handles so old they'd become retro popular again, and the water streaming out of them smelled of well water. The room smelled faintly of bleach and pine, the windows sparkled, but under the spotless surfaces, everything was worn, scratched, dented, stained. A cheery tree decorated with multicolored lights and ancient ornaments sat on the little table by the sofa.

He washed all the dishes carefully, then dried them with the threadbare tea towels draped over the oven's handle. Tilda and Nan put their heads together over a sheaf of paper, murmuring, while he covered the leftovers and set them neatly in the small fridge. The sums they discussed were small, with a few gaps in Nan's memory Tilda had to prompt her to fill. Daniel contrasted her gentle tone with the sharp precision she used on the call with the financier in London, and tried to assemble the pieces of Tilda into a coherent picture.

"I've got something for the pair of you," she said, after Tilda folded away the bank statements.

"Nan, you really didn't have to."

She rose, then made her way into the bedroom. While she rummaged around, Tilda nodded at the sofa. "That's my childhood bed. That very sofa. I slept with Nan until I was three or four, but I kicked."

With Tilda, conversational shifts came out of nowhere. He was tired enough to need a second to find the reference: their conversation at Christmas, in his room at his parents' house. "Okay."

"Surprised?"

What characterized true poverty was a complete disconnect from family and a sense of place. Love and belonging permeated this house, even if Tilda had slept on a sofa. "Not after a decade with the FBI. How long did you live here?"

"Until the year I turned eight. Mum finished her PhD that year, and came to collect me. She left when I was two, and came back for breaks, unless she was doing research or attending classes elsewhere."

"That must have been hard," he said absently. His brain was past the point of sloshing in his head, and now vibrated at a frequency barely audible to human ears. "Not having your mother around, I mean."

"I had Nan. I loved it here," she said. Her voice was low, intense. "You'll see later. Rocks and sea and sky, the wind in the grass. I loved it here."

"Here you are. It's not much, mind you," Nan said.

The box was wrapped in used paper and tied with a bow. Tilda smiled at it, smoothing her hands over the box then carefully opening it. Nestled in a bed of new tea towels, the kind Tilda preferred to dry dishes, were three jars of homemade currant jam.

"My favorite," she said softly, and leaned into her Nan's shoulder.

"I know."

"Nan used to feed me biscuits spread with this jam for tea," Tilda said.

"Not a proper tea, but I had to get her to eat somehow."

"I have a similar problem," Daniel said. The jars were neatly labeled in a script similar to his own grandmother's handwriting.

"Thank you," she said, and leaned forward to kiss Nan's cheek. "I'll have some on my toast in the morning, and think of you."

"You're welcome. It's not much—"

"It's perfect. Exactly what I want," Tilda said. "Something that reminds me of you. Of . . ."

Her voice trailed off. She smiled, bright as a scythe, bright as the tears in her eyes, smoothing the tea towels over and over.

"Nap," he said when they got back into the car.

"It's better not to sleep, and I want to go for a long walk," she said. Her eyes were bright, and wild.

"Nap," he repeated, more firmly, and started the engine. "Just an hour or so. I can't even go for a walk. I'll trip over my own feet."

They drove back into the village and checked into the inn. The owner knew Tilda by reputation and welcomed her warmly. In their room Tilda perched in the window seat, while Daniel set his phone to go off in an hour and stretched out on the bed in his clothes. He was asleep in seconds.

When the alarm went off Tilda was still sitting in the window seat, staring out at the cliffs enclosing the harbor, the ocean beyond. "Did you sleep?"

"I might have dozed for a few minutes," she said.

After quickly cleaning up they set off through the village, Tilda pointing out landmarks like the church, the school, the pub on their way to the path worn into the tough grass long ago. Dirt gave way to thick, tall grass and a split-rail fence. Her jacket knotted around her waist, Tilda stepped through the stile and set off along a narrow dirt path. Daniel followed her.

The wind patted him from all angles, the sunshine more constant but less powerful. Ahead of him, Tilda's hair lifted in the ocean-drenched breeze. When she turned to check on his progress, she looked shockingly young.

"Keep up," she called, mischief in her grin.

"I'm trying to enjoy the walk," he said. "Where are we going?"

She pointed to a promontory curving into the bay. A narrow beach hugged the base of the long cliff, the water dotted with huge stone towers left behind after the ocean carved away softer portions. "There," she said.

Mossy grass ran up to the very edge of the cliffs, and ran down the sides, clinging to any flat spots. The dirt trail was nearly invisible behind and ahead of them. While the wind's speed and intensity varied, its presence never did. Without the unseasonable temperatures, it would be a cold, damp visit.

Several yards ahead of him Tilda stopped and flung her arms out and her head back, exposing her throat and collarbones to the wind and sky. She said nothing, but the way her wedding ring glinted in the sun, the sheer exuberance of her tousled, dancing curls, the utter abandon screamed, *Home, home, I am home!*

He smiled, and followed, increasingly aware of seismic shifts under the continental plates of Tilda. She fit here, loved it here. He could see her working as a waitress in one of the restaurants, somehow capturing the essence of Cornwall for visiting tourists, bright smile and laughing eyes and wind and sunshine and sea. He could see her having affair after affair with wealthy businessmen down from London on holiday, laughing at their efforts to woo her and take her away from this wild place, rich only in gifts that couldn't be given, only received, spurning their offers of jewelry or a car or clothes, walking out of their bedrooms and back onto the moors. The wind would scour her clean of their scent. She wouldn't have a car here, either. She'd walk or bicycle everywhere, in her slim jeans and her Wellington boots, needing nothing they valued, wanting only whatever they could offer her that night, trading it for her freedom—

He tripped on a rock embedded in the dirt path and came back from his decidedly unromantic mental detour.

"All right, then?" she asked.

"Fine," he said. Who spent a walk by the sea with his new bride mentally conjuring up a different version of her, one where she loved and left as much as she laughed?

As he pondered this question, Tilda sat down on the edge of the rocks, nothing between her and a three-hundred-foot drop to the ocean, and slipped over the edge. He gave an inarticulate shout and lunged for her, going to his knee on the grass. She popped back up again like a jack-in-the-box, genuinely bewildered.

"What?" she said. She stood on a shelf of rock only as wide as her feet that was, as far as he could tell, supported by fuck-all underneath it.

He dropped his head to his upper arm and waited for his heart rate to slow into the double digits again. "I thought you went over the cliff."

"I'm sorry," she said, although her eyes were dancing.

"You're going to pay for that," he replied, and peered over the edge to see a tiny beach sheltered between two towering, hewn edges of the cliff. Now that he knew to look for it, he could see the path leading down the rocks, to the crescent of sand. "What's down there?"

"A very private, very sheltered beach."

That sounded appealing, but one of them had to be reasonable. "I don't know, Tilda," he said. "I've got size-twelve feet. A goat couldn't get down that path."

"I'll give you a really filthy blow job," she said so seriously he laughed.

"Deal. Let me go first. That way if I slip, I won't take you out on the way down."

In the end, he didn't fall, although there were a couple of near misses, and his knuckles were scraped and bloody by the time he set foot on the beach. The sunshine warmed the sand and rocks. All he could see was a two-hundred-degree swath of ocean.

Tilda sprawled out on the rocky sand and heaved a sigh of contentment. "We're really lucky with the weather. It's uncommonly warm and sunny."

"How did you know about this place?"

"Rory showed me, the summer I was fourteen," she said. Her first kiss, Daniel remembered, but he was reconstructing his impressions of a first kiss in this place, the sea and sky and the cries of the birds.

"You're different when you're with your grandmother."

"How so?"

"Calmer, softer, quieter," he said. "More receptive. You smile differently, hold yourself differently." Without the sharp angles, without the edge, but he kept that observation. She was vulnerable with Nan, something he never would have realized if he hadn't seen her here.

"Isn't that how people are supposed to be with their nans?"

"I suppose," he said. "Why didn't you want me to see pictures?"

"Nan put them away after Granddad died and Mum left for school. I think it's too hard for her to have them out. She doesn't have much room, either. Not really a packrat, our Nan."

He felt like a jerk for writing Nan and asking for a picture to give Tilda. He'd thought it would be thoughtful, and instead he'd put his foot in it.

"You didn't know," she said. "Don't think anything more about it."

Sun-warmed and protected by the cliffs, he dozed to the sound of the waves lapping irregularly at the beach, and awoke to the sensation of Tilda's mouth on his cock. For a moment the possibility of being seen seized him. He closed his fingers in Tilda's curls and tugged. "We shouldn't," he said.

"No one can see," she whispered. The breeze dried her saliva on his shaft, tightening the skin.

It was as filthy as she'd promised. Utterly exposed and completely hidden, he felt like he was at the end of the world, lost in time and space. She slicked his entire shaft with saliva, then tugged his jeans down far enough to lick at his balls. He came with his cock nudging the back of her throat and the rush of the ocean in his ears. The wind carried away his shout.

"I don't think I can climb the hill," he said.

She swished her hands in the ocean and dried them on her jeans. "The tide's coming in," she said matter-of-factly.

Properly motivated, he scrambled to his feet. The climb up the cliff was only slightly less terrifying than the climb down. They walked back to the inn with the sun setting into the ocean. He thought about the picture in his mother's house, the one that said *Home is where your story begins*. He thought about the albums Tilda deftly prevented Nan from showing him. He thought about their story, so new, about how little he'd known about Tilda's home, and wondered what kind of story they'd begun together.

— THIRTEEN —

New Year's Eve

The cabdriver heaved their bags from the trunk of the black London cab that amused Daniel to no end. "I'll get them," Daniel said, and handed him several bills. Tilda scanned the backseat one more time to be sure all the bags had made the transition from cab to street; they'd nearly left her shoulder bag in the rental car when they turned it in, and she wasn't eager to have to go back out again and track down her laptop, tablet, cell phone, and wallet in the back of a black cab.

When she looked up, the front door to the town house was open. Her mother stood in the doorway. "Hello, darling," she said, but made no move to come down the stairs and greet them.

Daniel glanced up, then at Tilda. There was no point in explaining that her mother would never greet them in the street, would never fly down the steps and envelop her daughter and new son-in-law in a hug that either would be considered common at best and hopelessly gauche at worst. Instead, she shifted her bag higher on her shoulder and reached for the smaller of the two suitcases.

"I've got them," Daniel murmured.

She climbed the steps. "Hello, Mum," she said, leaning in for a kiss.

"Come in, come in," she said to Daniel, who somehow managed to jockey their enormous suitcase through the narrow door without smearing the grime from the pavement on her mother's cream cabled leggings. She wore a heavy brown wrap sweater over the leggings, and her hair was swept back from forehead and temples. Her mother had the classic beauty of a forties screen star, high cheekbones and forehead, full mouth. Daniel didn't do anything as obvious as a double take, but as she watched, he did some very simple math and put together another piece of the puzzle.

Tilda closed the door. "Mother, this is Daniel Logan. Daniel, my mother, Elizabeth Davies."

"So lovely to meet you, Daniel," her mother said.

Daniel correctly deduced the body language and shook her hand rather than bending for a cheek kiss, as Tilda had. "It's a pleasure, Doctor Davies," he said.

"Elizabeth, please," her mother said. "How was the drive? I heard there was construction on the A30."

"There is, but traffic was light. We left the car outside the city and caught a cab here," Daniel said.

"You've got lovely weather for your visit."

"I'm glad to hear it," Daniel said.

And that covered the two English standbys, the weather and the state of the roads. Tilda smiled to herself.

"Although I think Tilda will see more office parks than anything else," Daniel added.

"Really, darling?" Her mother turned to look at her, genuine surprise on her face, leaving Tilda to wonder once again if her mother actually read her emails.

"I've got meetings with Quality Group," she said.

"How nice. We can discuss it over dinner," her mother said. She tucked her hair behind her ear. Silver strands gleamed in the black, and a very expensive pen was tucked over one ear. Tilda recognized the abstracted expression on her face. "Unless you'd like to have coffee in the reception room, but I'm in the middle of a rather tricky chapter and I'm sure you'd like to freshen up."

"Go back to work, Mum," she said. "We'll be fine."

"All right, darling. Lovely to see you. Help yourself to whatever," she said, gesturing vaguely down the hall toward the kitchen.

It was an automatic response. Her mother drifted into her study. The clicking of keys accompanied Tilda and Daniel past the towering Christmas tree decorated with white lights, up the stairs to the second floor.

"The reception room?" Daniel said under his breath.

"Living room."

"That's what a living room is called in England?"

"Only in Chelsea," she said. "In here."

She opened a door to a room whose bed was bare of linens. Surely her mother would have remembered to tell her household help to make up a guest room. No, wait, she was remembering the town house two streets over. "Hang on. Here."

She opened the door to the second guest room, the one with the en suite bath, and found a four-poster bed straight out of Elizabethan England, mounded with white bedding topped with white satin throw pillows, and stopped dead. Still preoccupied with trying not to bang the luggage into the cream wallpaper, Daniel nearly ran up her heels.

He stifled a laugh. "It's very . . . bridal," he said, and nudged her forward, into the hideous room. "Is this her idea of a joke?"

That was the problem with her mother. Perhaps it was a joke. Perhaps she was trying to do something lovely for Tilda, something romantic. Perhaps it was a not-so-subtle gesture to give her back what was long gone. Explaining the vast, labyrinthine history leading to these divergent possibilities to Daniel was beyond her. "White's very chic at the moment," she said.

"I'm not sure I can wait to see you in that bed," Daniel said under his breath. He set his small rolling case on the strip of hardwood left bare by the Turkish rug, then crossed the room to heft Tilda's larger bag on the luggage rack in the closet. She unzipped it and pulled out her toiletries bag.

"You may have to. Mother's dinner parties can linger until the wee hours, if the conversation gets going. I want to have a look at the storefront locations," she said and stepped past him into the toilet.

"I thought you were doing that tomorrow, with the real estate broker and Colin?" he called through the door.

She rinsed her face and began reapplying makeup. "I am, but I want to see the sites without someone telling me what I'm seeing." She ran her brush through her hair, and opened the door.

"You want to do some surveillance," he said with a little half smile. He was standing by the foot of the ridiculous bed, hands in his pockets, jacket and shirt miraculously unwrinkled, deliciously scruffy, but then Daniel always looked like he belonged. "Scope out the joint. Reconnoiter. See what you can see."

"Exactly," she said, and emptied her leather tote of all but the essentials—iPad, wallet, makeup case, lipstick, business-card case. Her cards still read *Matilda Davies*. The paperwork to change her name was staggering and would involve bureaucracies on two continents, as she was still a British citizen, with a passport issued in her maiden name, a green card also issued in her maiden name, not to mention her entire financial identity tied up in West Village

Stationery. She would make at least one more trip to the UK to close this deal, perhaps two, and there was some talk of going to Tokyo and Dubai to meet investors. The thought of dealing with the TSA if somehow her names didn't all align was enough to make her back away, hands up protectively. Daniel hadn't asked about changing her name, and she hadn't offered to.

"Let's walk. I could use a walk."

She followed him down the stairs, then peered around the door to her mother's study. "We're going out," she said. "Dinner's at eight?"

"Yes," her mother said, clearly distracted. "Tilda, I'm in the middle of a rather tricky conclusion—"

"We're leaving. We'll be back in time for dinner. Text me if you need anything."

Her mother seemed to remember their company. "Yes, of course, darling. Have fun showing Daniel the city."

She closed the front door behind her and stepped out into a gorgeous London winter day. Shifting her tote higher on her shoulder, she reached for Daniel's hand and set off down the pavement toward Marylebone. The quiet residential streets quickly filled as they approached.

"Good foot traffic," she noted.

"Zip your bag," Daniel responded absently. He was studying the buildings around them, but the cop never really stopped working. Tilda shoved her phone in the front pocket of her jeans and zipped the top of her leather tote. "Where are we going?"

"Bond Street and the Dover Street Market, and Primrose Hill," she said. She left him reading a sign on the side of a building and walked the length of the block. A nice mix of shops, restaurants, cafes. Further up the street she could see two art galleries, one name she recognized and a second she didn't. Crossing the street, she walked more slowly and examined the shop windows. Luxury goods, for the most part, the windows understated, elegant, the kind of angular theme in the shop windows that walked the fine line between artistic and incomprehensible. No sale signs, no price tags, even. If one wanted to inquire, one would have to go inside and ask, which meant one likely couldn't afford it. "It's the equivalent of the Upper East Side. Old money, which appreciates time-honored traditions, with new money buying in, eager to blend in. Let's get a coffee."

She claimed a table in one of the cafe's outdoor seating areas while Daniel ordered two large lattes at the counter. When he sat down she had her iPad out, making notes. Lots of window-shoppers, tourists gawking, a few art students making their way from the galleries to the Tube stop several streets over. Range Rovers, BMWs, and Mercedes lined the streets, or in rarer instances, idled at the curb while the chauffeur waited to ferry a woman to her next destination.

"I thought the people at Quality sent you reports on the location. Foot traffic, sales information, that kind of thing."

She sipped the latte. "They did," she said. "But data can be massaged. Locations have a particular feel. South of Houston isn't SoHo, London. SoHo isn't the West Village. Places, like people, have an energy all their own."

He looked up from the guidebook, and caught her eye. "You have a sixth sense for that."

"You do, too," she said.

"It's a matter of life or death for cops," he said, but his smile muted the seriousness. "If you don't hone that gut instinct, you end up walking into bad situations. A healthy radar keeps it from going from bad to worse."

"Do you teach that?"

He flipped the book over and sat back, ankle on his knee. The intersection of his Oxford and jeans, the brown leather belt, the way his jacket gaped to reveal his slim torso sent a slow, hot rush through her. "I only trained a couple of rookies, but when I did, I hammered away at the danger signs. The rest of it is pure instinct. You either know when someone's hiding something or you don't. You either see the killer in a pair of eyes, or you don't."

"But where you counsel people to turn around and walk away if they feel threatened or challenged, you keep going."

He shrugged. "That's the job."

"How were your instincts?"

"Sharp enough to keep me alive," he said. "Better than most, worse than some. One rookie I trained, Deshawn Richards, was like you. He could read nuances in a person or a group like they'd whispered all their secrets in his ear before he walked into it. He knew who had power, who meant harm, who would walk away when told to, who would get in our faces, who'd walk away and then come at us behind our backs. He had instincts. I had memory."

She smiled at him, caffeine and the adrenaline rush of the expansion coursing through her veins. She could almost, almost forget what lay ahead. "You're an odd one," she said.

He just lifted his eyebrows and grinned. "Wouldn't want you to get bored. I know how you feel about being bored."

"I know how *you* feel about being bored," she scoffed.

"I'm never bored with you," he said quietly.

The mood shifted, acquired an edge she didn't recognize. He reached across the table and clasped her left hand, running his thumb over her thin wedding ring, then lifted it to his mouth and kissed it. Then he went back to his book.

They lingered for another hour. Tilda took notes, formulated the questions she'd ask at the meeting tomorrow, and bought a bottle of water to drink on the walk to the next location. Daniel methodically plowed through the guidebook, and disappeared for twenty minutes, coming back with a more confident step.

"Ascertained our location in the space-time continuum?" she asked. When he nodded, she added, "Let's go," and zipped her tote.

The visit to Primrose Hill was a short trip made longer by a meander through a secondhand bookstore. Tilda repeated her process outside the second location while Daniel leafed through a 1950 edition of the *Parade's End* tetralogy.

"When's dinner?" he said absently.

"Drinks probably around eight, perhaps eight thirty. We won't sit down to eat until after nine."

"Let's eat something," Daniel said.

Another seat at another cafe directly across the street from the shop with a For Let sign in the window. Daniel produced two more lattes and a platter of bread, cheese, olives, and fruit, with a gigantic shortbread for dessert.

"I'm not sure," Tilda said. She knew London well enough to get around without consulting a laminated map, but beyond that, she was lost. "It doesn't feel like the West Village."

Daniel swallowed his mouthful of roll. "You can't expect it to feel like New York."

"Yes, but it needs to be close enough to replicate the success I've had there." She closed her eyes and let the energy surge up from her feet, pooling in her joints, knees and hips and elbows and shoulders, her spine and her jaw. "It's close. I'm just not sure." She found her tablet and opened the documents from the real estate agent and investor.

Daniel stifled a yawn. "I need a nap or I'm going to fall asleep in the soup course when it's served at ten."

"I think it's a cold soup, if that helps," she said, still focused on the spreadsheet. "Can you find your way back?"

"I can," he said, amused, "but you're coming with me. You need a nap, too. I saw you sitting in the inn's window seat when I woke up at two. And at four. You're going to crash."

"I wanted to watch the moon on the ocean," she said absently. "And I do not crash. As much traveling as I've done, I hardly feel jet lag."

"It takes the right combination of jet lag, sleeplessness, and stress, then you crash like an ocean liner sinking," he said. "Slowly, magnificently graceful as you slip beneath the waves, but it takes a crane to get you up again. Thirty minutes. Just a short nap."

"I just need to read through these—" So much was riding on this expansion. Everything she'd wanted the night she met Daniel. Quality Group joining forces with West Village Stationery would put her on the global map, taking her from a moderately success-ful shop owner into the rarefied air of an international brand. No one could take that away from her.

"Tilda. We are going to go back to your mother's house and we are going to lie down for thirty minutes. If you want to come back before this late-night meal your mother's calling a dinner, we'll have plenty of time."

She glanced in the plate-glass window of the antiques shop next to the cafe. Her skin was pale, and the shadows under her eyes weren't just a trick of the light. "Thirty minutes," she said.

He stood and held out his hand. She stuffed everything in her tote and took it. They hailed a cab on the corner and were back in Chelsea by five.

"Just taking a quick nap, Mum," Tilda called as they opened the door.

"Lovely, darling," her mother said.

"Has she moved from that office since we left?" Daniel asked as they climbed the stairs.

"Likely not," Tilda said.

Daniel stripped to his boxers and a T-shirt, then set his phone alarm. Hands on his hips, he cocked one eyebrow toward the bed piled with throw pillows. "What do we do with these?"

Tilda thrust both arms into the mound and swept them off the end of the bed. Daniel chuckled as he pulled back the duvet, then stretched out on his stomach. Tilda undressed to her bra and knickers. He was asleep before she lay down beside him.

She dreamed, something she rarely did at night, let alone while napping. In her dream she sat alone in a sage silk-papered dining room, dressed in a denim microskirt and her wedding ring, eating bangers and mash off elegant china.

Daniel didn't move when the alarm buzzed. She kissed his cheekbone, sandpaper-rough with stubble. "Daniel," she whispered.

He didn't even grunt. Amused, she pushed up the short sleeve of his T-shirt and kissed the bellied swell of his triceps. He had the lean look of a distance runner, his skeleton carrying nothing but skin and muscle. Tendons and veins stood out under the skin of his arm. In sleep, the furrow between his eyebrows had smoothed out, as had the tension around his mouth. He looked young, and vulnerable.

"Daniel," she tried again.

Nothing. His breathing didn't change, so she hooked one finger under the T-shirt's hem and pulled it up to reveal the small of his back. She placed another kiss in the fine dusting of dark gold hair there, then the dimple to either side.

No movement at all. "Wake up," she said in a singsong voice, and tugged down the wrinkled elastic edge of his boxers and kissed the place where his tailbone disappeared into the cleft of his buttocks. He really did have a very fine bottom. When she touched her tongue to the spot she just kissed, he shifted ever so slightly. She pulled the elastic down even more until it caught on either his hipbones or his erection, and continued to lick her way down the cleft, insinuating her hand under the elastic, between his thighs, to cup his balls.

At that touch he twitched and lifted his head to peer over his shoulder. His eyes were sleep-dazed, but arousal battled the exhaustion. She needed this. Sex with Daniel was rapidly becoming the only thing that grounded her in space and time. "Hi," she said.

"Door locked?" he asked. Sleep transformed his normally low voice to the resting purr of a motorcycle engine.

"Yes."

He rolled toward her, onto his back, revealing his torso. His body was built to go the distance, not bench-press a car, so he carried very little extra muscle, and almost no body fat. "Keep going," he said.

So she did, primly kneeling beside him while she lifted the elastic waistband clear of his erection, working the cotton down to his upper thighs. His shaft, thick and blood-hot, strained to his hipbones. She stroked him slowly while his hand wandered down the length of her spine to her hip, and back up again. She kept her touch light until his hand, on a return trip to her nape, pressed ever so gently to urge her forward. Flashing him a quick smile, she bent and licked the salty fluid from the tip, then took him in her mouth.

The angle was awkward, preventing her from taking him deeply, but she compensated with a firm stroke in time with her shallow bobs. Heat simmered between her thighs when his breathing hitched into a low, rough rasp. She tongued over the head, used her hand to spread saliva down the shaft. He was stone-hard in her mouth, his grip on her hip almost painfully tight.

"C'mere," he muttered when she pulled off to tease him.

He helped her get her panties off, then they shifted to give her room to straddle his shoulders. He ran his hands up her back to urge her forward, then grasped her hips and pulled her slick folds to his mouth. Even with the awkward angle his tongue quickly found her clit; he made a soft, rough, satisfied sound when she trembled in his grasp.

"God, Daniel," she gasped, arching at the confident touch.

A lift of his hips reminded her of her role in this stolen, silent moment. She sucked the first couple of inches of his shaft into her mouth and followed his pace, far too slow for her liking. She curled her hand under his heavy thigh, pulled his legs further apart, and stroked the tender skin there, prompting him to lift his hips. Only her hand around the base of his cock kept him from sliding deep. She took advantage, sucked and squeezed and hummed, all at once, his answering groan muffled against her sex.

She began to subtly rock her hips, pushing her clit into his rapacious mouth. He flattened one palm against her lower spine and slid two fingers into her, then crooked them against the bundle of nerves inside. She exhaled shakily around his cock, half gasping and half sobbing as her muscles quivered. Her own technique grew sloppy but he didn't seem to care in the slightest, rocking his cock through the tight circle of her hand, into her mouth in time to her own movements.

She came in a series of pulsing thuds, her cries muffled against his hipbone. She collapsed beside him, her head by his knees, her feet tucked under the overstuffed pillows. He turned and kissed her calf, then made a soft, humming noise and moved his fingers up to the crux of her thighs. "You in nothing but your bra is very hot," he said.

"Not awkward?" she asked with a smile.

"It's like I've left something undone," he said, and rolled onto his side. His big hand curved along her hip and ribs to stroke the place where silk and elastic met skin. "You know how I hate loose ends."

"My bra is a loose end, and this," she said, squeezing his erection, "isn't?"

He nodded, his smile now lifting the corners of his mouth. "Looks like we have several loose ends. How much time do we have?"

"Enough time for you to see to me properly," she replied.

"There's never enough time for that," he said, and crawled up her body, poised on hands and knees over her. "Never. You can't get enough of me."

It should sound arrogant, or teasing. Instead he sounded professorial, distant and factual, which shouldn't be hot, but was. She stared up at him, wondering how he'd managed to put his finger directly on the heart of the matter, wondering if he got the length and breadth of the truth he'd just brought out into the light. She couldn't get enough of anything, and some days, she'd give her heart to be satisfied.

"It turns me on when you use that voice," she said lightly.

"What voice?"

"That posh, distant voice. Like you're untouchable."

"I can work with that," he said. "Hands to yourself, miss."

She lay underneath him, let him draw desire up from the depths of her body to the surface of her skin, using only his mouth. He licked around the edges of her bra, shifted the straps from her shoulders to her upper arms with his teeth, leaving hot trails from the brush of stubble and skin. He kissed only what was exposed, leaving what lay hidden, the most sensitive flesh kept secret. By the time he set his mouth to her nipple through the silk covering it, the nub was taut and aching; by the time he left it to kiss along the dip of fabric, across her sternum, to her other nipple, the silk was saturated with his saliva and she could feel her sex grow heavy with longing. She writhed on the bed, her knees pushing against his until he obliging let her spread her legs, coming back to kneel between them.

That was better, until it was worse, because he gave her nothing, no pressure to grind against, nothing except his talented mouth on her nipples, and emptiness inside.

The doorbell rang. She stiffened, surfacing from the hot, edgy ache.

"Not our doorbell," Daniel said. He nudged her head back, exposing her throat to his mouth.

The front door opened; Tilda heard her mother's voice in conversation with someone. Then the door closed again, a car door slammed in the street outside.

"Who could that be?"

"Stop thinking about who's at the door and start thinking about this," he said. He captured her nipple between his teeth, pressure and hot breath against silk a tease when she wanted no barriers at all between his mouth and her skin. "I'm not going to make love to you until I take this off."

She moaned and undulated under him, lifting her hips as she skated her hands down his ribs to his cock. The bare, thick shaft, so close to where she wanted it, so maddeningly out of reach. She flattened her palms on his bottom pulling and lifting at the same time.

"Hands to yourself, please," he said again, rough amusement in his voice.

An expectant knock came from the rear of the town house. Another door opened, and this time the voices were louder, directly underneath them. A short conversation from which words like *oven* and *plates* rose through Tilda's heated mind like bubbles in a sauce, then a pause.

"Tilda?"

She froze. Daniel lifted his head and looked at the door.

"Tilda, darling! The chef's here!"

"Fuck," Daniel said, with feeling. He leaned forward and rested his forehead on hers. "Fuck, fuck, fuck."

He almost never swore. Tilda giggled, the sound stopped by his mouth claiming hers.

"Tilda!"

She turned her head to the side. "Yes, Mum!" she shouted back. Daniel winced and leaned away.

"The chef's here. Come down for a drink. When you're ready," she added as an afterthought.

"We're just getting in the shower now," Tilda called.

Daniel sat back on his heels and scrubbed his hands across his face. His erection jutted hard and flushed between his legs.

"A quickie," she whispered, and reached for him.

"I'm not wasting that build," he said. "I like the idea of sitting through dinner knowing you're slick and ready for me."

A slow smile spread across her face, because the idea appealed to her, too. "Fine," she said archly. Then she straddled his hips and engulfed his cock, giving him three sultry thrusts before lifting herself off again. "Oops," she said. His hands tightened at her waist; he groaned, but let her go.

She left her bra on while she cleaned her teeth and the water warmed, knowing he was watching her from his sprawl on the bed. The hot water streamed over her reddened nipples, prolonging the ebbing tide of arousal. Daniel's electric razor whirred in the background as she washed and rinsed and shaved her legs. "Trade me," she said.

When she opened the frosted glass door he was waiting with an open towel, and wrapped it around her before taking her place in the shower. She dried her hair, spritzed in a bit of shine and hold, then stepped into clean knickers and bra, then her wrap dress in shimmering gold silk, applied her makeup, darker around her eyes, a light gloss on her mouth. By the time she'd finished, Daniel had stepped out, dried off, and knotted the towel around his waist.

She watched him in the mirror as he shaved, the drops of water clinging to his cropped hair. He met her gaze. "You look like a bride should look," he said, and scraped away more stubble.

She tilted her head and studied herself while he finished and patted his jaw dry. To her eyes she neither looked, nor felt different than she had earlier in the month. "Do I?"

His hands drew up from her shoulders to lie along her jaw. His index finger gently touched her mouth. "Thoroughly kissed," he said, "and eager for more."

In the time it took her to thread a pair of gold hoops through her ears, fasten her watch around her wrist, and straighten the covers on the bed, Daniel was dressed in dark brown trousers, a blue Oxford, and a jacket. He helped her throw the errant pillows back on the bed, and smiled when she rolled her eyes.

"It's a boudoir."

"A marriage bower," he agreed.

"Imagine the same thing in lurid red satin," she said.

"A saloon girl's room," he said, so she was laughing when she walked down the stairs to find her mother holding open the front door to Andrew.

— FOURTEEN —

Her laugh didn't pause. Like a jetliner, always in motion, the sound seemed to lift her off her feet and carry her down the remaining steps and across the foyer to the door. "Hello, Andrew," she said, and presented her cheek for a kiss. "It's been ages."

"Over a decade, I believe," he said after they switched sides. He gave her hand a familiar squeeze she did not return.

"Andrew, this is my husband, Daniel Logan. Daniel, Andrew Everett-Dunn. He's a friend of Mum's."

"Nice to meet you," Daniel said.

"I'm a friend of the family, really. I've known Tilda since she was in school," Andrew said, shifting a silver-wrapped box to his left hand to shake Daniel's. "Welcome to London."

Her mother closed the door. "Can I get anyone a drink?"

"Love one," Andrew said, still holding on to the gift. "Scotch, neat."

"Daniel?"

"Sounds great," he said.

"Tilda, darling?"

"White wine for me," she said, and followed her mother to the drinks cabinet. "Mum, we said no gifts," Tilda said quietly.

"I know, darling, but what can you do? People couldn't show up without one. I thought we'd open them all together, darling, so Daniel feels more comfortable. That's how it's done in America, right?" The chef appeared with another bottle of Veuve Clicquot, and topped off her mother's glass. "You've been away for so long, and of course one must celebrate one's only daughter's wedding. It's such a surprise, too. These days so many people choose not to get married. Are you pregnant?"

"No, Mum," she said. "I'm not pregnant."

When they were all assembled in the reception room, they were a small but very prestigious group. Her mother; Andrew, who was now on faculty at Jesus College, Oxford; her long-standing research assistant after Andrew; Jessica, an archaeologist working in London; a writer for the *Guardian*; a novelist; her mother's current editor; her mother's prior editor; and her agent. They were evenly matched between men and women. The maid hired for the evening brought out trays of hors d'oeuvres. Daniel sat beside Tilda while she opened the presents: a lovely antique Tiffany silver picture frame, a pretty Wedgewood plate, a cheese board and knife. She peeked at a card written in her mother's angular, sweeping hand, and then lifted the top to find folded paper. Legal size, standard printer. She unfolded it and began reading.

It was the deed to her town house, the mortgage paid off by her mother, the property deeded to her. Daniel nudged her shoulder. "What is it?"

"Mum's given us the town house," she said.

A low murmur rippled through the room. "I bought it during a downturn," her mother said. "I expected to spend more time in

America, and thought it would serve as a base, but New York is your home now, darling."

"I don't know what to say, Mum," she said, and leaned over to kiss her mother's cheek. "Thank you."

"Thank you, Elizabeth," Daniel said.

"You're welcome," she said.

One last gift remained. A shiver chased across her nape when she picked it up, looked at the card, and saw Andrew's casually elegant scrawl, handwriting she knew as well as she knew her own. She unwrapped the box and lifted the lid to reveal a stunning Baccarat paperweight with a lotus flower inside the dome.

Her mother's face froze in a parody of a smile.

"It's beautiful," Tilda managed, turning it from side to side. The handiwork was exquisite, the flower suspended in the glass dome, the clear ground giving the sensation of weightlessness.

Daniel cupped his hand under hers and turned the paperweight to examine it more closely. "Beautiful," he echoed. "It will look really nice on your desk."

"Exactly what I thought. It seemed appropriate," Andrew said. He leaned back in his chair and crossed his legs, a little smile on his face. "For your business, which, I hear, is on the verge of taking off."

She looked at him. "Yes," she said. "It is."

After she opened the last present, little conversation groups formed while Tilda arranged the gifts on the drinks cabinet. She needed a moment to collect herself. She refilled her glass of wine, brushed the back of her hand over her forehead, and exhaled slowly. Dinner, then perhaps more conversation afterward, then everyone would leave and she could just sit down—

"Surely you don't wear his ring."

Andrew stood at her shoulder, his Scotch in his hand, smiling that familiar half smile that seemed to draw a curtain between them and the rest of the room. She straightened her shoulders and faced him. "I do. As you see."

His gaze flicked over her. "Marriage hasn't ruined you."

She sipped her wine and watched Daniel's conversation with the archaeologist, Daniel nodding and listening, the archaeologist gesturing expansively. "Pardon?"

"You've not transformed into a dull matron."

"I'm twenty-eight. Give me a few years and see what happens," she said, but even as she spoke, she couldn't imagine herself celebrating a five-year anniversary.

"I can imagine you with a babe at your breast," he mused, his voice a baritone rumble under the lighter conversation notes in the room. On the surface his voice was very similar to Daniel's, but while Daniel's tended toward a relatively even tone, Andrew's was pliable, serpentine. Daniel spoke in a rough cat's purr. Andrew's voice slithered.

Her mother's laugh tinkled down the scale, intruding into her thoughts. "Don't," she said.

He smiled. "Ten years and you're still the same. Impulsive. Burning bright," he said. His gaze lingered a moment too long on her mouth and throat, as if he could see the sex flush drawn to the surface of her skin by Daniel's fingertips. The memory of Daniel swirled together with the scent of Daniel's cologne, and her nipples tightened. "Does he know that about you?" Andrew asked, nodding at Daniel.

She sipped her wine and looked Andrew straight in the eye. "You shouldn't have," she said with a glance at the paperweight.

His gaze slid away for a split second. "Do you like it?"

"It's exquisite," she said. "Antique Baccarat. Where did you find it?" Knowing Andrew, it had been lying around the family pile since Baccarat manufactured it in the nineteenth century. But the green leaves and pink lotus flower hovering in the glass were entirely too coincidental.

"Picked it up at a church jumble sale in some village near Oxford," he said carelessly, too carelessly for the emotion to be real, although the story probably was. She knew him as well as he knew her, something he seemed not to understand.

"It's worth several thousand pounds," she said. "You really shouldn't have."

He shrugged away the value. "I rather liked the thought of something I gave you sitting on your desk," he said, trying for arch, not quite achieving it.

"You always were afraid of being forgotten," she said.

"While you were afraid of being ignored," he replied. "Have you forgotten me?"

Four sentences, less than five seconds, and the razor's edge of what lay between them hovered over her composure. She swallowed a larger sip of wine than she should have. "Long ago, Andrew. Long ago. As I should have," she said with a glance at his left hand. "You're not wearing your ring?"

He followed her glance to his hand, then slid it into his pocket of his Savile Row suit. "Milla and I have an understanding."

"I gathered as much," she said with a look at the paperweight. "Excuse me," she said.

The dinner tasted like sawdust to Tilda, but the rest of the room assured her mother it was delicious, seven courses with a palate-cleansing sorbet in between, served by the chef her mother hired. She and Daniel were seated next to each other in the center of the table draped in cream linen. Her mother sat at the head, with Rupert Bosworth-Jones, her agent, at the foot, an arrangement he rather wittily compared to the dynamics of their long-term relationship, which made everyone laugh. The chef placed plates in front of each person, then explained the ingredients and method of preparation, and withdrew.

Elizabeth brought everyone in the room up to speed on the current battle in Parliament to regulate the fisheries industry. When she paused to draw breath, Rupert cut in.

"Daniel," he said, "I'm afraid I missed this over cocktails, but what do you do?"

"I'm with the FBI," Daniel said.

"Ah," Rupert said. "And how did you meet our fair Tilda?"

"On a ledge dangling her feet twenty-two stories over Park Avenue South," Daniel said, prompting laughter.

"That's our fair Tilda," her mother said when the laughter subsided. "A fully developed flair for the dramatic."

"And you arrested her, then saw the error of your ways and saved her from an uncomfortable night in jail. In gratitude she offered to take you to dinner?"

"No, I sat down next to her on the ledge and asked her out. Any woman willing to take that kind of risk was a woman I wanted to meet."

More laughter. Tilda cut a tiny piece off her broiled salmon in lemon, tarragon, and garlic, let Daniel charm everyone, and did not look at Andrew.

"I hardly think that's the correct protocol for finding a woman one stiff breeze from falling to her death," Andrew said.

"That specific situation isn't covered in the manual," Daniel said. "And it got her off the ledge. Win-win."

She didn't need to glance up to see Andrew and Daniel exchanging looks.

"I knew where the real risk lay," she said languidly, flicking Daniel a look under her lashes. The words cut through the tension, prompting another, more polite round of laughs.

"Tilda, I understand you've other business in London," the agent said.

"I'm in talks with Quality Group to open boutiques in London and Tokyo as well as kiosks in their shops in airports in Europe and Asia," she said. At *Tokyo* Andrew flicked a glance her way but went back to his salad.

A murmur of interest rippled through the guests. "Oh, well done," the archaeologist said.

"Are multinational corporations really relevant to the future?" her mother asked.

"This is post-geographic," Tilda said. "The concept of individuals and commodities tied to specific nations or economic alliances no longer fits the marketplace, hence the airport locations."

"But London? And Tokyo?"

"Sophisticated diverse cities with their own brand," Tilda said. "Transportation hubs. We'll also have a presence at Kennedy."

"LaGuardia certainly wouldn't fit your brand," Rupert said. "I've never flown through a first-world airport that feels more like a third-world government office. One expects to see goats herded through the terminal in exchange for tickets."

"I've always loved beautiful stationery," one of the writers said when the laughter died. "There's nothing quite like the experience of pen and paper. It's the pen that makes it, the sensation of the ink flowing into the fibers, of ideas coming clear where before there was nothing. It's such an expression of the individual."

She made a mental note to send the woman a box of really good notecards. "Of course, electronic communication dominates in the modern world. As well it should for simple things like making an appointment or arranging to meet a friend for a movie. But one can make art in the moments that remain, the moments that really matter."

"But really, the ideas are the ultimate expression of the

individual," her mother said. "The medium in which they're communicated is far less relevant. Blank paper and ink is merely a tool to be used by the individual to create her own world."

"The medium of paper and ink and art becomes part of the message," Tilda said. "It conveys something to the recipient, that care was taken with every step of the process. It suggests that the individual takes as much care with her life."

"Well said, Matilda." Andrew lifted his glass in her direction. Tilda didn't need to look at her mother to know they wore the same expression.

"Well," the archaeologist mused after an awkward pause, "did anyone else see the latest *Who Do You Think You Are?* It's an historian's guilty pleasure, I confess."

"I'm always astonished people can lose track of their history so thoroughly," Andrew said. "Imagine not knowing one's grandfather stood with Richard II, or one's descended from the Tudors on one's mother's side."

"I can imagine that quite easily," Daniel said. "My family doesn't know our history beyond great-grandparents."

"You must admit that history in America is dipping a toe in a paddling pool. But . . . Logan . . . immigration from Ireland after the famine?"

Tilda glared at Andrew, and got a ghost of a wink in return.

"That's right," Daniel said, giving no sign he was aware of the subtle slight in the question.

"You know," the archaeologist said, "that show is a perfect example of the medium influencing the message. The visual impact of the individuals seeing their history unfold, in letters or diaries, or on beaches, adds such verisimilitude to the revelation, as if the human impact makes the story more real."

"The medium is the message," Rupert offered from the other end of the table. "Marshall McLuhan. The method of delivering the ideas shapes the ideas themselves, at the very least, their perception and reception. As anyone who's attempted to formulate a thoughtful argument whilst appearing on a panel show will note."

"Books were the most permanent form of communication," the archaeologist said. "Electronic information could be lost forever, until endless backups made it impossible to lose anything, including moments we would love to forget. A rant in an airport—"

"Or an unfortunate tweet—"

"Our lives are constantly archived and on display. Somehow the most ephemeral of mediums has become the most permanent."

"And yet we still appreciate a thank-you card on heavy paper, a handwritten note over a grammatical nightmare of a text. I received one from a student last term in which the entire content of the text consisted of the letters *t* and *u*. It feels rather hopeless to expect one's students to construct an argument engaging ideas ranging the length and breadth of recorded human history when they can't be bothered to properly capitalize and punctuate their texts."

"Do you find many young people are interested in stationery?" Rupert asked Tilda.

"The ones who find my store," she said. "I think, underneath it all, they're looking for something more than paper. They're searching for beautiful and permanent in a world built on disposable, on upgrades and new features and trends. They're searching, I believe, for something that matches the depth of their emotions."

"And they find it in paper," her mother said. She'd been watching the conversation flit from one person to another like a badminton birdie in the air.

"I don't know what they find," Tilda said finally. "I facilitate connection, a way to reach out to another person as best they can. Perhaps the permanence is in sustaining the beauty of that moment, the tangible elegance of it all. It fades away, of course. But they've had that moment. Can we really hope for more?"

There was a moment of silence. Then Rupert raised his glass. "To a lifetime of moments," Rupert said with a smile. "To Tilda and Daniel."

"To Tilda and Daniel," everyone echoed.

The candlelight flickered, casting shadows over the china and silver, the flowers, Daniel's warm glance, Andrew's hooded eyes, her mother's forced smile.

Dessert was an airy chocolate mousse topped with raspberries. Afterward they moved from the dining room back to the reception room for an after-dinner drink. The conversation lagged eventually and people started to leave. Tilda said good-bye from the reception room, while her mother stood by the door and ushered them into the spring night. The chef was finishing cleaning up in the kitchen.

"Dinner was lovely. Thank you."

"I'm so glad you thought so. You and your young man handled yourselves very well."

"We do occasionally go to dinner parties in New York, Mum."

"Andrew's gift was quite nice," she said. "Rather thoughtful."

"It was exactly the kind of thing I'd expect from him," Tilda said noncommittally. Inappropriate on every level except the obvious.

Her mother looked at her sharply. "Yes, what were you talking about over the drinks cabinet?"

"How much we've changed," she said. "Do you want me to stay up with you?"

"No, darling," her mother said. "Go on to bed. I'll just look over tomorrow's work, fix it in my mind."

Her mother's agent was the last to leave. On her way downstairs to retrieve the deed to the town house, Tilda paused at the top of the stairs when she heard her mother's voice, midsentence, unusually petulant. ". . . but honestly, Rupert, I didn't work as I have for the last twenty-five years so my daughter could marry a policeman and keep a shop!"

"Elizabeth, really, it's hardly a corner shop in the local high street. Daniel seems very attentive to her. She's done very well for herself."

She turned and tiptoed back to the bedroom, closing the door as quietly as possible. Inside, Daniel was unbuttoning his shirt. "That was interesting," he said noncommittally.

Tilda stifled a laugh that threatened to tip over into hysterical. "I apologize for Andrew."

Daniel pulled off his shirt and draped it over the back of a chair, then went to work on his shoelaces. "I am aware," he said, jerking free the knots, "of the English aristocracy's role in the Irish famine."

"As I said, I apologize. He was Mum's research assistant when I was finishing school, and he's a bit of a prat."

"Does your mother always question your decisions like that?"

"She questions everyone like that. Rupert deserves a commendation from the queen for putting up with her for twenty years, although the second house in Spain built with his commissions from her book deals and speaking engagements probably eases the sting of her calls," Tilda said.

"Your mother's friend invited me to the Roman excavation under the Bloomberg headquarters tomorrow," he said.

"Wonderful," she said. Her vision swam for a moment, unmoored by candlelight and too much to drink. "I think it's a closed site, so you're very lucky. Come here," she said, and reached for him.

He crossed the room and kissed her upturned mouth. "You haven't forgotten about me, have you?" she asked as she slid her palms over muscle and bone. *Flesh of my flesh, blood inked on the paper of my bones.*

She was, perhaps, a little drunk.

"You are unforgettable," he replied, and hitched her skirt up to the tops of her thighs. "Still ready for me?"

She nodded. Her dress dropped to the floor along with her panties. Her nipples, still reddened and hot from their earlier play, stiffened when the cool air swirled around them. Daniel hoisted Tilda's naked body against his, walked backward to the bed, and tumbled onto the duvet. She straddled him, jerking his belt buckle loose, unfastening his fly. He helped, releasing his shaft from his pants. His head thudded back against the bed as she sank down, but then he coiled and twisted and turned her under him.

It lasted less than a minute. She was so primed each thrust tightened the knots inside her until she snapped, and gasped into his shoulder. He came almost immediately, burying himself deep, his release soundless.

"I love you," he murmured into her throat.

"Love you, too," she whispered back.

Nothing felt real. City sounds were different in New York, or in Tokyo, and the unfamiliar room and bed only emphasized that even stillness was different the world over. She lay under him, wondering if her soul would be waiting for her back in New York, or if it were hovering over Cornwall, wondering why she'd left, where she was.

Daniel hoisted their rolling suitcases into the overhead bin while she unpacked her leather tote. Cashmere wrap for warmth, noise-canceling headphones, tablet loaded with her latest financials to review in case she couldn't sleep, travel pillow, earplugs, and eye mask because she really should sleep. Barring a mechanical problem, the flight would depart on time.

"How often did you make this trip?"

"Before I started talks with Quality? Once a year when I was in school. Two or three times now that I'm out, but I usually see Mum during one of those trips. She's very busy."

"You see your mother once a year."

"Perhaps twice if her teaching and speaking schedule allows." The seat-back pocket wouldn't hold both her iPad and her headphones case. Frustrated, she bundled her wrap on her lap and unzipped the headphones case. "I could afford one ticket home a year, which I needed to get home for the summer hols. I'd go to Cornwall. It was easier for Mum to come see both of us at once, rather than me trailing after her. After that, I was opening and running the shop."

Daniel took the case from her and tucked it in his seat-back pocket behind his bookmarked copy of *Parade's End*. "Your mother paid off the mortgage on a town house in the West Village for you but she wouldn't buy plane tickets home."

He wasn't asking. Daniel's professorial blazer, Oxford, and jeans weren't a fashion statement but an expression of his core personality. Her cop with the soul of a professor, entirely too smart to miss nuances of finances in relationships. Whatever romantic images he'd created of Tilda's boarding school life took on less-nostalgic tones after the dinner party. "She was angry with me for going to school in America," Tilda said matter-of-factly.

A truth, one of many surrounding her abrupt decision to accept NYU's full scholarship. She looked out the window at the rain-smeared tarmac. The baggage handlers shrouded in reflective jackets unloaded bags from a cart onto the conveyor belt, the luggage disappearing into the belly of the 767; if only one could stow away one's personal baggage so easily. "Quite angry, in fact. I didn't see her for nearly eighteen months."

"NYU's a pretty good school," Daniel said, his eyebrows raised.

"I had a place at Balliol. Mum arranged my tutorials herself."

Daniel looked at her. "You didn't exactly give up a spot at Oxford to go to play the drums in a punk rock band," he said gently. "I'm just trying to place you. Cornwall makes sense. Cornwall is the geophysical representation of you. Your mother makes sense with the boarding school, but not with Cornwall."

"Mum didn't fit there," she said. "Simple as that. She loathes Cornwall. She can build an academic career, buy a house in Chelsea, travel all over the world lecturing at the G8 summit or the Milken Institute, but no matter how successful she becomes, she's still from the same place. The class system is alive and well in England, if a bit less obvious than it used to be. Scratch Mum's surface and what you find is that shabby little village and that even shabbier little house, and she's ashamed of it."

"You're not."

She remembered watching the sea, unable to tear her eyes from the way it wrinkled and glittered under a cloud-scudded sky, staying awake to watch the moon arc across the waves. "Nan's from there. I'm from there. How could I possibly be ashamed of where I'm from?"

"Nan looked after you while your mother finished school," he said. "Then you went to St Andrews."

"Mum said the village school wasn't providing a proper education. More like they couldn't keep me in the building. She wants the best and settles for nothing until she has it. It's ruthless, but I admire that in her."

"Single-minded," he said. "Can your mother afford to give us the town house?"

"On her salary as a professor? No. On what she makes consulting with the world's largest corporations to increase their environmental awareness and responsibility? She might be able to buy the block."

"Isn't that a conflict of interest?"

"Mum is as honest as she is ruthless," Tilda said with a little smile. "A few years ago she discovered a massive pollution cover-up at one of the companies that hired her. She returned their fees, every penny, plus interest, then published a series of articles in the *Guardian* exposing the cover-up. Rather than losing business, she raised her rates, and her exclusivity. Bringing in Elizabeth Davies gets you an Oxford don, a plan of attack, and social capital you can't buy any other way. Her reputation is too hard won to compromise it, or let anyone else tarnish it."

He huffed in amusement, rolled onto his back, and covered his eyes with his arm. "You're your mother's daughter, aren't you?"

"Yes," she said, after a moment. "I suppose I am." She forced herself to stop fidgeting with the fringe on her wrap.

"Not to be rude, but how old is your mother?"

"Forty-five. She was seventeen when she had me."

Daniel didn't say anything else, just looked at her with that wise, knowing gaze that scared her more than any ledge. She cleared her throat, loosened her seat belt. "I think I'll work for a bit."

"Sure," he said.

It took another thirty minutes to load the remaining passengers and bags. In that time Tilda read through her emails, reminded her assistant of the three personal appointments remaining in the week, skimmed the Styles sections in the London *Times*. When the button dinged and the flight attendant asked them to shut off anything with a switch, she felt calmer. After a short delay as they waited in line to take off, the jet lumbered along the runway and lifted into the air.

In the air, she was fine.

"I'm going to have a sleep," she said.

Daniel turned on the overhead reading light. She arranged her mask, earplugs, and pillow. In the darkness his hand found hers and squeezed, then held hers while she envisioned the clean precision of black ink on white stationery, drafting her letter to Nan in her head.

– FIFTEEN –

February

As silently as he could in the predawn darkness, Daniel opened the cabinet by the sink and took down a glass, then ran it full of lukewarm tap water and drank. The Can Lake 50 ultramarathon he signed up to run took place in early October in Canandaigua; with a fifty-mile race on the horizon, if he slacked off his training now, he'd push too much too close to the race. Angie had pledged to run the 50K portion and was doing parallel training in Huntington. Normally they met on weekends for long runs, relying on her husband to meet them at waypoints with the energy drinks and bars they needed to get through the final miles.

On a day like today, gray and cold with clouds like a hangover, it was difficult to imagine the weather on race day. In the Finger Lakes district of upstate New York, it would be cooler, low humidity, and likely sunshine would highlight the fall foliage. But the weather suited Daniel's mood. Today they were getting in a run before going to a funeral.

The front door to his parents' house opened, and Angie stepped onto the braided rug and gently closed the door.

"Daniel, I really can't believe she's not going to make it to the funeral."

In deference to their parents, still sleeping upstairs after the emotional wake the night before, Angie's voice was low, but the tone came through loud and clear. Daniel slid his phone in the pocket of his running pants and zipped the pocket. Angie hadn't turned on the hall light, but Daniel didn't need to see her face to tell she was pissed off. In black tights and a fleece top zipped to under her chin, arms crossed, shoulders set, ponytail high on her head, she was the spitting image of her teenage self, wearing her field hockey uniform and furious with Mom for not letting her drive herself to the tournament.

At the wake last night he'd known he was going to pay for Tilda's absence when Angie got him alone.

"She's got a conference call."

"It's our uncle. Mom's brother. She's not coming?" Angie added.

"Quality wants to explore international venues as well as London. This is huge for her. There's a conference call scheduled with London and Tokyo at the same time as the funeral," Daniel said, and zipped up his fleece. "There's no point in her coming all the way out here when she'll have to prepare for the call, then miss the funeral to take it."

"There's the lunch afterward," Angie said.

"She'll probably miss that as well. These calls take a couple of hours, and there's usually a call to Colin afterward, to dissect who said what and who didn't say what."

"Daniel. That's bullshit and you know it." His sister rarely swore. Definitely pissed off. "You're a cop and you make the funerals, the birthday parties, holidays. It's Uncle Kiernan. He used to take us roller-skating, he helped us build the treehouse. He lived two streets away. Family comes first. Period."

"Angie, she met Uncle K once, at Christmas, when she met thirty other members of the family. We've been married for six weeks, and she's beyond busy."

Tilda had flown back to London to meet with the acquisitions team at Quality, and impressed the hell out of them. No surprise there. That meeting led to two more business trips, one to Dubai to talk to financiers, and another to Tokyo to research spaces and trends. The Asian market suited Tilda's business ethos down to the ground. But the travel had thrown off Tilda's body clock again. She was having a hard time sleeping at night, and staying awake during the day. Early in the morning when he went for a run he often found her in her study, either at her desk, going over proposals, or asleep on the chaise. When he got home late at night, he'd find her there again, working or asleep.

He'd thought a favorable reaction from Quality would ease her fears, and her workload. Instead, the opposite happened. After the New Year's trip to England, Tilda doubled down on work.

Angie hauled open the front door. "But you're here, more often than not. You might be late, but you're here, or you call."

"There are six different financiers and buyers on four continents weighing in on this deal," Daniel said. "This is a once in a lifetime opportunity that could make or break Tilda's career." He cut her off when she opened her mouth. "If you want to yell at me, do it while we're running."

They set off down the path to the driveway, then into the street, running in the direction of oncoming traffic. It was too early for much activity on residential streets; they'd avoid the main roads and highways heading into the city for the day. Daniel forced himself to slow his pace. His left knee clicked until the muscles loosened. Beside him his sister jogged grimly along, jaw set, pony-tail swinging in time to her stride but with a sharper snap than usual.

"I still don't get—"

Angie cut herself off, obviously biting her tongue. Some of his nervous energy released by the brisk pace, he said, "Get it off your chest, sis."

"You're infatuated. I haven't seen you like this since high school. Even when you were in uniform and we couldn't go to the bars without girls throwing themselves at you, you never got like this. You watch her like she's going to disappear."

That thought hit a little too close to home. "I love her. I can't explain that. You either love someone or you don't. I love her. I'm married to her."

"I'm just . . . I'm just worried. I admire her drive, the business she's built for herself, and I have no doubt that if she wants to be a global sensation that she'll be a global sensation. But you eloped with her after you'd known her for six months. That's not like you. You have to admit she's not like any woman you've dated before."

He didn't respond. Angie had opinions about the way things should be done. Always had. Always would. But those opinions were based on staying loyal to and taking care of the people in a close-knit family. Angie only wanted what was best for him. The problem was that sometimes the things that were best for you weren't the things that made you feel complete. When he was with Tilda, he felt whole.

"I love her." Three words, single syllables. They should say everything he needed to say and yet to someone on the outside they were meaningless.

"I just don't see how she'll make you happy."

Maybe he didn't want to be made happy. Maybe he didn't want

someone to slot him into the neat, orderly rows of How Things Are Done. Maybe he wanted someone who not only sat on ledges or slipped over cliffs, but also dared him to go over with her. "Not your problem, Angie."

"She's going to be a ton of work. High maintenance."

He was running eight miles in a sharp February wind because he liked the hard things, the harder the better, the more complicated and puzzling, the better. Challenges fed him. When they'd done the crosswords or Sudoku puzzles, he approached them with sheer delight, while Angie beat them into submission. "She's actually no maintenance at all. With Tilda, what you see is what you get."

They ran on in silence. Daniel pointed out a sheet of black ice, formed when the snow at the corner of a driveway melted in the sunshine, then froze after dark, then led the way down the path and along the trail. It was cooler down here. Darker.

"It just seems like . . . if you'd known each other a little longer . . . whatever *fling*," she said, making big gestures with her hands as she ran, "would have burned itself out."

"Opposites attract," he said, more flippantly than he meant, because the question struck a nerve.

"You're not going to manage her the right way," Angie went on. "You're analytical, rational, cerebral."

"I don't plan to manage her at all."

"Do you understand her? Really understand her?"

"Does any man really understand a woman?" he said. "I'm not sure I understand you, and I've known you thirty years."

"My point exactly. The whole ink and stationery is like something out of Edith Wharton. It's artificial, somehow. She's artificial," Angie said, her forceful exhales giving the words more emphasis than she meant. Or so Daniel hoped.

He laughed at the idea of Tilda as artificial. She burned too brightly to be fake. Fake didn't stand up to the kind of fire Tilda generated. "She's not artificial. She's anything but."

"You know what I mean. She's created."

He snapped a look at his sister, then avoided a pothole. "I actually don't know what you mean."

"The perfect sheath dresses in any color darker than hunter green, the Louis Vuitton, the cashmere, the capsule wardrobe."

Tilda's wardrobe was tiny, consisting of a few pieces of the highest quality, worn over and over until they had to be replaced. She made her own money and spent her own money, as did he. In her mind, classic applied to everything from shoes to clothes to stationery. But Angie's comment made something click into place inside him. In his time on the financial crimes task force, he'd learned that the things that were simple and classic often came with the highest price tag, as if simplicity and timelessness were the best disguise of all. "She doesn't chase fashion," Daniel said, struggling to find the right way to describe his wife when all he could come up with was, *She's Tilda.*

"She reminds me of a girl I knew in college. On the surface, everything looked perfect, the right clothes, no obvious accent, but no one knew anything about where she was from, where she went to school, who she'd been before she came to Bard. Eventually someone started digging and it turned out she was from some tiny coal town in West Virginia, all but grew up in a shack with no indoor plumbing, until her high school guidance counselor took an interest. She created herself out of nothing."

"Tilda isn't from a coal town in West Virginia," Daniel said. "She went to boarding school. Her mother lives in Oxford. She is exactly what she appears to be, an expat Brit living in New York for the last decade with a passion for clean lines and elegance."

"So maybe no one's dug deep enough to find her secrets," his sister said. "She's got them. I guarantee it."

"Fine, Long Island Medium, what do you think her secret is?"

"I don't know," his sister said on a hard exhale.

They'd picked up the pace in the middle of the run, going hard for a mile or two before scaling back to head for home. The pace pushed Angie to her limits, but she'd always used him as her bellwether for accomplishments and success. Separated by eleven months, Angie knew that if she could keep up with him in school or in athletics, then she could keep up with almost anyone. This kind of testing characterized their relationship from a very early age. He didn't worry about the arguing. No, he worried more when Angie shut down.

"She's covering something," Angie continued when they scaled back. "Whatever it is will be hidden in plain sight. Right in front of your nose."

Like your carping at me to cover your grief over losing Uncle K?

They ran to the end of the road, jogged to the end of the street, and walked along the block to the driveway. He reached out and pulled her close, then pressed a kiss into the fleece headband protecting her ears and forehead from the bitter cold. "I'm going to miss him, too," he said, and felt the shudder ripple through her shoulders.

This was what it meant to be part of a family, understanding that fights didn't mean that you loved each other any less. In fact, fights often meant that you both loved the other person, and trusted that they would hear the love through the argument. Angie fought with him because she loved him and she trusted him, and she knew that no matter what, family came first. He hadn't gone through the usual routine of introducing a woman to his family, letting them get to know each other, proposing marriage, and then throwing a big wedding. But he had done what was right for him. Eventually his family would accept that.

Angie's face was flushed, and sweat darkened the hair at her temples and nape as she climbed into the Tahoe to drive home and get ready for the funeral. Daniel showered and dressed, and met up with his parents in the kitchen. His mother's eyes were red but dry. Uncle Kiernan's death was expected; he'd battled lung cancer for two years. But losing a sibling hurt no matter how much time you had to prepare for it.

"What train is Tilda coming on?" his father asked. "I'll ask Jerry to pick her up at the station on his way to the church."

"She's not coming," Daniel said. "She's got a conference call today."

"Oh," his mother said quietly.

The soft sound pierced him. "I'm sorry, Mom," he said, and drew Tilda's condolence card from his inner breast pocket. He set it on the counter next to his mother's cup of coffee. "She sends her regrets. She said she'd try to call later. There are too many moving parts to these calls to reschedule them easily."

"I understand," his mother said. Her fingers trembled as she turned the card from end to end. "We knew this was coming. We just didn't know when, and she only met Kiernan once."

The only way Tilda would become part of his family was by coming to these kinds of family events. Weddings, funerals, soccer games. They'd eloped after knowing each other for mere months. It would get better, when the deal was done.

When the deal's done her travel schedule will get more brutal, a little voice reminded him. Lately she'd rarely been on the same continent as him, much less the same time zone. Just when she recovered from one stint of jet lag, she set off again. If this kept up much longer, she wouldn't know *where* she was, much less *who* she was.

"I'll drive, Dad," he said.

Without a word his father dropped the keys to the Land Rover in Daniel's outstretched hand. His father jealously retained driving privileges, but got in the backseat with his mother and wrapped his arm around her. She sobbed the whole way to the church, quiet choking sounds of grief that broke Daniel's heart. He dropped his parents off under the portico, parked the car, then took a couple of minutes to pull himself together before going into the church.

In the vestibule Jessie patted his arm imperiously. "Uncle Daniel, where's Aunt Tilda?"

"She couldn't make it, peanut," he said. "Business."

"Oh," Jessie said. "Tell her I'm trying out for the elite team next week, okay? She should come watch. I'm going to make it."

"I bet you will," Daniel said.

She turned to hurry after her mother. "Oh," she said. "I'm sorry for your loss."

He smiled at her, hearing Angie's coaching in the sentence. "Thanks, peanut. How are you holding up?"

"I'm being strong for mom," she said matter-of-factly. "Little K wanted to wear his Thomas sneakers to church, and Mom let him, but they both cried while she tied the laces. I'm really sad. I keep looking around for Uncle K, like he's going to be here because everyone's going to be here. But he's not here anymore."

Daniel was suddenly, starkly grateful that Angie, for all her fussing over the way things were done, had named her son after their favorite uncle. Jessie's little lip quivered, and her eyes filled with tears as her throat closed around a loss even grown-ups found difficult to voice. Heedless of her fancy black dress, Daniel went down on his heels and pulled her close. "I know, sweetheart. I know. It's hard. We're all going to miss him."

She found tissues in her little-girl purse, dried her eyes, then handed him one. "Can I sit next to you?"

"Sure, peanut," he said gently. Screw the pallbearer rules; if

Jessie wanted to sit next to him, he'd make room. "I'll sit at the end of the pew. Come on up after we sit down."

Daniel couldn't remember the homily, but he did remember the reflections from people who knew Kiernan well, and the weight of Jessie's head on his arm as she burrowed into him for comfort. He'd zoned out during the last hymn, transfixed by the weak light illuminating the stained glass window above the cross. The last time he'd gone to church was the previous summer, when the light poured through the window with such strength the glass seemed to become light itself. Deep blues and garnet reds and shards of yellow fell on the stone floor, the priest moving in and out of the light as he said mass. During the lunch afterward, people looked for Tilda, extended family who hadn't met her at Christmas. There was always a pause after he explained her absence.

What did Tilda do when members of her family died? She made contacts for people, introduced them, but he'd never once heard her talk about funerals. Funerals were like solstices, a tipping point, a change in angle to the earth's tilt that meant seeing life in a different light; what was once powerful enough to transform the entire building's atmosphere six months later was an afterthought. He thought about the difference between created and genuine, how people make sense until the light shifted and their real colors came through. He thought about the hidden coves and strips of beach in Cornwall, how the light poured down on them but only if you were willing to slip off a cliff and find them.

— SIXTEEN —

March

"Excuse me, miss. I need to speak to you privately."

The low murmur lifted the hair on Tilda's nape and sent a delicate shudder down her spine. She trusted that between the crowd around Sheba and her position in the dim light between spotlights in the Bleecker Street Gallery, no one noticed. "Hello, Daniel," she said.

He stepped closer, wrapping his arm around her waist before he kissed her cheek. "Sorry I'm late," he said. "I got caught up at work."

"No worries," she replied. "Did you get a glass of wine? Some hors d'oeuvres?"

"In a minute," he said. "I haven't seen much of you this week. When do you think this will let up?"

In the last month she'd been to Tokyo again, and on several conference calls at odd hours, adjusting for locations around the globe. As worn as the phrase was, she barely knew if she was coming or going. "I don't know," she admitted. "Probably around the same time your case does."

He gave a huff of laughter. "Touché."

His cheek pressed against her and his arms around her waist, he studied the piece in front of them. Sheba had taken one of her watercolor cathedral pieces of Saint John the Divine, sanded it down to rough paper, and layered it with text from her journal and sketches, covered that in a thin coat of something Tilda couldn't identify, sanded that down, added another sketch from a different angle. The resulting picture showed Saint John the Divine from multiple angles and drew in the viewer while resisting any attempts to make a cohesive statement.

"What do you think?" she said. It felt so good to relax into him, feel him take her weight without moving, and know that this was solid ground.

"It's interesting," he said. "I'm not sure what to make of it, but I'm also intrigued enough to stand here and keep trying."

She made a noncommittal noise and sipped her wine. He took the glass from her hand and tried it. "Nice," he commented.

Out of the corner of her eye she saw Colin watching them, his expression remarkably solemn for someone as young and naturally cheerful as he was. She didn't complete the eye contact, focusing instead on Daniel's hot, solid presence at her back. "Edith and I agreed that no matter how last millennium Sheba is, we would not skimp on the refreshments."

"Looks like a good choice," he said.

The turnout was astonishing. A line had queued up in front of the door before the opening, then social media worked to their advantage as people posted status updates and pictures. With thirty minutes to closing the crowd had died down slightly. Tilda retreated to the background, watching the room's dynamics, until

Cole Fleming and Marin Bryant-Fleming made their way through the crowd to her. "Hello," Tilda exclaimed with a smile. She leaned in to exchange a quick kiss with Marin and then another one with Cole. She introduced Daniel to Cole and Marin, and shook her head in denial when Marin told Daniel how grateful she was to Tilda for the introduction that changed her life. The two men left to track down more wine, and left Tilda and Marin standing in front of one of the biggest works in the show, a reworked representation of Central Park that featured the Met in winter, bare branches, black-painted iron railings, and curving paths.

Marin's blond head gleamed under the spotlights. "Thanks for the invitation," she said. She looked around the gallery. "The works are absolutely amazing. I've never seen anything like this before, and I feel like we're in on the ground floor of what will be an amazing retrospective of her career."

"Did you find something you couldn't live without?"

"Oh, yes," Marin said with the satisfaction of a woman who feels that she's gotten a very, very good deal. She tipped her head at the image to their left. A discreet Sold sticker had been affixed to a card Tilda printed for each piece, listing the work's title, medium, and price. "Don't tell Cole, but I bought that one for him. His apartment growing up overlooked the Met, and the Egyptian-themed playground. It's a surprise for his birthday next month."

Once again, Marin looked blissfully happy. Daniel and Cole returned with glasses of wine, and Daniel also cradled a napkin holding crackers, cheese, and a few grapes. They chatted for a few minutes and then Marin and Cole made their way to the gallery's glass door.

"One of your connections?" Daniel said. He offered Tilda the napkin holding the crackers and cheese, but she shook her head to decline. Knowing Daniel, that was his dinner.

"I introduced them," Tilda affirmed. "It's one of my most satisfying connections."

Daniel's brow furrowed a little more. "What did they need?"

"Each other," she said quietly. And while she was thrilled beyond measure to have been the instrument to their happiness, she felt that pang again, that unfamiliar emotion that was so difficult to identify. She didn't begrudge them their happiness. Far from it. She wondered if she would ever feel that happiness herself. She should feel it; she knew she should. She was married to an amazing man who loved her and supported her. All she had to do was claim what was already hers.

Why was that so difficult?

A sleek, polished woman wearing a vintage Chanel suit gave them a cool smile and an *excuse me*. Tilda turned in Daniel's arm as they stepped back, and kissed him properly. Colin and Penny were chatting near the door, Colin's head bent attentively, his gaze alternating between the art and Penny's vivid eyes while she talked. Good, Tilda thought. That was an excellent connection for both of them. Penny had a brilliant eye for marketing and design, and Colin worked for a global corporation in the business of selling expensive things to the very rich. With luck, the conversation and Penny's bare shoulders would focus his attention somewhere more likely to bear fruit.

Penny turned to answer a question posed by Edith, the gallery owner. Colin made eye contact with Tilda, detached himself from the conversation with a smile and a quiet word, and started toward her.

"Enjoying yourself, Colin?"

"Very much," he said, then tapped the side of his nose. "You sly girl. You never mentioned your connections in the art world."

Right response; she'd wanted to surprise Colin in a very good way, show him and through him Quality's upper management that she was exactly what they needed. But the tone sent her tumbling back through space and time. She stiffened ever so slightly. "This was a team effort. Penny knew exactly what I'd stumbled on, and Edith's was the only choice for an opening."

"That's exactly why Quality's so excited to do business with you," he said. "Imagine doing this on a global scale."

In an effort to settle her nerves, she slipped her arm through Daniel's. "Colin, allow me to introduce Daniel Logan. My husband."

"A pleasure," Colin said as they shook hands. "I was beginning to doubt you existed. What do you think?" he asked, gesturing expansively at the walls with the hand holding his wineglass.

"I just got here so I haven't had much of a chance to look around," Daniel said.

"The art is spectacular, really, a visceral statement on the fluid relationship between art and artist and the viewer's place in that relationship. And perspective," Colin added belatedly. Tilda felt Daniel's amused huff more than heard it. Colin was looking at the wall, so he didn't notice it. Tilda nudged Daniel with her elbow. "But from Tilda, it's rather surprising."

"Really?" Daniel said.

"Based on the shop, the stationery, the ink, the look of the shop's interior, well, her," he said, his gaze traveling from Tilda's sleeked-back curls to the tips of her Louboutins. Colin was far too well-bred to leer, which meant he was tipsy. Not drunk, just loose enough to take a few liberties with their professional relationship in front of her husband. "This kind of instinctual art isn't the kind of thing I expected Tilda to take on. I mean, look at her."

She felt her smile freeze on her face. *Yes, look at me. Tell me what you see, exactly. Dark clothes, dark hair, gray eyes, sharp angles and long, lean lines, demanding precision and perfection. Do you have any idea what it cost me to attain this, maintain this? Look at me, Colin, and tell me what you think you know.*

"If this surprises you, you don't know her very well," Daniel said. His baritone voice held the vibrating edge of honed steel. The talk and laughter in the room almost muted it, but Tilda heard it, felt the slight tightening of Daniel's hand on her hip.

Colin's eyes widened ever so slightly. "No," he said. "No, I rather suspect I don't. But these kinds of business instincts are exactly why we want her with Quality. You really must convince her to join us."

A nice recovery. Smooth. A bit of male bonding at the end, the two of them against Tilda. There was something about the voice, the accent, the aristocratic drawl, British public school, cultured and smooth and confident, that made her stomach do a flip in her abdomen.

Daniel's smile flashed in her peripheral vision, a hint of shark in it, although how she knew she couldn't say. "I don't convince her of anything," he said. "She knows exactly what she wants, and exactly how to get it. Colin, excuse us for a moment. Tilda, this way, please."

He took her hand and drew her through the crowd, using his shoulders and hips and voice in a way she'd never seen to clear a path. One hand still holding hers, he released the clip on the velvet rope blocking the stairs, and down they went, into the brick-walled basement. Edith had her office down here, and a bathroom off-limits to everyone except staff . . . and FBI agents. The restrooms were downstairs, behind Edith's office, and as gorgeous as the rest of Edith's space. The sink was a bronze trough set on a slab of rough-hewn granite, the fixtures brushed bronze, the door and bench seat made of similarly cut logs.

Daniel backed her into the granite slab. With her heels on she was almost exactly his height, so they were face-to-face, inches apart. Tilda stared at him, catching a glimpse of herself in the mirror on the stall door across from her. Gleaming, tousled hair, red lipstick, wide gray eyes accented by dark shadow and thick mascara. For a moment a ghost stared back at her, her younger self drawn out of the past by Colin's voice into this place and time, with Daniel.

"You okay? Tilda." His hands cupped her jaw. "You look like you're going to pass out."

"I'm fine," she said. "Jet lag. That's all. Just . . . touch me."

Without speaking she shifted her gaze to the mirror behind her. It was odd to look into Daniel's eyes via her own reflection. His gold brows drew down, as if he was trying to work out what she meant, his blue eyes the only flash of color in the room, other than her mouth.

He hunkered down on his heels in front of her, leaving her with the top of his head and the back of his body reflected in the mirror. She inhaled sharply when his hands closed around her ankles and skimmed their way up her calves, over her knees, to catch on the hem of her dress and coax it up. The fabric's movement stopped at her hips, while he continued to stand up. He leaned into her, looming over her so quickly he startled a gasp from her throat. Then he reached around and unzipped her dress just enough for the fabric to gap forward. Still silent, he tugged her bra straps down so the cups loosened and dropped away from her breasts.

Thirty seconds, perhaps fewer. Perhaps twenty, and she was naked in a bathroom with a hundred people milling about upstairs. She could love him for this alone, for understanding that she needed the physical connection of skin and blood and bone, not pretty words. Right now she felt like she had at Louise's party, when the noise and chaos and demands became too much, and she'd walked out onto the terrace for some air. Then Daniel found her.

Trapped in her dress, she gripped the rough edge of the countertop with her hands and stared up at him. The image in the mirror, the slim silver band on her ring finger, her disheveled appearance, his completely unruffled one, sent a shock wave through her. She flicked a glance at the door.

"I locked it."

Had he? She couldn't remember. He braced his hand beside hers, straightened his arms to bring his mouth in alignment with her breasts, and lapped at her nipples. She groaned and let her head fall back.

"What if someone comes in?"

"No one's going to come in," he said, and sank to his heels at her feet. The image in the mirror was beyond carnal, her body more than bare, Daniel's blond head at the crux of her thighs as he tugged her panties to midthigh.

She groaned again, slow and low and utterly helpless. Her head fell back and her eyes closed. Daniel's fingers closed over hers, then wove between them, holding her while his tongue slid into her folds and found her clit. In short order, her head dropped forward and her gaze slid out of focus, but not before she watched him show her exactly how well he knew her body.

"Shh," he said.

"I can't, Daniel, it's too much." Heat coiled out from her clit. She tried to spread her legs, heard stitches in her knickers give, and settled for another whimper. When she came it took everything she had to choke back her cries.

"Oh, God," she said.

He pulled his wallet from his front pocket. "Unzip me," he growled, then used his hips to hold her upright when releasing the counter proved her knees weren't ready to bear her weight. She fumbled with the belt, button, and zipper of his dress pants, then freed him from his boxers.

"You still carry a condom?" she asked, stroking him. Something about this found a setting on the dial she didn't know he had.

"Stop that, woman. Sometimes the mess isn't convenient," he said as he smoothed it down. "Like now. Up you go."

With one arm under her bottom he hoisted her to the right height, then braced his palm on the mirror. She wound her leg around his and muffled her moan in his suit jacket. His thrusts were shallow, working the bundle of nerves inside her with each quick, rough stroke.

"Can you—?"

"Yes, yes," she gasped. His tweed jacket rasped against her nipples, and the sensation of fine cotton and his tie against her bare breasts and abdomen excited her almost unbearably. Not to mention the sight of him in the mirror, so clearly in the act. Heat gathered sharp and tight in her core.

"I'm going to—"

"I'm there," she said almost inaudibly, and tipped over the edge again. He followed her with a groan that reverberated around the small room, and for one blissful, unsustainable moment he held her together, body and soul.

He flushed the condom and zipped up; she wet down some paper towels and cleaned up, then adjusted her bra and dress. When he stepped out of the stall, she smoothed down his lapels. "You know," she said conversationally, "most men, when confronted with a woman on the verge of fainting, sit her down and tell her to put her head between her legs while he gets her a glass of water."

He turned her to face the mirror and zipped up her dress. "I'm not most men," he said quietly, then turned her full circle to face him again. "More practically, there was nowhere to sit upstairs, and you don't take coddling well."

She smiled and pressed her face into his jacket. "I don't?"

"You get all tense and ruffled, like Jessie's cat when she goes from purring to hissing in a split second."

She smiled again, this time against the lump in her throat. It was true. "I do," she said.

"Anyway, I put my head between your legs," he said. "Close enough?"

This time the smile came with a huff of laughter. "Your filthy mouth."

"This entire relationship started because I have a filthy mouth. You love my filthy mouth."

"I do," she said again. "I really do. Were you staking your claim in front of Colin or making me feel better?"

"Yes." Completely seriously. The possessiveness startled her. He'd said she knew how to handle herself, and yet he'd done the most primitive, caveman thing possible. "Another man was looking at you in a way he had no right to look at you."

It wasn't fair to blame Colin because he reminded her of someone she wanted to keep in her past, but it was such a small moment of weakness, an alignment of the planets and stars and ley lines jerking her into a past she'd left behind. Colin just reminded her exactly why she couldn't reach out and claim what was rightfully hers. And yet she couldn't stop stepping onto the ledge; this time she'd brought Daniel onto the ledge with her.

"He's a man. Men look. Quite frankly, I encourage them to look. They often make stupid decisions when they do."

"It's your husband's job to remind them not to look," Daniel said. "Or be a little more subtle about it." His gaze skimmed her and apparently found her sufficiently refreshed to go back upstairs. "You're going to be pink for a while," he said, and stroked her cheek with the back of his index finger.

"I've brazened that out before," she said. "As have you, I suspect."

"You suspect right." He kissed her gently. "Let's go."

– SEVENTEEN –

March, Vernal Equinox

Until the swollen clouds opened to dump their contents on the city sidewalks, the task was simple: visit Sheba to celebrate the show's success. Stopping at the shops to buy sandwiches, salads, fresh fruit, two packages of cookies, and several bottles of mineral water was a chance to get out of a cold March rain. Fat drops pelted her Burberry and Wellingtons as she tightened one gloved hand around the plastic shopping bags' handles and tilted the umbrella against the wind with the other. Her coat was thoroughly soaked, rainwater trickling down her shins when she rang the buzzer at Sheba's door.

A click was all she got. "It's Tilda Davies," she said loudly, then the door lock clicked open.

Tilda climbed the stairs to the fifth floor. This time the door was cracked, heat billowing into the hallway. Tilda left the umbrella in the industrial hallway, shut the door behind her, and began the process of shedding a thoroughly wet coat. Her boots were cheerful, practical, and thoroughly unprofessional, and stayed on, although she dried them on the mat. When she turned back around, she found Sheba watching her, a mischievous smile on her lined face.

"You look like a drowned rat, child," Sheba said, then laughed.

Tilda scrubbed her fingertips across her scalp, sending droplets to the floor. "It's absolutely pouring out there," she said, and reached into her bag for the statement carefully zipped into the lining. She held it out to Sheba.

"How much?"

"Open it. It's just an estimate, mind you. Edith will have a check in a couple of weeks."

Sheba took the envelope, slit it with an X-ACTO knife, puffed air into the body of the envelope, and extracted the page. Tilda knew exactly how much it was, a considerable amount less the commissions paid to herself and Edith. Written in red ink at the bottom of the statements in Edith's careful hand was, *We really must do this again!* Sheba whooped and danced in a wide circle around the worktable before enveloping Tilda in a huge hug. "We did it!"

"I didn't do anything," Tilda said into Sheba's shoulder. "The palimpsests are your work. I just found someone to host the show."

Sheba let her go, twirling away to toss the statement on her worktable. "I've had twenty phone calls from critics and former gallery owners, another twenty from former students, and ten people I hadn't seen in ages stopped by. I'm practically a social butterfly."

Tilda said, "If you want to resume working with someone more familiar with the art world, I understand."

"No. No no no, child. Not a chance. You're my girl now. They want anything of mine, they have to come through you."

She blinked. Sheba didn't know about the impending Quality deal, or what it might mean for West Village Stationery; long-term relationships like this weren't her area. "I don't have the right connections to get you the prices you deserve. You need an agent from Sotheby's, or a dealer."

"Nope. No way. They didn't want me when I was a washed-up nobody. I need exactly what I've got. My Lady Matilda."

"I'm not a lady," Tilda said, but she couldn't help laughing. Sheba's delight was infectious, just as Daniel's calm grounded her. "It's a title bestowed on the children or wives of peers. My mother lectures at uni—"

"You brought lunch," Sheba said, and pulled the bottle of champagne from the bag.

"I thought we should celebrate."

Sheba wore a men's white long-sleeved undershirt under a paint-smeared wool sweater and equally ruined jeans. "I like the way you think," she said, and took the bottle over to the kitchen lining the back wall of the loft. "My son followed the tweet stream from LA. He says there was even a write-up in the LA papers."

"I've also been inundated with calls," Tilda said as she unpacked the white carrier bag. "Every art buyer in the city wants one of these, either for a museum or a private collector, but I think we should wait a bit. Build the anticipation rather than flooding the market."

"Agreed," Sheba said as she got down mismatched plates, followed by two very expensive champagne glasses. She handed Tilda serving spoons to scoop out salads. "In the meantime, take a few pieces that will look very good in your display cases."

Her gaze skimmed over Tilda, then lingered on the thin silver ring on her left hand. "I met your husband at the show."

Her husband. Daniel. Even three months after the wedding, she wasn't sure how she felt about it. There were moments that felt exactly like they did before Daniel asked her to marry him, moments like the one on the beach. But there were others when she felt like she was living someone else's life, when the ring glinted in the sun or someone noticed it and commented, usually with an enthusiasm that surprised Tilda. It felt odd for her, a permanency she never thought she'd claim. She told herself it took a while for the change in status to set in, that the honeymoon period was an adjustment on every level.

"What did you think?" she asked lightly as she set sandwiches on the plate.

Sheba tilted her head to the left, and smiled a slow, sweet, sad smile. "He's utterly enamored with you," she said, then turned back to the page in front of her. "What does he do?"

"He's with the FBI."

"He dresses like a teacher."

Tilda remembered the slight scratch of Daniel's wool vest, the rasp of the tweed against her sensitive skin. "He says he does it to fool criminals into thinking he's an easy mark."

"Does it work?" Sheba picked up the plates and nodded at the champagne glasses.

"Probably," Tilda said with a smile as they sat at the small table beside the windows. "Were you married?"

"No," Sheba said. There wasn't a hint of regret or explanation in her voice. Just a simple statement of fact. "Some people say that I gave up my art career in order to be with my son, but I never gave up art. It was just the two of us, and we took care of each other. He won a scholarship to a ballet school when he was sixteen and moved away from home. It was hard for me because I loved him, but it was what he wanted."

"It's a long way away."

"Based on your accent, you're a long way from your people, too."

"I am," Tilda said. "Tell me what you thought of the opening."

Sheba's conversation rambled through chats with people she'd known back in the seventies and eighties and touched on new connections made with students who knew only digital work, and carried them through the meal. For an outsider in the art world, she harbored very few resentments, not wasting her time with crowing over her staggering financial success or the critics' accolades. She simply reveled in being back in the thick of things. All in all, it was a very satisfying connection made, Tilda thought.

Sheba dusted cookie crumbs from her fingers, then crumpled her napkin to the center of her plate. "Let me show you the pieces I have ready," she said, tilting her head at an uneven stack in the corner under the window.

Tilda left her purse by the table, lifted the pile of pages, and set them on the worktable. She carefully looked at each one before setting it aside, once again struck by the seemingly random placement of objects, text, and color. While she studied the new material, she watched Sheba select a large sheet of thick paper from the random pile. Materials were fixed to the page, stiffening it, a pastel of a cherry tree in full blossom at the top. Sheba selected a knife from a haphazard stash and scraped away the neat edges of the pastel, turning clean edges jagged, revealing a midnight blue underneath. White text appeared as the edge spread. A Broadway show, Tilda thought. The font was popular in the seventies.

"The question I was asked most frequently was why you were doing this."

A smile danced across Sheba's face. "Students started showing up, wanting to do research papers on my work, wondering what happened to the great Bathsheba Clark. Their words, not mine. Like I'd died already, because no one wanted my art anymore. I didn't want people like that brooding over my paintings and sketchbooks and journals, trying to make sense of my life. My life! I've seen too many friends die and lose control of their estate, their history, afterward. I lived through the AIDS epidemic in the eighties, when it ravaged the artistic community. I've thought a great deal about what I want left behind when I die. I'm taking it apart, on my terms. Leaving nothing but the mystery."

Tilda again felt like she'd stumbled into the very antithesis of who she was and what she did. No clean lines or order here, just a purposeful deconstruction of an artistic life. "We should talk about prices. After that opening, we'll be able to add a zero to most items."

Sheba batted her hand dismissively. "You work that out with the gallery owner. I'm tempted to give them away in the park."

"How very Banksy of you. He charged sixty dollars a canvas."

"Seems about right to me," Sheba said.

She could add several zeroes to that price and still not run off buyers. "I'll take the lot," Tilda replied. "I'll talk to Edith; we'll divide the pages between her gallery and my shop while she works on the frames. Let me help you clean up." They washed the dishes together, then Tilda wiped down the counters and swept the floor. "Do you have someone who looks in on you?" she asked, eyeing the state of the kitchen.

"More in the last few days than ever before."

"I meant someone who helps you," she said gently. "Someone who cleans and keeps you in food so you can work."

"I can take care of myself," Sheba said.

"Of course, but . . ." She stopped, trying not to think about Nan, alone and growing old in her tiny cottage in Cornwall. "May I stop by anyway?"

"I'd like that," Sheba said. "You're a good listener. You pay attention. You study people. Why?"

"Pardon?"

"Most people can't be bothered with other folks. They want to talk about themselves, and you make it easy for them to do that. People want to tell you things. They think you can help them."

Tilda blinked at this dead to rights assessment of who she was and what she did. "I like hearing their stories. Sometimes, I can help them."

"Who hears your stories?"

Oddly enough, Daniel had asked her the very same thing, but in a different way. Tilda busied herself wrapping the palimpsests in several layers of plastic for the trip back to West Village Stationery. "There's not much to tell, not compared to your beautiful work."

"Everyone has a story," Sheba said.

Tilda looked up from the Bubble Wrap.

"Not everyone has the tools to tell it," Sheba added.

"I write letters," she said, surprising herself. "As long as you keep telling yours, we'll both be happy," Tilda said. "I'll see you in a few days, and I'll call before I come to see if you need anything in particular."

She took a cab back to the shop, where Penny was waiting with a giant golf umbrella. She covered the precious bag, not Tilda, on the dash to the shop's front door.

"I'm soaked," Tilda complained. She hadn't bothered to open her own umbrella.

"You'll dry out," Penny said unsympathetically. She left the umbrella in the stand by the door, dried her hands on her skirt, then began unwrapping the palimpsests. She made a noise somewhere between a gasp and a squeal, her hands flapping as she looked at the stash.

"You remind me of a dragon hyperventilating over his gold," Tilda said.

"If I could put these in a cave—a climate-controlled cave—and brood over them, I would. Oh my God. That's the corner of Houston and Avenue A. That's the Lower East Side series. I can't believe . . . What's this underneath? Is that a canvas? Poppies? She never did poppies. Is this unfinished work or—?" She ran her hands over her hair, visibly calming herself. "I would breathe fire at anyone who came in their vicinity. I would slay dragons to protect these."

"Sheba feels precisely the opposite," Tilda said, and leaned back against the desk.

"She does?"

"She started making these when art students wanted to talk to the formerly famous Bathsheba Clark."

"Formerly famous and currently the darling of the New York art scene," Penny said. "Famous for her most private work, her journals, a place to make mistakes and explore ideas where no one else sees them. She's making them public, but controlling the medium, and the message. She's pollinating the next generation of artists and opening herself up for everyone to see. Mistakes, miscues, wrong turns, the inspiration, they'd all be in those journals, but she controls how they appear. It's incredibly brave, and incredibly obstructive at the same time. She's revealing herself to the world, and yet hiding everything."

"Why is it so interesting to you?"

Penny thought about it for a minute. "It's not so much the art. It's her life. That's what I covet about these books, that's what I want. How does she see the world, and how does it become what she paints?"

"You want to know how to live a life."

"I guess so. A life like hers. Or yours."

"Mine?" Tilda said in disbelief.

"Yours." She looked around the shop, and in her expression

Tilda knew Penny's deepest fear, her deepest longing. It was a very familiar one, the kid outside the candy shop, the loner outside the clique, the person who thought she couldn't have the things other people have. It was Sheba in the art world that rejected her, the powerful man with a very unique set of sexual desires fulfilled by a dancer he could break in two with one hand, Penny inside Tilda's gleaming hardwood and steel and glass shop stocked with the finest paper goods on the market.

Oh yes, she knew it well, living on the outside, looking for acceptance, belonging, being something so brilliant it couldn't be ignored, or forgotten, or left behind. That's why she did what she did. No one should ever be excluded. Everyone belonged on the inside.

"I could have taken an art designer job for Bergdorf or Nordstrom," Penny said. "I came to work with you because I think you're going to do amazing things, and I want to be a part of something from the ground up."

"Thank you," Tilda said, genuinely touched. "But I don't know how I do it. I meet people who introduce me to other people. For every party I go to where someone says, 'You should talk to Bathsheba Clark,' I go to dozens that are just a swirl of faces and names."

Or Daniel. She'd met Daniel at a party, months earlier, when the only way to escape the forge of her past was to sit on a ledge and imagine flying.

"Well, I still want to watch. While I'm waiting to see what you do next, I'll brood over these," she said, spreading the six-by-eight-inch pages on the glass case under the bright lights.

"Brood quickly. I'm calling Edith at Bleecker Street Gallery to determine which ones we keep and which ones we hang."

"You got some mail."

Tilda flipped through it, her hands automatically plucking the finest stationery from the pack. The card from Colin was on paper she'd sold him.

Forgive me. —C

Simple and to the point. Given that they'd be working closely together if all the financiers came through for the deal, she had only one option. She tucked the card in a pocket, and texted him.

There's nothing to forgive. xx T

Edith couldn't come until tomorrow. When another customer opened the front door, Tilda gathered the palimpsests and took them into her office. The door closed, she spread them out again, and tried to work out why she couldn't stop staring at them.

— EIGHTEEN —

April

Two separate but distinct sensations brought Daniel out of sleep to float just under the surface of alertness. The first sensation was at the corner of his mouth, where Tilda's soft, sleep-full lips brushed against his. The second was at the top of his thigh, a hand covering the edge of his boxers, palm and fingers warm as they curved around to gently stroke the sensitive, hidden skin. The fact that the motion registered against his balls was no accident. He knew she knew exactly what she was doing—Tilda never did anything she didn't want to do—so his cock pulsed from morning wood to awake and aware with intention.

"Morning," he rasped.

"I believe so," she murmured against his cheek.

He heard the smile in her voice, and was absurdly grateful for it. "Wha' time's it?"

"Time for a blow job," she whispered in his ear.

Every hair stood up as a shiver crested along his nape. He worked a hand under her shoulders and pulled her across his body so she straddled him. He hated to lose the teasing pressure of her fingers, but the sense of loss disappeared when he rocked up against the sweet heat of her sex, only to return when she wriggled free from his grip on her hips. He groaned, a sound that hitched into a richer register when she started kissing her way down his body. She flicked her tongue against each nipple as she worked his boxers down to the tops of his thighs, then kissed the bottom of his sternum, his belly button. She stopped a mere breath from the head, then trailed her tongue from the flared head to the base, and back up again.

"Don't tease," he warned, and wove his fingers through her hair.

"But you're so much fun to tease," she murmured, her lips brushing his cock as they shaped the words.

Her hand wrapped around the shaft just below the head, she restricted herself to the tip, varying the suction, never taking him deep, her speed just slow enough to be maddening. Finally, she slid her hand down to the middle of his shaft and she took him deeper, the sound so slick and dirty in the early morning silence that it was almost enough to get him off.

Any blow job was a good blow job, sure, but a really good one could light up his spine and every nerve in his body, wipe his memory clean for a few moments. No past, and no future right now. Tilda loved it, and wasn't afraid to give him that hint of teeth, the rougher strokes. He wondered who'd taught her how to make it mind-blowing.

He kicked off his boxers, shifted into the center of the bed, and spread his legs. Dislodged by his movements, she gave a low, rough laugh but kept jacking him slowly. He slid his hands back into her hair and guided her down again, then settled in to have his vocabulary reduced to *fuck* and *yes*, and from there to word-less groans. He cupped her jaw and slid his thumb into her open mouth. She closed her lips around it and sucked, gaze locked on his. With her mouth closed the words became muted whimpers he could feel in the tips of his fingers resting on her throat.

He teetered on the edge between pleasure and release, his brain a whirling cloud of images and desires. Making up his mind, he tugged at her hair and growled, "Stop, no, not yet."

She kissed him, her mouth wet with saliva, her tongue rubbing against his before she pulled back to nip none-too-gently at his lips. "What do you want?"

He tugged her nightshirt over her head, then braced himself on his elbows, the better to watch. "Make it last," he commanded.

She gripped his cock and drew it toward her mouth, then paused.

He growled.

"Of course, sir," she purred, amused and aroused, with just a hint of subservience in her tone.

As he watched the carnal picture of his shaft disappearing into her mouth, his pulse pounded in his cheeks and throat. The sensation of hot, slick pressure engulfing his shaft slipped down to pool in his balls.

"Satisfactory?"

There was something so ridiculously hot about the way her mouth shaped that single word and infused it with a very British desire to please, overlaid with arrogance. She walked that edge like she owned it, sent heat sparking along his nerves. He loved that edge, too, and when he was this turned on, his brain responded to it.

"Keep going," he said. "I need more data."

She lowered her gaze in an attitude that would have been demure and humble if her eyelashes hadn't flickered just so. "God," he said. "You're so hot. I'm right there."

Her palm smoothed down his abdomen to cup his balls, warm pressure that sent him over the edge. His release pounded through him, big beats of pleasure that slowly subsided to pulses, then his racing heartbeat. He collapsed on his back, breathing hard, waiting for all the tremors and flashes to work their way out of his muscles and nerves. He pressed a kiss into her cheek, then the corner of her mouth. "Good morning."

"A very satisfactory morning," she said.

He chuckled, then looked at the clock. "We better get moving. Jessie's game starts at eleven."

Underneath him, her body tensed. "About that."

He lifted his head. "What about that?"

"I can't go. I'm going to England tonight for a quick round of meetings with Quality. I need to prepare."

"Tonight?" He swung his legs over the bed and sat up. "When did this come up?"

"Yesterday," she said, looking him right in the eye. "You got home late."

She'd been asleep, in bed for a change. He'd all but tiptoed around the room to avoid waking her. "Prepare on the train. Or the plane."

"Sheba also wants to talk," she said, and pushed off the bed.

He snagged her wrist as she walked past him, heading for the shower. "Sheba isn't your family. Jessie is."

"She's in the middle of the biggest creative production process she's had in twenty years. She's back at the top of the New York art scene. She needs a bit of reassurance, and she has no one else. Jessie has parents, siblings, grandparents, you."

The hand resting on his hip nudged, hinting at him to move, a hint he ignored. "These things with your family are all-day affairs. I need reliable Internet access and several hours to focus. You know how important this is to me."

At her request, he'd looked over the contract and proposal last week. "I have some concerns about the deal," he said quietly.

Her eyes narrowed. "It's a generous offer. They absorb all the risk," she said.

"For the vast majority of the reward, plus your involvement for five years."

"It will take that much time to build the brand," she said. "After that we negotiate based on results and the business direction."

"Tilda, you have no idea where you'll be in five years. It's a big commitment at a time in your life when—" He cut himself off. Based on her reaction to a pregnancy scare, telling her that locking herself into a global commitment when they might want to start a family was a bad idea.

"I don't have the cash to put into a project this large," she said from the bathroom. "What I have is myself. They have money, but they don't have a clear—" She reappeared in the bathroom door, her gray eyes as wary as a suspect held at knifepoint. "What time of life?"

"Five years is a long time, Tilda. If you're this busy, traveling this much, for the next five years, you'll be thirty-three, and I'll be thirty-seven before we start a family."

"We haven't talked about having children," she said.

Add that to the list of things they hadn't discussed before eloping. He ran his hands over his hair, then braced his elbows on his knees. "No," he said.

"I don't think now is the right time to have that conversation."

"Because we need to be on a train in an hour, or because we're both working the equivalent of two full-time jobs?"

"Either. I'm fairly sure we're not supposed to mix fights. Stick to one argument at a time."

In other words, kids were off the table. "It's important to Jessie that you be there. You told her you would be."

"She has games scheduled every weekend for the next three months. I'll go to another one. Tell her I'm sorry, and I'll bring her back a present from England."

He just looked at her. "Tilda, sweetheart, I know you don't know my family very well, but the only way you're going to get to know them is to spend time with them."

"I'm sorry," she said. "I don't have a choice. These aren't people I put on hold to wait for me. Colin is going to Dubai later in the week, and the CFO leaves for his holiday in Spain after our meetings. They're being quite kind to fit this in."

The shower door closed with a snick. Daniel cleaned himself up, brushed his teeth, then joined Tilda in the shower. She gave him a quick, apologetic kiss, then ducked out, leaving him alone under the spray.

He found her in her office, dressed in her at-home clothes, black yoga pants and a cashmere hoodie, her hair drying in dramatic swoops and curls around her face. The electric kettle was near to boiling on the metal tray that held her teas and cups. Arms folded, she stood looking at the spreadsheet in her hand. The lotus blossom paperweight rested on the leather box holding the requests received. Her list, organized differently from his ongoing thoughts and tasks kept in notebooks, but a list nonetheless. He lifted the paperweight, admiring the vivid pink blossom opening at the tips of the green stem, the way it seemed suspended in the glass, timeless and beautiful. In January a couple of minutes of research into Baccarat hallmarks told him he was holding several thousand dollars' worth of glass in his palm. Thoughtfully, he tilted the glass and watched the lotus flower catch the summer sunlight before replacing the paperweight back on her desk, and asked the question uppermost in his mind.

"Did you give me a blow job to preemptively apologize for missing Jessie's game?"

"Would you be mad at me if I did?" she asked without looking up from the spreadsheet.

He thrust his arms into his pullover and tugged it over his head. "Yeah. I would. Sex is sex. Apologies are apologies," he said. One hand on his hip, he cupped his other hand at the back of his head, trying to figure out what would lead her to do something like that. It was very uncharacteristic of Tilda, who was forthright almost to a fault. "Fights don't mean the end of the world, or the end of us. Angie and I fought all the time growing up. We've always forgiven each other. I trust that the fight is the fight, that it's not about something else."

"We would have had sex anyway," she pointed out.

"Doesn't matter."

The kettle clicked off, and the rolling boil eased. Tilda set the spreadsheet on her desk, then went not to the tray to make tea but to stand in front of him. "I'm sorry," she said quietly.

He looked down into her eyes, trying to put a name to the way she looked. Contrite, and worried, although he had no idea why she would be worried. People fought when they were in relationships. It was as unavoidable as death and taxes, and wasn't the end of the world. In this light her irises were so pale as to be nearly gray, her lashes and eyebrows and hair dark smudges around her eyes and temples. Her lips were still swollen from sex, a flushed red that drew his gaze, and made him bend forward to kiss her.

He stopped himself. Faced an uncomfortable truth. He was head over heels, balls to the wall in love with Tilda Davies. He could power square miles of the city with the way he burned for her, and while she said she loved him, what showed was respect. Admiration. Affection. Yes, she was English. Yes, they didn't talk about their feelings, stiff upper lip, keep calm and carry on. But if sex became transactional, they were in trouble. If sex didn't connect them, what did?

There was no way they could have that conversation now. "Let's talk about it later. Just . . . don't do it again."

She didn't flinch. "I won't."

On the train to Huntington, he pulled his Moleskine from his jacket pocket and flipped to a clean page.

Things Tilda Has Used Sex to Replace

1. *Emotions*
2. *Apologies*
3. *Emotions*

He stared out the window. The suburbs were blooming, green at the tips of branches, adding color to yards brown from winter. He'd never looked through the boxes, but he'd bet there was no letter from herself, listing qualities or characteristics she lacked in her life, and wanted fulfilled. She could give something to other people, some need that wasn't being met, their deepest desire, that she couldn't give herself. What was it his great-aunt used to say? The shoemaker's children are never shod? He sorted through his mental list of Tilda's qualities, her drive, her struggles with things he took for granted, like love and acceptance and continuity in relationships, and realized he'd missed a very vital point. Connected Tilda Davies, who knew someone who knew someone in every nook and cranny of the city, couldn't make connections for herself. Or, perhaps, she didn't make connections for herself because she didn't know how to handle them once they were made. She got people through what they considered to be the difficult part, the finding, the connecting, the beginning. The start was usually the most difficult portion for people. But what if that was the easy thing for Tilda, and what came after was the thing she didn't know how to do?

What if she'd been playing to her strengths until she met him, doing the thing everyone else admired and envied, but he'd forced her out of her comfort zone and into the unknown?

He ran down suspects, cases, promotions, marathons. Ultra-marathons. Once he decided he wanted her, Tilda Davies hadn't stood a chance. People forgot about his tenacity. He didn't mind, frequently encouraged it. Being underestimated in situations worked to his advantage. But his intention was never to tame her, or to own her. It was never about conquering; it was about possessing and being possessed in return.

She meant it when she said she wouldn't use sex as a preemptive apology again. He knew she meant it, but also knew he'd just boxed her in. It wasn't a cage, or a prison cell, but the strain in her eyes, the stark line of her jaw, told him he'd pushed her a little bit further out onto the ledge, the one he suspected they'd never really found their way off.

─ NINETEEN ─

May

Tilda flowed with the crowd exiting the subway car, along the platform, and through the turnstile to the station. Fifth Avenue was quieter than the subway, the grand shops not yet open, professionals in suits striding down the street, carrying cups of coffee, staring at phones. Phones were the easiest way to avoid eye contact and connection, but the previous night, on the flight home from Tokyo, she'd had to force herself to add a few lines to her letter to Nan. The habit started at boarding school, when she was so desperately lonely the only thing that kept her from crying was knowing she could write to Nan at the end of the day. She composed the lines as the day passed, storing them up for the few minutes she had to write before lights-out.

But lately, nothing she wrote felt real, true. Describing spring in Tokyo to Nan reminded her of another spring there, one she'd not written down and mailed to Cornwall. Her relationship with

Daniel left her equally wordless, forcing her to acknowledge another truth, that she lacked the language to describe something as deep and complicated as a marriage. She remembered the last time she couldn't make her experience real by converting life into ink on expensive paper. It was happening again, this time with a man she could not bear to lose, and the feeling of inevitability frightened her.

At least sex still told the truth about them; not even her unconscious attempt to sabotage the best-functioning part of their relationship worked. After Daniel left for Jessie's soccer game several weeks ago, she'd shoved the emotions aside by throwing herself into work. The momentum of avoidance carried her through a trip to London, then to Tokyo, the demanding immediacy of business keeping them in a state of suspended animation. Daniel was no less busy than she, working long hours, uncommunicative about the case, training for the ultramarathon when he wasn't working. Lately she felt like they circled each other, in constant motion, their orbits never quite intersecting.

They'd intersected the night before, when she walked through the front door of the town house and found Daniel uncharacteristically at home, and utterly wrecked. Officer Deshawn Richards, one of the rookie officers Daniel trained while with the NYPD, had been stabbed in the throat during a traffic stop. That's all Daniel had been able to say. The rest of the night had been silent, the tension of what weighed on them broken only by the sound of a whiskey bottle clinking against a tumbler. Feeling utterly inadequate compared to the depth of his grief, she'd nonetheless sat beside him until he was too drunk to do anything but sleep. She'd not slept at all herself, working through the night, into the next day, then crashing, only vaguely aware of Daniel's coming and going.

Today was the funeral. Her aversion was gut-deep and more

than jet lag, exhaustion, and stress combined, but she refused to bow to weakness, or tell Daniel anything less than the truth. The truth was, she had no calls today, no pressing appointments at West Village Stationery, no reason at all to skip this funeral. Remembering his response to her semi-playful blow job to apologize for missing Jessie's game, she wouldn't pull the sex card. Shame washed through her, memory triggered by the conversation. She'd not done it on purpose, but that was worse. It meant that the defects in her character were coming out again, and as much as she tried to tell herself she'd known this would happen, the memory of Daniel catching her at it, then calling her on it in his calm, measured way, burned to the bone.

She would brazen it out, dressed in black, holding a cappuccino to keep her awake. The imposing facade of St. Patrick's Cathedral loomed across the avenue as she crossed Fifty-second Street. Rain threatened but so far had held off, and the weather couldn't decide on spring or winter. The street was blocked, the hearse parked in front. Uniformed police officers from departments around the region lined the street on either side, an honor guard of men and women. Her phone in her hand, she slowed her pace.

"Excuse me," she said to the nearest NYPD officer. "I'm looking for Agent Daniel Logan."

"No one's allowed through," he said brusquely.

"I'm his wife."

That got his attention. "You have ID?"

"Yes, but not in his name," she said as she dug through her purse. She handed over her New York State ID card, then pulled out her phone and called Daniel.

"Hey, sweetheart. Where are you?" His voice was rough.

"I'm on the other side of the street with Officer Liu," she said, and handed the phone to the cop, who listened for a moment, then nodded and gave Tilda her phone back.

"Go on through, ma'am," he said. He waved to get the attention of the officer across the street from her, pointed at Tilda, then gave a white-gloved thumbs-up. The officer nodded. "She'll let you through."

"Thank you," she said, and loped across Fifth Avenue, her purse bumping from the crook of her arm. It was odd not to monitor the steady flow of cars and buses, but the size of the crowd and the solemn occasion had rerouted traffic. The crowd of uniformed police officers spilled out of the church and down the steps leading to the sidewalk. The sheer number of people clad in black or dark navy blue muted the city's normal spring sprays of white blossoms, pink cherry trees, and yellow daffodils.

The young female officer caught her eye. "Go around the side. He's in the vestry," she said.

But Tilda could already see Daniel's gold-and-silver head in the sea of dark blue caps. He pulled her in and took a deep, shuddering inhale. Uncertain where to put her hands, she patted his shoulder and upper arm, then his jaw. He was ruthlessly shaved, cut, and polished, his hair trimmed, his jaw silky smooth, but his eyes were red-rimmed, and under the smooth skin his jaw was tight.

"I'm sorry I'm late," she said, then added helplessly, "Daniel, I'm so sorry—"

He shook his head, then bent it. By the time he lifted his head he'd pulled himself back together. His face was set in an emotionless mask she'd never seen before. "Let's go," he said. "They're almost ready to start."

In one smooth motion he turned and put his hand at the small of her back, guiding her up the steps and into the cathedral's cool, dim interior, the ceiling lifted by air and sunlight illuminating the stained glass windows. Candles flickered in the niches. Daniel walked down the center aisle and guided her into a row of chairs. Tilda felt like she was adrift in a sea of black and blue.

"He left a wife, Michele, and four kids," Daniel said under his breath as they walked up the side aisle. They squeezed into two seats three rows behind the widow just as six white-gloved, uniformed men and two in suits bore the coffin to its place in front of the altar. Surreptitiously Tilda withdrew her phone from her pocket. She'd left the shop in Penny's capable hands, but a shipment from France was three days late. She swiped her thumb over the screen, then while the wheel spun glanced at the widow. She turned to the child seated next to her, her black veil swaying forward to expose a pale cheek. The little girl looked up at her mother, tears slipping along the tracks laid by an earlier bout of crying.

Tilda's breath came short. The girl wept silently, tears falling down her cheeks to dampen the Peter Pan collar of her black dress. Her mother bent forward and kissed her forehead, then swiped at her tears with her thumb before turning to the boy on her left. A woman Tilda assumed was a grandmother sat at the end of the row, holding the fourth child's hand.

Unable to connect to server.

She slipped her phone back in her pocket and fixed her gaze on the priest. His unhurried movements seemed appropriate to the situation, the religious equivalent of good black ink flowing onto time's white paper. She stood when Daniel stood, sat when he sat, reciting prayers and liturgical responses, stumbling through the unfamiliar prayers. They stood as the widow and her children filed out behind the flag-draped casket, followed by the rest of the family.

"Are you going to the cemetery?" she asked in an undertone.

"No," Daniel said. "It's a private internment, for family only. I'm going out with a bunch of the guys from the two-seven. I'll be home later."

"All right," she said, then went on tiptoe to kiss his cheek, wondering why she'd been there at all.

The door lock snicked, waking Tilda up. She rolled over and looked at the clock. Twenty past two. They'd closed down the bar, then. She lay where she was and listened to his slow progress up the stairs. Shuffling, and a couple of thuds where his shoes bumped into the step rather than clearing the riser. The light from the hall blinded her when he opened the door. His jacket was rumpled, his tie askew, the top buttons of his white shirt unfastened.

"Come here," she said.

He slumped on the edge of the bed. She slid to her knees on the floor in front of him and went to work on his shoelaces.

"I'm drunk," Daniel said matter-of-factly.

"It smells like very good whiskey," she said, and tugged off his left shoe.

"I haven't been this drunk in a very long time," he said, the words enunciated with the careful attention of the utterly legless.

"You don't have to explain," she said. She got his socks off, then started on the single remaining button on his jacket. He nominally helped her get it off his shoulders.

"Woke you up," he slurred.

"I haven't been asleep long," she said.

"Call?"

"Yes." Colin called her at seven London time, while he was still in his pajamas, eating porridge and fruit and toast.

"Sometimes I think you're on another continent," Daniel said.

She looked up at him, but his eyes were closed, so she went to work on his shirt buttons, then his belt and zipper. "Right now I'm right here," she said softly, and stripped him down to his T-shirt and boxers.

He sprawled on the covers. Eventually she shifted him until he was partially covered, then gave up and crawled over him, to her side of the bed.

"He was twenty-eight," Daniel said. "I trained him. Did you know that?"

"I did," she said. "You told me in London. Remember?"

"He could read people like nobody's business, knew what a suspect would do before he knew. The suspect. Not Deshawn. I'm not making sense."

"I understand," she said.

"This never should have happened to him. Other guys, sure, but not him. Do you think he felt it? The knife?"

"I don't know," she said. "Perhaps."

"We train for guns, but knives kill you just as dead. Married at twenty-one, four kids by twenty-seven. He wanted a better life for his kids. Better than his. He didn't know his dad. Was this better?"

"I don't know," she said. "He thought so."

He was asleep, that quickly, that deeply. When she woke up the next morning, he lay limp and heavy next to her. She showered and dressed and went to work, texting him as she walked.

Let me know when you wake up.

His text came just after noon, just as she finished processing the late shipment.

Come home for lunch.

She unlocked the front door just before one, gathered the mail from the doormat, and followed the sound of water running to the kitchen. He'd showered and dressed in jeans and an NYU

T-shirt over a thermal undershirt, but his eyes were bloodshot and he held his head rather carefully.

"I can't imagine you want to eat," she said as she flipped through the day's mail.

"I don't," he said. "I just wanted to see you."

She got a tub of Greek yogurt from the fridge and peeled off the top. "How are you feeling?"

"Hungover. You?"

"I'm fine," she said, distracted. Why wouldn't she be fine? "I sent a card to his widow."

"Thanks," he said, and slugged back more water.

"It's quite imposing, all those uniforms in one place."

One corner of his mouth quirked up. "You never saw me in uniform, did you?"

She smiled at him, then nodded at the little stash of law enforcement stuff on the counter—gun, badge, handcuffs—none of it the sort of thing she associated with Daniel except the black leather notebook where he recorded details, lists, information, phone numbers. He had a stash of them going back to his earliest days with the NYPD, the record of his daily life as a cop. "I believe you."

She abandoned the regular mail and turned to the contents of her post-office box. "What happens to their children?"

He swallowed more water. "There's a fund for widows and orphans. The department will take care of them. We can't make up for their father dying, but they won't be alone. Someone will go to games, watch dance recitals, bring them Christmas presents. We take care of our own."

Steel hummed in his voice, the shared *we*. Hungover, dehydrated, battered by loss, and Daniel just got tougher. Stronger. More determined.

"Good," she said. "That's good."

He came up behind her and set his water glass on the granite countertop. With the shades drawn the gray plank cabinets took on a cloudy-day cast. She sorted and opened the requests for Lady Matilda, idly fidgeting with the edges of the paper as she ran through her mental list.

"Hey," he said. "Don't worry about it." She bent her head; moments later, Daniel's mouth brushed against her nape. "He was on patrol, night shift. I work behind a desk. The biggest worry I have right now is managing the informant for the case I'm working on."

"I know," she said.

His arms came around her waist. She could feel the strength and power in his body, carefully arrayed to protect her, so why did she feel like she couldn't breathe?

"Hey," he said again.

She wore her heels and he was barefoot, so they were of a height. His erection swelled against her bottom, and his mouth worked against her nape, just lips and tongue to start, then teeth. The teeth were good, very good, sharp and insistently demanding she focus on her body. The mail forgotten, she shuddered and reached out blindly. One hand flattened against the cabinet her forehead thunked into while the other curled around the counter's edge.

He wove his fingers through hers to pin her left hand to the cabinet, then reached around her hips with his right. She tilted her head to the side to allow his mouth better access to her ear and the tendons in her neck. She whimpered and tried to turn to face him, but he leaned forward, pinning her to the counter. She settled for looking over her shoulder, mouth open and seeking his kiss.

The slick glide of his tongue against hers made her shudder. Daniel kissed her with the urgency of a man sliding down the dark well of lust. "Upstairs?" he asked.

"No," she said. "Here. Now."

She tugged her fingers free from his, then reached for her skirt, shifting and wriggling to pull it up to the tops of her thighs, then the top of her backside. Her breathing was loud enough, huffing against the cupboard and reverberating in her brain, but Daniel's . . . Daniel's exhale caught in his throat, turning into a rough little growl that sent shock waves of desire straight to her clit.

He still leaned against the cupboard, forearm braced by her head, other hand on the counter by her hip, giving her just enough room to get her skirt up and give him a good look. "God," he whispered, and that was rough, too.

She tucked her thumbs into the gossamer black panties and pulled them down. They caught on her thighs, but Daniel turned her to face him using a movement that was about hips and shoulders and chest because his hands were preoccupied with getting her panties to drop to the floor. He wrapped his arm around her waist and hoisted her up on the counter. She spread her knees, he stepped between them, and for a split second she thought about the familiarity of a long-term lover, the ease with which he put his hands on her hips and pulled her closer while she opened his threadbare jeans and worked them just low enough to release his cock.

Daniel braced both forearms on either side of her head, and watched her wrap her hand around his shaft and draw him forward. A shift, a tilt to her hips, and he slid right inside, going deep on the first stroke. A soft, shocked, disbelieving sound drifted into the air between them.

"Okay?" he murmured.

She could breathe again, like this, with him inside her, the familiar sensation of erotic desire coursing along her nerves, precursors to the impending storm of release. He stretched her deliciously, and waited until she gave a full-body undulation, snugging them up more tightly. She wrapped her legs around his waist and one arm around his neck, fisting the other hand in the loose denim at his hip to keep him close. He didn't flinch at taking her weight, just braced his bare feet more solidly against the slate floor and started to thrust, putting the power of his thighs and hips into each movement.

Someone was whimpering. It must have been her, because the sounds were too high to be Daniel, but someone was definitely whimpering into the hot, damp air between their bodies. She tilted her head a little to the side, and felt his hot temple slide along hers, so they both looked down at the dirty, erotic sight of his shaft, gleaming with her juices, gliding in and out. There was something so primitive and carnal about the possession. Electric heat cracked through her body, tightening muscles to bone.

"This is too good to be real," Daniel gasped.

One shoe, then the other, dropped to the kitchen floor, the sounds distant and unimportant in her brain. Each thrust sent a hard jolt of pleasure pulsing out from her core, building against her skin, until she was too hot, her dress too tight, her very skin on the verge of flaring into flame, like a match in that nanosecond before ignition.

"God," Daniel said, almost inaudible. "Yes. Yes."

In some distant part of her brain she knew reducing Daniel to single, hissed syllables was a significant accomplishment, but oh, she needed this, she needed it. All the auxiliary details coalesced, the catch and rub of her lace bra against her nipples, the incidental brush of his mouth against hers, the redness of his eyes, his cheeks, his throat. Her legs drew up even more, closing as her knees pressed against his lower ribs. With one hand he reached down and hooked his elbow under her knee, forcing it wide, lunging into her body on the next stroke, and the next. The impact against her clit sent her soaring into the void, with him just seconds behind her.

As the tremors eased, his lips sought hers, soft and sweet. Then he reached for a roll of paper towels and tore off a long segment.

"I need to take a shower," she said as she slid off the counter and dealt with the mess. "I can't go back to work smelling like I've had a quickie over lunch."

"Take the afternoon off," he said.

The words were quiet, a plea, if she didn't know better. "I can't," she said, and took a handful of paper towels. Sex certainly was less messy when condoms were involved. "I'm behind from that last trip to Tokyo. If I don't stay on top of things with Quality, they'll think I've lost interest."

A beat of silence passed before he answered. "Yeah. Sure," he said. "No problem. I'll probably go for a run."

She raised her eyebrows at him. "A run?"

"Not a long one. It'll flush out the toxins, one way or another."

He followed her up the stairs. He was dressed in running shorts, a long-sleeved NYU T-shirt, and his sneakers when she emerged. Something in the tight set of his jaw made her pause and reach for him. "I am sorry," she said.

"I know. You're busy."

They parted ways at the front door. She walked back to the shop knowing she was doing what she had to do, knowing she'd failed him, not knowing how to stop.

– TWENTY –

May

"Dessert?"

Seated at an intimate table for two under a tall ficus tree at the Four Seasons Restaurant, Tilda angled her knife and fork precisely across her plate. The silver gleamed in the light from the candle flickering in the middle of the table. Hushed talk flowed around them, the clink of silverware against china like the burble of water over rocks in a stream. Across the table Tilda flicked him a look, her eyes the color of the waxing moon outside, and muted by thick lashes.

"Perhaps just a coffee," she said.

"Coffee and dessert. It's your birthday. You have to have something sweet." He signaled the waiter, who cleared their plates, cleaned up a few stray crumbs from the bread basket, and handed them both dessert menus.

"The flourless chocolate torte," Daniel said.

"Decadent. I'll have the profiterole," Tilda said as she handed the menu to the waiter.

"And two decaf cappuccinos."

She tilted her head and studied him. "You really didn't have to do this."

"This is a belated Valentine's Day celebration, and it's your birthday," he said. "Which I knew only because I saw it on your birth certificate when we got married."

Lips pursed, one eyebrow raised, she gave him the look that said she was calling bullshit. "Really, Agent Logan?"

The banter relieved him. She'd been so distant since Deshawn's funeral, a distance he wanted to close, but without knowing why it existed, he wasn't sure how to go about handling it. There was no point in reassuring Tilda, but he could show her he cared, that he'd love her forever, that despite their hectic schedules and her weird, wired body clock, they were in sync. Show, don't tell. Actions speak louder than words. "All right, fine, I ran you through the system after I saw you at the party."

"Not after we met?"

"I was thinking about other things after we met."

Her smile lifted the corners of her mouth. "Such as?"

"What I'd ask you for," he said.

"You let me believe you knew about my little hobby, prattle on about letters when all you wanted was a date."

He smiled and said, "And you turned me down."

"And yet here we are. Married, even."

"Here we are." He sat back, and treated himself to a long, frankly assessing look. He could switch perspectives on Tilda, get lost in conversation with her, but pull back and see her as other people saw her. Tall, slim, dressed in a dark blue sheath, unrepentantly unruly curls in this age of poker-straight hair. The bones of her shoulders and collarbone peeked out from the neckline and sleeves of her dress. Her silver hoops winked in her ears and her wedding ring glinted on her left hand, but otherwise she wore no jewelry at all. As nearly as he could tell she owned inexpensive costume pieces, and rarely wore even those.

"We weren't together on my last birthday," she said.

"Would you have said anything this time around, or just let me realize we'd been together for a couple of years and never celebrated your birthday?"

She gave him that smile, that winking little smile. "It's not important."

"It's extremely important," he said, thinking of the red box in his jacket pocket.

"Did you celebrate birthdays in grand style when you were growing up?"

"Always," he said. "We'd have a family party, and a friends party. Bowling or laser tag or the movies, a sleepover in the basement. Some years there would be ten kids asleep in sleeping bags on the floor. My dad would make everyone waffles and sausage and we'd eat the rest of the cake before my friends went home."

"Your mother does that for the grandkids."

"She's carrying on tradition. When Angie's birthday came around, I used to go spend the night with a friend. Then, when we got older, my friends wanted to hang out at the house and check out Angie's friends."

"Your mum was okay with that?"

"She figured it was better to have us under her roof, where she could keep an eye on us, than somewhere else. All of our friends hung out at our house. What about you?"

"My birthday fell during the school term. We'd have treats after chapel, but otherwise, it was business as usual."

"You didn't celebrate afterward?"

"Nan made me a cake, of course, and my friends in the village would come by, but if I were in Oxford with Mum, well, Mum didn't give much credence to celebrating birthdays."

"How is Nan?"

"She's back from hospital. I called her earlier today. She's not pleased about being off her feet for a few weeks, and is convinced the farm will go to ruin without her doing everything, and won't admit to being in any pain."

"Are you going to go see her?"

"I added a couple of days to my next trip to London," she said, but the worry lines didn't smooth from her forehead.

Dessert and coffee arrived. He offered her a bite of the cake from his own fork. "Oh, that's good," she said. "Very rich."

"What was your best birthday?" he said as he waited for the server to process his credit card.

Her eyes went distant. "The year I was eight, I suppose. I was with Nan, and she invited all the girls in the village to her house for a tea party. Everyone brought presents, and we played games. Pin the tail on the donkey. In hindsight, I think she must have known . . ." Her voice trailed off. The waiter arrived and left the receipts with Daniel. Tilda gave her head a faint shake and smiled at him. "Do kids even play games like that at birthday parties these days?"

"Not the ones my nieces and nephews go to," he said as he signed the receipt. "Kids these days are organized to within an inch of their lives. Bounce castles and trampoline parks and miniature golf. I can't see my sister giving Jessie and Little K a donkey's tail with a pin in it."

"You could use tape," she said, obviously amused.

He stood and offered her his hand to help her up from her chair. She took it, her fingers chilly, so he laced his fingers with hers to warm them up. They walked through the foyer to the street, where Tilda stretched. "What a gorgeous night," she said.

It was Manhattan at its best, warm from the spring sunshine but not yet starting to stink from the summer heat. He looked at her shoes. Four-inch heels, as usual. "Can you walk in those?"

"To the West Village?" she asked incredulously. "I'd prefer not to."

"We're not going home."

"We're not?"

He tucked her hand in his elbow and turned uptown. "We're not."

"Daniel, what's going on?"

"It's a surprise," he said, the box in his jacket pocket bumping against his opposite hip. "It's not far. A few blocks."

"I don't really like surprises," she said.

"I've guessed as much," he said. "But this is a good surprise."

They strolled in silence, Tilda's long legs easily keeping up with him despite the heels. When they reached the imposing granite facade inscribed with *Waldorf Astoria* in polished gold letters, he put his hand at the small of her back to guide her up the steps. To his surprise, she balked under the brass-railed canopy. Tilda looked like a strong breeze would blow her away, but she could hold her ground.

"Really, what's going on? You don't have two hundred people in a ballroom waiting to jump out and shout *happy birthday* at me, do you?"

"I don't," he said.

"Then what are we doing here?"

"Celebrating your birthday," he said, and tugged gently at her hand. "Come on. I promise it's not a surprise party."

She ducked her head but let him pull her up the steps and into the opulent foyer. "Wait here," he said, and left her by the ornate clock topped with the Statue of Liberty while he checked in. He reclaimed his wife and walked across the marble floors to the elevator bank. When the doors whooshed shut behind them, Daniel closed the distance between him and Tilda and braced his hands on the hip-high brass railing. He leaned in to kiss her, because he had to kiss her, had to have that lush mouth under his if only for the duration of the ride to the twelfth floor.

"Don't," she said.

He paused, no more than a millimeter from her mouth, assessing her tone, the look on her face, the glitter in her eyes. The scent of her perfume and the shocking, earthy, blood-dark scent of lust rising from her skin went straight to his back brain, so he didn't pull back. "Why not?"

She somehow managed to work one index finger, the nails painted in clear, unchipped polish, into the infinitesimal space between his mouth and hers. The pad of her finger traversed the contours of his mouth from one corner to the other, the slick polish on the nail covering the same distance on her own mouth. Her gaze angled to one corner of the elevator, rising slowly through the building's core. "We should be discreet. Someone might be watching."

Discreet? Tilda? He remembered the bathroom at the art gallery, the ledge, and smiled at the sheer delight of it all, because he'd read her changing mood correctly. "That's what you want for your birthday?" he murmured. He didn't move, didn't back up, let her feel the heat and strength of his body, pressed against hers from knees to lips. "You want something private and intimate?"

For a long second she didn't respond at all. Then the elevator bell dinged and the doors opened. Without a word he stepped back and held out his hand, indicating she should precede him down the hallway. He watched her, tall and lean and swaying elegantly on her killer heels that sank into the carpet with every step. The muted lights caught her hair, raven black and gleaming. Once again he jerked from participant to observer. The color of her dress turned her eyes almost silver. She could have been a businesswoman returning to her hotel after a long day of meetings. She could have been an expensive call girl, the kind you could take to a cocktail party on the Upper East Side and fool everyone in the room. She could have been a yummy mummy, returning to her family after ducking out for some shopping.

She could have been his wife, gliding down the silent corridor to an anonymous hotel room. She could have been anything, anyone—virgin, fertility goddess—or she could have been exactly what she was. A woman. His wife.

As he reached past her to insert the key card into the lock, a wave of love washed through him. His wife. As mysterious as she was the day he met her, the day he married her. Once inside she set her tote by the dresser and looked around. Arrangements of white roses spilled from vases and containers on the dresser, nightstand, desk. Carefully dethorned single stems lay scattered on the king bed, which had been stripped to the bottom sheet. A bottle of champagne chilled in the bucket, next to two glasses. "You planned this," she said when she saw her vintage Louis Vuitton overnight bag sitting on the luggage rack. Packing for Tilda was easy. She traveled light, never more than one bag, no matter the length of the trip or the destination. Sometimes he got the feeling she'd be perfectly happy to live out of a suitcase, always in the air.

"I did," he said. "Happy birthday."

She made a little noise, then drew back the curtains covering the view onto Park Avenue and peered out at Manhattan's skyline. Hands in his pockets, he looked at her elegant profile washed clean by the city lights and felt his heart turn slow loops in his chest.

"It's lovely," she said finally.

The scent of white roses, clean and simple and pure, danced in the air molecules as he crossed the carpet, laid his hand alongside her jaw, and kissed her. She turned to him, her hands coming up to hold his lapels, her mouth soft and closed under his until he licked into it, coaxing it open. She bent her head and brushed her lips back and forth over his jaw, then to the spot where his pulse thumped above his collar. The move was so timid, so hesitant, so unlike her. A desire to protect her overwhelmed him.

"Shhhh," he said without knowing why. "Come here. I've got you."

He led her to the bed and unzipped her dress, slowly drawing the tab of the zipper down her back to reveal her spine, the bird's wings of her shoulder blades bisected by a black lace bra. He unfastened the hooks and slipped both dress and bra forward, down her arms to pool on the floor at their feet, leaving her in a matching pair of black lace panties and her heels.

She once again tucked her hands together just under her chin and bent her head. "Daniel," she said quietly.

The air hummed with something secretive, something deep and unspoken. "Lie down," he whispered into her nape.

She knelt on the bed, turning and tucking her feet under her bottom as she turned to face him. Sitting among the scattered roses on white sheets, she glowed like an ember. Hair, eyes, cheeks flushed, lips, the tips of her nipples, the black lace panties, her black heels. The sheer beauty of her took his breath away, while the blood pumping to his cock reduced him to one primitive word. *Mine.*

As she watched he shucked his jacket and tossed it on a chair, loosened his tie, then knelt on the bed next to her. He picked up one of the roses and trailed it along her jaw to her mouth. She exhaled shakily, a darker shade of red staining her cheeks and throat. He followed the line of her throat to the notch between her collarbones, twirling the rose for a moment, then bent and kissed the skin. Her scent, uniquely Tilda, wafted into the air, dissipating the smell of the rose.

The tops of her breasts received the same treatment, as he carefully brushed the petals against the curves while her nipples tightened into hard peaks. She shifted restlessly, trying to bring the dark buds into contact with the rose, inhaling shakily when he drew the flower down the side of her breast to avoid the contact.

"Your skin is almost the same shade of white as the rose," he said as he lifted the flower between her breasts, back to her mouth. Her lips parted and her tongue flicked out, but he pulled the flower back and down. This time he brushed the edges of the petals over each nipple before continuing down to tease the crux of her thighs.

She dropped back to her elbows and parted her legs. He brushed the flower over her mound again and again, until her head dropped back and she moaned. "Daniel," she said.

"Shh. Let me give you this."

She seemed to cycle through tension then relax back into the arousal he coaxed to the surface of her skin. When she lay all the way back, he dropped the rose beside her hip and retraced his steps with his mouth, from her forehead to her lips to her nipples to her abdomen. Her mouth tasted of dark coffee and rich chocolate, and her skin tasted faintly of sweat and musk. The scent of the flowers, the petal-soft texture of her skin, and he was drowning.

He kissed his way to the folds between her legs, but her hand in his hair stopped him. "No," she said. "Please. Now."

He sat back on his heels and unbuttoned his shirt, shrugging out of it, pulling his T-shirt over his head, then attacking his belt and zipper. She'd turned her head away. He followed her gaze to the mirror over the dresser, low enough to reflect everything on the bed. Her body, sprawled and flushed among the roses, wearing nothing but her wedding ring. Him on his knees beside her as he stripped.

Their eyes met. Her irises were pewter, fringed by her thick black lashes, and his heart knocked hard against his ribs. He tore his gaze away from the reflection to the woman underneath him as he aligned his cock with her opening and slid inside. Her body arched under his, seating him more firmly. Then he began to move. She was slick and tight and hot around him, burning in his arms, watching them in the mirror. He could feel her drawing tighter and tighter, clasping him inside and out, and risked a quick glance at the mirror. The sight nearly sent him over the edge, the sheer erotic thrill of seeing what he felt reflected back to him, burning into his brain. He saw each thrust in hips and buttocks, felt it glide along his cock and make heat pool in his balls. Tilda's toes were curled tightly, and the faint gasps he heard made her breasts rise against his chest, before panting out between her parted lips.

He wanted more. He angled his head to capture her lips, turning her head and drawing her into that intimate secret that was making love. Complex sensations buffeted him, fingernails in his back, heels digging into his calves. Tilda gasped under him, tiny stifled sounds all the more powerful for being muffled. But it wasn't like Tilda to hold back.

"I love you," he growled in her ear. "Tilda. I love you."

She lifted under him, her teeth clenched as she came. He slowed, thrusting through the contractions and fighting his own release until she shuddered and subsided under him. Only then did he drop into the abyss. Tilda panted under him, fingers trembling against his shoulders. Aftershocks burned through his muscles as he kissed her cheek, then her chin, then each of her closed eyelids.

"I love you, too," she whispered, the words little more than a huff of air against his ear. Her eyes opened slowly, like a cat awakening from a long sleep. When they focused on him, the expression was haunted, hunted even. Then she blinked, and it was gone. "When did you do all of this?"

"Earlier today. I took a couple of hours off work."

"Daniel, I don't know what to say. It's so much. You really didn't need to do this."

The complex sensations were still swirling in the air. He tried to get a handle on what she was thinking, feeling. "It's no bother. Or trouble. Or hassle." Doing things for the people he loved wasn't work. It was what made life worth living. He reached under the pillow for the towel he'd stashed there earlier in the day.

"Practical as well as romantic," she said.

Tilda handled the awkward parts of sex as gracefully as she handled everything else. He exchanged the towel for her overnight bag, then made a quick stop in the bathroom. When he came back out, in his boxers, she was wearing the nightgown he'd swiped from her side of the dresser, a practical gray cotton thing. It surprised him. She was so elegant in every other area of her life, but slept in what was basically an oversized V-neck T-shirt washed to softness.

"Do you want to spend the night?" she asked.

"Hell, yes," he said as he reached for his suit pants to hang them up. "It's part of the experience. And now, for your present."

She was rubbing the hotel's lotion into her hands as he spoke, but she looked up at him, her eyes wide. He straightened his shirt and tie on the hanger, then added his jacket, and pulled the box from the pocket. He hid it behind his back and sat on the edge of the bed.

One glance over his shoulder, and her eyes went huge in her face.

Damn. He'd forgotten about the mirror. "Sorry," he said and offered her the red leather box, embossed with gold, and the name *Cartier*. "I ruined the surprise."

"You didn't."

"I did."

"It's too much."

Probably. The thing cost an arm and a leg, but less than he would have spent on an engagement ring based on the two months' salary formula, if they'd done anything so quotidian as buy an engagement ring.

"You can't . . . you shouldn't have. *Cartier?*" She pronounced it perfectly, the *r* and *t* rolling off her tongue into the softened French syllable at the end. "My God."

"Tilda. It's your birthday. It's our first birthday together. We eloped, so I didn't buy an engagement ring, and we don't have a mortgage. You don't even know what it is."

"Daniel—"

"Open it."

She took the box from him and fumbled the little gold button to release the lid. Her fingers were shaking.

"Half their retail sales must go to packaging alone," he said, trying to lighten the mood.

The lid popped open. Tucked into the silk fold was a white gold bangle. She looked at it, then at him.

"It's a LOVE bracelet," he said.

"I know what it is," she breathed.

Of course she did. Luxury goods were her trade. She wasn't a bling person, but a simple bangle suited her down to the ground. The iconic bracelet symbolized eternal love. Celebrities wore them, grandparents bought them for their grandchildren, lovers bought them to mark anniversaries. He knew nothing about jewelry, but when he came across one during the course of an investigation, the memory got filed away in the back of his brain. *That's cool. That's the kind of symbol I like.*

The air conditioner ticked on, filling the room with a droning hum. He found the screwdriver that came with the bracelet and unfastened the two screws on either side of the bracelet. "May I?"

Without looking up she offered him her wrist. Without pinching her skin, he slid the slim metal tabs into the slots, then threaded the tiny screws and fastened the bracelet. It was perfect for her, elegant, simple, symbolic.

"It won't slide off, so you can't take it off at night or whenever," he said. It was something she'd wear for the rest of her life, through the births of their children, anniversaries, birthdays, holidays, vacations, nights where the only chance they had to talk was over a glass of wine. He could see her, slim and elegant and vibrantly alive at seventy-five, sipping wine and wearing that bracelet. The thought made his entire body tighten with a possessiveness he'd never felt before. "It's medieval, and of course if you hate it, I'll exchange it for the removable cuff version. Whatever you want. But . . . I loved it. I love you. I wanted you to wear it," he said as he lifted her wrist to his mouth and kissed the fine skin. The bracelet felt warm and heavy against his lips.

"I'm completely astonished. I don't know what to say except thank you." She leaned forward and kissed him, but her smile didn't quite reach her eyes.

"Happy birthday, Tilda," he said quietly, and let her tuck her face into his shoulder. Let her hide.

Four weeks later, in an unemotional voice, she asked him for a divorce, then left for yet another trip. Daniel felt like she'd stepped over the cliffs, and this time there was no convenient hidden ledge keeping her from falling all the way to the ground.

— TWENTY-ONE —

Solstice
7:28 p.m.

Colin parked illegally next to a fire hydrant that also happened to be in the shade under the tree in front of Fifteen Perry Street, and switched on his hazard lights. "We can't have your husband coming home and giving me a ticket."

Tilda snapped from the past to the present. Colin's car, outside her house, after a long morning at West Village Stationery, the bloody therapist's appointment with Daniel, then an afternoon discussion on the luxury goods trade with Colin. In six hours she had to get on a plane and fly to London. This was the longest day of the year, and the longest day of her life.

"The FBI doesn't write parking tickets," Tilda said as she searched her clutch for her house keys, taking refuge in an ordinary task to avoid remembering the look on Daniel's face when she threw those words at him. *If you really knew me.* There was no quicker way to wound Daniel than to imply he had misunderstood something.

He was trying so hard, and she didn't want to hurt him, but hurting him was inevitable, and sooner was better than later, right? She should have known better than to get involved with him, did know better. There was a price to pay for taking what she wanted; however, asking Daniel to pay that price was her mistake.

Oh, God. What had she done?

Colin peered past her at the front door. "Is he home?"

She looked out the windshield at the town house, narrow red brick with black shutters, matching black double front door with leaded glass windows. The only light on was the lamp in the front window. He could be home, or he could be at a bar with friends, or on Long Island with his family, or running. Daniel could be at work, making his methodical way through reams and reams of documents, following the root of all evil—money—to the source of the wrongdoing.

Or he could be at home, in jeans and a T-shirt, a beer in hand, waiting for Tilda. When she left the divorce papers on the dining room table, under the paperweight, she wasn't sure if she liked what she'd started, but she knew she had to do it. Despite her best hopes, they were incompatible. Now, outside their house, she was torn between two powerful emotions: stay, and run.

Eyebrows raised, Colin looked at her, obviously expecting an answer to his extraordinarily simple question. "He often works late at home."

In circumstances known only to residents of a city where the demand for apartments far outweighed the supply, they were still living together but only because Daniel moved to the guest bedroom on the second floor, conceding the entire top floor to Tilda.

"So you're not going to invite me in for a drink before our

flight leaves." Colin's smile was flirtatious, expecting to be turned down, but charmingly hopeful.

"Best not, Colin," she said.

He glanced at her left hand, bare of the wedding ring she'd worn for six months. She'd taken off both the ring and the bracelet the day she printed the paperwork for a uncontested divorce. "He's still living with you?"

"The housing market in New York is as tight as London's," she said. "It will take some time for him to find another flat."

"You're a difficult woman to read," Colin said. "I can't tell if I should offer you a shoulder to cry on or steal you away to a very posh hotel to celebrate your upcoming freedom."

"I'm actually rather allergic to posh hotels, and I'm not divorced yet," she said, more tartly than she'd intended. She'd never explained that particular allergy to Daniel. He knew she hated spinach, loved the sensation of fine fabric against her skin, and all but hibernated when it rained, but he didn't know how she felt about posh hotels. Because she'd never told him. And he, acting like any sane man who wanted to show a woman that he loved her, bought her one of the most prestigious luxury items on the market, and took her to the nicest hotel in the city to celebrate her birthday.

Her response was to ask him for a divorce. The memory of his face, shocked into a stillness not even he managed most of the time, made shame crawl up her spine and settle at the nape of her neck. No one asked for a divorce after her husband orchestrated a night like that, but she had. She'd waited a couple of weeks, fighting her fear, but in the end, the bracelet was an unspoken, ever-present reminder of what he felt, and what they would both lose.

The text requesting that she meet him at a therapist's office in Washington Square only confirmed what she should have known all along, and chose to ignore because this time she hoped things would be different. She would be different.

She owed him an explanation. That was the only question he asked when she handed him the paperwork. *Why?*

"Right," Colin said, unaware of this train of thought. "You know you're getting exactly what you want from Quality. West Village Stationery will have retail space in every luxury goods shopping hub in every major airport in the world, plus branches in London, Tokyo, and Dubai. They want you, Tilda. They really, really want *you*. Not Kate Spade. Not Tory Burch. You."

"Yes," she said. The list of names reminded her that she should have had her LOVE bracelet on. Colin spoke that language, the language of money and sophistication on a global scale. He had the right schools, the right accent, the right connections, and he'd been her advocate through this deal, less impartial than he should have been.

"Again with the unreadable," he said. "This is a very good thing. You're what? Thirty?"

"Twenty-eight."

"Twenty-eight, and on the verge of becoming a global household name."

It was unfathomable, really. No one could ignore her now. "I know," she said, but even as she spoke she felt the slow stomach loop of a wanting not resolved, transformed into a vibrating tension. She was in her favorite place, on the edge of something, divorce, global launch, getting what she'd always wanted and never been able to articulate. She should feel far more excited than she did.

"Right," Colin said. "I'm going to go home and pack. I'll see you at the departures terminal?"

"Yes, of course." Colin gave her a lingering cheek kiss before she slid out of the car. She trotted up the steps to the town house, and put her key in the lock.

The still air told her Daniel wasn't home. She stifled her disappointment. The catastrophic appointment this morning only proved she'd made the correct choice. She committed the cardinal sin of a woman entering marriage. She'd expected change, not in Daniel, but in herself, a fundamental reordering of the bedrock of her character.

This was too much to expect.

She paused by the dining room and looked at the papers on the table, underneath Andrew's expensive paperweight. She'd been foolish to think Daniel would sign them and be gone. He couldn't be rushed, very rarely got his feathers ruffled, did things in his own time, in his own way.

She climbed the stairs to the third floor, refusing to glance into the open doors on Daniel's level. In her bedroom she changed into her travel clothes, jeans, a T-shirt, a cardigan for warmth. Her flight to London left just before midnight. Twilight was falling by the time she finished packing, the indigo sky glowing outside her bedroom windows. She'd packed lightly, as it was unlikely she would see her mother on this trip, but she would make the drive to see Nan, check that her foot was healing and she had everything she needed.

Her suitcase packed, she found her phone and called Daniel. The call went straight to voice mail, which could mean he was working and unavailable, or could mean he didn't want to talk to her and had shut off his phone. A kernel of fear burrowed deep inside Tilda's chest. Daniel didn't avoid problems; he was likely working late. But she couldn't shake the sudden certainty that if she got on the plane and left, things would never be the same, that somehow taking flight would result in a more permanent devastation than asking for divorce.

Her mind was frantic, her nerves jittery, as if she'd begun something and already regretted the choice. To calm herself, she made a cup of tea, and settled at her desk, then withdrew from her leather tote her personal and business mail. There was a single letter to Lady Matilda, the once-steady flow drying up over the last few months as she focused more on business and less on her alter ego. With her sterling silver letter opener, she slit the side of the envelope and pulled out the letter.

Dear Lady Matilda—

I've never asked for anything like this before in my life, never mentioned it to another soul.

This was exactly the kind of person she maintained her list for, someone who yearned for connection, but had yet to find the right match. She was good at this, although sometimes she wondered if it wasn't a primary example of God's cruelty to give her the gift to connect others, so that every day she had to face her own cowardice. Daniel was the first person to ask what she would ask for if she put her name on her own list. She knew, of course, had always known what she longed for and did not have the courage to take for herself. No direct matches in mind, but there would be. There was always a connection, a match for those who dared to ask for what they wanted.

That's what she had to do. She had to ask Daniel for what she wanted, the divorce, the same way she expected people seeking introductions to write down their desires, their unmet needs. She had to put it on paper.

That was the last thing she wanted to do.

Pacing between her bedroom and her office, she tried Daniel's number again, with the same result. She was cold, her stomach churning, which was better than the flip-flops she felt when she looked at her suitcase packed and ready to carry down the stairs, load in a cab, and take to the airport. She wrapped her arms around her waist and bit her lip as she looked at her recent calls list. Her thumb brushed over the screen, sliding back and forth between Daniel's mobile and Colin's mobile, then settling on Colin's.

"Colin, I can't leave tonight," she said when he answered. "I need to talk to Daniel about something before I go to London."

"Having second thoughts?" he asked, his voice suddenly wary.

"No, not at all," she said hastily. "What I need to discuss with Daniel has nothing to do with the deal. But I can't leave without having this conversation. I'll take the eight a.m. flight tomorrow and be in London in time for a late dinner with the leadership team." So she wouldn't get any sleep before the meeting. She was beginning to feel like she'd never sleep again.

"I understand," he said, even though he couldn't possibly understand what she barely understood herself. In order to make this clear to Daniel, to give him the explanation that he deserved, she would have to write down in explicit detail a series of events that she had described to no other person, not even Nan.

"Thank you."

She sat down at her desk and withdrew her personal stationery from the desk's top drawer. The first sheet was engraved with her name, Matilda Davies, blank pages following, blank until she covered them with her handwriting and told the story known only to two other souls, previously inked only on her skin. She felt like she was moving on autopilot, carrying through actions begun not just a few days ago when she asked Daniel for a divorce, not even a year ago when she met Daniel sitting on a ledge, but long before that in a luxury hotel, in a foreign city. The consequences of her actions ten years ago had finally caught up with her, but she'd been run to ground and now there was nothing to do but face them. Writing it out would make it real in a way it hadn't been before. But it was already real, just as Daniel said the results of the pregnancy test were real, just not known. All she was doing was confessing to a sin already committed.

With one ear pricked to hear Daniel's key in the lock, or his footsteps on the stairs, she wrote. But by the time she had finished the letter hours later, it was clear Daniel wasn't coming home. Yes, the case that he'd been working on was moving along at a frenetic pace, but he'd never been called on to work until the wee hours of the morning. According to his best guess they wouldn't be able to get an indictment until the end of the summer.

She left the letter for him to find when he did come home. She left it on the kitchen counter in the spot where he habitually left his wallet, keys, mobile, gun, cuffs, badge, and the notebook where he kept his own lists, and went to bed.

Shortly after three a.m. her phone vibrated to indicate an incoming text. She snatched it up, but rather than Daniel's name, a text from her friend Louise flashed on the screen.

Hey got up for a wee Daniel's still out on our terrace. Is something wrong?

Air evaporated from her lungs. Daniel hadn't come home because he'd gone back to where it all began, Louise's rooftop terrace, to the ledge she'd coaxed him onto a year ago. The least she could do was meet him there now, and give him the letter that explained why he was there in the first place. Her hands shook as she thumbed a response to Louise.

Yes. I hate to ask but can I come over? I'm leaving for London in five hours and I need to see him before I go.

Louise's reply came as Tilda scuffed her feet into her ballet slippers and reach for her bag.

Of course will tell Pepo to let you up and leave the door unlocked xx

Tilda hurried down Perry Street toward Greenwich Avenue and hailed a cab. The ride to Park Avenue South took only a few minutes at this hour of the night, the streets eerily silent and empty. Pepo yawned as he buzzed her into the building. The elevator ride up twenty-two stories felt much the same as the cab ride—enclosed, isolated from the outside world. The silence rang in her ears, an odd, discordant humming that vanished when she stepped out into the hallway and saw Louise's door cracked ever so slightly. Tilda stepped inside onto the polished marble floors, then closed and locked the door behind her. The hallway leading to Louise's bedroom and bathroom was dark, so she tiptoed through the living room to the sliding glass doors that opened onto the terrace, and stepped through them.

Her eyes were already adjusted to the darkness, so she could easily see Daniel's back, narrow and straight, sitting on the ledge. What she hadn't expected was the glow of a cigarette's tip, the crackle of the paper and tobacco as he inhaled. The soles of her shoes scritched against the slate. He turned and looked over his shoulder, and his eyes widened ever so slightly when he saw her. He stubbed out the cigarette on the ledge and exhaled the last of the smoke into the still, warm air. Shame seared along the surface of her skin. It was a familiar feeling, but the remorse she felt for driving Daniel back to cigarettes was brand-new.

"Are you going to join me?" His baritone voice still sent shivers down her spine, reminding her that he might look insubstantial compared to heavily muscled street cops or gym rats, but inside, he was honed steel. The light from Louise's living room lamp picked out glints of silver in his tousled blond hair. His father went silver at a young age, and Daniel was as well. Thirty-two. He'd wear it well; Tilda felt a sharp pang when she realized she wouldn't be around to see it.

"If you'd like," she said. She walked up to the ledge, planted her bum on the inside, and then eased her legs over to dangle twenty-two stories above the street.

"This isn't where I thought you'd be," she said. She looked down at the envelope in her hand. "I should've guessed, though."

"I want to know where we went wrong. I came back here to try to puzzle it out."

Of course he did. Daniel solved puzzles for a living. She'd thought, when she married him, that it wouldn't matter, keeping this secret. It did. Her secret brought ruin with her from the past into the present she'd hoped not to taint.

Perhaps this was the price she had to pay to end what she never should have begun, this long walk down memory lane with the man who slid under her defenses with no intention other than loving her. Her blood heated even as her stomach turned flip-flops. "How are you getting on?"

"Not very well. But for some reason sitting up here makes it easier to bear. It's as if, up here, the last year never happened. I could go back to the beginning and start all over again, the way I should have started when I first saw you."

He looked as serious as he'd ever looked, even more serious than he had when he found her sitting on a ledge twenty-two stories above the Manhattan streets, as desperate as a junkie for some kind of adrenaline rush.

"There's nothing you could have done differently, Daniel, nothing you should have done differently. What's wrong with us is actually wrong with me, and it started long before we met."

She held out the letter to him. He took it, both of them holding on to the envelope a little longer than was necessary for the hand-off. Nothing bad would have happened if they dropped it, just a slow gentle drift to the streets, but for one crazy second she thought that both of them would go over the edge after it. She because it held the only part of her life she had never told another living soul, he because he had to know.

He took it from her and turned it over, looking at both the back and the front where she'd written his name in black ink. "This is your good stuff," he said.

She almost laughed. He meant the paper, not what was written on the sheets. That was beyond dangerous. That would end in total ruin. He now held in his hands the truth. He would know all her secrets, all her flaws.

"Read it," she said quietly. "I don't know that it will answer all your questions, but it should go a long way toward explaining why I asked you for a divorce."

She shifted her weight to swing her legs back over the ledge onto the safety of the terrace, but Daniel's grip on her wrist stopped her. "No," he said. "Stay here. We do this together."

– TWENTY-TWO –

Solstice

Inside an unfamiliar place the exhaustion seemed to drown her. On the street she could identify landmarks, follow Daniel's lead and use the sun and moon and stars to determine night or day. But so far off the ground, Manhattan's eerie, predawn silence rang in her ears. She'd known this was coming from the moment their story began. It might even be easy, because she was so tired, out of time, out of space. Numb. Dislocated, in the worse sense of the word.

Daniel read the first few lines, then looked at her. His gaze hit her like a searchlight, flashing over her from head to toe, white-hot and exposing. Shocking. She'd not seen him since the morning; she wore nothing provocative, a simple pair of dark jeans, a white T-shirt, a cardigan, her black leather tote on the terrace behind her. She had no defenses left. A strange floating sensation tilted the ledge a little; for a moment she felt she could simply float away like an untethered bunch of balloons.

Daniel's gaze sharpened, a blue scythe, the only brilliant color in the darkness. "Promise me you won't bolt," he said.

She nodded, although the response was more automatic than answer; he was using his cop voice, the one he performed like a party trick. She'd been up all night writing the letter. Her circadian rhythms and brain chemistry were completely disconnected from night and day, past and present.

She watched him for a length of time that was measured in seconds but felt like a lifetime, let herself drink in the sight of him, the compact strength, veins and dusting of blond hair on the backs of his hands, the deft way he handled the paper. Then she blinked, sandpaper lids rough enough to call moisture. Closing them felt so good. She could shut out Daniel's eyes while he read.

Daniel—

I wanted him.

Let me say first, let me make perfectly clear, that I not only consented to what happened, but I initiated everything.

I wanted him.

You wanted to take us back to the beginning, but we didn't begin here. None of us comes to a relationship as blank as a sheet of paper, and I am no exception. When I was seventeen, I lost my virginity in a room indistinguishable from the one you took me to on my birthday. That fall I was a rather unwilling companion for my mother during her first speaking tour. We traveled to twenty-three cities on three continents in six weeks, my mother, myself, and her research assistant, Andrew.

You remember Andrew.

It started out innocuously enough. Looks, mostly. A smile just a bit more knowing. I didn't seek him out, but I didn't avoid him, either. I didn't like him. He was everything I was supposed to want to be, but he subtly mocked what he was. He'd look at me. Wink. Roll his eyes. Bring me drinks, or sit next to me for a few minutes at one of the horrid receptions in New York, Philadelphia, Boston, Chicago, while I bored him with the current city's tourist report. I think Mum had read something in the Guardian *about preparing your child to leave the nest, and decided I needed a shove from the mother bird. I wanted to spend my gap year in Cornwall with Nan, so I resented being dragged all over the world on the twenty-first century version of the Grand Tour, sent off to see the sights to "foster independence" then sitting through the same lecture given over and over, the same jokes, attending obligatory cocktail parties, dinners, receptions. I watched Mum drop names and show off a little, for Andrew. Perhaps he saw what she was doing. Perhaps not.*

I did. While Mum worked at forming alliances to strengthen her future, I worked at drawing Andrew from her side. Mum found power in her way, and I found it in mine.

I won't insult you by asking if you've ever engaged in an illicit love affair. We never talked about that kind of first, the firsts that shame us, where we learn how deeply we can desire, how badly we can hurt. You won't know how those stolen, secret moments are electrified with passion and the fear of discovery. I kissed Andrew for the first time behind a closed door separating us from a reporter for the LA Times *who was interviewing Mum. I went on tiptoe and pressed* my mouth to his, felt his tongue touch mine for a second, perhaps two, before he pulled away. It's such a heady sound, the total silence when two people aren't breathing for fear of discovery.

He said we couldn't do it again.

I told him to stay away, if he could.

He couldn't.

The next day he drew me into the empty chapel at the Los Angeles Airport and kissed me. I can still remember the way his fingers felt along my jaw as he held my mouth for his, that sweet electric shock of his tongue against mine, my heart racing, the heat and weight of his body against mine.

He kissed me without desperation, as if we were getting acquainted, soft pressure, a nuzzle with his nose that changed the angle, caressing me with lip and breath and the shadow of his scruff until my mouth opened. His hand was heavy on my hip, holding me against the wall, inciting me to arch against him. He behaved as if this were completely normal, our right, even, and so I did, too.

I've not thought of this for years, but now I remember the strangest details, the contrast between his hair under my index finger while the collar of his shirt and blazer were stiff under my ring and pinky, the way tendrils of pleasure unfurled, climbing around my bones, spiraling through muscle, seeking the heat and light dancing along the surface of my skin. We flew to Tokyo from Los Angeles, to the city of lotus flowers and neon lights.

Do you know how seduction feels? We were discreet, even though I would sit next to him, studying, and feel the heat from his leg next to mine spread through my entire body until I was slick and hot with longing. When we met in hallways, in lobbies, in foyers of conference centers, in *these transitional spaces, I did all the things the song says. I stood too close. I looked too long. I lost my umbrella when it was raining so I could walk with him, I timed my exits and entrances so I was always in his line of sight. The more he gave me, for we were well beyond kissing but not quite to sex, the more I wanted him. Mum wanted him, too. I knew it, and I seduced him. I took the thing she wanted most, right from under her nose. He began to touch me in front of her. Elbows. They're not erotic. They're a gateway drug to the body, a chance for fingers to slip down the underside of a forearm and brush a palm. Or the small of a back, very proper, very gentleman-like, very much the price of admission to my hip or my shoulder.*

In Tokyo, Mum sent me to see gardens and Buddhist temples. Andrew volunteered to keep me company, cheer me out of my teenage sulk. As we walked we wove together then broke apart through pagodas and along garden paths, the spring heat and sunshine collecting in my hair, my skin. Every look felt fraught with significance, every shared moment imbued with a meaning and weight that belied the lightness inside me, like the lotus flowers blooming on the surface of dark green ponds, their long stems and roots anchoring them in a primordial dark. I felt like I was floating, until he looked at me, smiled, touched one long finger to a placard or pointed out a break in the view that seemed like a rip in the fabric of reality. Desire pulsed crazily in my palms, the soles of my feet. I could feel the sunshine on my lips, imagined his mouth replacing it, hotter, heavier, as full of promise. To break the spell I stood in front of him, reveled in the raw sexual heat eddying from him, a combination of body heat and desire.

We were standing on a bridge over a pond, and when he was ready to go, he put his hand on my hip. It was not an innocuous touch, the touch of an older-brother figure to a girl, but a lover's invitation. Not my shoulder, or my upper arm, but my hip. I remember the heat in his eyes when I looked up at him through my eyelashes, the way his eyes changed, the way his lips parted, the way he looked at me. It was a split second of awareness, but I knew he was mine, and he knew it, too. I drew him in and held him just by a look, a kiss, a touch. Now I would have him.

We went back to the hotel, to his room, and when the time came I was so eager, so ready to have him inside me. The first stroke was absolutely electric. I came. Twice. Not many girls do, during their first time, or so I'm told, but I . . . I absolutely loved it.

After that I had both the build and the release. I'd beg off an event with a headache or a paper to write for Mum (she read and reviewed the papers I wrote as thoroughly as she'd question any of her tutorial students) and he'd come back once Mum was settled into the conference to "work on the research." We discussed philosophers and bourgeois attitudes and the tedious conventional cultural mores we were flaunting. We grew reckless, incautious, until the day Mum came back to the room unexpectedly and saw Andrew splayed back on the couch, me on my knees in front of him.

Mum booked me on the next plane to London.

I hadn't thought about any of this until I opened Andrew's gift at Mum's party. I didn't write it down, you see. I wrote long letters to Nan, and in the writing it became real. This interlude in my life went unwritten, until now, because even as I was seducing the man my mother wanted for her lover, I knew it was wrong.

You wanted to know where our end began. This is where it began, if it is possible to trace such things to an event, but it is not an event. It is who I am, but this doesn't stop me from wanting what I cannot have. There is a price that comes with this. I pay it. I'm sorry I asked you to pay it, too.

But I'm also not sorry. I wanted you. The moment I saw you I wanted you in the way I want things that are not mine to hold. I was blinded by the way you gather sunlight, carry it with you, store it up for dark days. When you said you loved me, I forgot who and what I am, what I can and cannot have.

I'm sorry.

Tilda

While he read she floated in the sensation of feeling nothing at all, noting absence as a presence. It lasted for some indeterminate length of time, traffic noise rising in regular pulses from the street below, the same all over the world. She closed her eyes, dropped into it. It was over. She had nothing more to hide. She would close the deal, then go to Cornwall for a week and look after Nan herself while Daniel moved out. Penny could handle the day-to-day of West Village Stationery. Tilda could drowse in the sun and heal right alongside Nan, ground herself in the only place in the world that felt like home.

She opened her eyes, saw him in her peripheral vision, his solemn profile. The light from Louise's living room picked out the silver in his hair, the dusting of gold on the backs of his hands. In that moment, the space of a couple of heartbeats, no more, she loved him so passionately her throat closed. She loved him.

Then he turned to look at her, the movement slow, as if it cost him more than he could bear to pay. She recognized the look on his face. Wrecked. Ruined, even. She'd made that real. The consequences were written, black ink on white stationery, on Daniel's skin.

She held out her hand for the letter.

He gave it to her, but gripped her wrist when she took it. "Now we're going to talk."

TWENTY-THREE

Solstice

He saw it all in her eyes, the flash of love for him, the memory of where she was and what she'd written, the shame, then the shuttering as she put on the face she wore for the world. Flash, flash, flash, flash, gone, in the blink of her eyes. Four beats of his heart, slower than normal because he was an endurance runner. Two seconds, total. Four slow pulses, for her, because his heart would always and only beat for her.

But he knew, now. He had learned to read between Tilda's straight lines and elegant angles. He knew what she'd left out.

In ink the same color as blood, he mentally drafted a new list.

Tilda's Formative Experiences with Love and Belonging

1. Abandoned by father at birth
2. Left by mother at two

3. Reclaimed by mother at eight then left at boarding school
4. Seduced by a predator at seventeen and
5. Sent away by her mother for being seduced

Handle one fucked-up crisis at a time. Start with Andrew.
He was going kill Andrew.

The urge to shove a couple of changes of clothes into an overnight bag then get on the next flight to London, find Andrew at whatever library or archives he was currently living in, and beat him to a pulp spread through his brain like blood from a bullet wound. Fury bubbled inside him, hot and acidic, unfamiliar because he didn't often get angry, but when he remembered how Andrew had sat across from him at dinner, smiling, inquisitive, wishing them both well, all the while knowing what he knew . . . The *presumption*, the sheer fucking *intimacy* of that gift. A reminder of everything they'd done together, everything Andrew thought she still pined for, remembered in her secret heart of hearts, that formative experience that tainted her entire life.

Focus on Tilda. He'd seen it before, in children uprooted again and again by circumstances beyond their control. With addicts for parents, in households characterized by violence and abuse, and without a caring or stable presence to ground them, they slowly lost touch with who they were and where they came from. Their stories. So they made them up, parents who loved them but couldn't come claim them, a home life that matched the other kids', a future that included a family.

Tilda's story had been close enough to the truth to fool him. She told no lies, showed no visible wounds. She did what everyone else thought was difficult, and made it look easy in the process. She just left out great gaping swaths of what had happened to her, and he, who prided himself on seeing what everyone else missed, had swallowed the story whole. Even after the trip to England. She looked better than fine, burned brighter than a supernova, was taking names and making things happen *all over the goddamn world*, and he'd been fooled. A fool with charts and lists and spreadsheets, sure, but a fool to his very bones.

That didn't change how he felt about her.

He'd deal with that later.

At seventeen the line between seduction and statutory rape was a very, very fine one, and currently vibrating like piano wire. She was technically old enough to consent, acted like she knew who she was and what she wanted, but his heart ached for that Tilda, adrift in the world, aching for connection, seeking it out wherever she could. To learn that the people who should have known better counted her need for basic human connection as cheap entertainment for the terminal boredom of a book tour . . .

He'd kill Andrew, do the time, and chalk it up as a good deed.

But there was nothing to be gained by going to London and beating the ever-loving fuck out of an academic whose worst wound was probably repetitive motion injuries, then getting arrested for assault, and everything to lose, starting with Tilda. He'd heard one thing loud and clear in that letter: Tilda thought who she was made people abandon her. If he took off for England to engage in an uncharacteristic chest-beating display of alpha male showboating, he'd prove that again. Tilda could take care of herself. If she thought about it for ten minutes, she could come up with a dozen different ways to extract her pound of flesh from Andrew.

But she didn't waste time on revenge, or efforts to ingratiate herself with people who rejected her. She'd made herself absolutely unforgettable. Every time Andrew walked into an airport, opened a magazine, got a letter, he'd think of Tilda, and what he didn't have.

She sat beside him, as pale as the moon, thin like blades were thin, gleaming and deadly. She looked exhausted, pale, insubstantial, soulless. She should sleep for hours, days, but her body clock was so dysfunctional he wondered if she'd ever sleep regularly again. Emotion writhed inside him like a basket of colorful, poisonous snakes: love, lust, fury, hatred, shame, white-hot heat of revenge, all induced by the woman he loved. He'd foolishly thought love was enough. It was time to face the reality that maybe it wasn't.

Cases were ephemeral without motivation. "That's why Colin set you off at the gallery opening. He sounds like Andrew."

"It was the confidential, conspiratorial tone. Andrew used to talk to Mum about me the same way." She cleared her throat. "Mum saw it as Andrew and her against me. He used to laugh about it behind her back," she said.

Jesus, and there were layers of animosity in that flat assessment, because Tilda's mother was seventeen when she had Tilda, so thirty-four when her twenty-five-year-old research assistant started sleeping with her seventeen-year-old daughter. He could just see it, the teenage version of a toddler pulling on her mother's dress, *Mum . . . Mum . . . Mum . . . Mum . . .* then knocking over the vase full of flowers or coloring on the wall. In a way, Tilda was still doing that, but this time with West Village Stationery and Quality Group, a global scream for her mother to look at her, see her, really acknowledge her. He gave her points, though, for being true to herself. She could have followed her mother into academia, surrendered her soul to the utmost, when every victory would have been hollow and every failure gritty with ash, and likely not gotten much more in return. Instead, she'd prove she was worth the attention she garnered.

"Why did she invite him to the dinner party?"

"Andrew is very well connected, and Mum's too savvy to cut ties entirely when someone might prove useful in the future. They work in the same field." Her voice trailed off. "I think they had a relationship for a brief time after I went to university. For all I know, they're actually friends."

"Did Nan know?"

"I doubt it. I didn't tell her. That was the only time in my life I slacked off sending her letters. I can't see Mum telling her, either. It's too embarrassing."

So the only person Tilda would trust to love her despite this didn't know what she'd done. Fury flamed, turned on the only available outlet. "You said you lost your virginity to an older boy."

"Twenty-five is older."

"*Boy*, Tilda, means underage. Not a PhD candidate who's working for your mother."

She glared at him, her features sharp enough to cut, pale enough to freeze. The ledge trapped them in stillness, poised over space and yet completely constrained. And that, in a nutshell, was exactly what Tilda had learned about her sexuality: don't try to connect it to anything or anyone else, because that connection would burn her. "Would it be easier for you to frame me as a victim in all of this? It would give you a target, an outlet for your anger, a reason for me to be the way that I am. A better reason. A more palatable reason. You would have an explanation and I would have something to get over, a problem to solve. But that's not what happened. I loved it. It was inappropriate and hot and wrong and dirty and powerful."

Maybe that was true, for another woman without Tilda's disconnected, jarring childhood. Lots of people lost their virginity to adults who should know better, and went on about their lives with hardly a scar. Tilda had internalized the rejection. Only a blind man wouldn't see the dynamic between Tilda and her mother. Only a blind man wouldn't know what he was doing, what it meant to both of them. Andrew was many things, but not blind.

"He was an adult. He knew better. He should have said no."

"Americans are so rigid about sex," she started.

"That what he said?"

A rare blush tinted Tilda's cheeks, caught out repeating the bourgeois patter of the entitled, overeducated predator. "I was seventeen, Daniel. Do not make the mistake of thinking I was less sexual at seventeen than I am now. The boy, with the garage, my first kiss, he was sixteen."

His head whipped up. "You were twelve. You said you were twelve."

"And tall for my age. Mature. I liked it."

"Is that why you came to New York?" he asked, staring into the distance.

"Unbeknownst to Mum, I'd applied to NYU and been offered a full scholarship. I took it."

Cut her ties, in other words. He couldn't blame her, all she was doing was what she saw done, but the price she paid was a future with anyone. Walking away got you free, but at a price, and like any habit, it got easier every time you did it. Her whole family missed key points about what it means to be a family, in relationships, rituals and routines and connective tissue. Like going to funerals.

He started where he could. "Tilda. There is a difference between *I've made a mistake* and *I am a mistake*, or *I've done a bad thing* and *I am a bad thing*. There is a difference between guilt and shame. You are guilty of trying to get your mother's attention in a wildly inappropriate way, but you do not need to carry around the burden of shame for the rest of your life."

"All the self-help, I'm-ok-you're-ok talk is such crap," she said. "There is a reason why churches require penance. You're Catholic. You know this."

"No priest in the world would make you do penance for this."

"No one raped me. No one held me down, assaulted me, hit me, or threatened me with a knife to my throat."

No. They withheld attention until she was so deprived, so desperate for it she would do anything, even the most fucked-up, wrong thing possible to get it. His throat worked as he swallowed rocks of rage.

"We can go back to the way things were, casual encounters. This will die off eventually."

"That's what you want? Sex without love. You want what Andrew taught you? What your mother taught you you were worth?"

Her eyes were as opaque as rain. "That's what you wanted, isn't it? Asking for a date was just a prettier way of asking to go to bed with me."

"That's the card I sent you. That's not the first card I wrote." She stared at him.

"You still haven't seen the first draft. Unless you've been in my box in the armoire."

"Of course not. That's an invasion of privacy."

He laughed. He actually laughed, because he could not fucking believe the words coming out of her mouth. He scraped his palms over his head. "Look at the card, or ask me to show it to you, if we're still at the point where good conduct matters."

Silence. He let it stretch, until it became clear she wasn't going to answer him. They'd taught her, however inadvertently, to be ashamed of her need for love, and to doubt the motivations and tenacity of anyone who needed her in return. They'd taught her that the only thing she deserved was sex, not love. They'd taught her everyone belonged on her list except her.

"Why me, Tilda?"

She stared off into the distance toward the east, where the sun would rise. "I knew you wouldn't hurt me. I thought that perhaps that meant I wouldn't hurt you. I was wrong."

"I need time to process this," he said, then swung his legs back over the ledge. "Just . . . give me some time."

"Daniel."

He turned back to face her.

"I'm on the eight a.m. flight to London. If you're going to leave, would you please be gone when I get back?"

He couldn't help himself. He flinched, then just shook his head, turned, and left her sitting where it all began.

— TWENTY-FOUR —

Solstice +1

Tilda leaned back against the seat of the cab and wrapped her arms around her stomach. So that was it. She'd told him, and even though she said *if you're going to leave me*, she knew he would. No impulse decisions, no boiling emotions, just calm practicalities and a foolproof strategy for dealing with his emotions. He would go for a run, and when he came back, he would understand, and when he understood, he would leave.

Which was what she'd wanted. Like pulling off a plaster, or resetting a dislocated joint, she'd wanted this done. In theory the pain would lessen quickly. But right now the pain lanced through her, sharp and irregular, taking her breath away with each unpredictable pulse as she hurried up the steps and through the front door of her town house to claim her bag, then turn right back around and get back in the cab, and head for Kennedy Airport.

A little stack of Daniel's business cards sat on the table by the front door. Sorrow stabbed her when she saw them and realized that very likely when she got home they wouldn't be there. Her brain shied away from the image, taking refuge in a fast-moving bike messenger matching pace with her cab. Details. She would note them and write them down, a unique part of New York to describe for Nan. A deep tan, blade shades, a helmet that had seen better days, tattoos on his upper arms and forearms, messenger bag slung across his back. Drafting descriptive phrases was enough to get her through the TSA's pre-check line, into the terminal and to the gate where her flight to London was waiting for her. She settled into her seat, closed her eyes, and let the blessedly cool, humming interior of the plane envelope her.

She slept most of the way to London, landing in the summer's evening, reaching for her phone as soon as the plane's wheels touched down on the tarmac. She powered the phone on, and finished off the contents of her water bottle while she waited for it to boot. As soon as her phone connected with the network, it started to buzz frantically, downloading texts and emails and phone calls and voice mails all missed while she was in the air.

She checked her texts first, and found nothing of importance other than a text from Colin with the name, address, and phone number of the restaurant where she was to meet him and the leadership team from Quality. While she waited for the stewardess to open the cabin door, she checked her missed calls, scanning the list from bottom to top. Pauline, Penny, Pauline, Pauline, Mum, Pauline, Colin, Penny, Mum, a supplier, two friends, Pauline.

Pauline was the home health aide taking care of Nan. She'd never called before. Her mother rarely called, and certainly not after seeing Tilda the week prior. Her stomach cramped hard around nothing, as she missed all of the airline's in-flight meals. With trembling fingers she scrolled to Pauline's number and tapped call.

"'Lo?"

"Pauline, it's Tilda."

"Tilda. Oh, love. I'm so sorry. I'm so sorry. It was quick. I promise, it was quick."

The man seated next to her got to his feet and started rummaging through the overhead bin for his carry-on items. Tilda startled when the plane jerked and shuddered as the Jetway connected with it. Beneath her, the cargo bay door flopped open so they could begin unloading the luggage. "What happened?" Tilda managed.

"Didn't your mum call you? She didn't suffer, I'm sure of it." With that, Tilda's mind snapped free of its mooring. Words like *blood clot* and *ambulance* and *never seen anything like it* free-fell through her consciousness, into her stomach, which threatened to vomit back up the water. "By then, it was too late," Pauline finished. "I called you and when you didn't answer I called your mother. I thought she'd call you."

"She tried," Tilda managed.

Her seatmate gestured for Tilda to precede him off the plane. She yanked her bag from the overhead bin and stumbled down the aisle. "I just landed at Heathrow. I'm here on business."

"Well, your mum's arranged the funeral. You know how she is. Efficient," Pauline said, and hung up.

Tilda stood in the middle of the gate area, people milling around her, organizing their bags and coats and children, and stared at her phone. Then she called her mother next. "Tilda. Where have you been?"

"Nan's *dead*?"

"I left you a voice mail, darling. Did you not listen to it?"

"What happened?" Tilda asked, her voice trembling.

"A pulmonary embolism, which was a complication following the surgery on her ankle."

"What's . . . a what?"

"A blood clot formed deep in her leg, broke free, and traveled to her lungs. She died. Apparently it's a possible complication from prolonged immobilization. One can't always trust these home health aides."

"Pauline would have made sure Nan followed the doctor's protocols," Tilda said. She had. She'd been there for Nan, while Tilda had been everywhere and nowhere at all. "It's not her fault."

Silence on the other end of the line, then Tilda said, "When?"

"The funeral is scheduled for the day after tomorrow. Can you be here in time?"

That's not what she meant. She meant *When did Nan die?* But her mother missed the connection, and Tilda couldn't go back and reclaim it. "I'm already here. I've come to London to close the deal with Quality."

"That's a stroke of good luck."

Tilda barked out a laugh, then covered her eyes with her hand. "What if I hadn't been able to make it? Would you have buried her without me?"

"Tilda, darling, it's just a funeral."

"Mum, it's not just a funeral. It's when we—" she said, and even as she spoke the words, knew herself to be a hypocrite of the worst sort. She'd treated Daniel's funerals with no more care than her mother was treating Nan's. She swallowed but her voice still came out, heavy with an emotion her mother would deplore. "Celebrate her life. Say good-bye. Be there for each other."

"There's no point in discussing this, darling, because you're here and can attend the funeral. I've emailed you the arrangements. Based on that tedious noise in the background, I presume you're at Heathrow. Can you make your own way to Cornwall?

I need to finish a book review before I go there myself, otherwise, I would offer to pick you up and drive you there."

Tilda's breath left her in a rush. "I'll be fine, Mum," she said.

Her mother hung up. Slowly, Tilda drew the phone away from her ear and stared at the screen. The call time flashed, then faded away. She knew she should feel something, that her mother's behavior was inappropriate, but right now she couldn't feel anything other than bereft shock. Nan was dead. That fact, as unfathomable as it was, kept hitting her, little stinging darts to her chest, her gut, the nape of her neck. She looked around the terminal, filled with people coming and going, alone, in pairs, or as families.

Daniel. She should call Daniel. He would want to know. She tapped on his contact information and called his mobile, but the call went straight to voice mail. She left a message, not even sure what she was saying as she spoke, but trusting him to get the necessary information.

She caught a glimpse of a woman in the mirror, tall and slim, with tired black curls, and a stricken expression on her face. After a moment Tilda realized the woman in the mirror was her, and her soul had finally caught up with her. Moving slowly, feeling the ache of sheer exhaustion in her joints, she started walking to the bus stop that would take her to the station to catch the train to Cornwall.

Daniel braced his hip on the corner of his desk and plucked his phone from the stack of paperwork threatening to tip off the other side. "We need proof. In writing is best. Audio if you can't get it in writing. Ideally we want both."

Ryan Malone, top Wall Street trader turned whistleblower braced his head in his hands, scrubbed at his scalp with his fingers, then sat back and blew out his breath. "I don't know. If I push too hard, they're going to figure out what I'm up to. They never talked about it to me, you know?"

"So we'll develop a strategy," Daniel said. Tilda had called. He tapped the voice mail playback button and waited for her voice to come out of the ether. "I saw you in the *Post* with what's-her-name, the new face of Ralph Lauren."

Ryan shrugged and flashed him a grin that was starting to look ragged around the edges. "It's the best cover I could come up with. Watch the wolf of Wall Street tear it up over here," he said, making magician moves with his hands, "and ignore all the questions he's asking over there. Girls like her are a dime a dozen at the kind of party I go to," he said. "Want me to hook you up?"

Tilda's voice, oddly shaken, slid into Daniel's ear. Daniel felt a pain so deep and hollow it took his breath away. He was married to a singular woman he loved and needed as much as he needed air, so no, he didn't want an introduction to the kind of girl who came a dime a dozen. Receiver pressed to his ear, he waggled his ring finger at Ryan, then reached for a pen and paper to take a message.

1. Nan died
2. Pulmonary embolism
3. Funeral tomorrow

"You okay?" Ryan asked.

He sat there with the phone to his ear while the cheery automated voice ran through his options. *Press one to replay. Press two to forward. Press three to delete. Press four to return to the main menu.*

He replayed the message, and this time he heard the quiver in her voice, the careful, slow way she spoke, as if repeating what she couldn't believe.

Nan was dead. This was going to tear Tilda apart.

"My wife's grandmother just died," he said.

"God," Ryan said, his face immediately serious. "I'm sorry."

Daniel took a deep breath and forced his attention back to the man sitting in front of him, the man who held the keys to the case of his career. "I have to go. Right now."

— TWENTY-FIVE —

Tilda heard only her pulse, fluttering in her ears, her irregular, shallow breathing. The vicar's voice barely registered. Tilda wondered if he was closer to Nan, if that's why he sounded like he was speaking from the other end of a tunnel. His lips were moving, his Book of Common Prayer open in his hand as he led the mourners through the funeral rites, but sound came to her oddly distorted, an audio track out of sync with the video. She knelt beside her mother, folded her hands, bowed her head, but all she heard was the odd discordant silence that rang when loud machinery was shut off. Not echoes but rather the tympanic hum of the bones in her inner ear quivering with the strain of trying to hear something that was no longer there: Nan's voice.

"In the midst of life we are in death; from whom can we seek help? From you alone, O Lord, who by our sins are justly angered," the vicar said. He was young with a shock of ginger hair that stood out against his black robes, the black-clad mourners, and the walnut coffin, and painfully solemn about the rites, as if not quite comfortable with them yet. *That makes two of us,* Tilda thought. *I am not comfortable with this at all.*

Then the ringing began again. "Holy God, Holy and Mighty, Holy and merciful Savior, deliver us not into the bitterness of eternal death," the congregation repeated. The opening notes of a hymn burst into her consciousness, booming against her eardrums. She startled, heard voices behind her take up the first stanza of "Amazing Grace," Nan's favorite hymn. The music seemed to envelop her in an echoing drum. The notes ran at odd angles to each other, and tearing the sheet would leave jagged, uneven lines, pressing against her skin, her inner ears, her nostrils. She felt that if she opened her mouth the dark notes would slide down her throat, course through her stomach into her intestines, until she burst from it.

The last notes died away, intensifying the ringing in Tilda's ears. The pallbearers came forward to lift the coffin containing Nan's slight body and bear it out of the church. The vicar paused by their pew. Nan's Book of Common Prayer clasped in her gloved hands, Tilda followed her mother and grandmother as she'd always done. As she walked she saw bodies in black and navy blue, but faces were a blur.

The sunshine was grotesque, blinding her until she fumbled on her sunglasses. The procession moved slowly down the steps, the pallbearers pausing to keep the coffin level, a gentleness that closed Tilda's throat until it seemed like the ringing in her ears came not from the organ or the abrupt silence but rather from what she throttled in her own throat. The slate pathway was uneven, requiring all her concentration to keep her balance as she placed one foot in front of the other, the solid ground an unfamiliar and inhospitable place to be. She followed her mother, who followed the vicar, who followed the coffin to the graveyard, where the pallbearers set the coffin on the hoist that would lower it into the ground. She would send them notes edged in black, when she could find the right words, the right paper to say the unsayable. The vicar would know their names, addresses.

The thought of writing another letter made her stomach heave. Letters were for what was real. They were for Nan. Tilda had built her whole life, her whole career around the one thing that had grounded her since she was eight years old, and now Nan was gone.

Her mother sank into the first chair beside the grave as if her knees gave way at the sight of the obscene gash in the ground and the bald mound of dirt beside it. Perhaps the dirt made it real for her, as it did for Tilda. Tilda did not have the strength to push past her to the second chair, so she locked her knees and stood beside her mother, waiting while what seemed like the entire village formed a rough semicircle around the grave. A breeze shivered through the leaves.

She couldn't do this alone, and yet she deserved to do it alone. After all, she had left her husband to deal with his own grief not once, but twice. She'd been there for Deshawn's funeral only in body, not in spirit.

"You are dust, and to dust you shall return. All of us go down to the dust, yet even at the grave we make our song: alleluia, alleluia, alleluia." The vicar bent, his movements both awkward and real, and grasped a handful of dirt, letting it trickle through his fist, onto the polished walnut. He glanced at Tilda. She was supposed to do the same. It was a ritual, comforting, an anchor for the living in the scent and feel of Cornwall dirt, where it all began.

Could she claim an earlier beginning than the one she'd had in a hotel room in Tokyo?

Her mother's rigid shoulders forced Tilda to push the question aside. "Mum," she said softly. "Come on, Mum."

Like a child, she led her mother to the mound of dirt, where they reached down. Her mother gingerly scraped her palm over the dirt, her hand trembling while the little palm full of dirt clattered onto the coffin. Tilda scooped up a greedy handful. She had to feel something, the bite of a pebble into her palm, the grit under her fingernails, and nearly put the dirt to her mouth to swallow it, shove back the wail that threatened to claw its way out of her throat.

She'd lifted it. Everyone was staring at her, the vicar, her mother, the mourners.

Daniel.

Sunlight glinted off his gold-and-silver hair, refracting off the tears on his cheeks. He stood outside the semicircle of mourners. Tilda stared at him, her cupped hand spilling dirt into the trampled grass at her feet.

Daniel was there, and he was crying.

She made a choked little sound, swallowed hard, and he was in motion, striding around the mourners to stand beside her. "Shhh," he said. "It's okay."

His voice was deep, thick, like hot earth, dialing down the noise in her head, and his arm was steady around her waist. She let herself sag just a little, felt him catch her, then he cupped her fistful of dirt, his fingers gentle and strong on hers. He didn't force them open, just held her, let her tremble.

"I can't," she said, and clenched her fist more tightly. Nan loved this earth, loved the small world she lived in, a world so small that Tilda was the highlight, and Tilda couldn't bring herself to throw it into her grave. Tears streamed down her cheeks, ran along her throat to pool in the hollow. She was sniffing, her throat working, she couldn't do it, she couldn't. The clanging in her head was going to drive her insane if it didn't stop.

Then Daniel bent his head to hers. "Tilda," he whispered.

Her name. The name he'd used on the ledge a year earlier,

trying to establish a connection when he thought she was going to jump, not knowing she was already falling. The name he'd spoken at their wedding ceremony. The name he used when he was exasperated, amused, angry, aroused. It husked into her ears, mouse-quiet and clarion-clear, slicing through the roar like a pen on paper. Other sounds returned. A bird singing in the tree overhead, Daniel breathing, his heart thumping, or perhaps that was her own heart.

She extended her arm over the gaping wound in the ground and relaxed her fist. Dirt trickled into the earth's wound, pattered against the wood, slid to the earth underneath. The bird trilled above her. She opened her hand, and let it all stream into the grave.

"Sit down," he murmured. "Tilda, sweetheart, sit down before you fall down."

He supported her while she stumbled to the chair, and sat. The vicar's voice took up the unfamiliar cadences of the funeral rite. The bird sang. Daniel hunkered down on his heels next to her while she stared into the grave, and gently brushed the earth from her palm, into the grass.

She woke up in her old bedroom at Nan's house without any memory of getting from the graveside into the bed. She wore her dress but no shoes, and had the old quilt tucked around her. Twilight filled the room, casting the furniture in shadows, and the scent of Nan was so strong she forgot what had come before.

She untangled the quilt from her legs and sat up, then bent forward against the pounding in her skull. When the pain receded she got to her feet. Her stockings snagged on the floorboards as she shuffled to the door and leaned against it. Daniel sat at the counter in the kitchen, his suit jacket draped over the back of one of Nan's kitchen chairs, shirtsleeves rolled to his elbows. A cup of instant coffee sat beside the local newspaper. Her last letter to Nan leaned against the salt and pepper shakers. He looked up, his gaze skimming over her, but she couldn't read it. Read him. For the first time in their relationship, he was utterly unreadable.

"What time is it?"

"Gone seven," he replied.

She shuffled past him, into the bathroom, where her body went on autopilot. The trifold mirror covering the medicine cabinet reflected back a woman she did not recognize. For a moment she stared into the mirror, unable to process the swollen eyes, the reddened nose, the lines carved on either side of her mouth.

Without blinking, she opened the mirror, withdrew the painkillers, shook three into her palm, and swallowed them dry. Back in the main room she looked around, and saw pictures tucked behind lamps, between African violets on the end table, the albums spread over the coffee table.

"Where's Mum?"

Daniel got up and ran a glass of water, then held it out to Tilda. "She's gone back to Oxford."

Tilda stared at him. "What?"

"Drink this," Daniel said, and waited until she had taken the glass in front of him and swallowed half of it before answering. "She had two tutorials tomorrow. And a committee meeting she was chairing. She said she'd be in touch."

Tilda gripped the back of a chair, pulled it out from the table, and eased into it. Sitting seemed like enough, until she put her head in her hand. Colin and the deal belonged to another lifetime. "Is that what I'm supposed to do? Work? Because I don't know if I can do that. I called Colin right after I called you. I don't remember what I said to him other than Nan had died and I wasn't going to be able to meet them for dinner. It's entirely possible I hung up on him midsentence." She paused. "The deal feels like it was happening to another person in another life, and Mum went right back to work."

Daniel didn't say anything for a long moment. "People react differently to grief," he said finally. "Some people take comfort in work. When was the last time you ate?"

"I don't know," she said, and tried to remember, because he was here, taking care of her, and it meant so much to her. It meant everything, and she should answer his questions. "Um. Not today. Not yesterday. Um. Maybe yesterday. I didn't eat on the flight, or at the airport. I can't remember. I'm sorry. I can't remember."

He reached across the table and covered her hand with his own. "I'm going to make you something to eat," he said. "Toast and eggs."

He might as well have been asking her to hoist Nan's coffin out of the grave. "I don't think I can eat."

"Just try," he said, and got up.

For a while she just sat there while he got out the ancient cast iron pan and oiled it, cracked eggs and scrambled them, sliced bread for toast. The scent of the bread toasting made her stomach growl. When the food was ready he slid a plate of eggs and toast spread with currant jam in front of her, and added a cup of tea. She stared at the eggs, the steam rising from them, then at him.

"Just one bite," he said.

But her body betrayed her, because after one bite it wanted more. Ravenous thing. Rapacious thing. She finished the eggs, ate the toast down to the crust, and felt better. She looked at Daniel, who had cleared his plate, and saw *better* in his eyes.

"Thank you for coming," she said.

"You're welcome."

"Most of the village was there. I can't imagine anyone was in the shops. I saw Rupert in the crowd," she said, slowly. "A few of Mum's other friends. Not Andrew."

Daniel said nothing.

"He didn't come to the funeral. But you did. You came. This is what you do. You go to the funeral." It suddenly seemed the most meaningful thing anyone had ever done for her.

He nodded gravely, then cleared the table, tipping her crusts into the bin, running water in the sink to do the washing up. "I should do that," she said.

"You should go back to bed," he said without turning around. "You're dead on your feet."

She did. She undressed into the pajamas in the drawer, scented with ancient lavender sachets, and slid back into the bed, surrounded by the scent of Nan overlaid with the medicinal odors of wound care. She lay there long enough to watch the moon rise over the house, listening to Daniel get ready to leave. He'd gotten a room at the inn, she deduced. Maybe he'd already signed the papers. Her throat closed and tears prickled behind her eyes, but she didn't cry.

Grief left her defenseless. Ruined. In wreckage she found a single, pure need.

She got up and opened her bedroom door. "Daniel," she said. "Don't go."

The room was dim, moonlight bathing the worn wood floors in silver. He stood in the door, turned toward her, his shoulders broad against the starry sky. "Don't ask me to do that, Tilda. I know you're hurting, but I can't be that for you tonight."

"I don't want . . . I just . . ." She took a shuddering breath, and when she spoke again, her voice was very small. "I don't want sex. I just want to be close to you."

He looked at her, and for the first time in their short, whirlwind relationship, she let him see her exactly as she was. He locked the door again, then crossed the floor and met her by the bedroom door. She crawled back into bed, listening to him removing his suit, shirt, and tie. Then he lay down beside her. She let her eyes close and his warmth seep into her, right down to the bones.

She awoke the next morning to sunlight, birds, and Daniel lacing up his trainers. "Go back to sleep," he said without looking up. "I'm going for a run."

When the door closed behind him, she lay in Nan's bed, for the first time in months anchored by scent and light and sound in time and space. She thought about Daniel, setting off along the narrow road. Processing grief and hurt and uncertainty through intense physical exercise. The hills and cliffs would give him a challenge. Perhaps she should take it up, learn to leave it all behind on the pavement, rather than in hotel rooms.

Her entire body ached from the tension of the past few days, something she hadn't realized until she let go. Keeping it all together was so much work, so difficult. Picking up her former life was impossible.

Daniel would be gone for a couple of hours. All she could do right now was sleep.

She awoke again when the front door opened, bringing with it the scent of sea and grass, Daniel, and warm scones. When he appeared in the door to the bedroom his hair and T-shirt were damp with sweat. He had a bag from the tea shop in the village. "Breakfast," he said.

Lacking any clear direction for how to behave with him, she nodded, then got up. Her mouth tasted foul, and she wanted a shower, but he was sweaty and had brought back breakfast. "Can I just . . . if you don't mind?"

"Go ahead," he said, and took the newspaper into the garden.

Daniel was too much of a cop to not meet her eyes, but the muscles around them were tight, wary. She brushed her teeth, showered, and dressed in an ancient pair of jeans and a jumper. While he showered, she made tea, and coffee for him, then took Nan's tea tray to the garden. The Cornish coast on a June morning was a beautiful thing, blue sky to the horizon, gulls swooping over the cliffs, the scent of the fruit bushes blooming. But this year, no one would make jams and jellies and send Tilda a batch.

"Thank you for coming," she said again. It meant everything to her to have him there, beside her, for even a little longer, but words were utterly inadequate. Maybe that's why relationships were built on trust and a life together, because in the matters of birth and death and love, words were not only inadequate, but somehow wrong.

But with so few shared experiences to draw on, words were all she had.

"I'm glad to be here," he said, and slid her a glance. He meant it, the sincerity in his blue eyes real and potent. For a moment, connection hummed between them.

"When are you going back to New York?" she said when he joined her at the table.

Daniel broke a scone into smaller pieces. "My return ticket is booked for tomorrow. The informant's counting on a wild summer to get the information we need. I walked out of a planning meeting to catch a plane."

He'd walked out on the biggest case of his career to be with her. She nodded. "I know. Thank you." The tea scalded the roof of her mouth. She set the cup on the saucer and lay back on the chaise. She couldn't bring herself to ask him where he would be when she returned home.

They sat there while the sun climbed behind them, paused overhead, then descended into the sea. Daniel seemed as content as she was to simply watch clouds scud across the sky, the wind shift and crease the ocean, the tide rise and fall in the cove at the base of the village. At the end of the day he left, brought back more food. They ate while the moon rose, casting a mysterious and ethereal westward trail on the sea. They spoke of nothing, simply lay in the present and let the sun and moon and stars whirl around them, observed the call-and-response of the tides.

Daniel left the next day in time to catch an early evening flight to Kennedy; he'd go to sleep around midnight in his own bed after a seven-hour flight. No wonder Tilda was so lost. He'd often wondered what it took to bring Tilda Davies to a complete halt. He now had his answer. Death had flattened her down to the very ground.

She was asleep on the chaise when he came out to say good-bye, the quilt draped loosely over her body. He stood beside her, then sat on his heels and used the very tips of his fingers to stroke her hair back from her face. She was pale, bruised under her puffy eyes, no color in her cheeks and almost none in her lips. Her hair had dried without any guidance, so it curled in tufts and wisps around her ears. He brushed it back, whispered her name. *Tilda.* She continued breathing, dreaming without him. Faced with an impossible loss, impossible decisions, her mind tricked her body by demanding sleep.

She had no experience with grief. Her rootless childhood had ravaged her in more ways than one. She'd never lived in one place long enough to lose people who mattered to her, to feel the loss of a chunk of her soul like a physical ache. While home was a physical place, it was people, too. She had only the most tenuous connection to either, and that disappeared when a blood clot drifted from Nan's ankle to her lungs.

He ached for her, right down to his bones. He wanted to pull her into his arms and rock her like he'd rock a child; he wanted to strip her bare and show her how much life was still left; he wanted to rage at her; he wanted to go to his knees and worship her. But wanting her wasn't enough. She had to want him, and more than that, she had to want a life together.

The curl above her ear twisted loose. He tucked it away again. "Tilda," he whispered. "I'm not here because it's the right thing to do. I'm here because I love you."

Her breathing didn't change. Her eyelashes didn't flicker. She slept on. He kissed her cheek, then went to get a cab to the train station.

— TWENTY-SIX —

Tilda awoke in the late afternoon to an empty house and a sun headache. She ran herself a glass of water, and poked listlessly through the tiny house while she drank it. Opening cupboard doors. Closing them. She lifted the lid on the trunk at the foot of Nan's bed. An old linen sheet covered the contents, and Tilda closed it without disturbing them. At twilight she walked down to the sea, then to the pub for a quick supper. Talk quieted when she opened the door, but when she ordered a pint and a ploughman's platter to stay, a steady stream of residents kept her company during her meal, telling stories about Nan. She smiled through the inevitable tears, a paradox of emotion she couldn't explain or ignore, but simply felt.

Daniel sent a text while she was asleep. I'm home. She stroked the screen with her thumb, and wondered if he meant he'd arrived, or he was back at the town house. She would find out when she went home herself. In the meantime, she sat in Nan's house and tried to figure out what to do next. The answer, when framed in the context of what would Daniel do, seemed simple. She went to sit outside in the sun.

The next day she was drowsing on the chaise when a car door slammed, awakening her. She walked around the house to see who'd come to call and found the local solicitor and her mother on the slanted steps. "Hello, darling," her mother said, and gave her a quick kiss on the cheek.

Tilda accepted the kiss, but wrapped her arms protectively around her waist. "Hello, Mum."

"Hello, Ms. Davies," he said. "I'd like to speak to both you and Dr. Davies for a moment. May I come in?"

She let him in and made tea while he withdrew papers from his briefcase and settled himself at the table. After a polite sip, he cleared his throat. "I'm the executor of Mrs. Davies's estate. The short version of her will is this: your grandmother left the house and contents to you, Ms. Davies."

"To me?" Tilda said. She looked at her mother, who showed no signs of surprise at this turn of events. "Not to Mum?"

"No. I understand you live in America with no plans to return to England on a permanent basis. I'd be happy to recommend an agent, when you decide to sell."

"I'm not selling," she said. Her lips were numb. She cleared her throat, and repeated herself. "I'm not selling. Can you recommend someone reliable who might want to run the place?"

The attorney's brow furrowed for a moment. "There's a young lad in the village looking to try his hand with organic farming," he said. "I'll leave his name and number. I'm sure you can work out a suitable arrangement with him or with someone he recommends."

He neatly penned the name Joe Gloyne and a local phone

number on the pad of paper by Nan's rotary phone, then left. Tilda escorted the solicitor to the front door, then turned to look through the house's single room at her mother, standing on the flagstone terrace, staring out at the sea. Her back was straight, her shoulders rigid, a solitary, lonely figure. With a sudden, shocking clarity, Tilda realized she might never cross the gaping void between herself and her mother, not from her own mistakes or for lack of trying, but because her mother simply didn't want to be reached.

But life was far too short and far too precious for Tilda to deny herself the chance to love and be loved. As a child she'd asked for what she wanted, again and again, and been denied. She'd spent the last ten years staggering under a burden of shame and guilt without once asking for atonement. As an adult all she could do was let her mother, and herself, off the hook of anger and heartache.

"I'm sorry, Mum," she said in the silence hanging over the room after the door closed.

"Don't be, darling," her mother said, staring fixedly at the currant bushes running in tangles to the sea. "I didn't want the place, and your Nan knew that."

"That's not what I meant," she said quietly.

Her mother transferred her clear, analytical gaze from the tangled brambles to Tilda's face.

"I'm sorry for what happened with Andrew," Tilda said.

"The time for an apology was ten years ago," her mother said.

"Nonetheless, I am sorry, Mum."

"As am I," her mother said, and looked away again.

Tilda's heart was pounding, her underarms prickling from a nervous sweat, her stomach churning, but she had begun and she meant to go on. "But you should have protected me. A fatherless girl, left to her own devices in boarding schools and summer enrichment camps? You should have protected me," she said.

Her mother looked at her, her gray eyes as sharp and slicing as daggers. "I gave you the best of everything. The education and opportunities I never had, connections you spurned. As for protecting you . . . from *Andrew*? Andrew was hardly a threat to you. Lacking clear direction and a guiding hand, he has the initiative one would expect from someone who'd never had to do a proper day's work in his life, and his career has foundered for it. That was all you, my girl. How could I possibly protect you from yourself?"

"It would have been easy, Mum," Tilda said. She heard Daniel in her voice, even, sure, bedrock in her soul. "All you had to do was pay attention to me. That's all I wanted."

Her mother returned her attention to the sea. "I gave you everything, and you ask for more. Too much. From the very beginning, you asked too much of me."

She didn't clarify, or elaborate. The tide was flowing back out, ebbing from the harbor walls. Tilda watched and let the tide of grief carve away the rocks of anger and resentment and pain, revealing something else inside her. Pity, laced with forgiveness. She'd asked for it *from* her mother, and given it *to* her mother. It could be a gift to both of them, but only if her mother was willing to receive forgiveness as well as give it.

All she could do was offer it. She could do no more.

Claiming no interest in anything left in the cottage, her mother left at midafternoon.

Tilda cleaned out the fridge, sorted through Nan's knickknacks, the pictures on the mantel, and the albums tucked under the end table, then slept on sheets that smelled of Nan, and faintly of Daniel. The next day a man from the village brought his truck and loaded all of Nan's possessions but for the rocking chair and cedar chest into the back of it. Shipping them, and Nan's Mason Cash mixing bowl and the hand beater she used to scramble eggs or mix the milk into flour for tea biscuits, to New York would cost a fortune, but Tilda wanted them. When she'd finished, she opened all the windows and let the cool evening breeze blow through. She was booked on the evening flight to Kennedy, but before she hurled herself into the air again, there was one thing left to do.

She dragged the rocking chair through the door to the garden, and then positioned the cedar chest beside it. In the day's fading light she opened the lid, then shook out the sheet that had protected the most precious relics of Nan's life. She draped it over the rocking chair's polished arm, and turned back to see what the chest held.

It held neat stacks of letters tied with ribbon. Bewildered, her heart pounding, Tilda lifted them. They were her letters.

Nan, who said she didn't have time for foolish sentiment, had kept her letters. Judging by the ribbon-tied stacks, all of them, from . . . yes, the handwriting on the envelopes scrolled in reverse from her precise, angular script to the careful, rounded letters of the eight-year-old girl she'd been when she went to boarding school. Cradled in unsteady piles on her lap were all the letters she'd sent Nan, her entire history.

Her throat closed. Tears spilled down her cheeks as she smoothed her palm over the stacks. She was here, right here, in pen and ink. Despite sending away her past, it was right here, waiting for her to come back and claim it. The good and the bad, the funny and the sad, the mundane and the remarkable, it was all here, stored with Nan's treasures. In the other compartment lay her wedding day picture, taken by the judge's clerk who witnessed the ceremony.

Tilda studied the picture for quite a while. She didn't look like a bride, not in a garnet dress the light in the chamber dulled to near black. She carried no flowers. Daniel also wore a dark suit and a subdued tie. The background wasn't flowers or a gazebo or a lake, but rather law books and framed certificates and diplomas. She touched a smudge on the picture and realized Nan had sat there with the album, studying Tilda's face. The picture caught the moment she stood in front of the windows with Daniel, her head bowed, her hands clasped in his, the moment when he whispered her into the wedding.

Are you sure? Tilda, are you sure? We don't have to do this.

She stared at the picture for a very long time, taking in Daniel's concerned, loving expression. Her own face was so much more difficult to read, seemingly carved from alabaster marble, her lips parted, the line of her nape and jaw and forehead backlit by the light coming through the window. The pose was protective and possessive, surrender in her bowed neck, charged with the dark current of lust that characterized their early relationship. No wonder the judge and the clerk were looking elsewhere when they broke that little bubble of intimacy and turned back to the room.

Troubled, she set aside the framed picture and picked up the old-fashioned ones, made of leather, the snapshots tucked into little clips. There was just enough room left in the cedar chest to hold the pictures now displayed on end tables and the mantel, the old-fashioned albums she remembered collecting the day when she sorted through the living room. Nan always said she didn't have room for such silly things, that she remembered well enough what her only granddaughter looked like. Tilda was puzzled, until the light dawned.

When she came to visit, Nan put the pictures and albums away not because they made *her* uncomfortable, but because she knew they made *Tilda* uncomfortable. She'd been protecting Tilda to the last. Loving her as best she knew how, to the very end.

There was one album at the bottom of the chest, one Tilda hadn't seen before, made of dark blue leather that held a sheen of time and handling. She lifted it out and opened it to find pictures of her. A baby picture from the hospital, wearing the cap all newborns wore to keep them warm. Swaddled in a gorgeous hand-knit white lace shawl for her christening. Napping on her mother's chest while her mother napped, her head lolling back against the back of the sofa. In a pram, her mother pushing her self-consciously through the village.

These must be the pictures taken before she left for Oxford. The pictures displayed on the next few pages were relatively unremarkable, snapshots taken when Tilda and Mum came to visit Nan, carefully posed by the stone wall lining the path to the sea, or picking flowers in the field. Eating an ice cream after a visit to the shops, her eyes brimming with delight at the treat.

When she turned the next page, she stopped breathing. She was about eight, wearing a short ruffled dress and sandals, her hair a mop of black curls around her face, her eyes wide, unblinking. Haunted. Seen like this, the girl she was before she was sent to live with Nan, and the girl she was after that, her brokenness shone from the page like a searchlight over the sea. She remembered crying herself to sleep, night after night, until she stopped crying because no one was coming for her.

All her adult life she'd dragged this little girl from student housing to a series of apartments, then to the town house, and finally all over the world, repeating behaviors that looked wildly successful and cosmopolitan on the surface but were doomed to fail to give her what she wanted. Needed. Longed for. She remembered reading about indigenous tribes that, when on long journeys, would stop and wait for hours, or days, or weeks, for their souls to catch up with them. She'd lost her soul somewhere in her rootless, unfettered childhood. She wasn't sure where she'd left hers, perhaps in Tokyo, perhaps in Cornwall. Perhaps it had been waiting for her at the unclaimed baggage room in Heathrow all along.

At the bottom of the trunk lay a photograph of Granddad in an old-fashioned suit and tie, Nan's wedding photograph, Granddad in the same suit, Nan in a smart dark green dress that set off her hair and eyes. Pictures Nan had long since stowed away.

Tilda held them in her hands, trailed her fingertip over Nan's face. The motion left a slight smudge similar to the one left on her photograph by Nan's finger. Inspired, Tilda rummaged through Nan's tiny closet and came up with a vintage suitcase. Without so much as untying a ribbon she transferred the stacks to the musty suitcase, letters, albums, all of Nan's treasures.

It was time to go home. For the first time in her life, the name at the top of her list was her own.

She packed her suitcase once again, and took the train to Heathrow, cleared customs and immigration, then boarded the flight to JFK. Unwilling to check either of her bags, she staked out more than her share of allotted luggage space in the bins. The plane flew through a perpetual dusk, and distant gray sprawl of ocean beneath her, its textures and shifts smoothed to glass, the vast, empty dusk around her, lulled her to sleep. She awoke when the flight attendants began preparing the cabin for arrival. Out the window she sought the familiar landmarks lit up in the night sky: the Empire State Building, the Chrysler Building, the Freedom Tower at the tip of the island, Central Park's rectangular green swath. The setting sun gilded the Manhattan skyline. Tilda stared out the window, and felt it pierce her.

Standing in the taxi queue was far less beautiful, the wait hot and long. The cab smelled of onions and coffee. The cabbie dropped her and her two bags at the black door of Fifteen Perry

Street. After he left, she wrestled the bags through the doors, and then stopped in the foyer.

Home.

The divorce agreement still lay on the dining room table, although based on a fainter circle of dust Daniel had picked up the paperweight, then set it down again. Heart in the back of her throat, she flipped through to the last page.

He hadn't signed them. He'd thought about it, or at least looked at the paperweight. She hefted it, looked at the pink lotus flower suspended in the glass, then at the front windows. Still intact. A faint, involuntary smile crossed her face. How very, very like Daniel to think about hurling five grand of paperweight through the windows, but not do it.

She was so exhausted she couldn't make a list of all the things she needed to do, but was equally unable to sleep. So she left her new suitcase filled with the contents of Nan's cedar chest at the bottom of the stairs, and hauled the larger bag containing her clothes and toiletries up two flights to her bedroom. She paused on the second floor to peer into the guest room and bath. The bed was unmade, and Daniel's electric toothbrush and razor sat haphazardly on the counter, their charging lights blinking out of sync.

He hadn't signed the papers, and he was still here.

Unpacking took all of ten minutes. Dirty laundry, dry cleaning, toiletries neatly put away. She showered, changed into a pair of yoga pants and a long-sleeved T-shirt, then went back downstairs, ran a glass of water and went into the dining room.

She opened the vintage suitcase and took out the stacks of letters, neatly bundled and wrapped in faded ribbons, then sat down at the foot of the dining room table, facing the divorce papers. The knots in the ribbons gave way easily. She fanned them out along the length of the table, but ran out of room when she came to the head, where the divorce papers, paperweight, and pen still sat.

Very aware of what she was doing, she picked up the paper-weight and stuffed it in a drawer on the hutch, but laid the papers on a chair, still near the rows of letters but no longer blocking their flow. The pen she capped and pushed behind her ear, then resumed laying out the story of her life. She studied the letters as if she were studying a note from one of the people asking for an introduction. Most of the postmarks were from school, a few with international postage from the book tour, then New York.

Nothing from Tokyo, but she now had the letter she'd written Daniel about Tokyo. She went upstairs, got the letter from Daniel's nightstand, and tucked it in its proper place in the rows.

That was the first step, to reread the letters, starting with the most recent, and working her way back, excavating her self from these letters like artifacts on an archaeological dig.

Daniel's key turned the lock on the front door. It swung open, hit the suitcase on the floor, which scraped over the tile. "Tilda?"

"In here," she said, trusting him to navigate to the sound of her voice.

He appeared in the doorway in his suit and tie, his keys still in his hand. "Hi," he said.

"Hi," she said.

He braced his shoulder against the doorframe, tipped his head so it rested on the white wood. "Good flight?"

"Yes," she said. "It brought me home."

His gaze sharpened, then he nodded at the rows of envelopes on the dining room table. "What's this?"

"Every letter I ever sent Nan."

"Ah."

He looked at her, and she'd never felt more raw or vulnerable under his gaze. "Daniel, I don't know what to say."

"You don't have to say anything," he said not unkindly. "I'm going for a run. I'll be back later."

"All right," she said.

He came back downstairs wearing running shorts and a T-shirt. Before he left he handed her another glass of water.

She opened the last letter she'd sent to Nan, and read it. She'd promised herself she wouldn't cry anymore, that she knew what she needed to do and would work at it until it was done, but in hindsight the letter was so superficial and stupid and false, all the lies of omission she was telling herself, walls made of words and paper fibers and ink. She neatly folded the letter, inserted it back into its envelope, the only one on the table not handled by Nan, and went upstairs to sleep.

She awoke to Daniel sitting on the edge of the bed. "Tilda," he said.

In that moment she knew that she wanted to wake up every day for the rest of her life to Daniel's voice murmuring her name. His gaze, so troubled and caring, searched her face. "I love you. Daniel, believe me when I say that. I know I haven't given you any reason to but please, please believe me. I love you."

"I love you, too," he said. He smoothed her hair back from her face and smiled at her, so sweet and wistful and wary. What she'd done to him shamed her almost as much as what she'd done to Andrew.

"We need to talk," she started, then sat up straighter. "Why are you in a suit? Are you going back to work?"

His hand rested on her hip, warm, anchoring. "It's morning, Tilda. You've been asleep for thirteen hours."

"I need to go into work," she said, and started to lift the covers.

His hand tightened, not much, but enough. She felt the weight of it, weight she could have powered through a lifetime ago, before everything fell apart. "I called Penny and told her you were taking a couple more days off."

The weight of his hand mirrored the weight of her soul, unfamiliar but pleasantly heavy and warm. Carrying that weight would take some getting used to. "I've already asked her to do too much."

"She said you'd say that. She says to tell you not to short-circuit the process."

The instinct to avoid this through work was strong, but she ignored it. "We need to talk," she said again.

He smiled, somewhat involuntarily. "See? That wasn't so hard," he said before he grew serious again. "We do. But not today. Tonight."

"Shall we meet in the kitchen?"

"It's a date," he said, and squeezed her hip before leaving.

Getting out of bed was a breeze because her mouth tasted foul and her hair felt lank. She showered, brushed her teeth, dressed in loose-knit pajama pants and a T-shirt, went downstairs for breakfast, popped bread in the toaster, opened the door, and pulled out the currant jam.

Then she fell apart.

Half an hour later she pulled herself off the kitchen floor, put the jam away, and had a pear and a bowl of instant oatmeal for breakfast. She sat at the table on the patio and read her email, both work and personal, called a supplier, called several personal appointments she'd missed. Slate cleared, she went inside and looked at the letters stretched out on the dining room table. Her life, in neat rows. Craving sunshine and the summer breeze, she scooped up the divorce papers and the column of most recent letters from the table, and took them into the back yard with a cup of tea.

She was still sitting outside when Daniel came home. His footsteps paused for a moment, the fridge opened, closed, then he opened the screen door and walked down onto the flagstones, a beer in hand. He took in the stacks of letters, the plates dotted with crumbs, and said, "Have you been out here all day?"

She looked up. His tie was loosened, the top button undone, and his face was lined. "Most of it," she said. "Hard day?"

"Just long," he said, and pulled out a chair to sit next to her. "The next couple of months are going to be hell. Ready to talk?"

"Yes."

"The day you thought you were pregnant. Why did you call me?" he asked.

It was a good question. Why hadn't she just taken the test and dealt with the consequences on her own? But the first thing she thought when she realized exactly, precisely, how heart-stoppingly late she was, was *Call Daniel. Now.*

"I thought you should know," she said. She huffed out a laugh. Because he was Daniel. Because he was good with women on ledges, as she well knew. Because something told her he'd stand beside her in the bathroom, and afterward. In that moment she'd wanted the sheer animal comfort of someone to sit beside her while she waited for the test to return its answer, and that moment of weakness, as always, was her downfall.

"Why did you say yes?"

"I wanted to marry you," she said quietly. "Please believe me when I say that. I wanted to marry you. I wanted you. Wanting has never been my problem. My problem is having. Keeping what I want."

"That's not your problem, Tilda."

— TWENTY-SEVEN —

He looked at her, hated how the next few minutes would hurt her, but knowing she had to go through them. "What did your mother say to you after she saw you and Andrew?"

Tilda looked down, away, then slid him a glance, half love, half amusement, all hope.

"You really don't miss a trick, do you?" she said.

"I miss all kinds of tricks. I just try not to miss the same trick twice."

"You ruin everything."

He blinked, then realized she didn't mean him.

"That's what she said. *You ruin everything.*" She took a deep breath. "She looked at me like I was a whore, and said, *You ruin everything.* Then she walked away."

Rage throttled him. That's why Andrew was at the dinner party. His presence was a not-so-subtle reminder to Tilda of her past mistakes, ensuring they would haunt her for the rest of her life.

"I wasn't sure if she meant I'd ruined her life, the trip, or her reputation. I'd ruined her chances with Andrew, certainly. Perhaps simply by being born. I have no idea who my father is, but he disappeared like vapor before I was born. I ruined that for her, too. As near as I can tell there were two men in her life she actually wanted, and both times I ruined her chance at happiness."

He counted to ten. Then counted to ten again. He had to say something, before she interpreted his silence as judgment. "She's blaming you."

"Oh, I couldn't help being born," she said with a little laugh that sounded as harsh and brittle as his voice. "But I was trouble with Nan. Skipping school. Uncontrollable. That's why I was sent to boarding school. I'm certainly to blame with Andrew. She wanted him. He needed her, but wanted me. I wanted . . ." She went silent again. Daniel heard nothing but the rush of blood in his ears. "I wanted to make her *see me*, see who I am, see what I could do."

Silence. Daniel sat across from her, and waited. Something happened in Cornwall, beginning when she held a handful of Cornish dirt over her grandmother's coffin and let it trickle through her fingers. "I didn't want you to know this about me. You'd never do anything like that. You're a good person, a good man."

"Just because I wouldn't do that doesn't mean I judge you for doing it. You were seventeen, as alone as any child I've seen who wasn't in the foster-care system. Your mother . . . your mother defies description, and Andrew . . ."

Her cheeks bloomed pink. "Still. I'm ashamed of myself," she said finally.

"Why?" he said gently.

"What kind of horrible person does what I did—"

"A seventeen-year-old, passionate, determined person who knows she deserves better than what she's had."

"And what kind of pathetic person asks her husband to take her back because she's suffered one loss and is afraid of losing someone else? You'll think I'm here just because I'm scared of losing you and I'm afraid of being . . . without you. I'm not afraid to be alone, but the thought of life without you terrifies me."

"That would be great, Tilda, if you were here because you were scared and afraid of being alone. Because that's exactly why I'm here. I'm scared of losing you, of living the rest of my life without you."

Her gray eyes gleamed before she looked away, up at the trees, down at the flagstone patio. "You bought me the bracelet because you love me. You were loving me, and I couldn't bear to be in the room, because it wasn't just sex anymore. It was supposed to lead somewhere I didn't recognize, let alone know how to navigate. Sex had always led nowhere. No risk, no threat of connection. But that night at the hotel . . . you wanted it to lead somewhere. You wanted to connect it to our marriage. You were trying to make it mean something more than it had. And the bracelet. My God, Daniel. That bracelet."

Her eyes were a mixture of disbelief and joy and terror. "Not romantic? They're supposed to be romantic," he said offhandedly, but he knew better. "I felt like I was losing you. I knew I was. I just didn't know why."

Her face grew serious. "I didn't know how to take what you want to give. It's a skill, you see, learning the knack of being loved, a skill I don't have."

"Currently. One you don't have currently." He looked at her, calm, not a hint of amusement in his eyes.

Her back stiffened. "I don't want to be a project—"

"Goddammit, Tilda, I'm not a martyr. I'm not throwing myself on the pyre of your issues. I'm just better than the people who've left you. That's why I stay. Because you're amazing and I'm in love with you and I don't fucking quit just because things get tough."

"You swore," she said. She was half laughing, half crying.

"Sorry." He sat back and blew out his breath, then looked down at his clasped hands.

"I think that might be the most romantic thing anyone's ever said to me."

Her voice was dumbfounded. "Then I'm not sorry. You did a bad thing, Tilda," he said, without looking up. "You cut school, and got into trouble with boys, but *you* are not a bad thing, someone inherently destined to ruin every good thing that comes her way. But I can't prove that. Life isn't black ink on white paper, columns and numbers and script. It's a work of art that integrates the past into the future. It's impossible to *prove* a future in which I love you, you love me, and we never come to ruin. A future has to be lived. What you have to do is love me, and let me love you, day in and day out, year in and year out, until we die of old age, more in love than we are now." He gave her a sidelong glance, a smile quirking at the corner of his mouth. "How's that for a ledge?"

She clapped a hand to her mouth to muffle her disbelieving laugh. "That's a proper ledge. And to think I thought you weren't daring enough for me."

"People do tend to underestimate me," he said seriously.

"I won't make that mistake again." She swiped her eyes with the heels of her hands, then drew in a shaky breath. "That's all I do? Just . . . let you love me, and love you in return?"

"That's it."

She picked up the divorce papers from the table, and tore them in half, then in half again. The edges fluttered in the warm breeze until she secured them under the tea tray. "You asked me once who I'd put on the list for myself," she said. Quiet, but sure. This came from a completely different place in her, a place he'd not yet seen. That alone gave him hope. "You. I'd put you on the list for me. No one else. Nothing else. Not Quality, or a global brand. You."

"I'm yours," he said. "Have been since the moment I saw you, in fact."

"Sitting on a ledge," she said.

"Sitting on a ledge."

He leaned forward and kissed her, his hand around the nape of her neck. "Now what?"

"Dinner," he said, then stood and held out his hand. She put her hand in his, and squeezed his fingers when he helped her to her feet.

"Yes, please," she said, and gave him a quick kiss as she climbed the steps to the back door. She prepared dinner, nothing elaborate, a simple meal of cheese and olives, hummus and pita, a bright array of peppers and carrots for dipping.

That night, he moved his things back to the master suite on the third floor. Tilda gave him a shy, pleased smile as they got ready for bed, but while he half expected her to turn to him in the middle of the night, or to wake him as she so frequently had with her fingers trailing down his chest to his cock, or her mouth on his thighs, she did neither of those things. She had learned to mistrust her desires, and while he wanted her to be his wife in every sense of the word, he wouldn't rush her through that process of reclaiming her sexuality. When she was ready, she would come to him.

With that in mind, he didn't mention a trip to Huntington to see Jessie's soccer game. She was still so quiet inside, like she needed some time and space to read letters or look at pictures; when there was a lull in the case, while some of the parties involved vacationed in Seychelles, Daniel felt justified in taking a Saturday off.

"So you're not getting divorced anymore?" Angie sipped her coffee and watched Jessie's game on the field.

"No." He didn't tell Angie about the pictures and letters strewn over every flat surface in the house. Something mysterious, almost mythological was happening in that town house. If he had to hazard a guess, Tilda, who loved white paper and black ink, was falling in love with art. But he kept his hypothesis to himself. If he spoke of it, sent it into the wind too early, it might drift away and disappear.

"What happened?"

"Her grandmother died."

"You went to the funeral?"

"I went to the funeral."

Angie didn't say anything. She didn't have to say anything. Daniel tried to get his thoughts in order, to explain the seismic shifts of the human heart to someone who only knew bedrock.

"Mom taught us to write thank-you notes, right? Because that's what you do when you're a part of a family, or community. She taught us to be kind and gentle and giving. Thoughtful. But she taught us something else, too. She taught us how to be loved. Every day with the touches and the smiles and the affection, the attention, she taught us how to accept someone's love. To trust it. No one taught Tilda that. The only person she trusts to do it was her nan. Everyone else was suspect. Now Nan's dead, and she's trying to find her way. I'm walking with her."

Angie stared at him. To someone who grew up with that foundation, the lack of it was incomprehensible, like trying to explain air to a fish who'd never felt the yank of the hook. Her mother ripped big chunks right out of her soul. Andrew gave her sex, the lure of touch, the high of orgasm, with nothing underneath it. He was trying to give her bedrock.

Angie finished her coffee and tossed the paper cup in the trash can at the far end of the field. Jessie stole the ball from her opponent, only to lose it to the halfback. Her ponytail swung as she took off back up the field, her little face set with fierce determination. "She's the spitting image of you," Daniel said.

"My girl," Angie said fondly.

A red cab pulled into the parking lot, an unusual sight in suburban Long Island. Heads swiveled to watch Tilda get out of the backseat, claim her bag. She scanned the sidelines. His heart in his throat, Daniel lifted his arm and waved to get her attention. She waved back and set off toward them.

"Why didn't you two come together?" Angie asked.

"I didn't know she was coming," he said. His heart was pounding like it had the first time he saw her, skittering in his chest, his entire nervous system lit up like Times Square.

"Hi, Angie," she said, a little too brightly. It was as uncertain as Daniel had ever seen her. For Tilda, asking to be a part of the family was the riskiest thing she'd ever done. "I'm sorry I'm late."

"Not a problem," Angie said. "We're glad you're here. I'm so sorry to hear about your grandmother."

"Thank you," Tilda said. "I miss her terribly." Just then Jessie waved excitedly at Tilda, and Tilda waved back. "What's the score?"

"Two to one. We're up," Daniel said.

Tilda greeted his mom and dad, then stayed by his side through a celebratory lunch at Chuck E. Cheese's. The noise level was indescribable, games chirping and shrilling and blinking, like a children's casino in hell, but Tilda gamely ate pizza, drank a beer, and played Whac-A-Mole with Jessie, before Angie gave them a ride to the train station. The rain that had threatened all day finally spattered against the train's windows on the ride home. Her hand linked with his, Tilda watched houses and strip malls and roads flow past, then transferred her gaze from the suburbs to his face. "I understand," she said.

"Understand what?"

"Why you go to the soccer games. You go to the soccer games because you always go to the funerals."

"I never really thought about it, but yeah. Life's going to come at you. You have to take the joy when you can."

She sat in silence a little longer. "Take the joy when you can. I like that."

"Good," he said.

"I like that," she said again, but more quietly, and that was enough.

— TWENTY-EIGHT —

The morning Tilda went back to West Village Stationery, she surprised Penny in the act of rolling up the metal screen. She crossed Hudson, jaywalking between eddies of traffic. "Good morning," she said.

The screen clanged up while Penny turned, her eyes widening with surprise, then softening with sympathy. "Oh, honey, hi. How are you?"

"Fine," Tilda said, and accepted the quick hug that came with the cheek kiss. "I could sleep all day, and I cry at the drop of a hat, and I've got the mother of all headaches, but it looks like I'm going to stay married, so . . . fine? It was the hardest thing I've ever done, but I'm fine."

Penny squeezed her hand, then gave her a little smile. "You should take another week off. Everything is under control here."

"I really think work might do me good. And you haven't had a day off since I left." Tears sprang to her eyes. "Thank you," she whispered.

"You're welcome," Penny whispered back.

"The windows are fabulous," Tilda said. Penny had somehow created chameleons and whimsical spiders out of papier-mâché using outdated samples and incorrectly printed cards. The chameleons sunned by tide pools collected between large gray rocks. Tilda peered into the tide pools and saw glints of jewelry and silverware. "Fabulous."

"Palimpsests," Penny said archly, and tapped the side of her nose. "I was inspired."

They let themselves in, then locked the doors behind them. "We sold out of the stock Sheba gave us."

"I'm going to see her later this week," Tilda said. "I'll ask her if we can have a few more pieces."

"Double the price," Penny said. "I sold to three A-list movie stars using Black Cards to pay."

Tilda's eyes widened. "Really?"

"Really. Once we hold the second show, the sky will be the limit."

"How bad is the stack of mail?"

"I threw out junk mail, handled what was obviously business, and left the rest for you. Quality must have added you to a mailing list because you're getting invitations to all kinds of trade shows."

"About that," Tilda said quietly. She looked around the tiny shop, the oasis of gleaming wood and brightly lit shelves, and heard the words *this is enough* whisper in her soul. "I've decided not to take the deal."

Penny's face didn't change. "You're sure?"

"Yes," Tilda said, and waited for her to offer her resignation.

"Good. I mean, it was a great opportunity, but I've been thinking about some things we could do together. You and me."

Tilda felt her eyebrows rise. "What kinds of things?"

Penny reached under the counter and withdrew a portfolio. "I mocked up some invitations for Sheba's next show. They're not our usual style," she said as she opened the flap and fanned out the designs. An art deco look in silver and blue, a seventies look in an orange that shouldn't have worked, but did, an exquisitely layered Brooklyn Bridge creation of tissue paper from pencil drawing through ink sketches to the bridge's iconic swoops in fine black cord. "I thought we could put out some feelers in the couture stationery market. It's even more rarefied than what we sell now, but the market is there. With your connections and clientele, and my designs . . . we could see where it goes. When you're ready."

"On one condition," Tilda said. "I'll teach you the business side, and you'll teach me the creative side."

"I'm terrible with numbers."

"I don't have a creative bone in my body," Tilda said.

"Everyone is creative," Penny protested.

"Anyone can learn to make a balance sheet," Tilda said. "You've got the talent to branch out on your own, Penny. When you're ready, I want you to have the skills you need."

She sorted the mail and caught up on business correspondence. Then she closed the door to her office and called Colin.

"Miss Matilda," he said cheerily. "Bringing me good news on this fine summer day, I hope. Papers signed, everything tickety boo, yes?"

"Colin, I'm so sorry, but I'm going to have to let the deal go."

Over the phone connection, she heard a siren wail past. "Is this about the percentages?" Colin asked finally.

"It's about my grandmother dying, and about what's best for me right now."

"Tilda, darling, we're willing to wait a few weeks while you process your grief. More than that, and I can't guarantee that this offer will be available," he said. She heard the whoosh of steam, a barista calling out a mocha for Gerry. "Be very, very sure you want to take that chance."

It was no risk at all. She was a connoisseur of risk, and this was nothing compared to sitting on ledges or throwing her marriage away. If she took the extension on the offer, it would keep her and Quality up in the air. Even though Colin couldn't see her, she shook her head.

"I can't guarantee I'll be ready to move forward in a few months, let alone a few weeks," she said. "I'll send a note to the head of Quality, and explain my decision as best I can. It's an incredible offer, and I'm very grateful for the chance, but right now I need to be in New York, and only in New York."

She'd always suspected Colin used his charming public school persona to mask a rather sharp mind. "I understand," he said, and from his tone she knew he did. "Best of luck to you, and keep in touch."

"I will," she promised.

A week later, while Daniel was off on a long Sunday training run, Tilda packed the letters and pictures back into the vintage suitcase and trundled it through the West Village to SoHo along with a batch of homemade scones. Talk therapy still wasn't right for her. Instead, she was going to put her faith in the power of art to heal past wounds. After all, she represented the current darling of the art world, someone who knew all about getting lost and found again, and had the tools and language to help her work through it.

She owed this to Nan, to herself, to Daniel, to the life they would share. Art didn't feel like therapy. It felt like joy. If she followed joy, it couldn't be wrong.

Penny was waiting outside the building's door, clutching a coffee and a bundle of flowers for Sheba. "Good morning," Tilda said as she gave her a swift kiss on the cheek.

"I'm so nervous I'm shaking," Penny confessed. "Seeing her studio, watching her work. It's unbelievable."

"It certainly is," Tilda said, and then rang Sheba's bell.

Sheba was standing in her doorway when Tilda climbed the last flight of steps. The scent of strong Earl Grey tea drifted into the hall. "What's in there, child?"

"My life story," she said, pulling pages from envelopes and flattening them on the worktable. "One of my grandmother's letters to me, and one of mine to her. I have hundreds of these. You said once that I was a created thing, a work of art. I want to make these letters into art."

Sheba smoothed her palm over the pages. "An elegant hand," she said of Tilda's page. "All angles and lines. Your grandmother's writing is straight out of the copybooks from that era. Copperplate, I think they called it. What do you have in mind?"

"Absolutely no idea," Tilda admitted. "I'm going to scan them and the pictures I found to ensure I always have the text and picture, but then, once they're digital files, I thought I could print close-ups of certain words or pages, off center—"

"So you lose the context of the letter and keep only the lines and angles—"

"Exactly, yes, change the color of the font, or the page I print it on, include photos, that kind of thing—"

"Which you can do both digitally and with the actual letters and pictures—" Penny tossed out around a mouthful of scone.

"And create a palimpsest," Tilda finished. "I have no idea how to do this. Will you help me?"

"You know the word comes from Greek and Latin roots that mean 'twice scraped.'"

"No," Tilda said, but she was no longer surprised by the synchronicity.

Sheba considered her. "The Romans wrote on wax tablets, which were heated and reused again and again, and the practice carried over to parchment. Nothing was thrown away until it was exhausted. That image resonates with me," Sheba said. "Everything we've done and been is scraped over, melted down, but remains a part of what we become."

She wandered off, pausing to check the adhesive holding a sketch to a larger image, then went into her storage closet. She returned with a stack of her own work, which she set down beside Tilda. "Take your time, child," she said. Sheba crossed from the workspace to the kitchen, opened a drawer, and withdrew a key. "I miss having students. You two can use my space," she said, and set it on the table at Tilda's hip.

Yes. Tilda would take time and the actual historical documents, the letters and pictures, and transform them. She would claim her history, badly remembered, create something that revealed it, revealed her.

"Thank you," she said, and picked up the key. "Thank you very much."

The windows were open to Perry Street, the sheer curtains lifting on the early morning breeze. Dressed for a casual Sunday in a button-down blouse and jeans, Tilda sat in the garden, a cup of tea steaming in her right hand, the paperweight sitting before her. At this angle the lotus flower was foreshortened in the domed glass, distorted, nearly invisible. She sipped her tea and considered the paperweight.

The screen door opened and Daniel slid into the chair next to her, yawning and scratching his stubble. He wore only a pair of sleep shorts. With only a few weeks until the ultramarathon his body was little more than skin over muscle and bone. His shoulders and chest flexed as he yawned. "Morning."

"Good morning," she said. A slow beat of heat pulsed low in her belly. She wanted to kiss the fine edge where his beard gave way to his lips, and lower, where it smoothed out to the soft skin of his throat, below his ear. But for the first time in her life, she didn't know how to tempt a man into having sex with her, and he showed no signs of coming there on his own.

He looked at the paperweight and his gaze sharpened. "I need coffee to deal with that."

"There's a fresh pot on the counter," she said.

He emerged a few minutes later with a cup of coffee, then opened his arm and beckoned her in. Without hesitation she curled up on his lap, stroking down his throat, touching his pulse everywhere she could find it. He yelped when her bare feet found his inner thigh, and shifted her in his lap. After a sip of coffee he nodded at the papers and paperweight. "Time to talk about that?"

In response Tilda lifted the paperweight. "Yes," she said.

He made a noncommittal noise and sipped his coffee. His face, his dear face, was still a little puffy from sleep, the groove by his mouth cutting a little deeper from long days, late nights, and a difficult time at home. She leaned over, cupped his cheek with her hand, and kissed that groove. "What do you want me to do with it?"

"Whatever brings you peace," he said finally. "He never meant that for me, only you. What you do with it is up to you."

His ring gleamed in the sunlight striping across her thigh, and her heart seized in her chest. Daniel, oh, Daniel. Being so strong for her, never asking her to be anyone other than who she was, holding space for her to come to terms with her past.

He took it from her, tilted it to see the blossom from different angles. The morning light slid over the dome, then pierced deep, then disappeared again. "It's beautiful," he said. "Would you miss having it around?"

"No," she said candidly. "He meant it as Andrew has always meant things, a combination of arrogance and neediness. I want it gone."

Daniel hefted it one last time, then set it gently on the table. "Did you have any plans for it?"

"I rather thought we might sell it and use the money to take a rather nice honeymoon."

Daniel chuckled. "I like that idea," he said. "Very much. Where would you go?"

"Somewhere new to both of us," she said. "Somewhere warm, quiet, where we can see the stars. Near the ocean, too."

"It'll be nice to have an excuse to get out of the city's sloppy, frosty winter."

"That sounds perfect," she said quietly.

"What about the house?" he asked.

"What about the house?"

"Your mother gave us the house as a wedding present. Do you want to get rid of that, too?"

She thought about it for a second. "No. We began our life together in this house." Tilda's throat closed again. "Mum never lived here; it was a post-crash investment. She only stayed here once or twice. My memories here are of you. Us. I don't want to sell those."

He kissed her temple. No one ever talked about the joy, the unutterable exultation roots and shoots feel as they spread free from the kernel, the seed, the pod. The act of expansion was primitive, bone-deep, surging inside her; only once she began did she understand how much effort she'd expended to hold it back. She nuzzled into his throat and inhaled his scent, warm sleep and coffee.

"Are you running this morning?" she whispered.

"No," he said. "Tomorrow morning."

"Come upstairs with me?"

— TWENTY-NINE —

She lifted her mouth to his. Daniel opened his mouth, touched his tongue to hers, then waited as she rubbed her nose along his, then tilted her head to kiss him again. He fisted his hand in her hair, gripped her hip, and held her tight as his cock thickened to hardness. It had been so long since they'd had sex, and so much had happened in the interval. His heart started to pound, blood thrumming in his ears.

"I love you," she breathed against his lips. Then she lifted her chin, waiting for him to respond. Sitting in front of him, bare right down to the bottom of her soul. His eyes stung with a sudden wash of tears. This woman. This stubborn, strong, ridiculous, broken, defensive, searching, healing woman. This walking paradox of strength and vulnerability.

He stood, and extended his hand to her. "I love you, too. Come with me."

Her fingers were chilled. He led her up the stairs and down the hall to their bedroom, dropped her hand to arrange the cheval glass mirror in front of the bed, then picked up her hand again. He sat on the edge of the bed and guided her between his legs so they both faced the mirror. Both arms around her waist, he set his chin on her shoulder and looked in the mirror. His gaze sought out hers, asking a question he didn't need to put into words.

Color stood high on her cheeks. Her hair swooped across her forehead, down to her eyebrow. She nodded.

He set his mouth to her nape, kissed it softly, starting slow. It had been weeks since they'd had sex. He wasn't sure if they'd ever made love; he had, maybe she had, maybe she hadn't, but it was in the past. This was their present, their future, this slow drag of lips and tongue over skin and bone so exposed and yet so hidden and vulnerable. She shivered in his arms, her hands crossing to his elbows, holding him as he held her. Her head dropped forward, giving him access. He kept at it, alternating teeth and tongue, blowing on patches of damp skin, feeling her shivers turn into subtle undulations.

Using his cheek he urged her head to the side. She let it loll back to rest on his shoulder, offering him tendons and ear. He explored the different textures, bit down on her earlobe, holding the bite while he glanced in the mirror and found her watching them. Her eyes were wide, defenses down.

"See?" he said. He wanted to kiss the hinge of her jaw, so he tightened his arms and pulled her closer. Her eyelids drooped as her rear snugged up against his erection.

She looked at herself, peering straight into her own eyes as he unbuttoned her blouse, spread the fabric to reveal her breasts and belly. He cupped her breasts, stroked his fingertips over her nipples until they peaked, then lightly pinched them through the silky fabric. Her eyes closed, then opened again. She shifted in his lap, rubbing against his erection, her hands sliding up and down his forearms.

"Daniel," she murmured.

"Tilda." He waited until she opened her eyes again, her irises rings of pewter fast disappearing into her expanding pupils. "Tilda," he said into the slope where her collarbone met neck and shoulder. She all but purred at his voice, and he smiled into her shoulder. Such a ridiculous thing, what his voice meant to her. Smiling during sex felt so married. So right.

She gave a sweet little smile, languid and heated and totally present, letting him see her like this. He unfastened her jeans and worked them down her thighs. With her legs trapped closed, getting his hand between them wasn't easy, but he managed it, gently parting her folds. Slick heat greeted his fingertips, easing his way to her clit. She jolted when he circled it, subsiding as the first touch gave way to slow strokes. Her thighs tensed and released around his hand, and the flush on her cheeks crept down her throat to her collarbone. One hand slid up to his nape while the other gripped his forearm. She arched in his grip, head thrown back, throat flexed. When she went taut, her head dropped forward. For a split second their gazes met in the mirror. The connection shocked him, vibrating and alive and electric, then her eyes closed and she went under.

"Yes, yes," he whispered, and held her through it. "Tilda. Yes."

When it was over she was limp and pliant, muscles and tendons relaxing in stages. "More," she said, low and rough.

She roused herself enough to kick off her jeans and stretch out on the bed while he stripped himself efficiently. He braced himself above her, knees between her thighs, then hesitated, searching her face. Her brows flexed in uncertainty. She bit her lip, then slid her hands up his arms to his shoulders and flattened her palms on his shoulder blades. It wasn't much pressure, just enough to ask, aware of everything that had come before, acknowledging what it meant to go forward.

He lowered himself into her arms, shifted forward, and felt the sweet, electric heat of his cock nudging into her folds, then sliding deep. Eyes closed, she made a low sound somewhere between a groan and a purr. He dropped his forehead to hers and fought to remember how to breathe because this was as vulnerable as he'd ever made himself to another human being.

He was here, bared to her. Where was she?

Her eyes opened. A single tear tracked from the corner down her temple, into her hair. He stared at her and saw only Tilda, the old, wild Tilda and the new, open, alive Tilda. Just Tilda, as she was, as she would ever be, giving herself back to him.

He laid his thumbs on either side of her jaw, then bent and licked the shiny trail of her tear, kissed each eyelid, the tip of her nose, her lips. Her hands slid down to the base of his spine and she rolled her hips up, coaxing a thrust from him, then another, and another. It felt so good, hot and slick and slow and potent. She kissed his mouth, his jaw, his neck, her hands playing up the length of his spine and back down to cup his rear. Heat coiled low in his balls, then climbed up his shaft. Her knees drew up, disrupting the relentless play of fingers and mouth as she surrendered for a moment, head back, throat bared. He nipped at the straining tendon, and she laughed.

"Oh, slow, slow," she gasped, her voice high, breathy, urgent. "Not yet. Not yet."

"Shh," he replied, and slowed his pace. Her tight walls rippled around him, teasing him with the nearness of her release ebbing away. He worked one hand under her hips and tilted her up to meet him, sliding impossibly deeper with the new angle. Her ankles locked around his hips and she stopped caressing him, simply gripped his upper arms and lifted into each thrust.

He kissed her gently, a fleeting caress of lips. Her eyes opened almost immediately, glazed with pleasure, utterly defenseless to him, unwary and uncaring.

"God," he said, giving into a brief stutter of his hips.

"Oh, yes please," she said, and tightened everything: arms; legs; soft, clinging walls.

He tipped her over into the vortex, trapped her short, sharp cries with his mouth, and let them draw him into fire.

Afterward, she sprawled alongside him, her leg over his, her head tucked into the curve of his shoulder. He wrapped one arm around her back and idly scratched his abdomen with his hand.

"That was different," she said.

It took him a moment to remember the conversation at the courthouse, when he asked her if sex on their honeymoon was different from their premarital sex. He smiled at her. "Good."

She nodded. "Stay here," she said, and slid from underneath the covers to the armoire against the opposite wall. She opened the doors, then the drawer that until recently held all the detritus from her past, and got out something he couldn't see. She turned for the bed again, and he sat up with his back to the headboard. The pattern of sun-drenched leaves dappled her skin as she tucked her knees under her and her hair behind her ear, then opened her hand. In her palm rested her wedding band and the LOVE bracelet.

"I'm sorry I took them off," she said. "Would you . . . ?"

The bracelet took a minute to fix around her wrist, as the tiny screws had to be set with care to avoid stripping the threads. When he finished he lifted his fingers to his mouth and kissed her knuckles. She slid the bracelet down, then nodded at it. "I love it," she said. "Thank you."

He smiled. "You're welcome." Totally right for Tilda. It was then, and it was now, and it would be forever. The very definition of a symbol.

The ring was such a small thing, thin, platinum, size four and a half, and even at that loose enough to slip up to her knuckle when it was cold. He couldn't get it on his pinky past the first knuckle. As symbols went, it wasn't much of one. No diamonds or rubies, no bling, no intricate setting. He balanced the ring between his thumb and middle finger, and offered it to her. She held out her left hand, palm down. He slid it on, then continued the motion and wove their fingers together, left hand to left hand, palm to palm.

She stayed on her knees, as if she meant to get up. "Can I see the first card you wrote to me after we met? The one you didn't send?"

"Sure," he said easily, as if his heart rate didn't skyrocket at the thought of her seeing exactly what he wanted over a year ago.

"Where is it? Your shoebox?"

"It's in your file," he said, fighting to keep his voice steady.

"My received file?" she asked. "I didn't see anything from you in that file, and I looked through it a week or two ago."

"No. Your matched file."

"Why is it there?"

"Look at it and see."

She didn't move. "I didn't do anything for you. We haven't done anything outrageous sexually. We go to soccer games and funerals."

"And to dinner, and to gallery openings, and to breakfast at Sarabeth's, and to bed together. All you did was be you. Tilda," he said when she opened her mouth to protest. "Just read it."

— THIRTY —

Solstice, a year earlier
5.04 a.m.

Daniel had no memory of walking home from Louise's party, but here he was, at the front door of his apartment in Brooklyn. For hours he'd meandered through Manhattan's silent, half-lit streets, trying to process what just happened to him. He had a vague memory of pausing in the middle of the Brooklyn Bridge, watching the East River flow nearly three hundred feet beneath him. At that moment he'd felt like he could fly, electricity tingling on all his nerves, lighting up the synapses in his brain. It was an odd, unfamiliar sensation for a man whose specialty was the application of feet to pavement, wearing down the soles of running shoes as he churned through mile after mile. Even now, as he unlocked the door and climbed the stairs to his apartment, he felt like he'd been flung into the air.

By Tilda Davies. One conversation, lasting less than ten minutes, half of which he didn't understand. He had no idea what she was talking about on the ledge, the *process*, sending a *letter*, but he couldn't give less of a damn. Normally, not understanding something was like an itch he couldn't scratch, but whatever this was with not–Lady Matilda spurred a sense of deep knowing, beyond instinct, into a primal recognition unlike anything he'd felt before. His heart kept skittering and leaping in his chest, probably in response to the adrenaline his brain dumped into his nervous system every time he thought about sitting down on that ledge next to her, and watching the wind tousle her hair around her face.

And there went his heart again. He had to see her again. Had to. For the first time in his life, he was absolutely, utterly certain. No puzzle, no mystery, no questions asked, no doubt.

He stood in his darkened living room, looking around at his possessions as if they belonged to another man. Before he could stop himself he ripped open the packaging of the box of notecards he'd found on a dusty shelf at the back of an all-night bodega on his way home. Using the pen on top of his bureau he followed the protocol his mother drilled into him: salutation, body of note, signature. It took less than five seconds. With eyes blurry from lack of sleep, he looked at what he'd written.

No. It was a command, not a request; either way, he asked for too much, too risky, too crazy, even for a woman he met sitting on a ledge.

He hesitated, tapping his pen against the bureau. The longest day of the year was always followed by the longest night, the earth spinning in the black void, humans pinned to the surface by powerful forces, flung into the air by others, chasing the sun to hold the darkness at bay. She liked risk, but the line between crazy and sure was very thin. In this first draft he sounded crazy.

The sky outside his window lightened from midnight to dark

gray. Dawn was coming, and with daylight, sanity returned. Reluctantly, he set his first attempt aside and started over, with something more reasonable, one hundred percent more likely to succeed at getting him a second conversation with not–Lady Matilda.

But the first card lay at his elbow, taunting him. He picked it up and nearly tore it in two before throwing it in the recycling bin. Instead, he slid it into an envelope, and then into the box on his dresser that held his cuff links, watch, American flag pin, other various NYPD and FBI pins.

Someday, he'd show her how certain he'd been.

Dear Tilda,

Marry me.

Daniel